"N. K. Jemisin is a true superstar of fantasy literature"
The Ranting Dragon

"The world is so fully fleshed out that I could breathe its spices . . . Jemisin proves yet again that she is one of the important new writers in the SFF scene"
Kate Elliott, author of *Cold Magic*

"Astounding . . . Jemisin maintains a gripping voice and an emotional core that not only carries the story through its complicated setting, but sets things up for even more staggering revelations to come"
NPR

"To say Jemisin's worldbuilding is superb is an understatement"
Strange Horizons

"Jemisin might just be the best worldbuilder out there right now . . . [She] is a master at what she does"
RT Book Reviews

"Jemisin's graceful prose and gritty setting provide the perfect backdrop for this fascinating tale of determined characters fighting to save a doomed world"
Publishers Weekly

"N. K. Jemisin's *The Fifth Season* is a strikingly original fantasy novel"
Fantasy Faction

"The characters are truly wonderful"
BiblioSanctum

By N. K. Jemisin

The Inheritance Trilogy
The Hundred Thousand Kingdoms
The Broken Kingdoms
The Kingdom of Gods
The Awakened Kingdom (novella)

Dreamblood
The Killing Moon
The Shadowed Sun

The Broken Earth
The Fifth Season
The Obelisk Gate

THE OBELISK GATE

THE BROKEN EARTH: BOOK TWO

N. K. JEMISIN

www.orbitbooks.net

ORBIT

First published in the UK in 2016 by Orbit

1 3 5 7 9 10 8 6 4 2

A CIP catalogue record for this book
is available from the British Library.

ISBN 978-0-356-50836-8

Printed and bound in Great Britain by
Clays Ltd, St Ives plc

Papers used by Orbit are from well-managed forests
and other responsible sources.

MIX
Paper from
responsible sources
FSC® C104740

Orbit
An imprint of
Little, Brown Book Group
Carmelite House
50 Victoria Embankment
London EC4Y 0DZ

An Hachette UK Company
www.hachette.co.uk

www.orbitbooks.net

To those who have no choice but to prepare their children for the battlefield

MINIMAL PLATE
The Arctics
Tundra
NOMIDLATS
MAXIMAL PLATE

The Great Eastern Forest
Allia
The Rift
Yumenes-Allia Highroad
Yumenes
Alebid
Merz Desert
Meov
Western Coastals
Tirimo
Somidlats
Kiesh Treps
Lake Tekkaris
Mount Arok
The Stillness
distance in miles
0
1000
2000
The Antarctics
N
W
E
S

1

Nassun, on the rocks

HMM. NO. I'M TELLING THIS WRONG.

After all, a person is herself, and others. Relationships chisel the final shape of one's being. I am me, and you. Damaya was herself *and* the family that rejected her *and* the people of the Fulcrum who chiseled her to a fine point. Syenite was Alabaster *and* Innon *and* the people of poor lost Allia and Meov. Now you are Tirimo *and* the ash-strewn road's walkers *and* your dead children…and also the living one who remains. Whom you will get back.

That's not a spoiler. You are Essun, after all. You know this already. Don't you?

Nassun next, then. Nassun, who is just eight years old when the world ends.

There is no knowing what went through little Nassun's mind when she came home from her apprenticeship one afternoon to find her younger brother dead on the den floor, and her father standing over the corpse. We can imagine what she thought, felt, did. We can speculate. But we will not *know*. Perhaps that is for the best.

Here is what I know for certain: that apprenticeship I mentioned? Nassun was in training to become a lorist.

The Stillness has an odd relationship with its self-appointed keepers of stonelore. There are records of lorists existing as far back as the long-rumored Eggshell Season. That's the one in which some sort of gaseous emission caused all children born in the Arctics for several years to have delicate bones that broke with a touch and bent as they grew—if they grew. (Yumenescene archeomests have argued for centuries over whether this could have been caused by strontium or arsenic, and whether it should be counted as a Season at all given that it only affected a few hundred thousand weak, pallid little barbarians on the northern tundra. But that is *when* the peoples of the Arctics gained a reputation for weakness.) About twenty-five thousand years ago, according to the lorists themselves, which most people think is a blatant lie. In truth, lorists are an even older part of life in the Stillness. Twenty-five thousand years ago is simply when their role became distorted into near-uselessness.

They're still around, though they've forgotten how much they've forgotten. Somehow their order, if it can be called an order, survives despite the First through Seventh Universities disavowing their work as apocryphal and probably inaccurate, and despite governments down all the ages undermining their knowledge with propaganda. And despite the Seasons, of course. Once lorists came only from a race called Regwo—Westcoasters who had sallow-reddish skin and naturally black lips, and who worshipped the preservation of history the way people in less-bitter times worshipped gods. They used to chisel stonelore into mountainsides in tablets as high as the sky, so that all would see and know the wisdom needed to survive. Alas: in the Stillness, destroying mountains is as easy as an orogene toddler's temper tantrum. Destroying a people takes only a bit more effort.

So lorists are no longer Regwo, but most of them tint their lips black in the Regwo's memory. Not that they remember why, anymore. Now it's just how one knows a lorist: by the lips, and by the stack of polymer tablets they carry, and by the shabby clothes they tend to wear, and by the fact that they usually do not have real comm names. They aren't commless, mind. In theory they could return to their home comms in the event of a Season, although by profession they tend to wander far enough to make returning impractical. In practice, many communities will take them in, even during a Season, because even the most stoic community wants entertainment during the long cold nights. For this reason, most lorists train in the arts—music and comedy and such. They also act as teachers and caretakers of the young in times when no one else can be spared for such duty, and most importantly they serve as a living reminder that others have survived worse through the ages. Every comm needs that.

The lorist who has come to Tirimo is named Renthree Lorist Stone. (All lorists take the comm name Stone, and the use name Lorist, it being one of the rarer use-castes.) She is mostly unimportant, but there is a reason you must know of her. She was once Renthree Breeder Tenteek, but that was before she fell in love with a lorist who visited Tenteek and seduced the then-young woman away from a boring life as a glass-smith. Her life would have become slightly more interesting if a Season had occurred before she left, for a Breeder's responsibility in those times is clear—and perhaps that, too, is what spurred her away. Or maybe it was just the usual folly of young love? Hard to say. Renthree's lorist lover eventually left her on the outskirts of the Equatorial city of Penphen, with a broken heart and a head full of lore, and a wallet full of chipped jades and cabochons and one shoeprint-stained lozenge of mother-of-pearl. Renthree spent the mother-of-pearl to commission her own set of tablets from a knapper, used the jade chips to buy traveling supplies and to stay at an inn for the days it took the knapper to finish, and bought many strong drinks at a tavern with the cabochons. Then, newly outfitted and with wounds patched, she set out on her own. Thus does the profession perpetuate itself.

When Nassun appears at the way station where she has set up shop, it's possible that Renthree thinks about her own apprenticeship. (Not the seduction part; obviously Renthree likes older women, emphasis on women. The foolish dreamer part.) The day previous, Renthree passed through Tirimo, shopping at market stalls and smiling cheerfully through her black-daubed lips so as to advertise her presence in the area. She did not see Nassun, on her way home from creche, stop and stare in awe and sudden, irrational hope.

Nassun has skipped creche today to come and find her, and to bring an offering. This is traditional—the offering, that is, and not teachers' daughters skipping creche. Two adults from town are already at the way station, sitting on a bench to listen while Renthree talks, and Renthree's offering cup has already been filled with brightly colored shards faceted with the quartent's mark. Renthree blinks in surprise at the sight of Nassun: a gangly girl who is more leg than torso, more eyes than face, and very obviously too young to be out of creche so early when it isn't harvest season.

Nassun stops on the threshold of the way station, panting to catch her breath, which makes for a very dramatic entrance. The other two visitors turn to stare at her, Jija's normally quiet firstborn, and only their presence stops Nassun from blurting her intentions right then and there. Her mother has taught her to be very circumspect. (Her mother will hear about her skipping creche. Nassun doesn't care.) She swallows, however, and goes to Renthree immediately to hold out something: a dark chunk of rock, embedded in which can be seen a small, almost cubical diamond.

Nassun doesn't have any money beyond her allowance, you see, and she'd already spent that on books and sweets when word came that a lorist was in town. But no one in Tirimo knows that there's a potentially excellent diamond mine in the region—no one, that is, except orogenes. And then only if they're looking. Nassun's the only one who's bothered in several thousand years. She knows she should not have found this diamond. Her mother has taught her not to display her orogeny, and not to use it outside of carefully proscribed practice sessions that they undertake in a nearby valley every few weeks. No one carries diamonds for currency because they can't be sharded for change easily, but they're still useful in industry, mining, and the like. Nassun knows it has some value, but she has no inkling that the pretty rock she's just given to Renthree is worth a house or two. She's only eight.

And Nassun is so excited, when she sees Renthree's eyes widen at the sight of the glittering lump poking out of the black hunk of rock, that she stops caring that there are others present and blurts, "I want to be a lorist, too!"

Nassun has no idea what a lorist really does, of course. She just knows that she wants very very much to leave Tirimo.

More on this later.

Renthree would be a fool to refuse the offering, and she doesn't. But she doesn't give Nassun an answer right away, partly because she thinks Nassun is cute and that her declaration is no different from any other child's momentary passion. (She's right, to a degree; last month Nassun wanted to be a geneer.) Instead she asks Nassun to sit, and then she tells stories to her small audience for the rest of the afternoon, until the sun makes long shadows down the valley slope and through the trees. When the other two visitors get up to head home, they eye Nassun and drop hints until she reluctantly comes with them, because the people of Tirimo will not have it said that they disrespected a lorist by letting some child talk her to death all night.

In the wake of her visitors, Renthree stokes up the fire and starts making dinner from a bit of pork belly and greens and cornmeal that she bought in Tirimo the day before. While she waits for dinner to cook and eats an apple, she turns Nassun's rock in her fingers, fascinated. And troubled.

In the morning she heads into Tirimo. A few discreet inquiries lead her to Nassun's home. Essun's gone by this point, off to teach the last class of her career as a creche teacher. Nassun's gone off to creche, too, though she's biding her time till she can escape at lunchtime to go find the lorist again. Jija's in his "workshop," as he calls the offset room that passes for the house's basement, where he works on commissions with his noisy tools during the day. Uche is asleep on a pallet in the same room. He can sleep through anything. The songs of the earth have always been his lullaby.

Jija comes to the door when Renthree knocks, and for an instant she's a little taken aback. Jija is a Midlatter mongrel, same as Essun, though his heritage leans more toward the Sanzed; he's big and brown and muscular and bald-shaven. Intimidating. Yet the welcoming smile on his face is wholly genuine, which makes Renthree feel better about what she's decided to do. This is a good man. She cannot cheat him.

"Here," she says, giving him the diamond rock. She can't possibly take such a valuable gift from a child, not in exchange for a few stories and an apprenticeship that Nassun will probably change her mind about in a few months. Jija frowns in confusion and takes the rock, thanking her profusely after he hears her explanation. He promises to spread the tale of Renthree's generosity and integrity to everyone he can, which will hopefully give her more opportunities to practice her art before she leaves town.

Renthree leaves, and that is the end of her part in this tale. It is a significant part, however, which is why I told you of her.

There was not any one thing that turned Jija against his son, understand. Over the years he simply had noticed things about his wife and his children that stirred suspicion in the depths of his mind. That stirring had grown to a tickle, then an outright irritant by the point at which this tale begins, but denial kept him from worrying at the thought any further. He loved his family, after all, and the truth was simply…unthinkable. Literally.

He would have figured it out eventually, one way or another. I repeat: *He would have figured it out eventually.* No one is to blame but him.

But if you want a simple explanation, and if there can be any one event that became the tipping point, the camel straw, the broken plug on the lava tube . . . it was this rock. Because Jija knew stone, you see. He was an excellent knapper. He knew stone, and he knew Tirimo, and he knew that veins of igneous rock from an ancient volcano ran all through the surrounding land. Most did not breach the surface, but it was entirely possible that Nassun could by chance find a diamond sitting out where anyone could pick it up. Unlikely. But possible.

This understanding floats on the surface of Jija's mind for the rest of the day after Renthree leaves. The truth is beneath the surface, a leviathan waiting to uncurl, but the waters of his thoughts are placid for now. Denial is powerful.

But then Uche wakes up. Jija walks him into the den, asking him if he's hungry; Uche says he isn't. Then he smiles at Jija, and with the unerring sensitivity of a powerful orogene child, he orients on Jija's pocket and says, "Why is shiny there, Daddy?"

The words, in his lisping toddler-language, are cute. The knowledge that he possesses, because the rock is indeed in Jija's pocket and there's no way Uche could have known it was there, dooms him.

Nassun does not know that it started with the rock. When you see her, do not tell her.

When Nassun comes home that afternoon, Uche is already dead. Jija is standing over his cooling corpse in the den, breathing hard. It doesn't take a lot of effort to beat a toddler to death, but he hyperventilated while he did it. When Nassun comes in, there's still not enough carbon dioxide in Jija's bloodstream; he's dizzy, shaky, chilled. Irrational. So when Nassun pulls up sharply in the doorway of the den, staring at the tableau and only slowly understanding what she sees, Jija blurts, "Are you one, too?"

He's a big man. It's a loud, sharp blurt, and Nassun jumps. Her eyes jerk up to him, rather than staying on Uche's body, which saves her life. The gray color of her eyes is her mother's, but the shape of her face is Jija's. Just the sight of her pulls him a step away from the primal panic into which he has descended.

She tells the truth, too. That helps, because he wouldn't have believed anything else. "Yes," she says.

She's not really afraid in this moment. The sight of her brother's body, and her mind's refusal to interpret what she's seeing, have frozen all cognition within her. She's not even sure what Jija is asking, since understanding the context of his words would require her to acknowledge that what stains her father's fists is blood, and that her brother is not merely sleeping on the floor. She can't. Not right then. But absent any more coherent thought, and as children sometimes do in extreme situations, Nassun...regresses. What she sees frightens her, even if she does not understand why. And of the two of her parents, it is Jija to whom Nassun has always been closer. She's his favorite, too: the firstborn, the one he never expected to have, the one with his face and his sense of humor. She likes his favorite foods. He's had vague hopes of her following in his footsteps as a knapper.

So when she starts crying, she does not quite know why. And

as her thoughts skirl about and her heart screams, she takes a step toward him. His fists tighten, but she cannot see him as a threat. He is her father. She wants comfort. "Daddy," she says.

Jija flinches. Blinks. Stares, as if he has never seen her before.

Realizes. He cannot kill her. Not even if she is . . . no. She is his little girl.

She steps forward again, reaching out. He cannot make himself reach back, but he does hold still. She grabs his nearer wrist. He stands straddling Uche's body; she can't grab him around the waist the way she wants. She does, however, press her face against his bicep, so comfortingly strong. She does tremble, and he does feel her tears sliding down his skin.

He stands there, breath gradually slowing, fists gradually uncurling, while she weeps. After a time, he turns to face her fully, and she wraps arms around his waist. Turning to face her requires turning away from what he's done to Uche. It is an easy movement.

He murmurs to her, "Get your things. As if you were going to spend a few nights with Grandma." Jija's mother married again a few years back and now she lives in Sume, the town in the next valley over, which will soon be destroyed utterly.

"Are we going there?" Nassun asks against his belly.

He touches the back of her head. He's always done this, because she's always liked the gesture. When she was a baby, she cooed louder when he cupped her there. This is because the sessapinae are located in that region of the brain and when he touches her there, she can perceive him more completely, as orogenes do. Neither of them has ever known why she likes it so much.

"We're going somewhere you can be better," he says gently. "Somewhere I heard of, where they can help you." Make her a little girl again, and not . . . He turns away from this thought, too.

She swallows, then nods and steps back, looking up at him. "Is Mama coming, too?"

Something moves across Jija's face, subtle as an earthquake. "No."

And Nassun, who was fully prepared to go off into the sunset with some lorist, effectively running away from home to escape her mother, relaxes at last. "Okay, Daddy," she says, and heads to her room to pack.

Jija gazes after her for a long, breath-held moment. He turns away from Uche again, gets his own things, and heads outside to hitch up the horse to the wagon. Within an hour they are away, headed south with the end of the world on their heels.

* * *

In the days of Jyamaria, which died in the Season of Drowned Desert, it was thought that giving the lastborn to the sea would keep it from coming ashore and taking the rest.

—From "The Breeder's Stand," lorist tale recorded in Hanl Quartent, Western Coastals near Brokeoff Peninsula. Apocryphal.

2

you, continued

A WHAT?" YOU SAY.

"A moon." Alabaster, beloved monster, sane madman, the most powerful orogene in all the Stillness, and in-progress stone eater snack, stares at you. This has all of its old intensity, and you feel the will of him, the stuff that makes him the force of nature that he is, as an almost physical rider on that stare. The Guardians were fools to ever consider him tame. "A satellite."

"A *what?*"

He makes a little sound of frustration. He's completely the same, aside from being partially turned to stone, as the days when you and he were less than lovers and more than friends. Ten years and another self ago. "Astronomestry isn't foolishness," he says. "I know you were taught that, everyone in the Stillness thinks it's a waste of energy to study the sky when it's the ground that's trying to kill us, but Earthfires, Syen. I thought you would've learned to question the status quo a little better by now."

"I had other things to do," you snap, just like you always used to snap at him. But thinking of the old days makes you think of what you've been up to in the meantime. And that makes you think of your living daughter, and your dead son, and your soon-to-be-very-ex-husband, and you flinch physically. "And my name is Essun now, I told you."

"Whatever." With a groaning sigh, Alabaster carefully sits back against the wall. "They say you came here with a geomest. Have her explain it to you. I don't have a lot of energy these days." Because being eaten probably takes a toll. "You didn't answer my first question. Can you do it yet?"

Can you call the obelisks to you? It is a question that made no sense when he first asked it, possibly because you were distracted by realizing he was a) alive, b) turning to stone, and c) the orogene responsible for ripping the continent in half and touching off a Season that may never end.

"The obelisks?" You shake your head, more confused than refusing. Your gaze drifts to the strange object near his bed, which looks like an excessively long pink glassknife and feels like an obelisk, even though it cannot possibly be. "What do— no. I don't know. I haven't tried since Meov."

He groans softly, shutting his eyes. "You're so rusting useless, Syen. Essun. Never had any respect for the craft."

"I respect it fine, I just don't—"

"Just enough to get by, enough to excel but only for gain. They told you how high and you jumped no further, all to get a nicer apartment and another ring—"

"For privacy, you ass, and some control over my life, and some rusting respect—"

"And you actually *listened* to that Guardian of yours, when you don't listen to anybody else—"

"*Hey.*" Ten years as a schoolteacher have given your voice an obsidian edge. Alabaster actually stops ranting and blinks at you. Very quietly, you say, "You know full well why I listened to him."

There is a moment of silence. Both of you take this time to regroup.

"You're right," he says, at length. "I'm sorry." Because every Imperial Orogene listens—listened—to their assigned Guardian. Those who didn't died or ended up in a node. Except, again, for Alabaster; you never did find out what he did to his Guardian.

You offer a stiff nod of truce. "Apology accepted."

He takes a careful breath, looking weary. "Try, Essun. Try to reach an obelisk. Today. I need to know."

"Why? What's this about a still-light? What does—"

"*Satellite.* And all of it's irrelevant if you can't control the obelisks." His eyes are actually drifting shut. This is probably a good thing. He'll need his strength if he's to survive whatever is happening to him. If it's survivable. "Worse than irrelevant. You remember why I wouldn't tell you about the obelisks in the first place, don't you?"

Yes. Once, before you ever paid attention to those great floating half-real crystals in the sky, you asked Alabaster to explain how he accomplished some of his amazing feats of orogeny. He wouldn't tell you, and you hated him for that, but now you know just how dangerous the knowledge was. If you hadn't understood that the obelisks were amplifiers, *orogeny* amplifiers, you would never have reached for the garnet to save yourself from a Guardian's attack. But if the garnet obelisk hadn't been half-dead itself, cracked and stuffed with a frozen stone eater, it would have killed you. You didn't have the strength, the self-control, to prevent the power from frying you from the brain on down.

And now Alabaster wants you to reach for one deliberately, to see what happens.

Alabaster knows your face. "Go and see," he says. His eyes shut completely then. You hear a faint rattle in his breath, like gravel in his lungs. "The topaz is floating somewhere nearby. Call it tonight, then in the morning see…" Abruptly he seems to weaken, running out of strength. "See if it's come. If it hasn't, tell me, and I'll find someone else. Or do what I can myself."

Find who, to do what, you can't even begin to guess. "Will you still tell me what all this is about?"

"No. Because in spite of everything, Essun, I don't want you to die." He takes a deep breath, lets it out slowly. The next words are softer than usual. "It's good to see you."

You have to tighten your jaw to reply. "Yeah."

He says nothing more, and that's enough of a goodbye for both of you.

You get up, glancing at the stone eater who stands nearby. Alabaster calls her Antimony. She stands statue-still in the way they do, her too-black eyes watching you too steadily, and though her pose is something classical, you think there's a hint of irony in it. She stands with head elegantly tilted, one hand on her hip and the other upraised and poised with the fingers relaxed, waving in no particular direction. Maybe it's a come-hither, maybe it's a backhanded farewell, maybe it's that thing people do when they're keeping a secret and want you to know it, but they don't want to tell you what it is.

"Take care of him," you say to her.

"As I would any precious thing," she replies, without moving her mouth.

You're not even going to start trying to interpret that. You head back toward the infirmary entrance, where Hoa stands waiting for you. Hoa, who looks like an utterly strange human boy, who is actually a stone eater somehow, and who treats you as his precious thing.

He watches you, unhappily, as he has done since you realized what he was. You shake your head and move past him on your way out. He follows, at a pace.

It's early night in the comm of Castrima. Hard to tell since the giant geode's soft white light, emitted impossibly from the massive crystals that make up its substance, never changes. People are bustling about, carrying things, shouting to each other, going about their usual business without the necessary slowdown that would occur in other comms with the reduction of light. Sleeping will be difficult for a few days, you suspect, at least until you get used to this. That doesn't matter. Obelisks don't care about the time of day.

Lerna's been politely waiting outside while you and Hoa met with Alabaster and Antimony. He falls in as you come out, his expression expectant. "I need to go to the surface," you say.

Lerna makes a face. "The guards won't let you, Essun. People new to the comm aren't trusted. Castrima's survival depends on it remaining secret."

Seeing Alabaster again has brought back a lot of the old memories, and the old orneriness. "They can try to stop me."

Lerna stops walking. "And then you'll do what you did to Tirimo?"

Rusting hell. You stop, too, rocking a little from the force of that blow. Hoa stops as well, eying Lerna thoughtfully. Lerna's not glaring. The look on his face is too flat to be a glare. Damn. Okay.

After a moment, Lerna sighs and comes over. "We'll go to Ykka," he says. "We'll tell her what we need. We'll *ask* to go topside—with guards if she wants. All right?"

It's so reasonable that you don't know why you didn't even consider it. Well, you know why. Ykka might be an orogene like you, but you spent too many years being thwarted and betrayed by other orogenes at the Fulcrum; you know better than to trust her just because she's Your People. You should give her a chance because she's Your People, though.

"Fine," you say, and follow him to Ykka's.

Ykka's place is no larger than yours, and not distinct in any way despite being the home of the comm headwoman. Just another apartment carved by means unknown into the side of a giant glowing white crystal. Two people wait outside of its door, however, one leaning against the crystal and another peering over the railing at the expanse of Castrima. Lerna takes up position behind them and directs you to do the same. Only fair to wait your turn, and the obelisks aren't going anywhere.

The woman gazing out at the view glances over and looks you up and down. She's a little older, Sanzed, though darker complected than most, and her bushel of hair is ashblow with a slight kink to it, making it a frizzy cloud instead of just a coarse one. Got some Eastcoaster in her. And Westcoaster, too: Her gaze is through epicanthic-folded eyes, and it is assessing, wary, and unimpressed. "You the new one," she says. Not a question.

You nod back. "Essun."

She grins lopsidedly, and you blink. Her teeth have been filed to points, even though Sanzeds supposedly stopped doing that centuries ago. Bad for their reputation, after the Season of Teeth.

"Hjarka Leadership Castrima. Welcome to our little hole in the ground." Her smile widens. You stifle a grimace at the pun, though you're thinking, too, after hearing her name. It's usually bad news when a comm has a Leadership caste that isn't in charge. Dissatisfied Leaders have a nasty habit of fomenting coups during crises. But this is Ykka's problem to deal with, not yours.

The other person waiting, the man leaning on the crystal, doesn't seem to be watching you—but you notice how his eyes aren't moving to track whatever he's looking at, off in the distance. He's thin, shorter than you, with hair and a beard that make you think of strawberries growing amid hay. You imagine the delicate pressure of his indirect attention. You do *not* imagine the ping of instinct that tells you he is another of your kind. Since he doesn't acknowledge your presence, you say nothing to him.

"He came in a few months ago," Lerna says, distracting you from your new neighbors. For a moment you wonder if he means the strawberry-hay-haired man, and then you realize he's referring to Alabaster. "Just appeared in the middle of what passes for a town square within the geode—Flat Top." He nods toward something beyond you, and you turn, trying to understand what he means. Ah: there, amid the many sharp-tipped crystals of Castrima, is one that looks as if it's been sheared off halfway, leaving a wide hexagonal platform positioned and elevated near the center of the comm. Several stair-bridges connect to it, and there are chairs and a railing. Flat Top.

Lerna goes on. "There was no warning. Apparently the orogenes didn't sess anything, and the stills on guard duty didn't see anything. He and that stone eater of his were suddenly just... there."

He doesn't see you frown in surprise. You've never heard a still use the word *still* before.

"Maybe the stone eaters knew he was coming, but they rarely talk to anyone but their chosen people. And in this case, they didn't even do that." Lerna's gaze drifts over to Hoa, who's studiously ignoring him in that very moment. Lerna shakes his head. "Ykka tried to throw him out, of course, though she offered him a mercy killing if he wanted. His prognosis is obvious; gentle drugs and a bed would be a kindness. He did something when she called the Strongbacks, though. The light went out. The air and water stopped. Only for a minute, but it felt like a year. When he let everything come back on, everyone was upset. So Ykka said he could stay, and that we should treat his injuries."

Sounds about right. "He's a ten-ringer," you say. "And an ass. Give him whatever he wants and be nice about it."

"He's from the Fulcrum?" Lerna inhales in what seems to be awe. "Earthfires. I had no idea any Imperial Orogenes had survived."

You look at him, too surprised for amusement. But then, how would he know? Another thought sobers you. "He's turning to stone," you say softly.

"Yes." Lerna says it ruefully. "I've never seen anything like it. And it's getting worse. The first day he was here it was just his fingers that had... that the stone eater had... taken. I haven't seen how the condition progresses. He's careful to do it only when I or my assistants aren't around. I don't know if she's doing it to him somehow, or he's doing it to himself, or..." He shakes his head. "When I ask about it, he just grins and says, 'Just a bit longer, please. I'm waiting for someone.'" Lerna frowns at you, thoughtful.

And there's that: Somehow, Alabaster knew you were coming.

Or maybe he didn't. Maybe he was hoping for someone, anyone, with the necessary skill. Good chance of it here, with Ykka somehow summoning every rogga for miles. You'll only be what he was waiting for if it turns out you can summon an obelisk.

After a few moments, Ykka pokes her head out of the apartment through the hanging. She nods to Hjarka, glares at Strawberry-Hay until he sighs and turns to face her, then spies you and Lerna and Hoa. "Oh. Hey. Good. All of you come in."

You start to protest. "I need to talk to you in private."

She stares back at you. You blink, confused, thrown, annoyed. She keeps staring. Lerna shifts from foot to foot beside you, a silent pressure. Hoa merely watches, following your lead. Finally you get the message: her comm, her rules, and if you want to live here . . . You sigh and file in behind the others.

Inside, the apartment is warmer than in most of the comm, and darker; the curtain makes a difference, even though the walls glow. Makes it feel like night, which it probably is, topside. A good idea to steal for your own place, you think—before checking yourself, because you shouldn't be thinking long term. And then you check yourself again because you've lost Nassun and Jija's trail, so you *should* think long term. And then—

"Right," says Ykka, sounding bored as she moves to sit on a simple, low divan, cross-legged, with her chin propped on a fist. The others sit as well, but she's looking at you. "I'd been thinking about some changes already. You two arrived at a convenient time."

For a moment you think she's including Lerna in that "you two," but he sits down on the divan nearest hers, and there's something, some ease of movement or comfort in his manner, that tells you he's heard this before. She means Hoa, then. Hoa takes the floor, which makes him seem more like a child . . . though he isn't. It's strange how hard it is for you to remember that.

You sit down gingerly. "Convenient for what?"

"I still don't think this is a good idea," Strawberry-Hay says. He's looking at you, though his face is tilted toward Ykka. "We don't know anything about these people, Yeek."

"We know they survived out there until yesterday," says Hjarka, leaning to the side and propping her elbow on the divan's arm. "That's something."

"That's nothing." Strawberry-Hay—you really want to know his name—sets his jaw. "Our Hunters can survive out there."

Hunters. You blink. That's one of the old use-castes—a deprecated one, per Imperial Law, so nobody gets born into it anymore. Civilized societies don't need hunter-gatherers. That Castrima feels the need says more about the state of the comm than anything else Ykka has told you.

"Our Hunters know the terrain, and our Strongbacks, too, yeah," Hjarka says. "*Nearby*. Newcomers know more about the conditions beyond our territory—the people, the hazards, everything else."

"I'm not sure I know anything useful," you begin. But even as you say this, you frown, because you're remembering that thing you started noticing a few roadhouses ago. The sashes or rags of fine silk on too many of the Equatorials' wrists. The closed looks they gave you, their focus while others sat shell-shocked. At every encampment you saw them look their fellow survivors over, picking out any Sanzeds who were better equipped or healthier or otherwise doing better than average. Speaking to those chosen people in quiet voices. Leaving the next morning in groups larger than those in which they had arrived.

Does that mean anything? Like keeping to like is the old way, but races and nations haven't been important for a long time. Communities of purpose and diverse specialization are more efficient, as Old Sanze proved. Yet Yumenes is slag at the bottom of a fissure vent by now, and the laws and ways of the Empire no longer have any bite. Maybe this is the first sign of change, then. Maybe in a few years you'll have to leave Castrima and find a comm full of Midlatters like you who are brown but not too brown, big but not too big, with hair that's curly or kinky but never ashblow or straight. Nassun can come with you, in that case.

But how long would the both of you be able to hide what you are? No comm wants roggas. No comm except this one.

"You know more than we do," Ykka says, interrupting your woolgathering. "And anyway, I don't have the patience to argue about it. I'm telling you what I told him a few weeks back." She jerks her head at Lerna. "I need advisors—people who know this Season ground to sky. You're it until I replace you."

You're more than a little surprised. "I don't know a rusting thing about this comm!"

"That's my job—and his, and hers." Ykka nods toward Strawberry-Hay and Hjarka. "Anyway, you'll learn."

Your mouth hangs open. Then it occurs to you that she did include Hoa in this gathering, didn't she? "Earthfires and rustbuckets, you want a *stone eater* as an advisor?"

"Why not? They're here, too. More of them than we think." She focuses on Hoa, who watches her, his expression unreadable. "That's what you told me."

"It's true," he says quietly. Then: "I can't speak for them, though. And we aren't part of your comm."

Ykka leans down to give him a hard look. Her expression is something between hostile and guarded. "You have an impact on our comm, if only as a potential threat," she says. Her eyes flick toward you. "And the ones you're, uh, attached to, *are* part of this comm. You care what happens to them, at least. Don't you?"

You realize you haven't seen Ykka's stone eater, the woman with the ruby hair, for a few hours. That doesn't mean she isn't nearby, though. You learned better than to trust the appearance of absence with Antimony. Hoa says nothing in reply to Ykka. You're suddenly, irrationally glad he's bothered to stay visible for you.

"As for why you, and why the doctor," Ykka says, straightening, and speaking to you even if she's still eying Hoa, "it's because I need a mix of perspectives. A Leader, even if she doesn't want to lead." She eyes Hjarka. "Another local rogga, who doesn't bother to bite his tongue about how stupid he thinks I am." She nods to Strawberry-Hay, who sighs. "A Resistant and a doctor, who knows the road. A stone eater. Me. And you, Essun, who could kill us all." She smiles thinly. "Makes sense to give you a reason not to."

You have no real idea what to say, to that. You think, fleetingly, that Ykka should invite Alabaster to her circle of advisors, then, if the ability to destroy Castrima is a qualification. But that could lead to awkward questions.

To Hjarka and Strawberry-Hay you say, "Are you both from here?"

"Nope," says Hjarka.

"Yes," says Ykka. Hjarka glares at her. "You've lived here since you were young, Hjar."

Hjarka shrugs. "Nobody here remembers that except you, Yeek."

Strawberry-Hay says, "I was born and raised here."

Two orogenes, surviving to adulthood in a comm that didn't kill them. "What's your name?"

"Cutter Strongback." You wait. He smiles with half his mouth and neither of his eyes.

"Cutter's secret wasn't out, so to speak, while we were growing up," Ykka says. She's leaning against the wall behind the divan now, rubbing her eyes as if she's tired. "People guessed anyway. The rumors were enough to keep him from being adopted into the comm, under the previous headman. Of course, I've offered to give him the name a half-dozen times over now."

"If I give up 'Strongback,'" Cutter replies. He's still smiling in that paper-thin way.

Ykka lowers her hand. Her jaw is tight. "Denying what you are didn't keep people from knowing what you are."

"And flaunting it isn't what saved you."

Ykka takes a deep breath. The muscles in her jaw flex, relax. "And that would be why I asked you to do this, Cutter. But let's move on."

So it goes on.

You sit there throughout the meeting, trying to understand the undercurrents you're picking up on, still not believing you're even here, while Ykka lays out all of the problems facing Castrima. It's stuff you've never had to think about before: Complaints that the hot water in the communal pools isn't hot enough. A serious shortage of potters but an overabundance of people who know how to sew. Fungus in one of the granary caverns; several months' supply had to be burned lest it contaminate the rest. A meat shortage. You've gone from thinking obsessively about one person to having to be concerned with many. It's a bit sudden.

"I just took a bath," you blurt, trying to pull yourself out of a daze. "The water was nice."

"Of course you thought it was nice. You've been living rough for months, bathing in cold streams if you even bothered. A lot of the people in Castrima have never lived without reliable geo and adjustable faucets." Ykka rubs her eyes. The meeting's only been an hour or so, but it feels longer. "Everybody copes with a Season in their own way."

Complaining about nothing doesn't seem like coping to you, but okay.

"Being low on meat is an actual problem," Lerna says, frowning. "I noticed the last few comm shares didn't have any, or eggs."

Ykka's expression grows grimmer. "Yes. That's why." For your sake, she adds, "We don't have a greenland in this comm, if you haven't noticed yet. The soil around here is poor, all right for gardening but not for grass or hay. Then for the last few years before the Season started, everyone was so busy arguing about whether we should rebuild the old pre-Choking wall that nobody thought to contract with an agricultural comm for a few dozen cartloads of good soil." She sighs, rubbing the bridge of her nose. "Can't bring most livestock down the mine shafts and stairs, anyway. I don't know what we were thinking, trying to live down here. This is exactly why I need help."

Her weariness isn't a surprise, but her willingness to admit error is. It's also troubling. You say: "A comm can only have one leader, during a Season."

"Yeah, and that's still me. Don't you forget it." It could be a warn-off, but it doesn't sound like one. You suspect it's just a matter-of-fact acceptance of her place in Castrima: The people chose her, and for the time being they trust her. They don't know you, Lerna, or Hoa, and apparently they don't trust Hjarka and Cutter. You need her more than she needs any of you. Abruptly, though, Ykka shakes her head. "I can't talk about this shit anymore."

Good, because the looming sense of disjunct—this morning you were thinking of the road, and survival, and Nassun—is beginning to feel overwhelming. "I need to go topside."

It's too abrupt a change of subject, apparently out of the blue, and for a moment they all stare at you. "The rust for?" Ykka asks.

"Alabaster." Ykka looks blank. "The ten-ringer in your infirmary? He asked me to do something."

Ykka grimaces. "Oh. Him." You can't help smiling at this reaction. "Interesting. He hasn't talked to anyone since he got here. Just sits in there using up our antibiotics and eating our food."

"I just made a batch of 'cillin, Ykka." Lerna rolls his eyes.

"It's the principle of the thing."

You suspect Alabaster's been quelling the local microshakes and any aftershakes from the north, which would more than earn his keep. But if Ykka can't sess that for herself, explaining is pointless—and you're not sure you can trust her enough to talk about Alabaster yet. "He's an old friend." There. That's a good, if incomplete, summary.

"He didn't seem the type to have friends. You, either." She regards you for a long moment. "Are you a ten-ringer, too?"

Your fingers flex involuntarily. "I wore six rings, once." Lerna's head snaps around and he stares at you. Well. Cutter's face twitches in a way you can't interpret. You add: "Alabaster was my mentor, back when I was still with the Fulcrum."

"I see. And what does he want you to do, topside?"

You open your mouth, then close it. You can't help glancing at Hjarka, who snorts and gets to her feet, and Lerna, whose expression tightens as he realizes you don't want to speak in front of him. He deserves better than that, but still . . . he's a still. Finally you say, "Orogene business."

It's weak. Lerna's face goes blank, but his eyes are hard. Hjarka waves and heads for the curtain. "Then I'm out. Come on, Cutter. Since you're just a Strongback." She barks out a laugh.

Cutter stiffens, but to your surprise, he rises and follows her out. You eye Lerna for a moment, but he folds his arms. Not going anywhere. All right. In the wake of this, Ykka looks skeptical. "What is this, a final lesson from your old mentor? He's obviously not going to live much longer."

Your jaw tightens before you can help it. "That remains to be seen."

Ykka looks thoughtful for a moment longer, and then she nods decisively, getting to her feet. "All right, then. Just let me get some Strongbacks together and we'll be on our way."

"Wait, you're coming? Why?"

"Curiosity. I want to see what a Fulcrum six-ringer can do."

She grins at you and picks up the long fur vest you first saw her wearing. "Maybe see if I can do it, too."

You flinch violently at the idea of a self-taught feral attempting to connect to an obelisk. "No."

Ykka's expression flattens. Lerna stares at you, incredulous that you would achieve your goal and then scuttle it in the same breath. Quickly you amend yourself. "It's dangerous even for me, and I've done it before."

"'It'?"

Well, that does it. It's safer that she not know, but Lerna's right; you have to win this woman over if you're going to be living in her comm. "Promise me you won't try, if I tell you."

"I won't promise a rusting thing. I don't know you." Ykka folds her arms. You're a big woman, but she's a little bigger, and the hair doesn't help. Many Sanzeds like to grow their ashblow hair into big, poufy manes like hers. It's an animal intimidation thing, and it works if they've got the confidence to back it up. Ykka's got that and then some.

But you have knowledge. You push to your feet and meet her eyes. "You can't do it," you say, will her to believe. "You don't have the training."

"You don't know what kind of training I have."

And you blink, remembering that moment topside when the realization that you'd lost Nassun's trail nearly unhinged you. That strange, sweeping waft of power Ykka sent through you, like a slap but kinder, and somehow orogenic. Then there's her little trick of drawing orogenes from miles around toward Castrima. Ykka may not wear rings, but orogeny isn't about rank.

No help for it, then. "An obelisk," you say, relenting. You glance at Lerna; he blinks and frowns. "Alabaster wants me to call an obelisk. I'm going to see if I can."

To your surprise, Ykka nods, her eyes alight. "Aha! Always thought there was something about those things. Let's go, then. I definitely want to see this."

Oh. Shit.

Ykka shrugs on the vest. "Give me a half hour, then meet me at Scenic Overlook." That's the entrance to Castrima, that little platform where newcomers invariably gawk at the strangeness of a comm inside a giant geode. With that she brushes past you and out of the apartment.

Shaking your head, you eye Lerna. He nods tightly; he wants to go, too. Hoa? He simply takes up his usual place behind you, gazing at you placidly as if to say, *This was in doubt?* So now it's a party.

Ykka meets you at the overlook in half an hour. With her are four other Castrimans, who are armed and dressed in faded colors and grays for camouflage up on the surface. It's a harder procession, going up, than it was coming down: lots of uphill walking, many sets of stairs. You're not as out of breath as a few of Ykka's crew by the time it's done, but then you've been walking miles every day while they've been living safe and comfy in their underground town. (Ykka, you notice, only breathes a little harder. She's keeping in shape.) Eventually, though, you reach a false basement in one of the decoy houses topside. It's not the same basement that you entered through, which shouldn't surprise you; of course their "gate" has multiple entrances and exits. The underground passages are more complicated than you initially thought, though—something important to keep in mind, should you ever need to leave in a hurry.

The decoy house has Strongback sentries like the other one, some guarding the basement entrance and some actually in the house upstairs, keeping watch on the road outside. When the upstairs sentries give you the all clear, you head out into the late-evening ashfall.

After, what, less than a day in Castrima's geode? It's amazing how strange the surface seems to you. For the first time in weeks you *notice* the sulfur stench of the air, the silvery haze, the incessant soft patter of fat ash flakes on the ground and dead leaves. The silence, which makes you realize just how noisy Castrima-under is, with people talking and pulleys squeaking and smithies clanking, and the omnipresent hum of the geode's strange hidden machinery. Up here there's nothing. The trees have dropped their leaves; nothing moves through the curl-edged, desiccated detritus. No birdsong can be heard through the branches; most birds stop marking territory and mating during a Season, and song only attracts predators. No other animal sounds. There are no travelers on the road, though you can tell that the ash is thinner there. People have been by recently. Aside from that, though, even the wind is still. The sun has set, though there's still plenty of light in the sky. The clouds, even this far south, still reflect the Rifting.

"Traffic?" Ykka asks one of the sentries.

"Family-looking bunch about forty minutes ago," he says. He keeps his voice appropriately low. "Well equipped. Maybe twenty people, all ages, all Sanzeds. Traveling north."

That makes everyone look at him. Ykka repeats: "North?"

"North." The sentry, who has the most beautiful long-lashed eyes, looks back at Ykka and shrugs. "Looked like they had a destination in mind."

"Huh." She folds her arms, shivering a little, though it's not particularly cold outside; the cold of a Fifth Season takes months to set in fully. Castrima-under's just so warm that to someone used to that, Castrima-over's chilly. Or maybe Ykka's just reacting to the starkness of the comm around her. So many silent houses, dead gardens, and ash-occluded pathways where people once walked. You'd been thinking of the surface level of the comm as bait—and it is, a honeypot meant to draw in the desirable and distract the hostile. Yet it was also a real comm once, alive and bright and anything but still.

"Well?" Ykka takes a deep breath and smiles, but you think her smile is strained. She nods toward the low-hanging ash clouds. "If you need to *see* this thing, I don't think you're going to have much luck anytime soon."

She's right; the air is a haze of ash, and past the beaded, red-tinted clouds you can't see a damned thing. You step off the porch and look up at the sky anyway, unsure of how to begin. You also aren't sure *if* you should begin. After all, the first and second times you tried to interact with an obelisk, you almost died. Then there's the fact that Alabaster wants this, when he's the man who destroyed the world. Maybe you shouldn't do anything he asks.

He's never hurt you, though. The world has, but not him. Maybe the world deserved to be destroyed. And maybe he's earned a little of your trust, after all these years.

So you close your eyes and try to still your thoughts. There *are* sounds to be heard around you, you notice at last. Faint creaks and pops as the wooden parts of Castrima-over react to the weight of ash, or the changing warmth of the air. Several things scuttling among the dried-out stalks of a housegreen nearby: rodents or something else small, nothing to worry about. One of the Castrimans is breathing really loudly for some reason.

Warm jitter of the earth beneath your feet. No. Wrong direction.

There's actually enough ash in the sky that you can sort of grasp the clouds with your awareness. Ash is powdered rock, after all. But it's not the clouds you want. You grope along them as you would earth strata, not quite sure what you're looking for—

"Will this take much longer?" sighs one of the Castrimans.

"Why, got a hot date?" Ykka drawls.

He is insignificant. He is—

He is—

Something pulls you sharply west. You jerk and turn to face it, inhaling as you remember a night long ago in a comm called Allia, and another obelisk. The amethyst. *He didn't need to* see *it, he needed to* face *it.* Lines of sight, lines of force. Yes. And there, far along the line of your attention, you sess your awareness being drawn toward something heavy and . . . dark.

Dark, *so* dark. Alabaster said it would be the topaz, didn't he? This isn't that. It feels familiar, sort of, reminds you of the garnet. Not the amethyst. Why? The garnet was broken, mad (you're not sure why this word occurs to you), but beyond that it was also more powerful, somehow, though *power* is too simple a word for what these things contain. Richness. Strangeness. Darker colors, deeper potential? But if that's the case . . .

"Onyx," you say aloud, opening your eyes.

Other obelisks buzz along the periphery of your line of sight, closer, possible, but they don't respond to this near-instinctive call of yours. The dark obelisk is so far away, well past the Western Coastals, somewhere over the Unknown Sea. Even flying, it might take months to arrive. But.

But. The onyx *hears* you. You know this the way you once knew your children had heard you, even if they pretended to ignore you. Ponderously it turns, arcane processes awakening for the first time in an age of the earth, as it does uttering an assault of sound and vibration that shakes the sea for miles underneath. (How do you know this? You're not sessing this. You just know.)

Then it begins to come. Evil, eating Earth.

You flinch back along the line that leads to yourself. Along the way something snags your attention, and almost as an afterthought you call it, too: the topaz. It is lighter, livelier, much closer, and somehow more responsive, perhaps because you perceive a hint of Alabaster in its interstices like a curl of citrus rind added to a savory dish. He's prepped it for you.

Then you snap back into yourself and turn to Ykka, who's frowning at you. "You follow that?"

She shakes her head slowly, but not in negation. She caught some of it, somehow. You can see that in the look on her face. "I... that was... something. I'm not sure what."

"Don't reach for either one, when they get here." Because you're sure they're coming. "Don't reach for any of them. Ever." You're reluctant to say *obelisk*. Too many stills around, and even if they haven't killed you yet, stills never need to hear that something can make orogenes even more of a danger than they already are.

"What would happen if I did?" It's a question of honest curiosity, not challenge, but some questions are dangerous.

You decide to be honest. "You would die. I'm not sure how." Actually you're pretty sure she would spontaneously ignite into a white-hot screaming column of fire and force, possibly taking all of Castrima with her. But you're not a hundred percent sure, so you stick to what you know. "The—those things are like the batteries some Equatorial comms use." Shit. "Used. You've heard of those? A battery stores energy so you can have electricity even if the hydro's not flowing or the geo has—"

Ykka looks affronted. Well, she is Sanzed; they invented batteries. "I know what a rusting battery is! First hint of a shake and you've got acid burns on top of everything else, all for the sake of a bit of stored juice." She shakes her head. "What you're talking about isn't a *battery*."

"They were making sugar batteries when I left Yumenes," you say. She's not saying *obelisk*, either. Good; she gets it. "Safer than acid and metal. Batteries can be made more than one way. But if a battery is too powerful for the circuit you attach it to..." You figure that's enough to get the idea across.

She shakes her head again, but you think she believes you. As she turns and starts to pace in thought, you notice Lerna. He's been quiet all this time, listening to you and Ykka talk. Now he seems deep in thought, and that bothers you. You don't like that a still is thinking so hard about this.

But then he surprises you. "Ykka. How old do you think this comm really is?"

She stops and frowns at him. The other Castrimans shift as if uncomfortable. Maybe it bothers them, being reminded that they live in a deadciv ruin. "No clue. Why?"

He shrugs. "I'm just thinking of similarities."

You understand then. Crystals in Castrima-under that glow through some means you can't fathom. Crystals that float in the sky by some means you can't fathom. Both mechanisms meant to be used by orogenes and no one else.

Stone eaters showing an inordinate interest in orogenes who use either. You glance at Hoa.

But Hoa isn't looking at the sky, or at you. He's stepped off the porch and has crouched on the ashy ground just off the walkway, staring at something. You follow his gaze and see a small mound in what was once the front yard of the house next door. It looks like just another pile of ash, maybe three feet high, but then you notice a tiny desiccated animal foot poking out of one end. Cat, maybe, or rabbit. There are probably dozens of small carcasses around here, buried under the ash; the beginning of the Season likely caused a huge die-off. Odd that this carcass seems to have accumulated so much more ash than the ground around it, though.

"Too long gone to eat, kid," says one of the men, who's also noticed Hoa and clearly has no idea what the "kid" is. Hoa blinks at him and bites his lip with just the perfect degree of unease. He plays the child so well. Then he gets up and comes over to you, and you realize he's not playacting. Something really has unnerved him.

"Other things will eat it," he says to you, very softly. "We should go."

What. "You're not afraid of anything."

His jaw tightens. Jaw full of diamond teeth. Muscles over diamond bones? No wonder he's never let you try to lift him; he must be heavy as marble. But he says, "I'm afraid of things that will hurt you."

And . . . you believe him. Because, you suddenly realize, that's been the commonality of all his strange behavior so far. His willingness to face the kirkhusa, which might have been too fast even for your orogeny. His ferocity toward other stone eaters. He's protecting you. So few have ever tried to protect you, in your life. It's impulse that makes you lift a hand and stroke it over his weird white hair. He blinks. Something comes into his eyes that is anything but inhuman. You don't know what to think. This, though, is why you listen to him.

"Let's go," you say to Ykka and the others. You've done what Alabaster asked. You suspect he won't be displeased by the *extra* obelisk when you tell him—if he doesn't already know. Now, maybe, finally, he'll tell you what the rust is going on.

* * *

> Before, gather into stable rock for each citizen one year's supply: ten rullets of grain, five of legume, a quarter-tradet dry fruit, and a half storet in tallow, cheese, or preserved flesh. Multiply by each year of life desired. After, guard upon stable rock with at least three strong-backed souls per cache: one to guard the cache, two to guard the guard.
>
> —*Tablet One, "On Survival," verse four*

3

Schaffa, forgotten

YES. YOU ARE HIM, TOO, or you were until after Meov. But now he is someone else.

* * *

The force that shatters the *Clalsu* is orogeny applied to air. Orogeny isn't meant to be applied to air, but there's no real reason for it not to work. Syenite has had practice already using orogeny on water, at and since Allia. There are minerals in water, and likewise there are dust particles in air. Air has heat and friction and mass and kinetic potential, same as earth; the molecules of air are simply farther apart, the atoms shaped differently. Anyhow, the involvement of an obelisk makes all of these details academic.

Schaffa knows what's coming the instant he feels the obelisk's pulse. He is old, old, Syenite's Guardian. So old. He knows what stone eaters do to powerful orogenes whenever they get the chance, and he knows why it is crucial to keep orogenes' eyes on the ground and not the sky. He has seen what happens when a four-ringer—that's how he still thinks of Syenite—connects to an obelisk. He does genuinely care about her, you realize (she does not realize). It isn't all about control. She's his little one, and he has protected her in more ways than she knows. The thought of her agonizing death is unbearable to him. This is ironic, considering what happens next.

In the moment when Syenite stiffens and her frame becomes suffused with light, and the air within the *Clalsu*'s tiny forward compartment shivers and turns into a nearly solid wall of unstoppable force, Schaffa happens to be standing to one side of a hanging bulkhead rather than in front of it. His companion, the Guardian who has just killed Syenite's feral lover, is not so lucky: When the force slams him backward, the bulkhead juts out from the wall at just the right height and angle to shear his head off before giving way itself. Schaffa, however, flies backward unobstructed through the *Clalsu*'s capacious hold, which is empty because the ship hasn't been out on a piracy run in a while. There's room enough for his velocity to slow a little, and for the greatest force of Syenite's blow to move past him. When he finally does hit a bulkhead, it is with merely bone-breaking force and not bone-pulverizing force. And the bulkhead is buckling, crumbling along with the rest of the ship, when he hits it. That helps, too.

Then when jagged, knifelike spikes of bedrock from the ocean floor begin spearing through the explosion of debris, Schaffa is lucky again: None of them pierce his body. Syenite is lost in the obelisk by this point, and lost in the first throes of a grief that will send aftershakes through even Essun's life. (Schaffa saw her hand on the child's face, covering mouth and nose, pressing. Incomprehensible. Did she not know that Schaffa would love her son as he loved her? He would lay the boy down gently, so gently, in the wire chair.) She is part of something vast and globally powerful now, and Schaffa, once the most important person in her world, is beneath her notice. On some level he is aware of this even as he flies through the storm, and the knowledge leaves a deep burn of hurt in his heart. Then he is in the water and dying.

It is difficult to kill a Guardian. The many broken bones Schaffa has suffered and the damage to his organs would not be enough to do the job, in and of themselves. Even drowning wouldn't be a problem under ordinary circumstances. Guardians are different. But they do have limits, and drowning *plus* organ failure *plus* blunt force trauma is enough to breach them. He realizes this as he tumbles through the water, bouncing off shards of stone and debris from the destroyed ship. He can't tell which way is up, except that one direction seems faintly brighter than the other, but he is being dragged away from this by the swiftly sinking aft end of the ship. He uncurls, hits a rock, recovers, and tries to paddle against the downward current even though one of his arms is now broken. There's nothing in his lungs. The air's been beaten out of him, and he's trying not to inhale water because then he will surely die. He cannot die. He has so much left to do.

But he is only human, mostly, and as the terrible pressure grows and spots of blackness encroach on his vision and his whole body grows numb with the weight of the water, he cannot help sucking in a mighty lungful. It *hurts*: salt acid in his chest, fire in his throat, and still no air. On top of everything else—he can bear the rest, has borne worse in his long awful life—it is suddenly too much for the ordered, careful rationality that has guided and guarded Schaffa's mind up to this point.

He panics.

Guardians must never panic. He knows this; there are good reasons why. He does it anyway, flailing and screaming as he is dragged into the cold dark. He wants to live. This is the first and worst sin, for one of his kind.

His terror suddenly vanishes. A bad sign. It is replaced a moment later by an anger so powerful that it blots out everything else. He stops screaming and trembles with it, but even as he does so, he knows: This anger is not his own. In his panic, he has opened himself to danger, and the danger that he fears above all others has come striding through the door as if it owns the place already.

It says to him: *If you wish to live, that can be arranged.*

Oh, Evil Earth.

More offers, promises, suggestions and their rewards. Schaffa can have more power—power enough to fight the current, and the pain, and the lack of oxygen. He can live . . . for a price.

No. No. He knows the price. Better to die than pay it. But it is one thing to resolve to die, quite another to actually carry out that resolve in the midst of dying.

Something burns at the back of Schaffa's skull. This is a cold burn, not like the fire in his nose and throat and chest. Something there is waking up, warming up, gathering itself. Ready for the collapse of his resistance.

We all do what we have to do, comes the seducer's whisper, and this is the same reasoning Schaffa has used on himself too many times, over the centuries. Justifying too many atrocities. One does what one must, for duty. For life.

It's enough. The cold presence takes him.

Power suffuses his limbs. In just a few suddenly restarted

heartbeats, the broken bones have knitted and the organs have resumed their traditional function, albeit with a few work-arounds for the lack of oxygen. He twists in the water and begins to swim, sensing the direction he must go. Not up, not anymore; suddenly he finds oxygen in the water that he is breathing. He has no gills, yet his alveoli suddenly absorb more than they should be able to. It's only a little oxygen, though—not even enough to feed his body properly. Cells die, especially in a very particular part of his brain. He is aware of this, horribly. He is aware of the slow death of all that makes him *Schaffa*. But the price must be paid.

He fights it, of course. The anger tries to drive him forward, keep him underwater, but he knows that *everything* of him will die if he does. So he swims forward, but also upward, squinting through the murk at the light. It takes a long, dying time. But at least some of the rage within him is his own, fury that he has been forced into this position, rage at himself for succumbing, and that keeps him at it even as the tingling sets into his hands, his feet. But—

He reaches the surface. Breaches it. Concentrates hard on not panicking while he vomits up water, coughs out more, and finally sucks in air. It hurts so much. Still, with the first inhalation, the dying stops. His brain and limbs get what they need. There are still spots in his vision, still that awful coldness at the back of his head, but he is Schaffa. *Schaffa.* He holds on to this, digs in claws and snarls away the encroaching cold. Fire-under-Earth, he's still Schaffa, and he will not let himself forget this.

(He loses so much else, though. Understand: The Schaffa that we have known thus far, the Schaffa whom Damaya learned to fear and Syenite learned to defy, is now dead. What remains is a man with a habit of smiling, a warped paternal instinct, and a rage that is not wholly his own driving everything he does from this point on.

Perhaps you will mourn the Schaffa who is lost. It's all right if you do. He was part of you, once.)

He resumes swimming. After about seven hours—this is the strength his memories have bought him—he sees the still-smoking cone of Allia against the horizon. It's a longer distance than straight to shore, but he adjusts his direction to swim toward it. There will be help there, he knows somehow.

It is well past sunset now, fully dark. The water is cold, and he's thirsty, and he hurts. Thankfully none of the monsters of the deep attack him. The only real threat he faces is his own will, and the question of whether it will falter in the battle against the sea, or against the cold rage eating his mind. It does not help that he is alone save for the indifferent stars... and the obelisk. He sees it once, when he glances back: a wavering now-colorless shape against the sparkling night sky. It looks no farther away than when he first noticed it from the deck of the ship, and ignored it in favor of focusing on his quarry. He should have paid closer attention, studied it to see if it was approaching, remembered that even a four-ringer can be a threat under the right circumstances, and—

He frowns, pausing for a moment to float on his back. (This is dangerous. Fatigue immediately begins to set in. The power that sustains him can do only so much.) He stares at the obelisk. A four-ringer. Who? He tries to remember. There was someone... important.

No. He is Schaffa. That is all that is important. He resumes swimming.

Near dawn, he feels gritty black sand under his feet. He stumbles up out of the water, alien to himself and the movement of limbs on land, half crawling. The surf recedes behind him; there's a tree ahead. He collapses upon its roots and does something that resembles sleep. It's closer to a coma.

When he wakes, the sun's up and he is afire with pain of every kind: sore lungs, aching limbs, throbbing unhealed fractures in his nonessential bones, a dry throat, cracking skin. (And another, deeper ache.) He groans and something shadows his face. "You all right?" asks a voice that sounds like he feels. Rough, dry, low.

He peels his eyes open to see an old man crouching before him. The man's an Eastcoaster, thin and weathered, most of his curly white hair gone except a fringe round the back of his head. When Schaffa looks around, he sees that they are in a small, tree-shadowed cove. The old man's rowboat has been pulled onto the shore, not far away. A fishing rod pokes out of it. The trees of the cove are all dead and the sand beneath Schaffa blows with ash; they're still very close to the volcano that was Allia.

How did he get here? He remembers swimming. Why was he in the water? That part is gone.

"I—" Schaffa begins, and chokes on his own dry, swollen tongue. The old man helps him sit up, then offers him an open canteen. Brackish, leather-flavored water never tasted so sweet. The old man pulls it away after a few swallows, which Schaffa knows is wise, but he still groans and reaches after the canteen once. Only once, though. He is strong enough not to beg.

(The emptiness inside him is not just thirst.)

He tries to focus. "I'm." This time speaking is easier. "I... don't know if I'm all right."

"Shipwreck?" The old man cranes his neck to look around. In the near distance, very visible, is the ridge of knifelike stones that Syenite raised, from the pirates' island all the way to the mainland. "Were you out there? What was that, some sort of shake?"

It seems impossible that the old man does not know—but Schaffa has always been amazed at how little ordinary people understand about the world. (Always? Has he *always* been so amazed? Really?) "Rogga," he says, too tired to manage the three syllables of the non-vulgar word for their kind. It's enough. The old man's face hardens.

"Filthy Earth-spawned beasts. That's why they have to be drowned as babes." He shakes his head and focuses on Schaffa. "You're too big for me to lift, and dragging will hurt. Think you can get up?"

With help, Schaffa does manage to rise and stagger to the old man's rowboat. He sits shivering in the prow while the old man rows them away from the cove, heading south along the coast. Some of why he's shivering is cold—his clothes are still wet where he was lying down—and some of it is lingering shock. Some of it, however, is something entirely else.

(Damaya! With great effort he remembers this name, and an impression: a small frightened Midlatter girl superimposed over a tall, defiant Midlatter woman. Love and fear in her eyes, sorrow in his heart. He has hurt her. He needs to find her, but when he reaches for the sense of her that should be embedded in his mind, there is nothing. She is gone along with everything else.)

The old man chatters at him through the whole ride. He is Litz Strongback Metter, and Metter is a little fishing town a few miles south of Allia. They've been debating whether to move since that whole mess with Allia happened, but then suddenly the volcano went dormant, so maybe the Evil Earth isn't out to get them, after all, or at least not this time. He's got two children, one stupid and the other selfish, and three grandkids, all from the stupid one and hopefully not too stupid themselves. They don't have much, Metter's just another Coaster comm, can't even afford a proper wall instead of a bunch of trees and sticks, but folks gotta do what folks gotta do, you know how it is, everyone will take good care of you, don't you worry.

(*What is your name?* the old man asks amid the prattle, and Schaffa tells him. The man asks for more names than this, but Schaffa has only the one. *What were you doing out there?* The silence inside Schaffa yawns in answer.)

The village is an especially precarious one in that it is half on the shore and half on the water, houseboats and stilt-houses connected by jetties and piers. People gather round Schaffa when Litz helps him onto a pier. Hands touch him and he flinches, but they mean to help. It is not their fault that there is so little in them of what he needs that they feel wrong. They push him, guide him. He is beneath a cold shower of fresh water, and then he is put into short pants and a homespun sleeveless shirt. When he lifts his hair while washing it, they marvel at the scar on his neck, thick and stitched and vanishing into his hairline. (He wonders at it himself.) They puzzle over his clothing, so faded by sun and salt water that it has lost nearly all color. It looks brownish-gray. (He remembers that it should be burgundy, but not why.)

More water, the good kind. This time he can drink his fill. He eats a little. Then he sleeps for hours, with incessant angry whispering in the back of his mind.

When Schaffa wakes, it's late in the night, and there's a little boy standing in front of his bed. The lantern's wick has been turned down low, but it's bright enough in the room that Schaffa can see his old clothing, now washed and dry, in the boy's hands. The boy has turned one pocket inside out; there, alone on the whole garment, has it retained something of its original color. Burgundy.

Schaffa pushes himself up on one elbow. Something about the boy... perhaps. "Hello."

The boy looks so much like Litz that he needs only a few decades of weathering and less hair to be the old man's twin. But there is a desperate hope in the boy's eyes that would be completely out of place in Litz's. Litz knows his place in the world. This boy, who is maybe eleven or twelve, old enough to be confirmed by his comm... something has unmoored him, and Schaffa thinks he knows what. "This is yours," the boy says, holding up the garment.

"Yes."

"You're a Guardian?"

Fleeting almost-memory. "What is that?"

The boy looks as confused as Schaffa feels. He takes a step closer to the bed, and stops. (Come closer. Closer.) "They said you didn't remember things. You're lucky to be alive." The boy licks his lips, uncertain. "Guardians... guard."

"Guard what?"

Incredulity washes the fear from the boy. He steps closer still.

"*Orogenes.* I mean... you guard people from them. So they don't hurt anyone. And you guard them from people, too. That's what the stories say."

Schaffa pushes himself to sit up, letting his legs dangle over the edge of the bed. The pain of his injuries is nearly gone, his flesh repaired at a faster rate than normal by the angry power within him. He feels well, in fact, except for one thing.

"Guard orogenes," he says thoughtfully. "Do I?"

The boy laughs a little, though his smile fades quickly. He's very afraid, for some reason, though not of Schaffa. "People kill orogenes," the boy says softly. "When they find them. Unless they're with a Guardian."

"Do they?" It seems uncivilized of them. But then he remembers the ridge of spiky stones across the ocean, and his utter conviction that it was the work of an orogene. *That's why they have to be drowned as babes*, Litz had said.

Missed one, Schaffa thinks, then has to fight hysterical laughter.

"I don't want to hurt anyone," the boy is saying. "I will, one day, without... without training. I almost did when that volcano was doing things. It was so hard not to."

"If you had, it would have killed you and possibly many other people," Schaffa says. Then he blinks. How does he know that? "A hot spot is far too volatile for you to quell safely."

The boy's eyes alight. "You *do* know." He comes forward, sinks to a crouch beside Schaffa's knee. He whispers, "Please help me. I think my mother... she saw me, when the volcano... I tried to act like normal and I *couldn't*. I think she knows. If she tells my grandfather..." He inhales suddenly, sharply, as if he is gasping for air. He's holding back a sob, but the movement looks the same.

Schaffa knows how it feels to drown. He reaches out and strokes the boy's dense cloud of hair, crown to nape, and lets his fingers linger at the nape.

"There is something I have to do," Schaffa says, because there is. The anger and whispers within him have a purpose, after all, and this has become his purpose. *Gather them, train them, make them the weapons they are meant to be.* "If I take you with me, we must travel far from here. You'll never see your family again."

The boy looks away, his expression turning bitter. "They'd kill me if they knew."

"Yes." Schaffa presses, very gently, and draws the first measure of—something—from the boy. What? He cannot remember what it is called. Perhaps it has no name. All that matters is that it exists, and he needs it. With it, he knows somehow, he can hold on more tightly to the tattered remnants of who he is. (Was.) So he takes, and the first draught of it is like a sudden, sweet wash of fresh water amid gallons of burning salt. He yearns to drink it all, reaches for the rest as thirstily as he sought Litz's canteen, though he forces himself to let go for the same reason. He can endure on what he has now, and if he is patient, the boy will have more for him later.

Yes. His thoughts are clearer now. Easier to think around the whispers. He needs this boy, and others like him. He must go forth and find them, and with their help, he can make it to—

—to—

—well. Not everything is clearer. Some things will never come back. He'll make do.

The boy is searching his face. While Schaffa has been trying to put together the fragments of his identity, the boy has been wrestling with his future. They are made for each other. "I'll go with you," the boy says, having apparently spent the past minute thinking he has a choice. "Anywhere. I don't want to hurt anyone. I don't want to die."

For the first time since a moment on a ship a few days before, when he was a different person, Schaffa smiles. He strokes the boy's head again. "You have a good soul. I'll help you all I can." The boy's tension dissolves at once; tears wet his eyes. "Go and gather some things to travel. I'll speak with your parents."

These words fall from his mouth naturally, easily. He has said them before, though he doesn't remember when. He remembers, though, that sometimes things don't go as well as he says they will.

The boy whispers his thanks, grabs Schaffa's knee and tries to squeeze that thanks into him, then trots away. Schaffa pushes himself slowly to his feet. The boy has left the faded uniform behind, so Schaffa pulls this on again, his fingers remembering how the seams should lie. There should be a cloak, too, but that is gone. He can't remember where. When he steps forward, a mirror on the side of the room catches his eye, and he stops. Shivers, not in pleasure this time.

It is *wrong*. It is so wrong. His hair hangs lank and dry after the sun and salt's ravaging; it should be black and glossy, and instead it is dull and wispy, burnt. The uniform hangs off him, for he has spent some of the substance of his own body as fuel in the push to reach shore. The uniform's colors are also wrong and there is no reassurance in it of who he was, who he should be. And his eyes—

Evil Earth, he thinks, staring at the icy near-white of them. He did not know his eyes looked like this.

There is a creak on the floorboards near the door, and his alien eyes shift to one side. The boy's mother stands there, blinking in the light of the lantern she holds. "Schaffa," she says. "I thought I heard you up. And Eitz?"

That must be the boy's name. "He came to bring me these." Schaffa touches his clothing.

The woman comes into the room. "Huh," she says. "Now that it's all wrung out and dry, it looks like a uniform."

Schaffa nods. "I've learned something new of myself. I'm a Guardian."

Her eyes widen. "Truly?" There's suspicion in her gaze. "And Eitz has been bothering you."

"It was no bother." Schaffa smiles, to reassure her. For some reason, the woman's frown twitches and deepens. Ah, well; he has forgotten how to charm people, too. He turns and goes over to her, and she falls back a step at his approach. He stops, amused by her fear. "He, too, has learned something of himself. I'll be taking him away now."

The woman's eyes widen. Her mouth works in silence for a moment, then she sets her jaw. "I knew it."

"Did you?"

"I didn't want to." She swallows, her hand tightening; the little lantern flame wavers with whatever emotion flashes through her. "Don't take him. Please."

Schaffa tilts his head. "Why not?"

"It would kill his father."

"Not his grandfather?" Schaffa takes a step closer. (Closer.) "Not his uncles and aunts and cousins? Not you?"

She twitches again. "I...don't know how I feel, right now." She shakes her head.

"Poor, poor thing," Schaffa says softly. This compassion is automatic, too. He feels the sorrow deeply. "But will you protect him from them, if I do not take him?"

"What?" She looks at Schaffa in surprise and alarm. Can this truly have never occurred to her? Apparently not. "Protect... *him?*" That she asks this, Schaffa understands, is the proof that she is inadequate to the task.

So he sighs and reaches up, as if to put a hand on her shoulder, and shakes his head, as if to convey regret. She relaxes minutely and does not notice when his hand instead curves around her neck. His fingers settle into place and she stiffens at once. "Wh—" Then she falls down dead.

Schaffa blinks as she falls to the floor. For a moment he is confused. Was that supposed to happen? And then—his own thoughts freshened further by the dollop of *something* that she has given him, such a tiny amount of it relative to what Eitz possessed—he understands. This thing is only safe to do with orogenes, who have more than enough to share. The woman must have been a still. But Schaffa feels better. In fact—

Take more, whispers the rage at the back of his mind. *Take the others. They threaten the boy, which threatens you.*

Yes. That seems wise.

So Schaffa rises and moves through the quiet, dark house, touching each member of Eitz's family and devouring a piece of them. Most of them do not wake. The stupid son gives more than the rest; almost an orogene. (Almost a Guardian.) Litz gives the least, perhaps because he is old—or perhaps because he is awake and fighting against the hand Schaffa has clamped over his mouth and nose. He is trying to stab Schaffa with a fishknife pulled from under his pillow. What a pity that he must suffer such fear! Schaffa twists Litz's head around sharply to get at the nape of his neck. There's a snapping sound as he does this, which he doesn't even notice until the flow of *something* out of Litz goes soft and dead and useless. Ah, yes, belatedly Schaffa remembers that it does not work on the dead. He'll be more careful in the future.

But it is so much better, now that the taut ache inside him has gone still. He feels... not whole. Never that, again. But when there is so much of another presence inside him, even a little regained ground is a blessing.

"I am Schaffa Guardian... Warrant?" he murmurs, blinking as the last part finally comes to him. What comm is Warrant? He cannot remember. He is glad to have the name regardless. "I have done only what was necessary. Only what is best for the world."

The words feel right. Yes. He has needed the sense of purpose, which now sits like lead at the back of his brain; amazing that he did not have it before. Now, though? "Now I have work to do."

Eitz finds him in the living room. The boy is breathless, excited, carrying a small satchel. "I heard you and Mama talking. Did you... tell her?"

Schaffa crouches to be on eye level with him, taking him by the shoulders. "Yes. She said she didn't know how she felt, and then she said nothing more."

Eitz's face crumples. He glances toward the corridor that

leads to the adults' rooms in the house. Everyone down that corridor is dead. The doors are closed and quiet. Schaffa has left Eitz's siblings and cousins alive, however, because he is not a complete monster.

"Can I say goodbye to her?" Eitz asks softly.

"I think that would be dangerous," Schaffa says. He means it. He doesn't want to have to kill the boy yet. "These things are best done cleanly. Come; you have me now, and I will never leave you."

The boy blinks at this and straightens a little, then nods shakily. He's old for such words to have the power on him that they do. They work, Schaffa suspects, because Eitz has spent the past few months living in terror of his family. It is nothing to play on such a lonely, weary state of mind. It isn't even a lie.

They leave the half-dead house behind. Schaffa knows that he should take the boy…somewhere. Somewhere with obsidian walls and gilded bars, a place that will die in a cataclysm of fire in ten years, so perhaps it is good that he is too damaged to remember this location. In any case the angry whispers have begun steering him in a different direction. Somewhere south. Where he has work to do.

He puts his hand on Eitz's shoulder to comfort the boy, or perhaps to comfort himself. Together they walk into the predawn dark.

* * *

Don't be fooled. The Guardians are much, much older than Old Sanze, and they do not work for us.

—Last recorded words of Emperor Mutshatee, prior to his execution

4

you are challenged

YOU'RE TIRED AFTER CALLING THE OBELISK. When you get back to your room and stretch out for half a moment on the bare pallet that came with the apartment, you fall asleep so fast you don't even realize you're doing it. In the dead of the night—or so your body clock says, since the glowing walls haven't changed—your eyes blink open and it's like only a moment has passed. But Hoa is curled beside you, apparently actually sleeping for once, and you can hear Tonkee snoring faintly in the room next door, and you feel much better than you did, if hungry. Well rested, for perhaps the first time in weeks.

The hunger spurs you up and into the apartment's living room. There's a small hempen satchel on the table, which Tonkee must've acquired, partially open to reveal mushrooms and a small pile of dried beans and other cachefood. That's right: As accepted members of Castrima, you now get a share of the comm's stores. None of it is the kind of food you can just eat for a snack, except maybe the mushrooms, but you've never seen those before, and some varieties of mushrooms need to be cooked to be edible.

You're tempted, but...*is* Castrima the sort of comm that would give dangerous foodstuffs to newcomers without warning them?

Hmm. Right. You fetch your runny-sack, rummage in it for the remaining provisions you brought to Castrima with you, and make a meal out of dried oranges, cachebread crusts, and a lump of bad-tasting jerky that you traded for at the last comm you passed, and which you suspect is hydro-pipe rat meat. Food is that which nourishes, the lorists say.

You've just choked the jerky down, and are sitting there sleepily pondering how merely summoning an obelisk took so much out of you—as if anything regarding the obelisks can be described with the adjective *merely*—when you become aware of a high, rhythmic scraping sound outside. You dismiss it immediately. Nothing about this comm makes sense; it will probably take you weeks if not months to get used to its peculiar sounds. (Months. Are you giving up on Nassun so easily?) So you ignore the sound even as it grows louder and closer, and you keep yawning, and you're about to get up and head back to bed when it belatedly dawns on you that what you're hearing is *screaming*.

Frowning, you go to the door of the apartment, pulling open the thin curtain. You're not particularly concerned; your sessapinae haven't even twitched, and anyway if there's ever a shake down here in Castrima-under, everyone's dead no matter how quickly they leave their homes. Outside there are lots of people up and about. A woman passes right by your door, carrying a big basket of the same mushrooms you almost ate; she nods at you distractedly as you come out, then almost loses her load as she tries to turn toward the noise and nearly bumps into a man pushing a covered, wheeled bin that stinks to the sky and is probably from the latrines.

In a comm with no functional day-night cycle, Castrima effectively never sleeps, and you know they have six work shifts instead of the usual three because you've been put on one. It won't start till midday—or twelvebell, as the Castrima folk say—when you're supposed to look for some woman named Artith near the forge.

And none of this is relevant because through the scatter and jut of Castrima's crystals, you can see a small cluster of people coming into the big rectangular tunnel-mouth that serves as the entrance to the geode. They're running, and they're carrying another person, who's doing all the screaming.

Even then, you're tempted to ignore it and go back to sleep. It's a Season. People die; there's nothing you can do about it. These aren't even your people. There's no reason for you to care.

Then someone shouts, "*Lerna!*" And the tone of it is so panicked that you twitch. You can see the squat gray crystal that houses Lerna's apartment from your balcony, three crystals away and a little below your own. His door-curtain jerks open and he hurries out, shrugging on a shirt as he runs down the nearest set of steps. Heading for the infirmary, where the cluster of running folk seems to be going as well.

For reasons that you cannot name, you glance back at your own apartment doorway. Tonkee, who sleeps like petrified wood, hasn't come out—but Hoa is there, statue-still and watching you. Something about his expression makes you frown. He doesn't seem to be able to do the emotionless stoneface of his kin, maybe because he doesn't have a face of actual stone. Regardless, the first thing you interpret of his expression is . . . pity.

You're out of the apartment and running for the ground level in the next breath, almost before you've thought about it. (You think as you run: The pity of a disguised stone eater has galvanized you as the screams of a fellow human being haven't. Such a monster you are.) Castrima is as frustratingly confusing as always, but this time you're aided by the fact that other people have started running along the bridges and walkways in the direction of the trouble, so you can just go with the flow.

By the time you get there, a small crowd has formed around the infirmary, most of the people milling about in curiosity or concern or anxiety. Lerna and the cluster of people carrying their injured companion have gone inside, and the awful screech is obvious now for what it is: the throat-tearing howl of someone in appalling pain, pain beyond bearing, who nevertheless is somehow forced to bear it.

It is not an intentional thing that you start pushing forward to get inside. You know nothing about giving medical care... but you do know pain. To your surprise, though, people glance at you in annoyance—then blink and shift aside. You notice those who look blank being pulled aside for quick whispers by those whose eyes have widened. Oh-ho. Castrima's been talking about you.

Then you're inside the infirmary, and you nearly get knocked down by a Sanzed woman running past with some sort of syringe in her hands. Can't be safe to do that. You follow her over to an infirmary bed where six people hold down the person doing the screaming. You get a look at the person's face when one of them shifts aside: no one you know. Just another Midlatter man, who has clearly been topside to judge by the gray layer of ash on his skin and clothing and hair. The woman with the syringe shoulders aside someone else and ostensibly administers the syringe's contents. A moment later, the man shudders all over, and his mouth begins to close. His scream dies off, slowly, slowly. Slowly. He jerks once, mightily; his holders all shift with the strength of his effort. Then at last, mercifully, he subsides into unconsciousness.

The silence almost reverberates. Lerna and the Sanzed healer keep moving, though the people who have been holding the man down draw back and look at each other as if asking what to do now. In the now-silent confusion, you cannot help glancing off toward the far end of the infirmary, where Alabaster still sits unnoticed by the infirmary's new guests. His stone eater stands where you last saw her, though her gaze is also fixed on the tableau. You can see Alabaster's face over the beds; his eyes slide over to meet yours, but then they shift away.

Your attention is recaptured by the man on the bed as some of the people around him step back. At first you can't tell what the problem is, other than that his pants seem oddly *wet* in patches, caked with muddy ash. The wetness isn't red, it's not blood, but there's a smell that you're not sure how to describe. Meat in brine. Hot fat. His boots are off, baring feet which still spasmodically twitch a little, the splayed toes relaxing only reluctantly even in unconsciousness. Lerna is cutting open one pants leg with a pair of scissors. What you notice first, as he peels away the damp cloth, are the small round blue hemispheres that dot the man's skin here and there, each perhaps two inches in diameter and an inch of rounded height, shiny and foreign to his flesh. There are ten or fifteen of them. Each sits at the center of a patch of bloated pink-brown flesh covering perhaps a handspan of the man's legs. You think the lumps are jewels, at first. That's kind of what they look like, metallic over the blue, and beautiful.

"Fuck," says someone, voice soft with shock, and someone

else says, "What the rust." Someone else pushes into the infirmary behind you after a moment's argument with the people who've blocked off the door. She comes to stand beside you and you look over at Ykka, whose eyes widen in confusion and revulsion for an instant before she schools her expression to blankness. Then she says, sharply enough to jerk people out of staring, "What happened?"

(You notice, belatedly or perhaps right in time, that another stone eater is in the room, not far beyond the tableau. She's familiar—the red-haired one who greeted you along with Ykka when you first came to Castrima. She's watching Ykka now, avidly, but her stone gaze occasionally drifts toward you, too. You suddenly become hyperaware that Hoa did not follow you from the apartment.)

"Outer perimeter patrol," says another ash-covered Midlatter man, to Ykka. He doesn't look like a Strongback, too small. Maybe he's one of the new Hunters. He comes around the bedside group and fixes his gaze on Ykka as if she is all that prevents him from staring at the injured man until his mind breaks. "We were out by the s-salt quarry, thinking it might be a good place for hunting. There was some kind of sinkhole near a stream runnel. Beled—I don't know. He's gone. I heard them both scream at first, but I didn't know why. I was upstream, looking at some animal tracks. By the time I got there it was just Terteis there, looking like he was trying to climb out of the ash. I helped him out, but they were on him already, and more were crawling up his shoes so I had to cut them off—"

A hiss jerks your eyes away from the speaking man. Lerna is shaking his hand, holding out the fingers stiffly as if they hurt.

"Get me the rusting forceps!" he says to another man, who twitches and turns to do so. You've never heard Lerna curse before.

"Some kind of boil," says the Sanzed woman who injected the man. She sounds disbelieving; she's speaking to Lerna, as if trying to convince him rather than herself. (Lerna just keeps grimly probing the edges of the burns with his uninjured hand, ignoring her.) "Has to be. He fell into a steam vent, a geyser, an old rusted-out geo pipe." Which would make the bugs just a coincidence.

"—or they would've gotten on me, too." The other Hunter is still talking in his hollow voice. "I thought the sinkhole was just loose ash, but it was really . . . I don't know. Like an anthill." The Hunter swallows, sets his jaw. "I couldn't get the rest off, so I brought him here."

Ykka's lips press together, but she rolls up her sleeves and goes over, pushing through the other shocked people nearby. She yells, "Back up! If you don't mean to help with this, get out of the rusting way." Some of the milling people start pulling others away. Someone else grabs for one of the jewel-objects and tries to pull it off, then jerks their hand away, yelping as Lerna did. The object changes, two pieces of the shiny blue surface flaking away and lifting before clapping back into place—and suddenly it shifts in your head. It's not a jewel; it's a bug. Some kind of beetle, and the iridescent shell is its carapace. In the moment that it lifted its wing covers, you saw that its round body was translucent, with something jumping and bubbling inside. You can sess the heat of it even from where you are, hot as a boil. The man's flesh steams around it.

Someone gives Lerna the forceps and he tries to pull one of the beetles off. Its wing covers lift again, and a thin jet of something skeets across Lerna's fingers. He yelps and drops the forceps, jerking back. "Acid!" someone says. Someone else grabs his hand and tries to quickly wipe off the stuff, but you know what it is even before Lerna gasps, "No! Just water. Scalding water."

"Careful," says the other Hunter, belatedly. One of his hands bears a line of blisters, you notice. You also notice that he doesn't look back at the infirmary table or any of the people there.

This is too horrible to watch. The rusting bugs are boiling the man to death. But when you look away, you see that Alabaster is watching you again. Alabaster, who himself is covered in burns, but who *should be dead*. No one stands near the epicenter of a continent-spanning fissure vent and gets only patchy third-degree burns. He should've been ashes scattered over Yumenes's melted streets.

You realize this as he gazes at you, though his expression is indifferent to another man's trial by fire. It is a familiar sort of indifference—Fulcrum-familiar. It is the indifference that comes of too many betrayals, too many friends lost for no good reason, too many "too horrible to watch" atrocities seen.

And yet. The reverberation of Alabaster's orogeny is carelessly powerful, diamond-precise, and so achingly familiar that you have to close your eyes and fight off memories of a heaving ship deck, a lonely highroad, a windy rock island. The torus that he spins is devastatingly small—barely an inch wide, so attenuated that you cannot find its hairpin fulcrum. He's still better than you.

Then you hear a gasp. You open your eyes to see one of the bugs shiver, hiss like a living teakettle—and then freeze over. Its legs, which had been hooked into the boiled flesh around it, pop loose. It's dead.

But then you hear a soft groan, and the orogeny dissipates. You look over to see that Alabaster has bowed his head and hunched over. His stone eater slow-grind crouches beside him, something in her posture indicating concern even if her face is as placid as ever. The red-haired stone eater—in internal exasperation you decide to call her Ruby Hair, for now—is gazing at him, too.

That's it, then. You look back at the man—and your gaze catches on Lerna, who's looking at the frozen bug in fascination. His eyes lift, sweep the room, stutter across yours, stop. You see the question there, and start to shake your head: No, you did not freeze the bug. But that isn't the right question, and maybe isn't even the question he's asking. He doesn't need to know if you did. He needs to know if you *can*.

Lerna, Hoa, Alabaster; today you are driven by silent, meaningful gazes, it seems.

The hot points of the insects sess like geothermal vents as you step forward and focus your sessapinae. Lots of controlled pressure in their tiny bodies; that's how they make the water boil. You lift a hand toward the man out of habit so everyone will know you're doing something, and you hear a curse, a hiss, a scramble of feet and jostling bodies as people move back from you, away from any torus you might manifest. Fools. Don't they know you only need a torus when you have to pull from the ambient? The bugs have plenty of what you need. The difficulty will lie in confining your draw just to them and not the man's overheated flesh underneath.

Ykka's stone eater takes a slow step closer. You sess her movement, rather than seeing it; it's like a mountain shifting toward you. Then Ruby Hair stops as suddenly there is another mountain in its way: Hoa, stock-still and quietly cold. Where did he come from? You cannot spare another thought for these creatures right now.

You begin slowly, using your eyes as well as your sessapinae to determine exactly where to stop... but Alabaster has shown you the way of it. You spin the torus from their hot little bodies as he did, one by one. As you do this, some of them crack open with a loud and violent hiss, and one of them even pops off, flying off toward the side of the room. (People move out of its way even faster than they moved out of yours.) Then it is done.

Everyone stares at you. You look at Ykka. You're breathing hard because that degree of fine focus is much, much harder than shifting a hillside. "Need anything shaken?"

She blinks, sessing instantly what you mean. Then she grabs your arm. There is—what? An inversion. A channeling-away, as you would do to an obelisk, except there is no obelisk, and you aren't doing the channeling even though it's your orogeny. All at once you hear people exclaim outside, and you glance through the infirmary's door. The infirmary is a built-building, not carved from one of the giant crystals of the geode; inside it's lit only by electric lamps. Outside, however, through the uncurtained doorway, you can see the geode crystals glowing noticeably brighter, all over the comm.

You stare at Ykka. She nods back at you in a matter-of-fact, collegial way, as if you should have any clue what she's just done or as if you should be comfortable with a feral doing something that a ringed Fulcrum orogene can't. Then Ykka steps over to grab another pair of forceps to help. Lerna's pulling on one of the beetles again despite his scalded fingers, and this time the thing is coming off. A proboscis as long as its body slides out of the boiled flesh, and—you can't look anymore.

(You glimpse Ruby Hair again, from the corner of your eye. She's ignoring Hoa, who stands still as a statue between you, and now she's smiling at Ykka. Her lips are parted just a little. You glimpse a hint of shining teeth. You blot this from your awareness.)

So you retreat to the far end of the infirmary, to sit down beside Alabaster's cushion pile. He's still bent over, breathing like a bellows, although the stone eater has taken hold of his shoulder with one viselike hand to keep him mostly upright. Belatedly you realize he's holding one of his stumpy wrists to his belly, and—oh, Earth. The gray-brown rock that once only capped his right wrist now sleeves up to his elbow.

He lifts his head; sweat sheens his face. He looks as weary as if he just shut down another supervolcano, although this time he's at least conscious, and smiling.

"Ever the good pupil, Syen," he murmurs. "But rusting Earth, is it costly to teach you."

The shock of understanding rings through you like silence. *Alabaster can't do orogeny anymore.* Not without . . . consequences. Impulse makes you look at Antimony, and your gorge rises as you realize the stone eater's gaze is fixed on his newly stoned arm. She doesn't move, however. After a moment Alabaster manages to straighten, throwing a grateful look at her for the supportive hand. "Later," he says softly. You know this means *eat my arm later.* She adjusts her hand to support him from behind instead.

The urge to push her aside, put your hand in place to hold him up, is so powerful that you can't look at this, either.

You push yourself up, brush past everyone else to get outside the infirmary, and then you sit down on the low, flattened tip of a crystal that is only just beginning to grow out of the geode wall. No one bothers you, though you feel the pressure of gazes and hear the echo of whispers. You don't mean to stay long, but you do. You don't know why.

Eventually a shadow falls over your feet. You look up to see Lerna standing there. Beyond him, Ykka is walking away with another man who is trying to talk to her; she seems to be angrily ignoring him. The rest of the crowd has dispersed at last, though you can see through the open doorway that there's still more people in the infirmary than usual, perhaps visiting the poor half-cooked Hunter.

Lerna isn't looking at you. He's staring at the far wall of the geode, which is lost in the hazy glow from dozens of crystals between here and there. He's also smoking a cigarette. The stench of it, and the yellowish color of the outer wrapping, tells you it's a mellow: derminther mela leaves and flower buds, mildly narcotic when dried. The Somidlats are famous for them, to the degree that the Somidlats can be famous for anything. You're still surprised to see him smoking one, though. He's a doctor. Mellows are bad for you.

"You all right?" you ask.

He doesn't answer at first, taking a long drag on the cigarette. You're starting to think he won't speak, when he says, "I'm going to kill him when I go back in there."

Then you understand. The bugs burned through skin,

muscle, maybe even down to bone. With a team of Yumenescene doctors and cutting-edge biomestric drugs, maybe the man could be kept alive long enough to heal—and even then he might never walk again. With just whatever equipment and medicines Castrima has to hand, the best Lerna can do is amputate. The man might survive it. But this is a Season, and every comm-dweller must earn their shelter from the ash and cold. Few comms have use for a legless Hunter, and this comm is already supporting one burned invalid.

(Ykka walking away, ignoring a man who sounds like he is arguing for a life.)

So Lerna is very much not all right. You decide to change the subject, slightly. "I've never seen anything like those bugs."

"The locals say they're called boilbugs, though no one knew why before now. They breed around streams, carry water inside themselves. Animals eat them during droughts. Usually they're carrion eaters. Harmless." Lerna flicks ash from his forearm. He's wearing only a loose sleeveless shirt due to Castrima's warmth. The skin of his forearms is flecked with . . . something. You look away. "Things change during a Season, though."

Yes. Cooked carrion probably lasts longer.

"You could've gotten those things off him the instant you walked in the door," Lerna adds.

You blink. Then it registers in your mind that this statement was an attack. It's so mildly delivered, from such an unexpected quarter, that you're too surprised to be angry. "I couldn't," you say. "At least, I didn't know I could. Alabaster—"

"I don't expect anything from him. He came to die here, not live here." Lerna pivots to face you, and all of a sudden you realize that his placid manner has been concealing absolute rage. His gaze is cool, but it's visible in everything else: his white lips, the flex of muscle in his jaw, his flaring nostrils. "Why are *you* here, Essun?"

You flinch. "You know why. I came to find Nassun."

"Nassun's out of your reach. Your goals have changed; now you're here to survive, same as the rest of us. Now you're *one of us*." His lip curls in something that might be contempt. "I'm saying this because if I don't make you understand, you might have a rusting fit and kill us all."

You open your mouth to reply. He takes a step toward you, though, and it's so aggressive that you actually sit up. "Tell me you won't, Essun. Tell me I won't have to leave *this* comm in the dead of the night, hoping nobody you've pissed off catches me and slits my throat. Tell me I'm not going to have to go back out there, to fight for my life and watch people I try to help die again and again and again, until I get eaten by rusting *bugs*—"

He cuts himself off with a choked sound, turning away sharply. You stare at his tense back and say nothing, because there's nothing you can say. This is the second time he's mentioned your murder of Tirimo. And is that surprising? He was born there, grew up there; Lerna's mother was still living there when you left. You think. Maybe you killed her, too, that last day.

There's nothing you can say, not with guilt souring your mouth, but you try anyway. "I'm sorry."

He laughs. It doesn't even sound like him, it's so ugly and angry. Then he resumes his former posture, gazing at the far geode wall. He's more in control of himself now; the muscle in his jaw isn't jumping quite so much. "Prove you're sorry."

You shake your head, in confusion rather than refusal. "How?"

"Word's spreading. A couple of the biggest gossips in the comm were with Ykka when she met you, and apparently you confirmed what a lot of the roggas have been whispering among themselves." You almost flinch at his use of *rogga*. He was such a polite boy once. "Topside, you said this Season won't end for thousands of years. Was that an exaggeration, or the truth?"

You sigh and rub a hand over your hair. It's a thick, curly mess at the roots. You need to retwist your locks, but you haven't because you haven't had time and because it feels like there's no point.

"Seasons always end," you say. "Father Earth keeps his own equilibrium. It's just a question of how long it will take."

"How long?" It's barely a question. His tone is flat, resigned. He suspects the answer already.

And he deserves your honest, best guess. "Ten thousand years?" For the Yumenes Rifting to stop venting and the skies to clear. Not long at all by the usual scale of tectonics, but the real danger lies in what the ash might set off. Enough ash covering the warm surface of the sea, and the ice might grow at the poles. That means saltier seas. Drier climates. Permafrost. Glaciers marching, spreading. And the most habitable part of the world should that happen, the Equatorials, will still be hot and toxic.

It's the winter that really kills, during Seasons. Starvation. Exposure. Even after the skies clear, though, the Rift could cause an age of winter that lasts *millions* of years. None of which matters, because humanity will have gone extinct long before. It'll be just the obelisks floating over plains of endless white, with no one left to wonder at or ignore them.

His eyelids flicker. "Hnh." To your surprise, he turns to face you. Even more surprising is that his anger seems to be gone, though it has been replaced by a kind of bleakness that feels familiar. It's his question, though, that floors you:

"So what are you planning to do about it?"

Your mouth actually falls open. After a moment you manage to reply, "I wasn't aware there was anything I *could* do about it." Just like you hadn't thought there was anything you could do about the boilbugs. Alabaster is the genius. You're the grunt.

"What are you and Alabaster doing with the obelisks?"

"What is *Alabaster* doing," you correct. "He just asked me to summon one. Probably because—" It hurts to say. "He can't do that kind of orogeny anymore."

"Alabaster made the Rift, didn't he?"

You close your mouth fast enough that your teeth clack. You've just said Alabaster can't do orogeny anymore. Enough Castrimans hear that they're living in an underground rock garden because of him, and they'll find a way to kill him, stone eater or not.

Lerna smiles lopsidedly. "It's not hard to put together, Essun. His wounds are from steam, particulate abrasion, and corrosive gas, not fire—characteristic of being in close proximity to an erupting burn. I don't know how he survived, but it's left its mark on him." He shrugged. "And I've seen you destroy a town in five minutes without breaking a sweat, so I've got an inkling of what a ten-ringer might be capable of. What are the obelisks for?"

You set your jaw. "You can ask me six different ways, Lerna, and I'll give you six different versions of 'I don't know,' because I don't."

"I think you at least have an idea. But lie to me if you want." He shakes his head. "This is your comm now."

He falls silent after that, as if expecting a response from you. You're too busy vehemently rejecting the idea to respond. But he knows you too well; he knows you don't want to hear it. That's why he says it again. "*Essun Rogga Castrima.* That's who you are now."

"No."

"Leave, then. Everyone knows Ykka can't really hold you if you put your mind to leaving. I know you'll kill us all if you feel the need. So, go."

You sit there, looking at your hands, which dangle between your knees. Your thoughts are empty.

Lerna inclines his head. "You aren't leaving because you aren't stupid. Maybe you can survive out there, but not as anything Nassun would ever want to see again. And if nothing else, you want to live so that you can eventually find her again… however unlikely that is."

Your hands twitch once. Then they resume dangling limply.

"When this Season doesn't end," Lerna continues, and it is so much worse that he does it in that same weary monotone which asked how long the Season would last, like he is speaking utter truth and knows it and hates it, "we'll run out of food. Cannibalism will help, but it's not sustainable. At that point the comm will either turn raider or simply dissolve into roving bands of commless. But even that won't save us, long term. Eventually the remnants of Castrima will just starve. Father Earth wins at last."

It's the truth, whether you want to face it or not. And it's further proof that whatever happened to Lerna during his brief commless career changed him. Not really for the worse. It's just made him the kind of healer who knows that sometimes one must inflict terrible agony—rebreak a bone, carve off a limb, kill the weak—in order to make the whole stronger.

"Nassun's strong like you," he continues, softly and brutally. "Say she survives Jija. Say you find her, bring her here or any other place that seems safe. She'll starve with the rest when the storecaches empty, but with her orogeny, she could probably force others to give her their food. Maybe even kill them and have the remaining stores for herself. Eventually the stores will run out, though. She'll have to leave the comm, scrape by on whatever forage she can find under the ash, hopefully while not running afoul of the wildlife or other hazards. She'll be one of the last to die: alone, hungry, cold, hating herself. Hating you. Or maybe she'll have shut down by then. Maybe she'll just be an animal, driven only by the instinct to survive and failing even at that. Maybe she'll eat herself in the end, the way any beast might—"

"Stop," you say. It's a whisper. Mercifully, he does. He turns away again instead, taking another long drag of his half-forgotten mellow.

"Have you talked to anyone since you got here?" he asks finally. It's not really a change of subject. You don't relax. He nods toward the infirmary. "Anyone but Alabaster and that menagerie you've been traveling with? More than a meeting; *talked*."

Not enough to count. You shake your head.

"The rumor's spreading, Essun. And now everyone's thinking

about how slowly their children will die." He finally flicks away the mellow. It's still burning. "Thinking about how they can't do anything about it."

But you can, he doesn't need to say.

Can you?

Lerna walks away so abruptly that you're surprised. You hadn't realized he was done. It's an ingrained flinch at the idea of waste that makes you go pick up his discarded cigarette. Takes you a moment to figure out how to inhale without choking; you've never tried before. Orogenes aren't supposed to ingest narcotics.

But orogenes aren't supposed to live, either, during a Season. The Fulcrum had no storecaches. No one ever mentioned it, but you're pretty sure that if a Season ever hit Yumenes hard enough, the Guardians would have swept the place and slaughtered every one of you. Your kind is useful in preventing Seasons, but if the Fulcrum ever so failed in its duty, if ever the worthies of the Black Star or the Emperor had felt a whiff of a thought of a tremor, you and your fellow Imperial Orogenes would not have been rewarded with survival.

And why should you have been? What survival skills does any rogga offer? You can keep people from dying in a shake, yay. Fat lot of good that does when there's no food.

"Enough!" You hear Ykka's voice from a short distance away, though you can't see her around the ground-level crystals. She's shouting. "It's done! You want to be there for it or stay here wasting breath on me?"

You get up, your knees aching. Head in that direction.

Along the way, you pass a young man whose face is streaked

with tears of fury and incipient grief. He storms past you back to the infirmary. You keep going and eventually see Ykka standing near the side of a high, narrow crystal. She's planted a hand against its wall and stands with her head bowed, her bush of hair falling around her face so you can't see it. You think she's shaking a little.

Maybe that's your imagination. She seems so coldhearted. But then, so do you.

"Ykka."

"Not you, too," she mutters. "I don't want to hear it, Bugkiller."

Belatedly you realize: By killing the boilbugs, you made this a harder choice for her. Before, she could have ordered the Hunter killed as a mercy, and the bugs would have been at fault. Now it's pragmatism, comm policy. That's on her.

You shake your head and step closer. She straightens and turns in an instant, and you sess the defensive orientation of her orogeny. She doesn't do anything with it, doesn't set a torus or start an ambient-draw, but then, she wouldn't, would she? Those are Fulcrum techniques. You don't really know what she's going to do, this strangely trained feral, to defend herself.

Part of you is curious, in a detached sort of way. The other part notes the tension on her face. So you offer her the still-lit mellow.

She blinks at it. Her orogeny settles into quiescence again, but her eyes lift and study yours. Then she tilts her head, bemused, considering. Finally she puts one hand on her hip, plucks the mellow from your fingers with the other, and takes a long drag. It works quickly; after a moment she turns to lean back against the crystal, her face settling into weary rather than tense lines as she blows out curls of smoke. She offers it back. You settle beside her and take it.

It takes another ten minutes to finish the cigarette, passing it back and forth between the two of you. Both of you linger, however, after it's done, by unspoken agreement. Only when you hear someone begin to utter loud, broken sobs from the infirmary behind you do you nod to each other, and part ways.

* * *

It is unfathomable that any sensible civilization would be so wasteful as fill prime storage caverns with corpses! No wonder these people died out, whoever they were. I estimate another year before we can clear all of the bones, funeral urns, and other debris, then perhaps another six months to fully map and renovate. Less if you can get me those blackjackets I requested! I don't care if they cost the Earth; some of these chambers are unstable.

There are tablets in here, though. Something in verses, though we can't read this bizarre language. Like stonelore. Five tablets, not three. What do you want to do with them? I say we give the lot to Fourth so they'll stop whining about how much history we're destroying.

—Report of Journeywoman Fogrid Innovator Yumenes to the Geneer Licensure, Equatorial East: "Proposal to Repurpose Subsurface Catacombs, City of Firaway." Master-level review only.

INTERLUDE

A dilemma: You are made of so many people you do not wish to be. Including me.

But you know so little of me. I will attempt to explain the context *of me, if not the detail. It begins—I began—with a war.*

War *is a poor word. Is it war when people find an infestation of vermin in some unwanted place and try to burn or poison it clean? Though that, too, is a poor metaphor, because no one hates individual mice or bedbugs. No one singles out for vengeance* that one, that one right there, three-legged splotch-backed little bastard, *and all its progeny down the hundreds of verminous generations that encompass a human life. And the three-legged splotch-backed little bastards don't have much chance of becoming more than an annoyance to people—whereas you and all your kind have cracked the surface of the planet and lost the Moon. If the mice in your garden, back in Tirimo, had helped Jija kill Uche, you would have shaken the place to pebbles and set fire to the ruins before you left. You destroyed Tirimo anyway, but if it had been personal, you'd have done worse.*

Yet for all your hatred, you still might not have managed to kill the vermin. The survivors would be greatly changed—made harder, stronger, more splotch-backed. Perhaps the hardships you inflicted would have fissioned their descendants into many factions, each with different interests. Some of those interests would have nothing to do with you. Some would revere and despise you for your power. Some would be as dedicated to your destruction as you were to theirs, even though by the time they had the strength to actually act on their enmity, you would have forgotten their existence. To them, your enmity would be the stuff of legend.

And some might hope to appease you, or talk you around to at least a degree of peaceful tolerance. I am one of these.

I was not always. For a very long time, I was one of the vengeful ones... but what it keeps coming back to is this: Life cannot exist without the Earth. Yet there is a not-insubstantial chance that life will win its war, and destroy the Earth. We've come close a few times.

That can't happen. We cannot be permitted to win.

So this is a confession, my Essun. I've betrayed you already and I will do it again. You haven't even chosen a side yet, and already I fend off those who would recruit you to their cause. Already I plot your death. It's necessary. But I can at least try my damnedest to give your life a meaning that will last till the world ends.

5

Nassun takes the reins

MAMA MADE ME LIE TO YOU, Nassun is thinking. She's looking at her father, who's been driving the wagon for hours at this point. His eyes are on the road, but a muscle in his jaw jumps. One of his hands—the one that first struck Uche, ultimately killed him—is shaking where it grips the reins. Nassun can tell that he is still caught up in the fury, maybe still killing Uche in his head. She doesn't understand why, and she doesn't like it. But she loves her father, fears him, worships him, and therefore some part of her yearns to appease him. She asks herself: *What did I do to make this happen?* And the answer that comes is: *Lie. You lied, and lies are always bad.*

But this lie was not her choice. That had been Mama's command, along with all the others: *Don't reach, don't ice, I'm going to make the earth move and you'd better not react, didn't I tell you not to react, even listening is reacting, normal people don't listen like that, are you listening to me, rusting* stop, *for Earth's sake can't you do anything right, stop crying, now do it again*. Endless commands. Endless displeasure. Occasionally the slap of ice in threat, the slap of a hand, the sickening inversion of Nassun's torus, the jerk of a hand on her upper arm. Mama has said occasionally that she loves Nassun, but Nassun has never seen any proof of it.

Not like Daddy, who gives her knapped stone kirkhusa to play with or a first aid kit for her runny-sack because Nassun is a Resistant like her mama. Daddy, who takes her fishing at Tirika Creek on days when he doesn't have commissions to fulfill. Mama has never lain out on the grassy rooftop with Nassun, pointing at the stars and explaining that some deadcivs are said to have given them names, though no one remembers those. Daddy is never too tired to talk at the ends of his workdays. Daddy does not inspect Nassun in the mornings after baths the way Mama does, checking for poorly washed ears or an unmade bed, and when Nassun misbehaves, Daddy only sighs and shakes his head and tells her, "Sweetening, you knew better." Because Nassun always does.

It was not because of Daddy that Nassun wanted to run away and become a lorist. She does not like that her father is so angry now. This seems yet another thing that her mother has done to her.

So she says, "I wanted to tell you."

Daddy does not react. The horses keep plodding forward. The road stretches before the cart, the woods and hills inching past around the road, the bright blue sky overhead. There aren't a lot of people riding past today—just some carters with heavy wagons of trade goods, messengers, some quartent guards on patrol. A few of the carters, who visit Tirimo often, nod or wave because they know Daddy, but Daddy does not respond. Nassun doesn't like this, either. Her father is a friendly man. The man who sits beside her feels like a stranger.

Just because he doesn't reply doesn't mean he's not listening.

She adds, "I asked Mama when we could tell you. I asked her that a lot. She said never. She said you wouldn't understand."

Daddy says nothing. His hands are still shaking—less now? Nassun cannot tell. She starts to feel uncertain; is he angry? Is he sad about Uche? (Is *she* sad about Uche? It does not feel real. When she thinks of her little brother, she thinks of a gabby, giggly little thing who sometimes bit people and still shit his diaper occasionally, and who had an orogenic presence the size of a quartent. The crumpled, still thing back at their house cannot be Uche, because it was too small and dull.) Nassun wants to touch her father's shaking hand, but she finds herself oddly reluctant to do so. She isn't sure why—fear? Maybe just because this man is so much a stranger, and she has always been shy of strangers.

But. No. He is Daddy. Whatever is wrong with him now, it's Mama's fault.

So Nassun reaches out and grips Daddy's nearer hand, hard, because she wants to show him that she is not afraid, and because she is angry, though not at Daddy. "I wanted to tell you!"

The world blurs. At first Nassun isn't sure of what's happening, and she locks up. This is what Mama has drilled her to do in moments of surprise or pain: lock down her body's instinctive fear reaction, lock down her sessapinae's instinctive grab for the earth below. And under no circumstances is Nassun to react with orogeny, because normal people do not do that. *You can do anything else*, Mama's voice says in her head. *Scream, cry, throw something with your hands, get up and start a fight*. Not orogeny.

So Nassun hits the ground harder than she should because she has not quite mastered the skill of not reacting, and she still stiffens up physically along with not reacting orogenically.

And the world blurs because she has not only been knocked off the driver's seat of the wagon, but she has actually rolled off the edge of the Imperial Road and down a gravel-strewn slope, toward a small creek-fed pond.

(The creek that feeds it is where, in a few days, Essun will bathe a strange white boy who acts as if he has forgotten what soap is for.)

Nassun flops to a stop, dazed and breathless. Nothing really hurts yet. By the time the world settles and she begins to understand what's happened—*Daddy hit me, knocked me off the wagon*—Daddy has scrambled down the slope and is crying her name as he crouches beside her and helps her to sit up. *Really* crying. As Nassun blinks away dust and the stars that obscure her vision, she reaches up in confusion to touch Daddy's face, and finds it streaked wet.

"I'm sorry," he says. "I'm so sorry, sweetening. I don't want to hurt you, I don't, you're all I have left—" He jerks her close and holds her tightly, although it hurts. She has bruises all over. "I'm so sorry. I'm so—rusting—sorry! Oh, Earth, oh, Earth, you evil son of a ruster! Not this one! You can't have this one, too!"

These are sobs of grief, long and throat-scraping and hysterical. Nassun will understand this later (and not very much later). She will realize that in this moment, her father is weeping as much for the son he murdered as for the daughter he has injured.

In the moment, however, she thinks, *He still loves me*, and starts crying, too.

So it is while they are like this, Daddy holding Nassun tight, Nassun shaking with relief and lingering shock, that the rippling shockwave of the continent being ripped in half up north reaches them.

They are nearly a whole day's travel down the Imperial Road. Back in Tirimo, a few moments previous, Essun has just shunted the force of the wave so that it splits and goes around the town—which means that what comes at Nassun is incrementally more powerful. And Nassun has been knocked half-insensible, and she is less skilled, less experienced. When she sesses the onrush of the shake, and the sheer power of it, she reacts in exactly the wrong way: She locks up again.

Her father lifts his head, surprised by her gasp and sudden stiffness, and that is when the hammer lands. Even he sesses the loom of it, though it comes too fast and too powerfully to be anything but a jangle of *run run RUN RUN* at the back of his mind. Running is pointless. The shake is basically what happens when a person doing laundry flaps the wrinkles out of a sheet, writ on a continental scale and moving with the speed and force of a casual asteroid strike. On the scale of small, stationary, crushable people, the strata heave beneath them and the trees shake and then splinter. The water in the pond beside them actually leaps into the air for a moment, suspended and still. Daddy stares at it, apparently riveted to this single static point amid the relentless unpeeling of the world everywhere else.

But Nassun is still a skilled orogene even if she is a half-addled one. Though she did not muster herself in time to do what Essun did and break the force of the wave before it hits, she does the next best thing. She drives invisible pylons of force into the strata, as deep as she can, grabbing for the very lithosphere itself. When the kinetic force of the wave hits, incremental instants before the planetary crust above it flexes in reaction, she snatches the heat and pressure and friction from it and uses this to fuel her pylons, pinning the strata and soil in place as solidly as if glued.

There's plenty of strength to draw from the earth, but she spins an ambient torus anyway. She keeps it at a wide remove, because *her father* is within it and she cannot cannot cannot hurt him, and she spins it hard and vicious even though she doesn't need to. Instinct tells her to, and instinct is right. The freezing eye-wall of her torus, which disintegrates anything coming into the stable zone at its center, is what keeps a few dozen projectiles from puncturing them to death.

All of this means that when the world comes apart, it happens everywhere else. For an instant there is nothing to see of reality save a floating globule of pond, a hurricane of pulverized everything else, and an oasis of stillness at the hurricane's core.

Then the concussion passes. The pond slaps back into place, spraying them with muddy snow. The trees that haven't shattered snap back upright, some of them nearly bending all the way in the other direction in reactive momentum and breaking there. In the distance—beyond Nassun's torus—people and animals and boulders and trees that have been flung into the air come crashing down. There are screams, human and inhuman. Cracking wood, crumbling stone, the distant screech of something man-made and metallic rending apart. Behind them, at the far end of the valley they have just left, a rock face shatters and comes down in an avalanche roar, releasing a large steaming chalcedony geode.

Then there is silence. In it, finally, Nassun pulls her face up from her father's shoulder to look around. She does not know what to think. Her father's arms ease around her—shock—and she wriggles until he lets her go so that she can get to her feet.

He does, too. For long moments they simply stare around at the wreckage of the world they once knew.

Then Daddy turns to look at her, slowly, and she sees in his face what Uche must have seen in those last moments. "Did you do this?" he asks.

The orogeny has cleared Nassun's head, of necessity. It is a survival mechanism; intense stimulation of the sessapinae is usually accompanied by a surge of adrenaline and other physical changes that prepare the body for flight—or sustained orogeny, if that is needed. In this case it brings an increased clarity of thought, which is how Nassun finally realizes that her father was not hysterical over her fall purely for her sake. And that what she sees in his eyes right now is something entirely different from love.

Her heart breaks in this moment. Another small, quiet tragedy, amid so many others. But she speaks, because in the end she is her mother's daughter, and if Essun has done nothing else, she has trained her little girl to survive.

"That was too big to be me," Nassun says. Her voice is calm, detached. "What I did is this—" She gestures around them, at the circle of safe ground that surrounds them, distinct from the chaos just beyond. "I'm sorry I didn't stop all of it, Daddy. I tried."

The *Daddy* is what works, just as her tears saved her before. The murder in his expression flickers, fades, twists. "I can't kill you," he whispers, to himself.

Nassun sees the waver of him. It is also instinct that she steps forward and takes his hand. He flinches, perhaps thinking of knocking her away again, but this time she holds on. "*Daddy*," she says again, this time putting more of a needy whine into her voice. It is the thing that has swayed him, these times when he has come near to turning on her: remembering that she is his little girl. Reminding him that he has been, up to today, a good father.

It is a manipulation. Something of her is warped out of true by this moment, and from now on all her acts of affection toward her father will be calculated, performative. Her childhood dies, for all intents and purposes. But that is better than *all* of her dying, she knows.

And it works. Jija blinks rapidly, then murmurs something unintelligible to himself. His hand tightens on hers. "Let's get back up to the road," he says.

(He is "Jija," now, in her head. He will be Jija hereafter, forever, and never Daddy again except out loud, when Nassun needs reins to steer him.)

So they go back up, Nassun limping a little because her backside is sore where she landed too hard on the asphalt and rocks. The road has been cracked all down its length, though it is not so bad in the immediate vicinity of their wagon. The horses are still hitched, though one of them has fallen to her knees and half entangled herself in the tack. Hopefully she hasn't broken a leg. The other is still with shock. Nassun starts working on calming the horses, coaxing the downed one back up and talking the other out of near-catatonia, while her father goes to the other travelers whom they can see sprawled around the road. The ones who were within the wide circumference of Nassun's torus are okay. The ones who were not . . . well.

Once the horses are shaky but functional, Nassun goes after Jija and finds him trying to lift a man who has been flung into a tree. It's broken the man's back; he's conscious and cursing, but Nassun can see the flop of his now-useless legs. It's bad to move him, but obviously Jija thinks it's worse to leave him here like this. "Nassun," Jija says, panting as he tries for a better grip on the man, "clear the wagon bed. There's a real hospital at Pleasant Water, a day away. I think we can make it if we—"

"Daddy," she says softly. "Pleasant Water isn't there anymore."

He stops. (The injured man groans.) Turns to her, frowning. "What?"

"Sume is gone, too," she says. She does not add, *but Tirimo is fine because Mama was there.* She doesn't want to go back, not even for the end of the world. Jija darts a glance back down the road they have walked, but of course all they can see are shattered trees and a few overturned chunks of asphalt along the road... and bodies. Lots of bodies. All the way to Tirimo, or so the eye suggests.

"What the rust," he breathes.

"There's a big hole in the ground up north," Nassun continues. "*Really* big. That's what caused this. It's going to cause more shakes and things, too. I can sess ash and gas coming this way. Daddy... I think it's a Season."

The injured man gasps, not entirely from pain. Jija's eyes go wide and horrified. But he asks, and this is important: "Are you sure?"

It's important because it means he's listening to her. It is a measure of trust. Nassun feels a surge of triumph at this, though she does not really know why.

"Yes." She bites her lip. "It's going to be really bad, Daddy."

Jija's eyes drift toward Tirimo again. That is conditioned response: During a Season, comm members know that the only place they can be sure of welcome is there. Anything else is a risk.

But Nassun will not go back, now that she is away. Not when

Jija loves her—however strangely—and has taken her away and is *listening* to her, *understanding* her, even though he knows she is an orogene. Mama was wrong about that part. She'd said Jija wouldn't understand.

He didn't understand Uche.

Nassun sets her teeth against this thought. Uche was too little. Nassun will be smarter. And Mama was still only half-right. Nassun will be smarter than her, too.

So she says softly, "Mama knows, Daddy."

Nassun's not even sure what she means by this. Knows that Uche is dead? Knows who has beaten him to death? Would Mama even believe that Jija could do such a thing to his own child? Nassun can hardly believe it herself. But Jija flinches as if the words are an accusation. He stares at her for a long moment, his expression shifting from fear through horror through despair . . . and slowly, to resignation.

He looks down at the injured man. He's no one Nassun knows—not from Tirimo, wearing the practical clothes and good shoes of a message runner. He won't be running again, certainly not back to his home comm, wherever that is.

"I'm sorry," Jija says. He bends and snaps the man's neck even as he's drawing breath to ask, *For what?*

Then Jija rises. His hands are shaking again, but he turns and extends one of them. Nassun takes it. They walk back to the wagon then, and resume their journey south.

* * *

The Season will always return.

—*Tablet Two, "The Incomplete Truth," verse one*

6

you commit to the cause

"A WHAT?" ASKS TONKEE, SQUINTING AT you through a curtain of hair. You've just come into the apartment after spending part of the day helping one of the work shifts fletch and repair crossbow bolts for the Hunters' use. Since you're not part of any particular use-caste, you've been helping out with each of them in turn, a little every day. This was on Ykka's advice, though Ykka's skeptical about your newfound determination to try to fit into the comm. She likes that you're trying, at least.

Another suggestion was for you to encourage Tonkee to do the same, since thus far Tonkee's done nothing but eat and sleep and bathe on the comm's generosity. Granted, a certain amount of the lattermost has been necessary for the sake of comm socialization. At the moment Tonkee is kneeling over a basin of water in her room, hacking at her hair with a knife to chop out the matted bits. You're keeping well back because the room smells of mildew and body odor and because you think you see something moving in the water along with her shed hair. Tonkee may have needed to wear filth as part of her commless disguise, but that doesn't mean it wasn't actual filth.

"A moon," you say. It's a strange word, brief and round; you're not sure how much to stretch out the *oo* sound in the middle. What else had Alabaster said? "A . . . satellite. He said a geomest would know."

She frowns more while sawing at a particularly stubborn hank. "Well, I don't know what he's talking about. Never heard of a 'moon.' The obelisks are my area of expertise, remember?" Then she blinks and pauses, letting the half-hacked hank dangle. "Although, technically, the obelisks themselves are satellites."

"What?"

"Well, 'satellite' just means an object whose motion and position are dependent on another. The object that controls everything is called a primary, the dependent object is its satellite. See?" She shrugs. "It's something astronomests talk about when you can get any sense out of them. *Orbital mechanics.*" She rolls her eyes.

"What?"

"Gibberish. Plate tectonics for the sky." You stare, disbelieving, and she waves a hand. "Anyway, I told you how the obelisks followed you to Tirimo. Where you go, they go. That makes them satellites to your primary."

You shudder, not liking the thought that comes into your head—of thin, invisible tethers anchoring you to the amethyst, the nearer topaz, and now the distant onyx whose dark presence is growing in your mind. And oddly, you also think of the Fulcrum. Of the tethers that bound you to it, even when you had the apparent freedom to leave it and travel. You always came back, though, or the Fulcrum would've come after you—in the form of the Guardians.

"Chains," you say softly.

"No, no," Tonkee says distractedly. She's working on the hank again, and having real trouble with it. Her knife has gone blunt. You leave for a moment and go into the room that you share with Hoa, fetching the whetstone from your pack. She blinks when you offer it to her, then nods thanks and starts sharpening the knife. "If there was a chain between you and an obelisk, it would be following you because you're *making* it follow you. Force, not gravity. I mean, if you could make an obelisk do what you wanted." You let out a little breath of amusement at this. "But a satellite reacts to you regardless of whether you try to make it react. It's drawn to your presence, and the weight you exert upon the universe. It lingers around you because it can't help itself." She waves a wet hand distractedly, while you stare again. "Not to ascribe motivations and intentions to the obelisks, of course; that would be silly."

You crouch against the far wall of the room to consider this while she resumes work. As the remainder of her hair begins to loosen, you recognize it at last, because it's curly and dark like your own, instead of ashblow and gray. A little looser in the curl, maybe. Midlatter hair; another mark against her in the eyes of her family, probably. And given the bog-standard Sanzed look of her otherwise—she's a bit on the short and pear-shaped side, but that's what comes of the Yumenescene families not using Breeders to improve themselves—it's something you would've remembered about her from that long-ago visit she made to the Fulcrum.

You don't think Alabaster was talking about the obelisks when he mentioned this moon thing. Still—"You said that thing we found in the Fulcrum, that *socket*, was where they built the obelisks."

It's immediately clear you're back on ground that Tonkee is actually interested in. She sets the knife down and leans forward, her face excited through the dangling uneven remainder of her hair. "Mmm-hmm. Maybe not all of them. The dimensions of every obelisk recorded have been slightly different, so only some—or maybe even just one—would have fit in that socket. Or maybe the socket changed every time they put one in there, adapting itself to the obelisk!"

"How do you know they *put them* in there? Maybe they first... grew there, then were faceted or mined and taken away later." This makes Tonkee look thoughtful; you feel obliquely proud to have considered something she hasn't. "And 'they' who?"

She blinks, then sits back, her excitement visibly fading. Finally she says, "Supposedly, the Yumenescene Leadership is descended from the people who saved the world after the Shattering Season. We have texts passed down from that time, secrets that each family is charged with keeping, and which we're supposed to be shown upon earning our use and comm names." She scowls. "My family didn't, because they were already thinking about disowning me. So I broke into the vault and *took* my birthright."

You nod, because that sounds like the Binof you remember. You're skeptical about the family secret, though. Yumenes didn't exist before Sanze, and Sanze is only the latest of the countless civilizations that must have come and gone over the Seasons.

The Leadership legends have the air of a myth concocted to justify their place in society.

Tonkee continues, "In the vault I found all sorts of things: maps, strange writing in a language like none I've ever seen, objects that didn't make sense—like one tiny, perfectly round yellow stone, about an inch in circumference. Someone had put it in a glass case, sealed and plastered with warnings not to touch. Apparently the thing had a reputation for punching holes in people." You wince. "So either there's some truth to the family stories, or amazingly, being rich and powerful makes it easy to assemble quite the collection of valuable ancient objects. Or both." She notices your expression and looks amused. "Yeah, probably not both. It's not stonelore, anyway, just . . . words. Soft knowledge. I needed to harden it."

That sounds like Tonkee. "So you snuck into the Fulcrum to try to find the socket, because somehow this proves some rusty old story your family passed down?"

"It was on one of the maps I found." Tonkee shrugs. "If there was truth to part of the story—about there being a socket in Yumenes, deliberately hidden away by the city's founders—then that did suggest there might be truth to the rest, yes." Setting the knife aside, Tonkee shifts to get comfortable, idly brushing the shed hairs into a pile with one hand. Her hair is painfully short and uneven now, and you really want to take the scissors from her and shape it. You'll wait till she's given it another wash first, though.

"There's truth to other parts of the stories, too," Tonkee says. "I mean, a lot of the stories are rust and mellow-smoke; I don't want to pretend otherwise. But I learned at Seventh that the obelisks go as far back as history goes, and then some. We have evidence of Seasons from ten, fifteen, even twenty thousand years ago—and the obelisks are older. It's possible that they even predate the Shattering."

The first Season, and the one that nearly killed the world. Only lorists speak of it, and the Seventh University has disavowed most of their tales. Out of contrariness, you say, "Maybe there wasn't a Shattering. Maybe there have always been Fifth Seasons."

"Maybe." Tonkee shrugs, either not noticing your attempt to be obnoxious, or not caring. Probably the latter. "Mentioning the Shattering was a great way to set off a five-hour argument in the colloquium. Stupid old farts." She smiles to herself, remembering, and then abruptly sobers. You understand at once. Dibars, the city that housed Seventh, is in the Equatorials, only a little west of Yumenes.

"I don't believe it, though," Tonkee says, when she's had a moment to recover. "That we've always had Seasons."

"Why not?"

"Because of us." She grins. "Life, I mean. It's not different enough."

"What?"

Tonkee leans forward. She's not quite as excited as she gets about obelisks, but it's clear that just about any long-hidden knowledge sets her off. For a moment, in the gleam of her open, cheeky face, you see Binof; then she speaks and becomes Tonkee the geomest again. "'All things change during a Season,' yes? But not enough. Think of it this way: Everything that grows or walks on land can breathe the world's air, eat its food, survive its usual shifts in temperature. We don't have to *change* to do that; we are precisely the way we need to be, because that's how the world works. Right? Maybe people are the worst of the lot, because we have to use our hands to make coats instead of just growing fur... but we can make coats. We're built for that, with clever hands that can sew and brains that can figure out how to hunt or grow animals for fur. But we aren't built to filter ash out of our lungs before it turns into cement—"

"Some animals are."

Tonkee gives you an ugly look. "Stop interrupting. It's rude."

You sigh and gesture for her to go on, and she nods, mollified. "Now. *Yes*, some animals grow lung-filters during a Season—or start breathing water and move into the ocean where it's safer, or bury themselves and hibernate, or whatever. We've figured out how to build not just coats, but storecaches and walls and stonelore. But these are afterthoughts." She gestures wildly, groping for the words. "Like... when a cartwheel blows a spoke and you're halfway between comms, you improvise. See? You put a stick or even a bar of metal into the space where the broken spoke was, just to keep the wheel strong enough to last until you can reach a wheelwright. That's what's happening when kirkhusa suddenly develop a taste for meat during a Season. Why don't they just eat meat all the time? Why haven't they *always* eaten meat? Because they were originally built for something else, they're still *better* at eating something else, and eating meat during Seasons is the slapdash, last-minute fix nature threw in to keep kirkhusa from going extinct."

"That's..." You're a little awed. It sounds crazy, but it feels right, somehow. You can't think of any holes to poke in the theory, and you're not sure you want to. Tonkee's not someone you mean to go toe-to-toe with in a battle of logic.

Tonkee nods. "That's why I can't stop thinking about the obelisks. People built them, which means that as a species we're at least as old as they are! That's a lot of time to break things, start over, and break them again. Or, if the Leadership stories are true...maybe it's enough time to put a fix in place. Something to tide us over till the real repairs can be made."

You frown to yourself. "Wait. The Yumenescene Leadership thinks the obelisks—leftover deadciv junk—are the fix?"

"Basically. The stories say the obelisks held the world together when it would have come apart. And they imply there might someday be a way to end the Seasons, involving the obelisks."

An end to all Seasons? It's hard even to imagine. No need for runny-sacks. No storecaches. Comms could last forever, grow forever. Every city could become like Yumenes.

"It would be amazing," you murmur.

Tonkee glances sharply at you. "Orogenes might be a kind of fix, too, you know," she says. "And without the Seasons, you'd no longer be needed."

You frown back at her, not sure whether to be disquieted or comforted by that statement, until she starts finger-combing her remaining hair and you realize you've run out of things to say.

* * *

Hoa is gone. You're not sure where. You left him behind in the infirmary, staring down Ruby Hair, and when you returned to your apartment to try to get a few more hours' sleep he was not beside you when you woke. His little bundle of rocks is still in your room, next to your bed, so he must be planning to return soon. It's probably nothing. Still, after so many weeks, you feel oddly bereft without his strange, subtle presence. But perhaps this is just as well. You have a visit to make, and it might go easier without... hostility.

You walk to the infirmary again slowly, quietly. It's early evening, you think—always hard to tell in Castrima-under, but your body is still acclimated to the rhythms of the surface. For now, you trust in that. Some of the people out on the platforms and walkways stare as you pass; this comm spends plenty of time gossiping, clearly. That doesn't matter. All that does is whether Alabaster has had time enough to recover. You need to talk.

There's no sign of the dead Hunter's body from that morning; everything's been cleaned up. Lerna's inside, in fresh clothing, and he glances at you as you come in. There's still a distance in his expression, you note, though he only meets your gaze for a moment before nodding and turning back to whatever he's doing with what look like surgical instruments. There's another man near him, pipetting something into a series of small glass vials; the man doesn't even look up. It's an infirmary. Anyone can come in.

It's not until you're halfway down the infirmary's long central aisle, walking between the rows of cots, that you consciously notice the sound you've been hearing all along: a kind of hum. It seems monotonous at first, but as you concentrate on it, you detect multiple tones, harmonies, a subtle rhythm. Music? Music so alien, so difficult to parse, that you're not sure that word really applies. You can't figure out where it's coming from, at first. Alabaster is still where you saw him that morning, on a pile of cushions and blankets on the floor. No telling why Lerna hasn't put him on a cot. There are flasks on a nightstand nearby, a roll of fresh bandages, some scissors, a pot of salve. A bedpan, thankfully unused since its last cleaning, though it still stinks near him.

The music is coming from the stone eater, you realize in wonder as you settle into a crouch before them. Antimony sits cross-legged near Alabaster's "nest," utterly still, looking as though someone bothered to sculpt a woman sitting cross-legged with one hand upraised. Alabaster's asleep—though in an odd, nearly sitting-up posture that you don't understand until you realize he's leaning back against Antimony's hand. Maybe that's the only way he can sleep comfortably? There are bandages on his arms today, shiny with salve, and he's not wearing a shirt—which helps you see that he's not as badly damaged as you first thought. There are no patches of stone on his chest or belly, and only a few small burns around his shoulders, most of those healed. But his torso is nearly skeletal—barely any muscle, ribs showing, belly almost concave.

Also, his right arm is much shorter than it was that morning.

You look up at Antimony. The music is coming from somewhere inside of her. Her black eyes are focused on him; they haven't moved with your arrival. It's peaceful, this strange music. And Alabaster looks comfortable.

"You haven't been taking care of him," you say, looking at his ribs and remembering countless evenings putting food in front of him, glaring while he wearily chewed it, conspiring with Innon to get him to eat at the group meals. He always ate more when he thought people were looking. "If you were going to steal him from us, the least you could've done was feed him properly. Fatten him up before you ate him, or something."

The music continues. There is a very faint, stone-grating sound as her black cabochon eyes shift to you at last. They're such alien eyes, despite their superficial resemblance to human. You can see the dry, matte material that comprises the whites of her eyes. No veins, no spots, no off-white coloring that would indicate weariness or worry or anything else human. You can't even tell if there are pupils within the black of her irises. For all you know, she can't even see with them, and uses her elbows to detect your presence and direction.

You meet those eyes and realize, suddenly, that there's so little left in you which is capable of fear.

"You took him from us and we couldn't do it alone." No, that is a lie of incompleteness. Innon, a feral, had no hope against Guardians and a trained Fulcrum orogene. You, though? You're the one who fucked everything up. "*I* couldn't do it alone. If Alabaster had been there... I hated you. Afterward, while I was wandering, I vowed to find a way to kill you. Put you in an obelisk like that other one. Bury you in the ocean, far enough out that no one will ever dig you up."

She watches you and says nothing. You can't even read the catch of her breath, because she doesn't breathe. But the music stops, dying into silence. That's a reaction, at least.

This really is pointless. But then the silence looms louder, and you're still feeling kind of pissy, so you add: "Shame. The music was pretty."

(Later, lying in bed and considering the day's errors, you will think belatedly, *I am as crazy now as Alabaster was back then.*)

A moment later Alabaster stirs, lifting his head and uttering a soft groan that throws your thoughts and your heart ten years away before they circle back. He blinks at you in disorientation for a moment, and you realize he doesn't recognize you with your hair twice as long and your skin weathered and your clothes Season-faded. Then he blinks again, and you take a deep breath, and you're both back in the here and now.

"The onyx," he says, his voice hoarse with sleep. Of course he knows. "Always biting off more than you can chew, Syen."

You don't bother to correct him on the name. "You said an obelisk."

"I said the rusting topaz. But if you could call the onyx, I've underestimated your development." His head cocks, his expression thoughtful. "What have you been doing, these last few years, to have refined your control so much?"

You can't think of anything at first, and then you can. "I had two children." Keeping an orogene child from destroying everything in its vicinity took a lot of your energy, in those earliest years. You learned to sleep with one eye open, your sessapinae primed for the slightest twitch of infant fear or toddler pique—or, worse, a local shake that might prompt either child to react. You quelled a dozen disasters a night.

He nods, and belatedly you remember waking up during the night in Meov sometimes to find Alabaster blearily awake and watching Corundum. You remember teasing him, in fact, on his worrying, when Coru was clearly no threat to anyone.

Earth burn it, you hate figuring out all this stuff after the fact.

"They left me with my mother for a few years after I was born," he says, almost to himself. You'd guessed this already, given that he speaks a Coaster language. How his Fulcrum-bred mother had known it, though, is a mystery that will never be solved. "They took me away once I was old enough to be threatened effectively, but before that, she apparently prevented me from icing Yumenes a few times. I don't think we're meant to be raised by stills." He paused, his gaze distant. "I met her years later by chance. Didn't know her, though she somehow recognized me. I think she's—she *was*—on the senior advisory board. Topped out at nine rings, if I recall." He falls silent for a moment. Perhaps he's contemplating the fact that he killed his mother, too. Or maybe he's trying to remember something of her other than a hurried meeting between two strangers in a corridor.

His focus sharpens abruptly, back to the present and you. "I think you might be a nine-ringer now."

You can't help surprise and pleasure, though you cover both with the appearance of nonchalance. "I thought things like that didn't matter anymore."

"They don't. I was careful to wipe out the Fulcrum when I tore Yumenes apart. There are still buildings where the city was, perched on the edges of the maw, unless they've fallen in since. But the obsidian walls are rubble, and I made sure Main went into the pit first." There's a deep, vicious satisfaction in his voice. He sounds like you a moment ago, as you imagined murdering stone eaters.

(You glance at Antimony. She's gone back to watching Alabaster, her hand still supporting his back. You could almost think of her as doing it out of devotion or kindness, if you didn't know his hands and feet and forearm were in whatever passes for her stomach.)

"I only mention rings so you can have a point of reference."

Alabaster stirs, sitting up carefully and then, as if he heard your thought, extending his stubby, stone-capped right arm. "Look inside this. Tell me what you see."

"Are you going to tell me what's going on, Alabaster?" But he doesn't answer, just looking at you, and you sigh. All right.

You look at his arm, which stops at the elbow now, and wonder what he means by *look inside*. Then, unbidden, you remember a night when he willed poison out of the cells of his own body. But he had help for that. You frown, impulsively glancing at the strangely shaped pink object behind him—the thing that looks like an overly long, big-handled knife, and which is actually, somehow, an obelisk. The spinel, he called it.

You glance at him; he must have seen you eye it. He doesn't move: not a twitch of his burned and stone-crusted face, not a flicker of his nonexistent eyelashes. All right, then. Anything goes, as long as you do what he says.

So you stare down at his arm. You don't want to chance the spinel. No telling what it will do. Instead, first you try letting your awareness go into the arm. This feels absurd; you've spent your life sessing layers of earth miles underground. To your surprise, however, your perception *can* grasp his arm. It's small and strange, too close and almost too tiny, but it's there, because at least the outermost layer of him is rock. Calcium and carbon and flecks of oxidized iron that must have once been blood, and—

You pause, frowning, and open your eyes. (You don't remember closing them.) "What is that?"

"What *is* that?" The side of his mouth that hasn't been seamed by a burn lifts in a sardonic smile.

You scowl. "There's something in this stuff that you're—" Becoming. "—this stone stuff. It's not, I don't know. It's rock, and not."

"Can you sess the flesh further down the arm?"

You shouldn't be able to. But when you narrow your focus to the limit that you can, when you squint and press your tongue to the roof of your mouth and wrinkle your nose, it's there, too. Big sticky globules all bouncing against one another—You withdraw at once, revolted. At least stone is clean.

"Look again, Syen. Don't be a coward."

You could be annoyed, but you're too old for this shit now. Setting your jaw, you try again, taking a deep breath so you won't feel queasy. Everything's so *wet* inside him, and the water isn't even sequestered away between layers of clay or—

You pause. Narrow your focus still further. Between the gelidity, moving, too, but in a slower and less organic way, you suddenly sess the same thing you found in the stone of him. Something else, neither flesh nor stone. Something immaterial, and yet it is there for you to perceive. It glimmers in threads strung between the bits of him, crossing itself in lattices, shifting constantly. A... tension? An energy, shiny and streaming. Potential. Intention.

You shake your head, pulling back so you can focus on him. "What is that?"

This time he answers. "The stuff of orogeny." He makes his voice dramatic, since his facial expressions can't change much. "I've told you before that what we do isn't logical. To make the earth move we put something of ourselves into the system and make *completely unrelated things* come out. There's always been something else involved, connecting the two. This." You frown. He sits forward, growing more animated with his excitement, just the way he used to in the old days—but then something creaks on him, and he flinches with pain. Carefully he sits back against Antimony's hand again.

But you're hearing him. And he's right. It hasn't ever really made sense, has it, the way orogeny works? It shouldn't work at all, that willpower and concentration and perception should shift mountains. Nothing else in the world works this way. People cannot stop avalanches by dancing well, or make storms happen by refining their hearing. And on some level, you've always *known* that this was there, making your will manifest. This...whatever it is.

Alabaster has always been able to read you like a book. "The civilization that made the obelisks had a word for this," he says, nodding at your epiphany. "I think there's a reason we don't. It's because no one for countless generations has wanted orogenes to *understand* what we do. They've just wanted us to do it."

You nod slowly. "After Allia, I can see why no one would've wanted us to learn how to manipulate obelisks."

"Rust the obelisks. They didn't want us to create something better. Or worse." He takes a deep breath carefully. "We're going to stop manipulating stone now, Essun. That stuff you see in me? *That's* what you have to learn to control. To perceive, wherever it exists. It's what the obelisks are made of, and it's how they do what they do. We have to get you to do those things, too. We have to make you a ten-ringer, at least."

At least. Just like that. "*Why?* Alabaster, you mentioned something. A...moon. Tonkee doesn't have a clue what that is. And all the things you've said, about causing that rift and wanting me to do something worse—" Something moves at the periphery of your vision. You glance up and realize the man who's been working with Lerna is coming with a bowl in his hands. Dinner, for Alabaster. You drop your voice. "I'm not, by the way. Helping you make things worse. Haven't you done enough already?"

Alabaster glances at the oncoming nurse, too. Watching him, Alabaster says in a low voice, "The Moon is something this world used to have, Essun. An object in the sky, much closer than the stars." He keeps switching between calling you one name and another. It's distracting. "Its loss was part of what caused the Seasons."

Father Earth did not always hate life, the lorists say. *He hates because he cannot forgive the loss of his only child.*

But then, the lorists' tales also say the obelisks are harmless.

"How do you know—" But then you stop, because the man has reached you, so you sit back against a nearby cot, digesting what you've heard while he spoon-feeds Alabaster. The stuff is watery mash of some kind, and not much of it. Alabaster sits there and opens his mouth for the feeding like a babe. His eyes stay on you throughout. It's unnerving, and finally you have to look away. Some of the things that have changed between you, you cannot bear.

Finally the man is done, and with a flat look in your direction that nevertheless conveys his opinion that you should have been the one to administer the food, he leaves. But when you straighten and open your mouth to ask more questions, Alabaster says, "I'm probably going to need to use that bedpan soon. I can't control my bowels very well anymore, but at least they're still regular." At the look on your face, he smiles with only a hint of bitterness. "I don't want you to see that any more than you want to see it. So why don't we just say you should come back later? Noon seems to work better for not interfering with any of my gross natural functions."

That isn't fair. Well. It is, and you deserve his censure, but it's censure that should be shared. "Why did you do this to yourself?" You gesture at his arm, his ruined body. "I just..." Maybe you could take it better if you understood.

"The consequence of what I did at Yumenes." He shook his head. "Something to remember, Syen, for when you make your own choices in the future: Some of them come with a terrible price. Although sometimes that price is worth paying."

You can't understand why he sees this, this horrible slow death, as a price worth paying for anything—let alone for what he got out of it, which was the destruction of the world. And you still don't understand what any of it has to do with stone eaters or moons or obelisks or anything else.

"Wouldn't it have been better," you cannot help saying, "to just... live?" To have come back, you cannot say. To have made what little life he could with Syenite again, after Meov was gone but before she found Tirimo and Jija and tried to create a lesser version of the family she'd lost. Before she became you.

The answer is in the way his eyes deaden. This was the look that was on his face as you stood in a node station once, over the abused corpse of one of his sons. Maybe it's the look that was on his face when he learned of Innon's death. It's certainly what you saw in your own face after Uche's. That's when you no longer need an answer to the question. There is such a thing as too much loss. Too much has been taken from you both—taken and taken and taken, until there's nothing left but hope, and you've *given* that up because it hurts too much. Until you would rather die, or kill, or avoid attachments altogether, than lose one more thing.

You think of the feeling that was in your heart as you pressed a hand over Corundum's nose and mouth. Not the thought. The thought was simple and predictable: *Better to die than live a slave.* But what you *felt* in that moment was a kind of cold, monstrous love. A determination to make sure your son's life remained the beautiful, wholesome thing that it had been up to that day, even if it meant you had to end his life early.

Alabaster doesn't answer your question. You don't need him to anymore. You get up to leave so that he can at least keep his dignity in front of you, because that's really all you have left to give him. Your love and respect aren't worth much to anyone.

Maybe you're still thinking of dignity when you ask one more question, so that the conversation doesn't end on a note of hopelessness. It's your way of offering an olive branch, too, and letting him know that you've decided to learn what he has to teach you. You're not interested in making the Season worse or whatever he's on about...but it's clear that he needs this on some level. The son he made with you is dead, the family you built together has been rendered forever incomplete, but if nothing else he's still your mentor.

(You need this, too, a cynical part of you notes. It's a poor trade, really—Nassun for him, a mother's purpose for an ex-lover's, these ridiculous mysteries for the starker and more important why of Jija murdering his own son. But without Nassun to motivate you, you need something. Anything, to keep going.)

So you say, with your back to him: "What did they call it?"

"Hn?"

"The obelisk-builders. You said they had a word for the stuff in the obelisks." The silvery stuff thrumming between the cells of Alabaster's body, concentrating and compacting in the solidifying stone of him. "The stuff of orogeny. What was their word, since we don't have one anymore?"

"Oh." He shifts, perhaps readying himself for the bedpan. "The word doesn't matter, Essun. Make one up if you like. You just need to know the stuff exists."

"I want to know what they called it." It's a small piece of the mystery he's trying to shove down your throat. You want to wrap your fingers around it, control the ingestion, at least taste some of it along the way. And, too, the people who made the obelisks were powerful. Foolish, maybe, and clearly awful for inflicting the Seasons upon their descendants, if they are indeed the ones who did so. But powerful. Maybe knowing the name will give you power somehow.

He starts to shake his head, winces as this causes him pain somewhere, sighs instead. "They called it *magic*."

It's meaningless. Just a word. But maybe you can give it meaning somehow. "Magic," you repeat, memorizing. Then you nod farewell, and leave without looking back.

* * *

The stone eaters knew I was there. I'm certain of it. They just didn't care.

I observed them for hours as they stood motionless, voices echoing out of nowhere. The language they spoke to each other was . . . strange. Arctic, perhaps? One of the Coastals? I've never heard the like. Regardless, after some ten hours I will admit that I fell asleep. I woke to the sound of a great crash and crunch, so loud that I thought the Shattering itself was upon me. When I dared to lift my eyes, one of the stone eaters was scattered chunks upon the ground. The other stood as before, save for one change, directed right at me: a bright, glittering smile.

—*Memoir of Ouse Innovator (nat Strongback) Ticastries, amateur geomest. Not endorsed by the Fifth University.*

7

Nassun finds the moon

The journey south for Nassun and her father is long and fraught. They make most of the journey with the horse cart, which means that they travel faster than Essun, who is on foot and behind them to an increasing degree. Jija offers rides in exchange for food or supplies; this helps them move faster still because they don't need to stop and trade often. Because of this pace, they stay ahead of the worst of the changing climate, the ashfall, the carnivorous kirkhusa and the boilbugs and all the worse things brewing in the lands behind them. They're going so quickly when they pass through Castrima-over that Nassun barely feels Ykka's summons—and when she does it is in her dreams, drawing her down and down into the warm earth amid white crystalline light. But she dreams this ten miles past Castrima, since Jija thought they could go a little farther that day before camping, and thus they do not fall prey to the honeypot of invitingly whole, empty buildings.

When they do have to stop at comms, some are only in lockdown and haven't yet declared Seasonal Law. Hoping the worst of it won't come so far south, probably; it's rare for Seasons to affect the whole continent at once. Nassun never speaks of what she is to strangers, but if she could, she would tell them that there is nowhere to hide from this Season. Some parts of the Stillness will suffer the full effects later than others, but eventually it will be bad everywhere.

Some of the comms they stop at invite them to stay. Jija's older, but still hale and strong, and his knapping skills and Resistant use-caste make him valuable. Nassun's young enough to be trained in nearly any needed skill, and she's visibly healthy and tall for her age, already showing signs of growing into her mother's strong Midlatter frame. There are a few places they stop, strong comms with deep stores and friendly people, where she wishes they could stay. Jija always refuses, though. He's got some destination in mind.

A few of the comms they pass try to kill them. There's no logic to this, since one man and a little girl cannot possibly have enough valuables between them to be worth murdering, but there isn't much logic in a Season. They run from some. Jija takes a longknife to a man's head to get them out of a comm that has let them through the gates and then tried to close them in. They lose the horses and the cart, which is probably what the comm wanted, but Jija and Nassun escape, which is what matters most. It's on foot from there, and slower, but they are alive.

At another comm, whose people don't even bother to warn them before aiming crossbows, it is Nassun who saves them. She does this by wrapping her arms around her father and setting her teeth in the earth and dragging every iota of life and heat and movement out of the whole comm until it is a gleaming frosted confection of ice-slivered slate walls and still, solid bodies.

(She will never do this again. The way Jija looks at her afterward.)

They stay in the dead comm for a few days, resting in empty houses and replenishing their supplies. No one bothers this comm while they are there because Nassun keeps the walls iced as a clear *danger here* warn-off. They cannot stay long, of course. Eventually the other comms in the area will band together and come to kill the rogga whom they will assume threatens them all. A few days of warm water and fresh food—Jija cooks one of the comm's frozen chickens for a real treat—and they move on. Before the bodies thaw and start stinking, see.

And so it goes: Bandits and scammers and a near-fatal gas waft and a tree that fires wooden spikes when warm bodies are in proximity; they survive it all. Nassun has a growth spurt, even though she is always hungry and rarely full. By the time they finally approach the place that Jija has heard about, she is three inches taller, and a year has passed.

They are out of the Somidlats at last, edging into the Antarctics. Nassun has begun to suspect that Jija means to take her all the way to Nife, one of the few cities in the Antarctic region, near which a satellite Fulcrum is said to be located. But he turns them off the Pellestane-Nife Imperial Road and they begin going eastward, stopping periodically so that Jija can consult with people along the way and see if he's going in the right direction. It is after one of these conversations, conducted always in whispers and always after Jija thinks Nassun has gone to sleep, and only with people whom Jija considers level-headed after a few hours of chitchat and shared food, that Nassun finally learns where they are going. "*Tell me*," she hears Jija whisper to a woman who was out scouting for a local comm, after they have shared an evening meal of meat she caught around a fire Jija built, "*have you ever heard of the Moon?*"

The question holds no meaning for Nassun; neither does the word at the end of it. But the woman inhales. She directs Jija to shift over to the southeast-running regional road instead of the Imperial Road, and then to divert due south at the turning of a river they'll soon reach. Thereafter Nassun pretends to be asleep, because she can feel the woman's narrow-eyed gaze on her. Eventually, though, Jija shyly offers to help warm her bedroll. Then Nassun has to listen while her father works to make the woman moan and gasp in repayment for the meat—and to make her forget that Nassun is there. In the morning they move on before the woman wakes so that she will not follow and try to hurt Nassun.

Days later they divert at the river, heading into the woods along a tree-shadowed path that is barely more than a tamped-down paler ribbon amid the forest scrub and undergrowth. The sky has not been completely shadowed for long in this part of the world; most of the trees still have leaves, and Nassun can even hear animals leaping about and darting away as they pass. Occasionally birds twitter or croon. There are no other people on this path, though obviously some have passed recently or the path would be even more overgrown than it is. The Antarctics are a stark, sparsely populated part of the world, she remembers reading in the textbooks of another life. Few comms, fewer Imperial roads, winters that are harsh even outside a Season. The quartents here take weeks to travel across. Swaths of the Antarctics are tundra, and the southernmost tip of the continent is said to become solid ice, which extends far into the sea. She's read that the night sky, if they could see it through the clouds, is sometimes filled with strange dancing colored lights.

In this part of the Antarctics, though, the air is almost steamy despite the light chill. Beneath their feet, Nassun can sess the heavy, pent churn of an active shield volcano—actually erupting, just very slowly, with a trickle-trickle of lava flow further south. Here and there on the topography of her awareness Nassun can detect gas vents and a few boils that have come to the surface as hot springs and geysers. All this moisture and the warm ground are what keep the trees green.

Then the trees part, and before them looms something that Nassun has never seen before. A rock formation, she thinks—but one that seems to consist of dozens of long, columnar ribbons of brown-gray stone that ripple in an upslope, gradually slanting high enough to qualify as a low mountain or a tall hill. At the top of this river of stone, she can see bushy green tree canopies; the formation plateaus up there. Atop that plateau Nassun can glimpse something through the trees, which might be a rounded rooftop or storecache tower. A settlement of some kind. But unless they climb along the columnar ribbons, which looks dangerous, she's not sure how to get up there.

Except... except. It is a scratch on her awareness, rising to a pressure, itching into certainty. Nassun glances at her father, who is staring at the river of stone, too. In the months since

Uche's death, she has come to understand Jija better now than ever before in her life, because her life depends on it. She understands that he is fragile, despite his outward strength and stolidity. The cracks in him are new but dangerous, like the edges of tectonic plates: always raw, never stable, needing only the merest brush to unleash aeons' worth of pent-up energy and destroy everything nearby.

But earthquakes are easy to manage, if you know how.

So Nassun says, watching him carefully, "This was made by orogenes, Daddy."

She has guessed that he will tense, and he does. She has guessed that he will need to take a deep breath to calm himself, which he also does. He reacts to even the thought of orogenes the way that Mama used to react to red wine: with fast breath and shaking hands and sometimes freezing or weak knees. Daddy could never even bring things that were burgundy-colored into the house—but sometimes he would forget and do it anyway, and once it was done there was no reasoning with Mama. Nothing to be done but wait for her shakes and rapid breathing and hand-wringing to pass.

(Hand-*rubbing.* Nassun did not notice the distinction, but Essun was rubbing one hand. The old ache, there in the bones.)

Once Jija is calm enough, therefore, Nassun adds, "I think only orogenes can get up that slope, too." She's sure of this, in fact. The stone columns are *moving*, imperceptibly. This whole region is a volcano in exquisitely slow eruption. Here it pushes up a steady incremental lava flow that takes years to cool and thus separates itself into these long hexagonal shafts as the stuff contracts. It would be easy for an orogene, even an untrained one, to push against that upwelling pressure, taste some of that slow-cooling heat, and raise another column. Ride it, to reach that plateau. Many of the stone ribbons before them are paler gray, fresher, sharper. Others have done this recently.

Then Daddy surprises her by nodding jerkily. "There are... there should be others like you in this place." He never says the o-word or the r-word. It's always *like you* and *your kind* and *that sort*. "It's why I brought you here, sweetening."

"Is this the Antarctic Fulcrum?" Maybe she was wrong about where that was.

"No." His lip curls. The fault line trembles. "It's better."

It's the first time he's ever been willing to speak of this. He's not breathing much faster, either, or staring at her in that way he so often does when he's struggling to remember that she's his daughter. Nassun decides to probe a little, testing his strata. "Better?"

"Better." He looks at her, and for the first time in what feels like forever, he smiles at her the way he used to. The way a father should smile at his daughter. "They can cure you, Nassun. That's what the stories say."

Cure her of what? she almost asks. Then survival instinct kicks in and she bites her tongue before she can say the stupid thing. There is only one disease that afflicts her in his eyes, only one poison he would journey halfway across the world to have drawn out of his little girl.

A cure. *A cure*. For orogeny? She hardly knows what to think. Be... other than what she is? Be normal? Is that even possible?

She's so stunned that she forgets to watch her father for a moment. When she remembers, she shivers, because he has been watching *her*. He nods in satisfaction at the look on her face, though. Her surprise is what he wanted to see: that or maybe wonder, or pleasure. He would have reacted poorly to dislike or fear.

"How?" she asks. Curiosity he can tolerate.

"I don't know. But I heard about it from travelers, before." Just as there is only one *your kind* that he ever means, there's only one *before* that matters, for both of them. "They say it's been around for maybe the last five or ten years."

"But what about the Fulcrum?" She shakes her head, confused. If anywhere, she would have thought...

Daddy's face twists. "Trained, leashed animals are still animals." He turns back to the rise of flowing stone. "I want my little girl back."

I haven't gone anywhere, Nassun thinks, but knows better than to say.

There's no path to illustrate the way to go, no signs to indicate anything nearby. Part of that could be Seasonal defenses; they've seen a few comms that protected themselves not just with walls but seemingly insurmountable obstacles and camouflage. Doubtless the members of the comm know some secret way to get up to the plateau, but without this knowledge, Nassun and Jija are left with a puzzle to solve. There's also no easy way past the rise; they could go around it, see if there are steps on the other side, but that might take days.

Nassun sits down on a log nearby—after checking it carefully for insects or other creatures that might have turned aggressive since the start of the Season. (Nassun has learned to treat nature and her father with the same wary caution.) She watches Jija pace back and forth, pausing now and again to kick at one of the ribbons where it rises sharply from the ground. He mutters to himself. He'll need time to admit what must be done.

Finally he turns to her. "Can you do it?"

She stands up. He stumbles back as if startled by the sudden movement, then stops and glowers at her. She just stands there, letting him see how much it hurts her that he fears her so.

A muscle flexes in his jaw; some of his anger fades into chagrin. (Only some.) "Will you have to kill this forest, to do it?"

Oh. She can understand some of his worry now. This is the first green place they've seen in a year. "No, Daddy," she says. "There's a volcano." She points down under their feet. He flinches again, glaring at the ground with the same naked hatred he occasionally flashes at her. But it is as pointless to hate Father Earth as it is to wish the Seasons would end.

He takes a deep breath and opens his mouth, and Nassun is so expecting him to say *all right* that she is already beginning to form the smile that he will need, in reassurance. Thus they are both caught completely off guard when a loud clack resounds through the forest around them, setting off a flock of birds she didn't know was there. Something chuffs into the ground nearby, making Nassun blink with the faint reverberations of the blow through the local strata. Something small, but striking with force. And then Jija screams.

Once, Nassun froze in reaction to being startled. Mama's training. Some of that conditioning has slipped over the past year, and although she grows still, she sinks her awareness into the earth nevertheless—just a few feet, but still. But she freezes in two kinds of ways as she sees the heavy, huge, barbed metal bolt that has been shot through her father's calf. "*Daddy!*"

Jija is down on one knee, clutching his leg and making a sound through his teeth that is less than a scream, but no less agonized. The thing is huge: several feet long, two inches in circumference. She can see the way it has pushed aside his flesh on its terrible path. The tip is buried in the ground on the other side of his calf, effectively pinning him in place. A harpoon, not a crossbow bolt. It even has a thin chain attached to the blunt end.

A chain? Nassun whirls, following it. Someone's holding it. There are feet pounding on the strata nearby, crunching leaves as they move. Darting shadows flicker past tree trunks and vanish; she hears a call in some Arctic language she's heard before but does not know. *Bandits*. Coming.

She looks at Daddy again, who is trying to take deep breaths. His face is pale. There's so much blood. But he looks up at her with his eyes wide and white with pain, and suddenly she remembers the comm where the people attacked them, the comm she iced, and the way he looked at her afterward.

Bandits. *Kill them*. She knows she must. If she does not, they will kill her.

But her father wants a little girl, not an animal.

She stares and stares and breathes hard and cannot stop staring, cannot think, cannot *act*, can do nothing but stand there and shake and hyperventilate, torn between survival and daughterhood.

Then someone leaps down the lava-flow ridge, bouncing from one ribbon of rock to the other with a speed and agility that is—Nassun stares. No one can do that. But the man lands in a crouch amid the gravelly soil at the foot of the ridges with a heavy, ominous thud. He's solidly built. She can tell he's big even though he stays low as he half rises, his gaze fixed on something in the trees beyond Nassun, and draws a long, wicked glassknife. (And yet, somehow, the weight of his landing on the ground does not reverberate on her senses. What does that mean? And there is a . . . She shakes her head, thinking maybe it's an insect, but the odd buzzing is a sensation and not a sound.)

Then the man is off, running straight into the brush, his feet pushing against the ground with such force that clods of dirt kick up in his wake. Nassun's mouth falls open as she turns to follow him, losing track amid the green, but there are shouts in that language again—and then, in the direction that she saw the man run, a soft, guttural sound, like someone reacting to a hard blow. The moving people amid the trees stop. Nassun sees an Arctic woman stand frozen in the clear gap between a tangle of vines and an old, weathered rock. The woman turns, inhaling to call out to someone else, and in a near-blur the man is behind her, punching her in the back. No, no, the knife—And then he is gone, before the woman falls. The violence and speed of the attack are stunning.

"N-Nassun," Jija says, and Nassun jumps again. She actually forgot him for a moment. She goes over, crouching and putting her foot on the chain to prevent anyone from using it to hurt him further. He grips her arm, too hard. "You should, unh, run."

"No, Daddy." She tries to figure out how the chain is fastened to the harpoon. The weapon's shaft is smooth. If she can get the chain loose or cut off the barbed point, they can just drag Daddy's leg off of it to free him. But what then? It's such a terrible wound. Will he bleed to death? She doesn't know what to do.

Jija hisses as she jiggles the end of the chain experimentally, trying to see if she can twist it loose. "I don't...I think the bone..." Jija actually sways, and Nassun thinks the white of his lips is a bad sign. "Go."

She ignores him. The chain is welded to a loop at the end of the shaft. She fingers it and thinks hard, now that the strange man's appearance has broken her deadlock. (Her hand's shaking, though. She takes a deep breath, trying to get hold of her own fear. Somewhere off in the trees, there is a gurgling groan, and a scream of fury.) She knows Jija has some of his stoneknapping tools in his pack, but the harpoon is steel. Wait—metal breaks if it's cold enough, doesn't it? Could she, maybe, with a high narrow torus...?

She's never done this before. If she does it wrong, she'll freeze off his leg. Yet somehow, instinctively, she feels certain that it *can* be done. The way Mama taught her to think about orogeny, as heat and movement taken in and heat and movement pushed out, has never really felt right to her. There is truth to it; it works, she knows from experience. But something about it is... off. Inelegant. She has often thought, *If I don't think about it as heat*... without ever finishing that thought in a productive way.

Mama is not here, and death is, and her father is the only person left in the world who loves her, even though his love comes wrapped in pain.

So she puts a hand on the butt end of the harpoon. "Don't move, Daddy."

"Wh-what?" Jija is shaking, but also weakening rapidly. Good; Nassun can work with her concentration uninterrupted. She puts her free hand on his leg—since her orogeny has always flinched away from freezing *her*, even back when she couldn't fully control it—and closes her eyes.

There is something underneath the heat of the volcano, interspersed amid the wavelets of motion that dance through the earth. It's easy to manipulate the waves and heat, but hard to even *perceive* this other thing, which is perhaps why Mama taught Nassun to look for waves and heat instead. But if Nassun can grasp the other thing, which is finer and more delicate and also more precise than the heat and waves... if she can shape it into a kind of sharp edge, and file it down to infinite fineness, and slice it across the shaft like *so*—

There is a quick, high-pitched hiss as the air between her and Jija stirs. Then the chain tip of the harpoon shaft drops loose, the shorn faces of metal glimmering mirror-smooth in the afternoon light.

Exhaling in relief, Nassun opens her eyes. To find that Jija has tensed, and is staring beyond her with an expression of mingled horror and belligerence. Startled, Nassun whirls, to see the knife-wielding man behind her.

His hair is black, Arctic-limp, and long enough to fall below his waist. He's so very tall that she falls onto her butt turning to look at him. Or maybe that's because she's suddenly exhausted? She does not know. The man is breathing hard, and his clothing—homespun cloth and a pair of surprisingly neat, pleated old trousers—is splattered liberally with blood centering on the glassknife in his right hand. He gazes down at her with eyes that glitter bright as the metal she just cut, and his smile is very nearly as sharp-edged.

"Hello, little one," the man says as Nassun stares. "That's quite the trick."

Jija tries to move, shifting his leg along the harpoon shaft, and it is awful. There is the abortive sound of bone grating on metal, and he groan-coughs out an agonized cry, grabbing spasmodically for Nassun. Nassun catches his shoulder, but he's heavy, and she's tired, and she realizes in sudden horror that she lacks the strength to fight the man with the glassknife if that should be necessary. Jija's shoulder shakes beneath her hand, and she's shaking nearly as hard. Maybe this is why no one uses the stuff underneath the heat? Now she and her father will pay the price for her folly.

But the black-haired man hunkers down, moving with remarkably slow grace for someone who showed such swift brutality only moments before. "Don't be afraid," he says. He blinks then, something flickering and uncertain in his gaze. "Do I know you?"

Nassun has never before seen this giant with the icewhite eyes and the world's longest knife. The knife is still in his hand, though now it dangles at his side, dripping. She shakes her head, a little too hard and fast.

The man blinks, the uncertainty clears, and the smile returns. "The beasts are dead. I came to help you, didn't I?" Something is off about the question. He asks it as if he seeks confirmation: *didn't I?* It's too sincere, too heartfelt somehow. Then he says, "I won't let anyone hurt you."

Perhaps it is only coincidence that his gaze slides over to her father's face after he says this. But. Something in Nassun unclenches, just a little.

Then Jija tries to move again and makes another pained sound, and the man's gaze sharpens. "How unpleasant. Let me help you—" He sets down the knife and reaches for Jija.

"Stay the rust back—" Jija blurts, trying to move back and jerking all over with the pain of this. He's panting, too, and sweating. "Who are you? Are you?" His eyes roll toward the flowing ridge of hex-stone. "From?"

The man, who has drawn back at Jija's reaction, follows his gaze. "Oh. Yes. The comm's sentries saw you coming along the road. Then we saw the bandits moving in, so I came to help. We've had trouble with that lot before. It was a convenient opportunity to eliminate the threat." His white gaze shifts back to Nassun, flicking at the sheared-off harpoon along the way. He has never stopped smiling. "But *you* should not have had trouble with them."

He knows what Nassun is. She cringes against her father, though she knows he is no shelter. It's habit.

Her father tenses, his breath quickening to a rasp. "Are . . . are you . . ." He swallows. "We're looking for the Moon."

The man's smile widens. His accent is something Equatorial; Equatorials always have such strong white teeth. "Ah, yes," he says. "You've found it."

Her father slumps in relief, to the degree that his leg allows. "Oh . . . oh. Evil Earth, at last."

Nassun can't take it anymore. "What is *the Moon?*"

"Found Moon." The man inclines his head. "That is the name of our community. A very special place, for very special people." Then he sheaths the knife and extends one hand, palm up, offering. "My name is Schaffa."

The hand is held out only to Nassun, and Nassun doesn't know why. Maybe because he knows what she is? Maybe only because her hand isn't covered with blood, as both of Jija's are. She swallows and takes the hand, which immediately and firmly closes around hers. She manages, "I'm Nassun. That's my father." She lifts her chin. "Nassun *Resistant Tirimo.*"

Nassun knows that her mother was trained by the Fulcrum, which means that Mama's use name was never "Resistant." And Nassun is only ten years old now, too young for Tirimo to recognize with a comm name even if she still lived there. Yet the man inclines his head gravely, as if it is not a lie. "Come, then," he says. "Let's see if between the two of us, we can't get your father free."

He rises, pulling her up with him, and she turns toward Jija, thinking that with Schaffa here they can maybe just lift Jija off the shaft and that if they do it fast enough maybe it won't hurt him too much. But before she can open her mouth to say this, Schaffa presses two fingers to the back of her neck. She flinches and rounds on him, instantly defensive, and he raises both hands, wagging the fingers to show that he's still unarmed. She can feel a bit of damp on her neck, probably a smear of blood.

"Duty first," he says.

"What?"

He nods toward her father. "I can lift him, while you shift the leg."

Nassun blinks again, confused. The man moves over to Jija, and she is distracted from wondering about that strange touch by her father's cries of pain as they work him free.

Much later, though, she will remember an instant after

that touch, when the tips of the man's fingers glimmered like the cut ends of the harpoon. A gossamer-thin thread of light-under-the-heat had seemed to flicker from her to him. She will remember, too, that for a moment that thread of light illuminated others: a whole tracework of jagged lines spreading all over him like the spiderwebbing that follows a sharp impact in brittle glass. The impact site, the center of the spiderweb, was somewhere near the back of his head. Nassun will remember thinking in that instant: *He's not alone in there.*

In the moment it is no matter. Their journey has ended. Nassun is, apparently, home.

* * *

The Guardians do not speak of Warrant, where they are made. No one knows its location. When asked, they only smile.

—*From lorist tale, "Untitled 759," recorded in Charta Quartent, Eadin Comm, by itinerant Mell Lorist Stone*

8

you've been warned

YOU'RE IN LINE TO PICK up your household's share for the week when you hear the first whisper. It's not directed at you, and it's not meant to be overheard, but you hear it anyway because the speaker is agitated and forgets to be quiet. "Too Earthfired many of 'em," an older man is saying to a younger man, when you pull yourself out of your own thoughts enough to process the words. "Ykka's all right, earned her place, didn't she? Gotta be a few good ones. But the rest? We only need *one*—"

The man is shushed by his companion at once. You fix your gaze on a distant group of people trying to haul some baskets of mineral ore across the cavern by use of a guided ropeslide, so that when the younger man looks around he won't see you looking at them. But you remember.

It's been a week since the incident with the boilbugs and it feels like a month. This isn't just losing track of days and nights. Some of the strange elasticity of time comes from your having lost Nassun, and with her the urgency of purpose. Without that purpose you feel sort of attenuated and loose, as aimless as compass needles must have been during the Wandering Season. You've decided to try settling in, recentering your awareness, exploring your new boundaries, but that isn't helping much. Castrima's geode defies your sense of size as well as time. It feels cluttered when you stand near one of the geode's walls, where the view of the opposite wall is occluded by dozens of jagged, crisscrossing quartz shafts. It feels empty when you pass entire crystals' worth of unoccupied apartments, and realize the place was built to hold many more people than it currently does. The trading post on the surface was smaller than Tirimo—yet you're beginning to realize that Ykka's efforts at recruitment for Castrima have been exceptionally successful. At least half of the people you meet in the comm are new, same as you. (No wonder she wanted some new people on her improvised advising council; *newness* is a group trait here.) You meet a nervous metallorist and three knappers who are nothing like Jija, a biomest who works with Lerna two days a week, and a woman who once made a living selling artful leather crafts as gifts, who now spends her days tanning skins that the Hunters bring in.

Some of the new people have a bitter look, because like Lerna they did not intend to join Castrima. Ykka or someone else deemed them useful to a community that once consisted solely of traders and miners, and that meant the end of their journey. Some of them, however, are palpably feverish in their determination to contribute to and defend the comm. These are the ones who had nowhere to go, their comms destroyed by the Rifting or the aftershakes. Not all of them have useful skills. They're youngish, usually, which makes sense because most comms won't take in people who are elderly or infirm during a Season unless they have very desirable skills—and because, you learn upon talking with them, Ykka demands that a very specific question be put to most newcomers: *Can you live with orogenes?* The ones who say yes get to come in. The ones who *can* say yes tend to be younger.

(The ones who say no, you understand without having to ask, are not permitted to travel onward and potentially join other comms or commless bands to attack a community that knowingly harbors orogenes. There's a convenient gypsum quarry not far off, apparently, which is downwind. Helps to draw scavengers away from Castrima-over, too.)

And then there are the natives—the people who were part of Castrima long before the Season began. A lot of them are unhappy about all the new additions, even though everyone knows the comm couldn't have survived as it was. It was simply too small. Before Lerna they had no doctor, only a man who did midwifery, field surgery, and livestock medicine as a sideline to his farrier business. And they had only two orogenes—Ykka and Cutter, though apparently no one knew for sure that Cutter was one until the start of the Season; now there's a story you want to hear someday. Without orogenes, Castrima-under becomes a deathtrap, which makes most of the natives reluctantly willing to accept Ykka's efforts to attract more of her kind. So the old Castrimans look at you with suspicion, but the good thing is that they look at all the newcomers the same way. It's not your status as an orogene that bothers them. It's that you haven't yet proven yourself.

(It is surprising how refreshing this feels. Being judged by what you do, and not what you are.)

Lately you've spent your mornings on a work crew doing

water-gardening: sprouting seeds in trays of wet cloth, then moving the resulting seedlings to troughs of water and chemicals that the biomests devise so that they can grow. It's soothing work, and reminds you of the housegreen you had back in Tirimo. (Uche sitting amid the edible ferns, making horrible faces as he chewed on a mouthful of dirt before you could stop him. You smile at this memory before the hurt blanks your face again. You still can't smile over things Corundum did, and that's been ten—no, eleven—years now.)

In the evenings you go to Ykka's, to talk with her and Lerna and Hjarka and Cutter about the affairs of the comm. This includes stuff like whether to punish Jever Innovator Castrima for selling fans—since market economies are illegal during a Season per Imperial Law—and how to stop Old Man Crey (who isn't that old) from complaining again that the communal baths are too tepid. He's getting on everyone's nerves. And who's going to step in if Ontrag, the potter, keeps breaking the bad practice pottery of the two people apprenticed to her? It's how Ontrag was taught, but that's also how one teaches people who *want* to learn pottery. Ontrag's apprentices are only there because Ykka ordered them to learn the old woman's skill before she kicks off. At the rate things are going, they might kill her themselves.

It's ridiculous, mundane, incredibly tedious stuff, and... you love it. Why? Who knows. Perhaps because it's similar to the sorts of discussions you had back during the two times you were part of a family? You remember arguing with Innon about whether to teach Corundum Sanze-mat early, so he wouldn't have an accent, or later, and only if Coru ever wanted to leave Meov. You had an argument with Jija once because he believed putting fruit in the cold cache ruined the taste, and you didn't care because it made the fruit last longer. The arguments that you have with the other advisors are more important: Your decisions affect more than a thousand people now. But they have the same silly, pedantic feel. Silly pedantry is a luxury that you've rarely been able to enjoy in your life.

You've gone topside again, standing silent on the porch of a gateway house in the falling ash. The sky's a little different today: thinnish gray-yellow instead of thickish gray-red, and the pattern of the clouds is long and wavelike in lieu of the chains of beads you've seen since the Rifting. One of the Strongback guards says, looking up, "Maybe things are getting better." The yellow of the clouds almost feels like sunlight. You can see the sun itself now and again, a pale and strengthless disc occasionally framed by the gentle drifting curves.

You don't tell the guard what you can sess, which is that the yellow clouds contain more sulfur than usual. Nor do you say what you know, which is that if it rains right now, the forest that surrounds Castrima and currently provides a significant portion of the comm's food will die. Somewhere up north, the rift that Alabaster tore has simply belched out a great waft of the gas from some long-buried underground pocket. Cutter, who's come up here with you and Hjarka, glances at you, face carefully blank; he knows, too. But he doesn't say anything, either, and you think you know why: Because of the guard, and his wistful hope that things are getting better. It would be cruel to break that hope before it fades on its own. You like Cutter better for this moment of shared kindness.

Then you turn your head a little and the feeling vanishes. There's another stone eater nearby, lurking in the shadows of a house not far off. This one is male-ish, butter-yellow marble laced with veins of brown, with a swirling cap of brass hair. He isn't looking at anyone, isn't moving, and you wouldn't have even noticed him if not for the bright metal of his hair, so striking against the haze of the day. You wonder, for the third or fourth time, why they cluster around Castrima. Are they trying to help, as Hoa helps you? Are they expecting more of you to turn to delicious, chewable stone? Are they just bored?

You can't deal with these creatures. You push Butter Marble from your mind and look away, and later when you're ready to set off and you glance that way again, he is gone.

The three of you are up here, following one of the Hunters through the forest, because they want you to come and see something. Ykka's not along for the trip because she's mediating a dispute between the Strongbacks and the Resistants about shift length or something. Lerna's not here because he's started teaching a class in wound care to anyone who wants to attend. Hoa's not here because Hoa's still missing, as he has been for the past week. But with you are seven of the Castrima Strongbacks, two Hunters, and the blond white woman you met on your first day in Castrima, who has since introduced herself as Esni. She's been accepted into the comm as a Strongback, despite being barely over a hundred pounds and paler than ash. Turns out she was the head of a drover clan before the Rifting, which means she knows how to wrangle large animals and people with outsized egos. She and her people voluntarily joined Castrima because it was much closer than their home comm down in the Antarctics. The air-dried, pickled, salt-cured remnants of their last cattle herd have constituted Castrima's only meat stores since the Rifting.

No one talks as you walk. The silence of the forest, save for the rustling of small creatures through the undergrowth and the occasional tap-tap of wood-boring animals in the distance, demands more of the same. The woods are changing, you see as you tromp through them. The taller trees lost their leaves months ago, sap drawing down to protect against the encroaching cold and the souring surface soil. But correspondingly, the shrubs and mid-level trees have grown thicker foliage, drinking in what little light they can capture, sometimes folding their leaves down at night to shed ash. This makes the ash thinner off the roads, so much that you can sometimes see the ground litter.

Which is good, because it makes the newest parts of the landscape stand out that much more: the mounds. They're three or four feet high, usually, built of cemented ash and leaves and twigs, and on a brighter day like this they are easy to spot because they steam faintly. Occasionally you see small bones, the remains of paws or tails, poking through the base of each mound. Boilbug nests. Not many... but you don't remember any, a week ago when you walked past this area of the forest. (You would've sessed the heat.) It's a reminder that while most plants and animals struggle to survive in a Season, a rare few do more: deprived of their usual predators and given ideal conditions, they thrive, breeding wildly wherever they can find a food source, relying on numbers to ensure the species' continuation.

Not good, regardless. You find yourself checking your shoes frequently, and you notice the others doing the same.

Then you've reached the top of a ridge that overlooks a spreading forest basin. It's clear the basin is outside the zone of protection that Castrima's orogenes maintain, because broad swaths of the forest here are flattened and dead in the aftermath of the Rifting. You'd be able to see hundreds of miles if not for the ash, but since this is such a bright, low-ash day, you can see perhaps a few dozen. It's enough.

Because there, hazy in the golden light, you can see something standing above the flattened forest: a cluster of what must be stripped saplings or long branches set into the ground in an attempt at straightness, although many of them list to one side or the other. At the tip of each is a flapping bit of dark red cloth to draw the eye. You can't tell whether the red is dye or something else, because mounted on each of these stakes is a body. The stakes jut from the bodies' mouths or other parts; they are impaled upon them.

"Not our people," says Hjarka. She's looking through a distance glass, adjusting it while one of the Hunters hovers nearby, hands half-upraised to catch the precious instrument should Hjarka fumble it or, knowing Hjarka, toss the thing away. "I mean, it's hard to tell from this distance, but I don't recognize them, and I don't think we've ever sent anyone out that far. And they look filthy. Commless band, maybe."

"One that bit off more than it could chew," mutters one of the Hunters.

"All our patrols are accounted for," says Esni, folding her arms. "I don't keep track of anybody but the Strongbacks, I mean, the Hunters do their own thing—but we do note goings and comings." She's already studied the bodies through the distance glass, and it was her call that members of the comm leadership be brought topside to see for themselves. "I figure the culprits are travelers. A late group trying to make it back to a home comm, better armed than the commless who attacked them. And luckier."

"Travelers wouldn't do this," says Cutter quietly. He's usually quiet. Hjarka's the one you always expect to be difficult, but she's actually predictable and far more easygoing than her fierce appearance would suggest. Cutter, though, opposes nearly everything you or Ykka or the others suggest. He's a stubborn little ruster under that quiet demeanor. "The impaling, I mean. No reason to stop for that long. Someone spent time cutting down those poles, sharpening them, digging holes to post them, positioning them so they could be seen for miles around. Travelers…travel."

Cutter's much harder to read than Hjarka, too, you notice now. Hjarka is a woman who has never been able to hide the breadth and vigor of what she is, so she doesn't bother to try. Cutter is a man who's spent his life concealing the strength of mountains behind a veneer of meekness. Now you know what that looks like from the outside. But he's got a point.

"What do you think it is, then?" You guess wildly. "Another commless band?"

"They wouldn't do this, either. At this point they're not wasting bodies anymore."

You wince, and see several other people in the group sigh or shift. But it's true. There are still animals to hunt, but the ones that aren't hibernating are fierce enough or armored enough or toxic enough to be costly prey for anything but very well-prepared hunters. Commless rarely have good working crossbows, and desperation makes for poor stealth. And as the boilbugs have shown, there's new competition for any carcasses.

Of course, if Castrima doesn't find a new source of meat soon, you and the others won't be wasting bodies anymore, either. That wince served many purposes.

Hjarka lowers the distance glass at last. "Yeah," she sighs, responding to Cutter. "Fuck."

"What?" You feel stupid, suddenly, as if everyone has started speaking another language.

"Somebody's marking territory." Hjarka gestures with the distance glass, shrugging; the Hunter deftly plucks it from her hand. "Doing this is a warn-off, but not to other commless—who don't give a shit and will probably just pull the bodies down for snacks. To *us*. Letting us know what they'll do if we cross their boundaries."

"Only comm in that direction is Tettehee," says one of the Hunters. "They're friendly, have been for years. And we're no threat to them. Not much water in that direction to support other comms; the river wends away to the north."

North. That bothers you. You don't know why. There's no reason to mention this to the others, but still . . . "When's the last time you heard from this Tettehee?" Silence greets you, and you look around. Everyone's staring. Well, that answers that. "We need to send somebody to Tettehee, then."

"'Somebody' who might end up on a pole?" Hjarka glares at you. "Nobody's expendable in this comm, *newcomer*."

It's the first time you've ever sparked her ire, and it's a lot of ire. She's older, bigger, and in addition to her sharpened teeth, there's her glare, which is black-eyed and fierce. But she reminds you, somehow, of Innon, so you feel anything but anger in response.

"We're going to need to send out a trading party anyway." You say it as gently as you can, which makes her blink. That's the inevitable conclusion of all the talks you've had lately about the comm's deepening meat deficit. "We might as well use this warn-off to make sure that party is armed, and a large enough group that no one can tackle them without paying for it."

"And if whoever did this has a larger, better-armed group?"

It's never just about strength, during a Season. You know that. Hjarka knows that. But you say, "Send an orogene with them."

She blinks in genuine surprise, then lifts an eyebrow. "Who'll kill half our people trying to defend them?"

You turn away from her and hold out a hand. None of them move away from you, but then none of them are from comms large enough to have been visited often by Imperial Orogenes; they don't know what your gesture means. They gasp, though, and move back and murmur when you spin a five-foot-wide torus in the brush a few paces away. Ash and dead leaves swirl into a dust devil, glittering with ice in the sulfurous afternoon light. You didn't have to spin it that fast. You're just being dramatic.

Then you use what you dragged from that torus and turn, pointing at the stand of impaled bodies down in the basin. At this distance it's impossible to tell what's happening at first—but then the trees in the area shiver and the poles begin to sway wildly. A moment later a fissure opens, and you drop the poles and their grisly ornaments into the ground. You pull your hands together, slowly so as not to alarm anyone, and the trees stop shivering. But a moment later, everyone feels the faint judder of the ridge you're standing on, because you've let a little of the aftershake come this way. Again, you didn't have to. You just had a point to make.

It's commendable that Hjarka just looks impressed and not alarmed when you open your eyes and turn to her. "Nice," she says. "So *you* can ice someone without killing everyone around you. But if every rogga could do that, people wouldn't have a problem with roggas."

You really hate that rusting word, no matter what Ykka thinks.

And you're not sure you agree with Hjarka's assessment. People have problems with roggas for a lot of reasons that have nothing to do with orogeny. You open your mouth to reply—and then stop. Because now you can see the trap Hjarka's set, the only way this conversation's going to end, and you don't want to go there... but there's no avoiding it. Rusting fuck.

So that's how you end up in charge of a brand-new Fulcrum, sort of.

* * *

"Stupid," Alabaster says.

You sigh. "I know."

It's the next day, and another conversation about the principles of the unreal—how an obelisk works, how their crystalline structure emulates the strange linkages of power between the cells of a living being, and how there are theories about things even smaller than cells, somehow, even though no one has seen them or can prove that they exist.

You have these conversations with Alabaster every day, in between your morning work shift and evening politicking, because he is filled with a sense of urgency spurred by his own impending mortality. The sessions don't last long, because Alabaster has limited strength. And the conversations so far haven't been very useful, mostly because Alabaster is a terrible teacher. He barks orders and gives lectures, never answering your questions when you ask them. He's impatient and snappish. And while some of this can be chalked up to the pain that he's in, the rest is just Alabaster being himself. He really hasn't changed.

You are frequently surprised at how much you've missed him, the irascible old ass. And because of this, you hold your temper... for a while, anyway.

"Someone's got to teach the younger ones, anyway," you say. Most of the comm's orogenes are children or adolescents, simply because most ferals don't survive childhood. You've heard rumors that some of the older orogenes are teaching them, helping them learn not to ice things when they stub their toes, and it helps that Castrima is as stable as the Equatorials once were. But that's ferals teaching ferals. "And if I fail to do whatever it is you keep insisting that I do—"

"None of them are worth rust. You'd sess that yourself, if you'd bothered to pay any attention to them. It's not just about skill, it's also natural talent; that's the whole reason the Fulcrum made us breed, Essun. And most of them will never be able to get past energy redistribution." This is the term that the two of you have concocted for orogeny done with heat and kinetics—the Fulcrum's way. What Alabaster is now trying to teach you, and what you're struggling to learn because it relies on things that make no sense whatsoever, is something you've started calling *magic redistribution*. That isn't right, either; it's not redistribution, but it'll do until you understand it better.

Alabaster's still on about the orogeny class you've agreed to teach, and the children who will fill it. "It's a waste of your time to teach them."

This dismissal, inexplicably, starts to eat through your patience. "It's never a waste of time to educate others."

"Spoken like a simple creche teacher. Oh, wait."

It's a cheap shot, disrespecting the vocation that gave you years of camouflage. You should let it go, but it feels like salt on a glass-cut and you snap. "Stop. It."

Alabaster blinks, then scowls to the degree that he can. "I don't have a great deal of time for coddling, Syen—"

"*Essun.*" Right now, here, it matters. "And I don't rusting care if you're dying. You don't get to talk to me like this." And you get up, because suddenly you're rusting *done.*

He stares at you. Antimony is there as always, supporting him in silence, and her eyes shift to you for a moment. You think you read surprise in them, but that's probably just projection. "You don't care if I'm dying."

"No, I don't. Why the rust should I? You don't care if any of the rest of us die. You *did this to us.*" Lerna, at the other end of the room, glances up and frowns, and you remember to lower your voice. "You'll kick off sooner and more easily than the rest of us. *We* get to starve to death, well after you're dust in the ash. And if you can't be bothered to actually teach me anything, then fuck you; I'll figure out how to fix things myself!"

So you're halfway across the infirmary, your steps brisk and your hands fisted at your sides, when he snaps, "Walk out that door and you *will* starve to death. Stay and you have a chance."

You keep walking, yelling over your shoulder, "*You* figured it out!"

"It took me ten years! And—fucking, flaking rust, you hard-headed, steel-hearted—"

The geode jolts. Not just the infirmary building but the whole damned thing. You hear cries of alarm outside, and that does it.

You stop and clench your fists and slam a counter-torus against the fulcrum that he's positioned just underneath Castrima. It doesn't dislodge his; you're still not precise enough for that, and anyway you're too angry to try very hard. The movement stops, however—whether because you stopped it or because you've surprised him so much that he stopped it, you don't care.

Then you turn back, storming at him in such a fury that Antimony vanishes and is suddenly standing beside him, a silent sentinel warning. You don't care about her, and you don't care that Alabaster is bent again, making a low strained wheezing sound, or any of it.

"Listen to me, you selfish ass," you snarl, bending down so the stone eater will be the only one to hear. 'Baster's shaking, in visible pain, and a day ago that would've been enough to stop you. Now you're too angry for pity. "I have to live here even if you're just waiting to die, and if you make these people hate us because you can't rein it in—"

Wait. You trail off, distracted. This time you can see the change as it happens to his arm—the left one, which had been longer. The stone of him creeps along slowly, steadily, making a minute hissing sound as it transmutes flesh into something else. And nearly against your will you shift your sight as he has taught you, searching between the gelid bubbles of him for those elusive tendrils of connection. You see, suddenly, that they are brighter, almost like silver metal, tightening into a lattice and aligning in new ways that you've never seen before.

"You're such an arrogant ruster," he snarls through his teeth. This breaks through your astonishment about his arm, replacing it with affront that *he* of all people has called *you* arrogant.

"*Essun.* You act like you're the only one who's made mistakes, the only one who ever died inside and had to keep going. You don't know shit, won't listen to shit—"

"Because you won't tell me anything! You expect me to listen to you, but you don't share, you just demand and proclaim and, and—and I'm not a child! Evil Earth, I wouldn't even speak to a child this way!"

(There is a traitor part of you that whispers, *Except you did. You spoke to Nassun like this.* And the loyal part of you snarls back, *Because she wouldn't have understood. She wouldn't have been safe if you'd been gentler, slower. It was for her own good, and—*)

"It's for your own rusting good," Alabaster grates. The progression of the stone down his arm has stopped, only an inch or so this time. Lucky. "I'm trying to protect you, for Earth's sake!"

You stop, glaring at him, and he glares back, and silence falls.

There is the clink of something heavy and metallic being put down behind you. This makes you glance back at Lerna, who is looking at you and has folded his arms. Most of the people in Castrima, even the orogenes, won't know what the jolt was all about, but he does because he saw the body language, and now you've got to explain things to him—hopefully before he doses Alabaster's next bowl of mush with something toxic.

It's a reminder that these are not the old days and you cannot react in the old ways. If Alabaster has not changed, then it's up to you. Because you have.

So you straighten and take a deep breath. "You've never taught anyone anything, have you?"

He blinks, frowning in apparent suspicion at your change of tone. "I taught you."

"No, Alabaster. Back then you did impossible things and I just watched you and tried not to die when I imitated you. But you've never tried to intentionally disseminate information to another adult, have you?" You know the answer even without him saying it, but it's important that he say it. This is something he needs to learn.

A muscle in his jaw flexes. "I've tried."

You laugh. The defensive note in his voice tells you everything. After another moment's consideration—and a deep breath to marshal your self-control—you sit down again. This leaves Antimony looming over you both, but you try to ignore her. "Listen," you say. "You need to give me a reason to trust you."

His eyes narrow. "You don't trust me by now?"

"You've destroyed the world, Alabaster. You've told me you want me to make it worse. I'm not hearing a whole lot here that screams, 'Obey me without question.'"

His nostrils flare. The pain of the stoning seems to have faded, though he's drenched with sweat and still breathing hard. But then something in his expression shifts, too, and a moment later he slumps, to the degree that he is able.

"I let him die," he murmurs, looking away. "Of course you don't trust me."

"No, Alabaster. The Guardians killed Innon."

He half smiles. "Him, too."

Then you know. Ten years and it's like no time has passed at all. "No," you say again. But this is softer. Strengthless. He's said he wouldn't forgive you for Corundum . . . but perhaps you're not the only one he doesn't forgive.

A long silence passes.

"All right," he says at last. His voice is very soft. "I'll tell you."

"What?"

"Where I've been for the past ten years." He glances up at Antimony, who still looms over both of you. "What this is all about."

"She isn't ready," the stone eater says. You jump at her voice.

Alabaster tries to shrug, winces as something twinges somewhere on his body, sighs. "Neither was I."

Antimony stares down at both of you. It's not really that different from the way she's been staring at you since you came back, but it feels more pent. Maybe that's just projection. But then, suddenly, she vanishes. You see it happen this time. Her form blurs, becoming insubstantial, translucent. Then she drops into the ground as if a hole has opened beneath her feet. Gone.

Alabaster sighs. "Come sit beside me," he says.

You frown immediately. "Why?"

"So we can have sex again. Why the rust do you think?"

You loved him once. You probably still do. With a sigh you get up and move to the wall. Gingerly, though his back is unburned, you prop yourself for comfort, then rest a hand against his back to hold him up, the way Antimony so often does.

Alabaster's silent for a moment, and then he says, "Thank you."

Then... he tells you everything.

* * *

Breathe not the fine ashfall. Drink not the red water.
Walk not long upon warm soil.

—*Tablet One, "On Survival," verse seven*

9

Nassun, needed

Because you are Essun, I should not need to remind you that all Nassun knew before Found Moon was Tirimo, and the ash-darkening world of the road during a Fifth Season. You know your daughter, don't you? So it should be obvious therefore that Found Moon becomes something she never believed she had before: a true home.

It is not a newcomm. At its core is the village of Jekity, which was a city before the Choking Season some hundred years before. During that Season, Mount Akok blanketed the Antarctics with ash—but that is not what nearly killed Jekity, since the city had vast stores and sturdy wood-and-slate walls at the time. Jekity the city died because of human errors, compounded: A child lighting a lantern spilled oil, which set off a fire that swept the western end of the comm and burned a third of it before people managed to get it under control. The comm's headman died in the fire, and when three qualified candidates stepped forward to take his place, factionalism and infighting meant that the burned section of the wall didn't get rebuilt quickly enough. A tibbit-run—small, furred animals that swarm like ants when food is scarce enough—swept into the comm and took care of anyone too slow to get off the ground... and the comm's ground-level storecaches. The survivors lasted for a time on what was left, then starved. By the time the sky cleared five years later, less than five thousand souls remained of the hundred thousand who'd begun the Season.

The Jekity of now is even smaller. The poor, unskilled repairs made to the wall during Choking are still in place, and while the stores have been elevated and replenished sufficiently to meet Imperial standards, this is only on paper: The comm has done a bad job of rotating old, spoiled stores out and laying in new. Strangers have rarely asked to join Jekity over the years. Even by Antarctic standards, the comm is seen as ill-fated. Its young people usually leave to talk or marry their way into other, growing communities where jobs are more plentiful and the memory of suffering does not linger. When Schaffa found this sleepy terrace-farming comm ten years before, and convinced the then-headwoman Maite to allow him to set up a special Guardian facility within the comm's walls, she hoped that it was the beginning of a turnaround for her home. Guardians are a healthy addition to any community, aren't they? And indeed, there are now three Guardians in Jekity including Schaffa, along with nine children of varying ages. There were ten, but when one of the children caused a brief but powerful earth-shake amid a temper tantrum one evening, the child vanished. Maite did not ask questions. It's good to know the Guardians are doing their jobs.

Nassun and her father do not know this as they move into the comm, though others will eventually tell them. The healers—an elderly doctor and a forest herbalist—spend seven days getting Jija out of danger, because he develops a fever not long after the surgery on his wound. Nassun tends him the whole while. When it becomes clear that he'll survive, however, Schaffa introduces them to Maite, who's delighted to learn that Jija is a stoneknapper. The comm has not had one for several decades, so they've been sending orders to knappers in the comm of Deveteris, twenty miles away. There's an old, empty house in the comm with an attached kiln, and while a forge would've been more useful, Jija tells her he can make it work. Maite gives it a month to be sure, and listens when her people tell her that Jija is polite and friendly and sensible. He's physically hearty, too, since he's recovering from that wound like a proper Resistant, and since he managed to survive the road with no companion but a little girl. Everyone notices how well behaved and devoted his daughter is, too—not at all what anyone would expect of a rogga. Thus, at the end of the month, Jija receives the name *Jija Resistant Jekity*. They induct him with a ceremony that most of the comm has never seen before, so long has it been since anyone new joined the comm. Maite herself had to look up the details of the ceremony in an old lore-book. Then they throw a party, which is very nice. Jija tells them he's honored.

Nassun remains just *Nassun*. No one calls her Nassun Resistant Tirimo, though she still introduces herself that way upon meeting new people. Schaffa's interest in her is simply too obvious. But she causes no trouble, so the people of Jekity are as friendly toward her as they are toward Jija, if in a slightly more guarded fashion.

It is the other orogene children who unashamedly embrace Nassun for everything she is.

The oldest of them is a Coaster boy named Eitz, who speaks with a strange choppy accent that Nassun thinks of as exotic. He's eighteen, tall, long-faced, and if there is a perpetual shadow in his expression, it does nothing to mar his beauty in Nassun's eyes. He's the one who welcomes Nassun on the first day after it becomes clear that Jija will live. "Found Moon is *our* community," he says in a deep voice that makes Nassun's heart race, leading her to the small compound that Schaffa's people have built over near Jekity's weakest wall. It's up a hill. He leads her toward a pair of gates that swing open as they approach. "Yumenes had the Fulcrum, and Jekity has this: A place where you can be yourself, and always be safe. Schaffa and the other Guardians are here for us, too, remember. This is ours."

Found Moon has walls of its own, shaped from the shafts of columnar rock that dominate this area—but these are uniformly sized and perfectly even in conformation. Nassun doesn't even have to sess them to realize they have been raised by orogeny. Within the compound are a handful of small buildings, a few new but most parts of old Jekity left abandoned as the comm's population dwindled. Whatever those used to be, they have since been refurbished into a house for the Guardians, a mess hall, a wide tiled practice area, several ground-level storesheds, and a dormitory for the children.

The other children fascinate Nassun. Two are Westcoasters, small and brown and black-haired and angle-eyed. Sisters, and they look it, named Oegin and Ynegen. Nassun has never seen Westcoasters before, and she stares until she realizes they are staring at her in turn. They ask to touch her hair and she asks to touch theirs back. This makes them all realize how strange and silly a request that is, and they giggle and become instant friends without a head petted between them. Then there is Paido, another Somidlatter, who looks like he's got more than a little Antarctic in him because his hair is bright yellow and his skin is so white that it nearly glows. The others tease him about it, but Nassun tells him that sometimes she burns in the sun, too—though she carefully doesn't mention that this takes the better part of a day rather than minutes—and his face alights.

The other children are all from lower Somidlats comms, and all have visible Sanzed in them. Deshati was in training to become a stoneknapper before the Guardians found her, and she asks Nassun all sorts of questions about her father. (Nassun warns her off talking to Jija directly. Deshati understands at once, though she is sad about it.) Wudeh gets sick when he eats certain kinds of grain and is very small and frail because he doesn't get enough good food, though his orogeny is the strongest of the bunch. Lashar looks at Nassun coldly and sneers at her accent, though Nassun can't tell the difference between how she speaks and how Lashar does. The others tell her it's because Lashar's grandfather was an Equatorial and her mother is a local comm Leader. Alas, Lashar is an orogene, so none of that matters anymore... but her upbringing tells.

Shirk is not Shirk's name, but she won't tell anyone what that really is, so they started calling her that after she tried to duck out of chores one afternoon. (She doesn't anymore, but the name stuck.) Peek is similarly nicknamed, because she is tremendously shy and spends most of her time hiding behind someone else. She has only one eye, and a terrible scar down the side of her face—where her grandmother tried to stab her, the others whisper when Peek is not around. Her real name is Xif.

Nassun makes ten, and they want to know everything about her: where she came from, what kinds of foods she likes to eat, what life was like in Tirimo, has she ever held a baby kirkhusa because they are so soft. And in whispers they ask about other things, once it becomes clear that Schaffa favors her. What did she do on the day of the Rifting? How did she learn such skill with orogeny? This is how Nassun discovers that it is rare for their kind to be born to orogene parents. Wudeh comes the closest, because his aunt realized what he was and taught him what she could in secret, but this amounted to little more than how not to ice people by accident. Some of the others only learned that lesson the hard way—and Oegin grows very quiet during this conversation. Deshati actually didn't know she was an orogene until the Rifting, which Nassun finds incomprehensible. She is the one who asks the most questions, but quietly, when the others are not around, and in a tone of shame.

Another thing Nassun discovers is that she is much, much, *much* better than any of them. It is not simply a matter of training. Eitz has had years more training than her, and yet his orogeny is as thin and frail as Wudeh's body. Eitz is in control of it, enough to do no harm, but he can't do much good with it, either, like find diamonds or make a cool spot to stand in on a hot day or slice a harpoon in half. The others stare when Nassun tries to explain the lattermost, and then Schaffa comes away from the wall of a nearby building (one of the Guardians is always watching while they gather and train and play) to take her for a walk.

"What you do not understand," Schaffa says, resting a hand on her shoulder as they walk, "is that an orogene's skill is not just a matter of practice, but of innate ability. So much has been done to breed the gift out of the world." He sighs a little, sounding almost disappointed. "There are few left who are born with a high level of ability."

"My father killed my brother because of it," Nassun says. "Uche had more orogeny than me. All he ever did was listen with it, though, and say weird things sometimes. He made me laugh."

She keeps the words soft because they still hurt to say, and because she's said them so rarely. Jija never wanted to hear it, so she has had no one with whom she could discuss her grief until now. They're over by the southern terraces of Jekity, successive platforms high above the floor of a lava-plain valley. The terraces are still heavily planted with grains, greens, and beans. Some of the plants are beginning to look sickly from the thinning sunlight. This will probably be the last harvest before the ash clouds get too thick.

"Yes. And that is a tragedy, little one; I'm sorry." Schaffa sighs. "My brethren have done their job too well, I think, in warning the populace about the dangers of untrained orogenes. Not that any of those warnings were false. Just... exaggerated, perhaps." He shrugs. She feels a flash of anger that this *exaggeration* is why her father looks at her with such hate sometimes. But the anger is nebulous, directionless; she hates the world, not anyone in particular. That's a lot to hate.

"He thinks I'm evil," she finds herself saying.

Schaffa looks at her for a long moment. There is something confused in his gaze for a moment, a wondering sort of frown that he gets from time to time. Not quite intentionally, Nassun sesses him in a fleeting pass, and yes—those strange silvery threads are flaring within him again, lacing through his flesh and tugging on his mind from somewhere near the back of his head. She stops as soon as his expression clears, because he is fiendishly sensitive to her uses of orogeny, and he does not like her doing anything without his permission. But when he is being tugged by the bright threads, he notices less.

"You aren't evil," he says firmly. "You are exactly as nature made you. And that is *special*, Nassun—special and powerful in ways that are atypical even for one of your kind. In the Fulcrum, you would have rings by now. Perhaps four, or even five. For one your age, that's amazing."

This makes Nassun happy, even though she doesn't fully understand. "Wudeh says the Fulcrum rings go up to ten?" Wudeh has the most talkative of the three Guardians, agate-eyed Nida. Nida sometimes says things that don't make sense, but the rest of the time she shares useful wisdom, so all the kids have learned to simply tune out the gibbering.

"Yes, ten." For some reason, Schaffa seems displeased by this. "But this is not the Fulcrum, Nassun. Here, you must train yourself, since we have no senior orogenes to train you. And that's good, because there are . . . things you can do." His face twitches. Flicker of silver through him again, then quiescence. "Things you are needed to do, which . . . things that Fulcrum training cannot do."

Nassun considers this, for the moment ignoring the silver. "Things like making my orogeny go away?" She knows her father has asked this of Schaffa.

"That would be possible, when you reach a certain point of development. But to reach that point, it is best that you learn to use your powers with no preconceptions." He glances at her. His expression is noncommittal, but somehow she knows: He does not want her changing into a still, even if it does become possible. "You're lucky to have been born to an orogene who was skilled enough to manage you as a child. You must have been very dangerous in your infancy and early years."

It's Nassun's turn to shrug at this. She lowers her gaze and scuffs at a weed that has worked its way up between two basalt columns. "I guess."

He glances at her, his gaze sharpening. Whatever is wrong with him—and there is something wrong with all of Found Moon's Guardians—it vanishes whenever she tries to hide something from him. It is as if he can sess obfuscations. "Tell me more of your mother."

Nassun does not want to talk about her mother. "She's probably dead." It seems likely, though she remembers feeling her mother's effort to shunt the Rifting away from Tirimo. People would've noticed that, though, wouldn't they? Mama always warned Nassun against doing orogeny during a shake, because that is how most orogenes get discovered. And Uche is what happens when orogenes get discovered.

"Perhaps." His head cocks, like that of a bird. "I've seen the marks of Fulcrum training in your technique. You are . . . precise. It's unusual to see in a grit—" He pauses. Looks confused again for a moment. Smiles. "A child of your age. How did she train you?"

Nassun shrugs again, thrusting her hands into her pockets. He will hate her, if she tells him. If not that, he will surely at least think less of her. Maybe he will give up.

Schaffa moves to sit on a nearby terrace wall. He also keeps watching her, smiling politely. Waiting. Which makes Nassun think of a third, worse possibility: What if she refuses to tell him, and he gets angry and kicks her and her father out of Found Moon? Then she will have nothing left but Jija.

And—she sneaks another look at Schaffa. His brow has furrowed slightly, not in displeasure but concern. The concern does not seem false. He is concerned about *her.* No one has shown concern for her in a year.

Thus, finally, Nassun says, "We would go out to a place near the end of the valley, away from Tirimo. She would tell Daddy she was taking me out hunting for herbs." Schaffa nods. That is something that children are normally taught in comms outside the Equatorial node network. A useful skill, should a Season come. "She would call it 'girl time.' Daddy used to laugh."

"And you practiced orogeny there?"

Nassun nodded, looking at her hands. "She would talk to me about it, when Daddy wasn't home. 'Girl talk.'" Discussions of wave mechanics and math. Endless quizzes. Anger when Nassun did not answer quickly, or correctly. "But at the Tip—the place she took me to—it was just practice. She had drawn circles on the ground. I had to push around a boulder, and my torus couldn't get any wider than the fifth ring, and then the fourth, and then the third. Sometimes she would throw the boulder at me." Terrifying to have three tons of stone rumbling along the ground toward her, and to wonder, *If I can't do it, will Mama stop?*

She had done it, so that question remains unanswered.

Schaffa chuckles. "Amazing." At Nassun's look of confusion, he adds, "That is precisely how orogene children are—were—trained at the Fulcrum. But it seems your training was substantially accelerated." He tilts his head again, considering. "If you had only occasional practice sessions, to conceal them from your father..."

Nassun nods. Her left hand flexes closed and then open again, as if on its own. "She said there wasn't time to teach me the gentle way, and anyway I was too strong. She had to do what would work."

"I see." Yet she can feel him watching her, waiting. He knows there's more. He prompts, "It must have been challenging, though."

Nassun nods. Shrugs. "I hated it. I yelled at her once. Told her she was mean. I told her I hated her and she couldn't make me do it."

Schaffa's breathing is, when the silver light is not stuttering or flickering within him, remarkably even. She has thought before that he sounds like a sleeping person, so steady is it. She listens to him breathe, not asleep, but calming nevertheless.

"She got really quiet. Then she said, 'Are you sure you can control yourself?' And she took my hand." She bites her lip then. "She broke it."

Schaffa's breath pauses, just for an instant. "Your hand?"

Nassun nods. She draws a finger across her palm, where each

of the long bones connecting wrist to knuckle still ache sometimes, when it is cold. After he says nothing more, she can continue. "She said it didn't m-matter if I hated her. It didn't matter if I didn't *want* to be good at orogeny. Then she took my hand and said don't ice anything. She had a round rock, and she hit my, my... my hand with it." The sound of stone striking flesh. Wet popping sounds as her mother set the bones. Her own voice screaming. Her mother's voice cutting through the pounding of blood in her ears: *You're fire, Nassun. You're lightning, dangerous unless captured in wires. But if you can control yourself through pain, I'll know you're safe.* "I didn't ice anything."

After that, her mother had taken her home and told Jija that Nassun had fallen and caught herself badly. True to her word, she'd never made Nassun go to the Tip with her again. Jija had remarked, later, on how quiet Nassun had become that year. *Just something that happens when girls start to grow up*, Mama had said.

No. If Daddy was Jija, then Mama had to be Essun.

Schaffa is very quiet. He knows what she is now, though: a child so willful that her own mother broke her hand to make her mind. A girl whose mother never loved her, only *refined* her, and whose father will only love her again if she can do the impossible and become something she is not.

"That was wrong," Schaffa says. His voice is so soft she can barely hear it. She turns to look at him in surprise. He is staring at the ground, and there is a strange look on his face. Not the usual wandering, confused look that he gets sometimes. This is something he actually remembers, and his expression is... guilty? Rueful. Sad. "It's wrong to hurt someone you love, Nassun."

Nassun stares at him. Her own breath catches, and she

doesn't notice until her chest aches and she is forced to suck in air. It's wrong to hurt someone you love. It's wrong. It's wrong. It has always been wrong.

Then Schaffa lifts a hand to her. She takes it. He pulls, and she falls willingly, and then she is in his arms and they are very tight and strong around her the way her father's have not been since before he killed Uche. In that moment, she does not care that Schaffa cannot possibly love her, when he has known her for only a few weeks. She loves him. She needs him. She will do anything for him.

With her face pressed into Schaffa's shoulder, Nassun sesses it when the silver flicker happens again. This time, in contact with him, she also feels the slight flinch of his muscles. It is barely a fluctuation, and might be anything: a bug bite, a shiver in the cooling evening breeze. Somehow, though, she realizes that it is actually pain. Frowning against his uniform, Nassun cautiously reaches toward that strange place at the back of Schaffa's head, where the silver threads come from. They are *hungry*, the threads, somehow; as she gets closer to them, they lick at her, seeking something. Curious, Nassun touches them, and sesses... what? A faint tug. Then she is tired.

Schaffa flinches again and pulls back, holding her at arm's length. "What are you doing?"

She shrugs awkwardly. "You needed it. You were hurting."

Schaffa turns his head from side to side slowly, not in negation, but as if checking for something he expects to be there, which is now gone. "I am always hurting, little one. It's part of what Guardians are. But..." His expression is wondering. By this, Nassun knows the pain is gone, at least for now.

"You're always hurting?" She frowns. "Is it that thing in your head?"

His gaze snaps back to her immediately. She has never been afraid of his icewhite eyes, even now as they turn very cold. "What?"

She points at the back of her own skull. It is where the sessapinae are located, she knows from lectures on biomestry in creche. "There's a little thing in you. Here. I don't know what it is, but I sessed it when I met you. When you touched my neck." She blinks, understanding. "You took something then to make it bother you less."

"Yes. I did." He reaches around her head now, and sets two of his fingers just at the top of her spine, beneath the back edge of her skull. This touch is not as relaxed as other times he has touched her. The two fingers are stiffened, held as if he's pantomiming a knife.

Only he isn't pantomiming, she realizes. She remembers that day in the forest when they reached Found Moon and the bandits attacked them. Schaffa is very, very strong—easily strong enough to push two fingers through bone and muscle like paper. *He* wouldn't have needed a rock to break her hand.

Schaffa's gaze searches hers and finds that she understands precisely what he's thinking about doing. "You aren't afraid."

She shrugs.

"Tell me why you aren't." His voice brooks no disobedience.

"Just..." She cannot help shrugging again. She can't really figure out how to say it. "I don't... I mean, if you have a good reason?"

"You have no inkling of my reasons, little one."

"I *know.*" She scowls, more out of frustration with herself than anything else. Then an explanation occurs to her. "Daddy didn't have a reason when he killed my little brother." Or when he knocked her off the wagon. Or any of the half-dozen times he's looked at Nassun and thought about killing her so obviously that even a ten-year-old can figure it out.

An icewhite blink. What happens then is fascinating to watch: Slowly Schaffa's expression thaws from the contemplation of her murder into wonder again, and a sorrow so deep that it makes a lump come to Nassun's throat. "And you have seen so much purposeless suffering that at least being killed for a reason can be borne?"

He's so much better at talking. She nods emphatically.

Schaffa sighs. She feels his fingers waver. "But this is not a thing that can be known beyond my order. I let a child live once, who saw, but I should not have. And we both suffered for my compassion. I remember that."

"I don't want you to suffer," Nassun says. She puts her hands on his chest, wills the silver flickers within him to take more. They begin to drift toward her. "It always hurts? That isn't right."

"Many things ease the pain. Smiling, for example, releases specific endorphins, which—" He jerks and takes his hand from the back of her neck, grabbing her hands and pulling them away from him just as the silver threads find her. He actually looks alarmed. "That will kill you!"

"You're going to kill me anyway." This seems sensible to her.

He stares. "Earth of our fathers and mothers." But with that, slowly, the killing tension begins to bleed out of his posture.

After a moment, he sighs. "Never speak of—of what you sess in me, around the others. If the other Guardians learn that you know, I may not be able to protect you."

Nassun nods. "I won't. Will you tell me what it is?"

"Someday, perhaps." He gets to his feet. Nassun hangs on to his hand when he tries to pull away. He frowns at her, bemused, but she grins and swings his hand a little, and after a moment he shakes his head. Then they head back into the compound, and that is the first day Nassun thinks of it as *home.*

* * *

Seek the orogene in its crib. Watch for the center of the circle. There you will find [obscured]

—*Tablet Two, "The Incomplete Truth," verse five*

10

you've got a big job ahead of you

You've called him crazy so many times. Told yourself that you despised him even as you grew to love him. Why? Perhaps you understood early on that he was what you could become. More likely it is that you suspected long before you lost and found him again that he *wasn't* crazy. "Crazy" is what everyone thinks all roggas are, after all—addled by the time they spend in stone, by their ostensible alliance with the Evil Earth, by not being human enough.

But.

"Crazy" is also what roggas who obey choose to call roggas that don't. You obeyed, once, because you thought it would make you safe. He showed you—again and again, unrelentingly, he would not let you pretend otherwise—that if obedience did not make one safe from the Guardians or the nodes or the lynchings or the breeding or the disrespect, then what was the point? The game was too rigged to bother playing.

You pretended to hate him because you were a coward. But

you eventually loved him, and he is part of you now, because you have since grown brave.

* * *

"I fought Antimony all the way down," Alabaster says. "It was stupid. If she'd lost her grip on me, if her concentration had faltered for an instant, I would have become part of the stone. Not even crushed, just...mixed in." He lifts a truncated arm, and you know him well enough to realize he would have waggled his fingers. If he still had fingers. He sighs, not even noticing. "We were probably into the mantle by the time Innon died."

His voice is soft. It's gotten quiet in the infirmary. You look up and around; Lerna's gone, and one of his assistants is sleeping on an unoccupied bed, snoring faintly. You speak in a soft voice, too. This is a conversation for only the two of you.

You have to ask, though even thinking the question makes you ache. "Do you know...?"

"Yes. I sessed how he died." He falls silent for a moment. You reverberate with his grief and your own. "Couldn't help sessing it. What they do, those Guardians, is magic, too. It's just... wrong. Contaminated, like everything else about their kind. When they shake a person apart, if you're attuned to that person, it feels like a niner."

And of course you were both attuned to Innon. He was a part of you. You shiver, because he's trying to make you *more* attuned, to the earth and orogeny and the obelisks and the unifying theory of magic, but you don't ever want to experience that again. It was bad enough seeing it, knowing the horror that resulted had once been a body you held and loved. It had felt much worse than a niner. "I couldn't stop it."

"No. You couldn't." You're sitting behind him, holding him upright with one hand. He's been gazing away from you, somewhere into the middle distance, since he began telling this story. He does not turn to look at you now over his shoulder, possibly because he can't do so without pain. But maybe that's comfort in his voice.

He continues: "I don't know how she manipulated the pressure, the heat, to keep it from killing me. I don't know how I didn't go mad from knowing where I was, wanting to get back to you, realizing I was helpless, feeling like I was suffocating. When I sessed what you did to Coru, I shut down. I don't remember the rest of the journey, or I don't want to. We must have . . . I don't know." He shudders, or tries to. You feel the twitch of muscles in his back.

"When I came to, I was on the surface again. In a place that . . ." He hesitates. His silence goes on for long enough that your skin prickles.

(I've been there. It's difficult to describe. That isn't Alabaster's fault.)

"On the other side of the world," Alabaster finally says, "there is a city."

The words don't make sense. The other side of the world is a great expanse of trackless blankness in your head. A map of nothing but ocean. "On . . . an island? Is there a landmass there?"

"Sort of." He can't really smile easily anymore. You hear it in his voice, though. "There's a massive shield volcano there, though it's under the ocean. Biggest one I've ever sessed; you could fit the Antarctics into it. The city sits directly above it, on the ocean. There's nothing visible around it: no land for farming, no hills to break tsunami. No harbor or moorings for boats. Just . . . buildings. Trees and some other plants, of varieties I've never seen elsewhere, gone wild but not a forest—sculpted into the city, sort of. I don't know what to call that. Infrastructures that seem to keep the whole thing stable and functioning, but all strange. Tubes and crystals and stuff that looks alive. Couldn't tell you how a tenth of it worked. And, at the center of the city, there's . . . a hole."

"A hole." You're trying to imagine it. "For swimming?"

"No. There's no water in it. The hole goes into the volcano, and . . . beyond." He takes a deep breath. "The city exists to contain the hole. Everything about the city is built for that purpose. Even its name, which the stone eaters told me, acknowledges this: *Corepoint*. It's a ruin, Essun—a deadciv ruin like any other, except that it's intact. The streets haven't crumbled. The buildings are empty, but some of the furniture is even usable—made of things not natural, undecaying. You could live in them if you wanted." He paused. "I did live in them, when Antimony brought me there. There was nowhere else to go and no one else to talk to . . . except the stone eaters. Dozens of them, Essun, maybe hundreds. They say they didn't build the city, but it's theirs now. Has been, for tens of thousands of years."

You're mindful of how much he hates being interrupted, but he pauses anyway. Maybe he's expecting commentary, or maybe he's giving you time to absorb his words. You're just staring at the back of his head. What's left of his hair is getting too long; you'll have to ask Lerna for scissors and a pick soon. There are absolutely no suitable thoughts in your head, besides this.

"It's something you can't help thinking about, when you're confronted with it." He sounds tired. Your lessons rarely last more than an hour, and it's been longer than that already. You would feel guilty if you had any emotion left in you right now other than shock. "The obelisks hint at it, but they're so..." You feel him try to shrug. You understand. "Not something you can touch or walk through. But this city. Recorded history goes back what, ten thousand years? Twenty-five if you count all the Seasons the University's still arguing about. But *people* have been around for much longer than that. Who knows when some version of our ancestors first crawled out of the ash and started jabbering at each other? Thirty thousand years? Forty? A long time to be the pathetic creatures we are now, huddling behind our walls and putting all our wits, all our learning, toward the singular task of staying alive. That's all we make now: Better ways to do field surgery with improvised equipment. Better chemicals, so we can grow more beans with little light. Once, we were so much more." He falls silent again, for a long moment. "I cried for you and Innon and Coru for three days, there in that city of who we used to be."

You ache, that he included you in his grief. You don't deserve it.

"When I... they brought me food." Alabaster skips past whatever he would've said so seamlessly that at first the sentence doesn't make sense. "I ate it, then tried to kill them." His voice turns wry. "Took me a while to give that up, actually, but they kept feeding me. I asked them, again and again, why they'd brought me there. Why they were keeping me alive. Antimony is the only one who would speak to me at first. I thought they were deferring to her, but then I realized they just didn't speak my language. Some of them weren't used to interacting with people at all. They stared, and sometimes I had to shoo them away. I seemed to fascinate some, disgust others. The feeling was mutual.

"I learned some of their language, eventually. I had to. Parts of the city *talked* in that language. If you knew the right words, you could open doors, turn on lights, make a room warmer or colder. Not everything still worked. The city *was* breaking down. Just slowly.

"But the hole. There were markers all around it, lighting up as you got closer." (You suddenly remember a chamber at the Fulcrum's heart. Long narrow panels igniting in sequence as you walked toward the socket, glowing with no discernible fire or filament.) "Barriers big as buildings in themselves, which sometimes glowed at night. Warnings that would write themselves in fire on the air before you, sirens that would sound if you got too near. Antimony took me to it, though, on the first day that I was... functional. I stood on one of the barriers and looked down into a darkness so deep that it..."

He has to stop. After he swallows, he resumes.

"She'd told me already that she took me from Meov because they couldn't risk me being killed. So there, at Corepoint's heart, she told me, 'This is why I saved you. This is the enemy you face. You are the only one who can.'"

"*What?*" You're not confused. You think you understand. You just don't want to, so you decide that you must be confused.

"That's what she said," he replies. Now he's angry, but not at you. "Word for word. I remember it because I was thinking *that* was the reason Innon and Coru died and you got thrown to the rusting dogs: because sometime in the ass-end of history, some of our so-smart ancestors decided to dig a hole to the heart of the world for no rusting reason. No; for power, Antimony said. I don't know how that was supposed to work but they did it, and they made the obelisks and other tools to harness that power.

"Something went wrong, though. I got the sense that even Antimony didn't know exactly what. Or maybe the stone eaters are still arguing about it and nobody's come to a consensus. Something just went wrong. The obelisks...misfired. The Moon was flung away from the planet. Maybe that did it, maybe some other things happened, but whatever the cause, the result was the Shattering. It really happened, Essun. That's what caused the Seasons." The muscles in his back flex a little against your hand. He's tense. "Do you understand? *We* use the obelisks. To stills, they're just big strange rocks. That city, all those wonders...that deadciv was *run by orogenes*. We destroyed the world just like they always say we did. *Roggas*."

He says it so sharply and viciously that his whole body reverberates with the word. You feel how he stiffens as he says it. Vehemence hurts him. He knew it would and said it anyway.

"What they got wrong," he continues, sounding weary now, "are the loyalties. The stories say we're agents of Father Earth, but it's the opposite: We're his enemies. He hates us more than he hates the stills, because of what we did. That's why he made the Guardians to control us, and—"

You're shaking your head. "'Baster...you're speaking as if it, the planet, is real. Alive, I mean. Aware. All that stuff about Father Earth, it's just stories to explain what's wrong with the world. Like those weird cults that crop up from time to time. I heard of one that asks an old man in the sky to keep them alive every time they go to sleep. People need to believe there's more to the world than there is."

And the world is just shit. You understand this now, after two dead children and the repeated destruction of your life. There's no need to imagine the planet as some malevolent force seeking vengeance. It's a rock. This is just how life is supposed to be: terrible and brief and ending in—if you're lucky—oblivion.

He laughs. This hurts him, too, but it's a laugh that makes your skin prickle, because it's the laugh of the Yumenes-Allia highroad. The laugh of a dead node station. Alabaster was never mad; he's just learned so much that would have driven a lesser soul to gibbering, that sometimes it shows. Letting out some of that accumulated horror by occasionally sounding like a frothing maniac is how he copes. It's also how he warns you, you know now, that he's about to destroy some additional measure of your naivete. Nothing is ever as simple as you want it to be.

"That's probably how they thought," Alabaster says, when his laugh goes quiet. "The ones who decided to dig a hole to the world's core. But just because you can't see or understand a thing doesn't mean it can't hurt you."

You know that's true. But more importantly, you hear the knowledge in Alabaster's voice. It makes you tense. "What have you seen?"

"Everything."

Your skin prickles.

He takes a deep breath. When he speaks again, it's a monotone. "This is a three-sided war. More sides than that, but only three that you need to concern yourself with. All three sides want the war to end; it's just a question of how. We're the problem, you see—people. Two of the sides are trying to decide what should be done with us."

That phrasing explains a lot. "The Earth and . . . the stone eaters?" Always lurking, planning, wanting something unknown.

"No. They're people, too, Essun. Haven't you figured that out? They need things, want things, feel things, same way we do. And they've been fighting this war much, much longer than you or I. Some of them from the very beginning."

"The beginning?" What, the Shattering?

"Yes, some of them are that old. Antimony is one. That little one who follows you, too, I think. There are others. They can't die, so . . . yeah. Some of them saw it all happen."

You're too floored to really react. Hoa? Seven-ish years old, going on thirty thousand. *Hoa?*

"One side wants us—people—dead," Alabaster says. "That's one way to end things, I suppose. One side wants people . . . neutralized. Alive, but rendered harmless. Like the stone eaters themselves: Earth tried to make them more like itself, dependent on itself, thinking that would make them harmless." He sighs. "I guess it's reassuring to know the planet can cock up, too."

Your flinch is a delayed reaction, because you've still got Hoa in mind. "He used to be human," you murmur. Yes. It's just a disguise now, a long-discarded set of clothes donned again for old times' sake, but once upon a time, he was a real flesh-and-blood boy who looked like that. There's nothing Sanzed in him because *the Sanzed did not exist as a people in his day.*

"They all did. It's what's wrong with them." He's very tired now, which may be why he speaks more softly. "I can barely remember things that happened to me fifty years ago; imagine trying to remember five thousand years ago. Ten thousand. Twenty. Imagine forgetting your own name. That's why they never answer, when we ask them who they are." You inhale in realization. "I don't think it's what they're made of that makes stone eaters so different. I think it's that no one can live that long and not become something entirely alien."

He keeps saying *imagine*, and you can't. Of course you can't. But you can think of Hoa in that moment. Being fascinated by soap. Curling against you to sleep. His sorrow, when you stopped treating him like a human being. He'd been trying so hard. Doing his best. Failing in the end.

"You said three sides," you say. Focusing on what you can, instead of mourning what you can't. Alabaster is beginning to slouch, leaning harder against your hand. He needs to rest.

Alabaster is silent for so long that you think he might have fallen asleep. Then he says, "I slipped out one night, when Antimony wasn't there. I'd been there . . . years? Time got loose after a while. No one but them to talk to, and sometimes they forget that people need to talk. Nothing in the earth to listen to except the grumbling of the volcano. The stars are all wrong on that side of the world . . ." He trails off for a moment. Loose time, catching up with him. "I'd been looking at diagrams of the obelisks, trying to understand what their builders intended. My head hurt. I knew you were alive, and I missed you so much I was sick with it. I had this sudden, wild, half-rusted thought: Maybe, through the hole, I could get back to you."

If only he had a hand left that you could take. Your fingers twitch against his back instead. It's not the same.

"So I ran to the hole and jumped in. It's not suicide if you don't mean to die; that's what I told myself." Another felt smile. "But it wasn't... The things around the hole are mechanisms, but not just for warning. I must have triggered something, or maybe that was how they were meant to work. I went down, but it wasn't like falling. It was controlled, somehow. Fast, but steady. I should have died. Air pressure, heat, the same things Antimony took me through without the rock involved, but Antimony wasn't there and I should have died. There are lights along the shaft at intervals. Windows, I think. People actually used to live down there! But mostly, it's just the dark.

"Eventually... hours or days later... I slowed down. I had reached—"

He stops. You feel the prickle of goose bumps rise on his skin.

"The Earth *is* alive." His voice grows harsh, hoarse, faintly hysterical. "Some of the old stories are just stories, you're right, but *not that one.* I understood then what the stone eaters had been trying to tell me. Why I had to use the obelisks to create the Rift. We've been at war with the world for so long that we've forgotten, Essun, but *the world* hasn't. And we have to end it soon, or..."

Alabaster pauses, suddenly, for a long and pent moment. You want to ask what will happen if a war so ancient doesn't end soon. You want to ask what happened to him down there at the core of the Earth, what he saw or experienced that has so plainly shaken him. You don't ask. You're a brave woman, but you know what you can take, and what you can't.

He whispers: "When I die, don't bury me."

"Wh—"

"Give me to Antimony."

As if she has heard her name, suddenly, Antimony reappears, standing before you both. You glare at her, realizing that this means Alabaster has reached the end of his strength and that the conversation must end. It makes you resent his weakness, and hate that he is dying. It makes you seek a scapegoat for that hatred.

"No," you say, looking at her. "She took you from me. She doesn't get to keep you."

He chuckles. It's so weary that your anger breaks. "It's either her or the Evil Earth, Essun. Please."

He begins to list to one side, and maybe you're not as much of a monster as you think, because you give up and get up. Antimony blurs in that stone-eaterish way, slow except when they aren't, and then she is crouched beside him, using both hands now to hold and support him as he slips into sleep.

You gaze at Antimony. You've thought of her as an enemy all this time, but if what Alabaster says is true...

"No," you snap. You're not really saying it to her, but it works either way. "I'm not ready to think of you as an ally yet." Maybe not ever.

"Even if you were," says the voice from within the stone eater's chest, "I'm *his* ally. Not yours."

People like us, with wants and needs. You want to reject this, too, but oddly it comforts you to know that she doesn't like you, either. "Alabaster said he understood why you did what you did. But I don't understand why he did what *he* did, or what he wants now. He said this was a three-sided war; what's the third side? Which side is he on? How does the Rift…help?"

No matter how you try, you cannot imagine Antimony as having once been human. Too many things work against it: the stillness of her face, the dislocation of her voice. The fact that you hate her. "The Obelisk Gate amplifies energies both physical and arcane. No single point of surface venting produces these energies in sufficient quantity. The Rift is a reliable, high-volume source."

Meaning…You tense. "You're saying that if I use the Rift as my ambient source, channel it through my torus—"

"No. That would simply kill you."

"Well, thanks for the warn-off." You're beginning to understand, though. It's the same problem you keep having with Alabaster's lessons; heat and pressure and motion are not the only forces in play here. "You're saying the earth churns out magic, too? And if I push that magic into an obelisk…" You blink, recalling her words. "Obelisk Gate?"

Antimony's gaze has been focused on Alabaster. Now her flat black eyes slide to finally meet yours. "The two hundred and sixteen individual obelisks, networked together via the control cabochon." While you stand there wondering what the rust a control cabochon is, and marveling that there are more than two hundred of the damned things, she adds, "Using *that* to channel the power of the Rift should be enough."

"To do what?"

For the first time, you hear a note of emotion in her voice: annoyance. "To impose equilibrium on the Earth-Moon system."

What. "Alabaster said the Moon was flung away."

"Into a degrading long-ellipsis orbit." When you stare blankly, she speaks your language again. "It's coming back."

Oh, Earth. Oh, rust. Oh, no. "*You want me to catch the fucking Moon?*"

She just stares at you, and belatedly you realize you're practically shouting. You throw a guilty look at Alabaster, but he hasn't woken. Neither has the nurse on the far cot. When she sees that you're quiet, Antimony says, "That is an option." Almost as an afterthought, she adds, "Alabaster made the first of two necessary course corrections to the Moon, slowing it and altering the trajectory that would have taken it past the planet again. Someone else must make the second correction, bringing it back into stable orbit and magical alignment. Should equilibrium be reestablished, it's likely the Seasons will end, or diminish to such infrequency as to mean the same thing to your kind."

You inhale, but you get it now. Give Father Earth back his lost child and perhaps his wrath will be appeased. That's the third faction, then: those who want a truce, people and Father Earth agreeing to tolerate one another, even if it means creating the Rift and killing millions in the process. Peaceful coexistence by any means necessary.

The end of the Seasons. It sounds... unimaginable. There have always been Seasons. Except now you know that isn't true.

"Then it isn't an option," you say finally. "End the Seasons or watch everything die as this Season burns on forever? I'll—" *Catch the Moon* sounds ridiculous. "I'll do what you stone eaters want, then."

"There are always options." Her gaze, alien as it is, abruptly shifts in a subtle way—or maybe you're just reading her better. Suddenly she looks human, and very, very bitter. "And not all of my kind want the same thing."

You frown at her, but she says nothing more.

You want to ask more questions, try harder to understand, but she was right: You weren't ready for this. Your head's spinning, and the words stuffed into it are starting to blur and jumble together. It's too much to deal with.

Wants and needs. You swallow. "Can I stay here?"

She does not respond. You suppose it wasn't really necessary to ask. You get up and move to the nearest cot. Its head is against the wall, which would put your head behind Alabaster and Antimony, and you don't feel like staring at the back of the stone eater's head. You grab the pillow and curl up with your head at the foot of the bed instead, so you can see Alabaster's face. Once, you slept better when you could see him, across the expanse of Innon's shoulders. This is not the same reassurance . . . but it's something.

After a while, Antimony begins to sing again. It's strangely relaxing. You sleep better than you have in months.

* * *

Seek the retrograde [obscured] in the southern sky.

When it grows larger, [obscured]

—*Tablet Two, "The Incomplete Truth," verse six*

11

Schaffa, lying down

Him again. I wish he hadn't done so much to you. You don't like being him to any degree. You will like less knowing that he is part of Nassun... but don't think about that right now.

* * *

The man who still carries the name of Schaffa even though he hardly qualifies as the same person, dreams fragments of himself.

Guardians don't dream easily. The object embedded deep within the left lobe of Schaffa's sessapinae interferes with the sleep-wake cycle. He does not often need sleep, and when he does, his body does not often enter the deeper sleep that enables dreaming. (Ordinary people go mad if they are deprived of dreaming-sleep. Guardians are immune to that sort of madness... or perhaps they're just mad all the time.) He knows it's a bad sign that he dreams more often these days, but it cannot be helped. He chose to pay the price.

So he lies on a bed in a cabin and groans, twitching fitfully, while his mind flails through images. It's poor dreaming because his mind is out of practice, and because so little remains of the material that might have been used to construct the dreams. Later he will speak of this aloud, to himself, as he clutches his head and tries to pull the scattering bits of his identity closer together, and that's how I'll know what torments him. I will know that as he thrashes, he dreams...

...Of two people, their features surprisingly sharp in his memory though all else has been stripped away: their names, their relationship to him, his reason for remembering them. He can guess, seeing that the woman of the pair has icewhite eyes rimmed with thick black eyelashes, that she is his mother. The man is more ordinary. Too ordinary—carefully so, in a way that immediately stirs a suspicion in Schaffa's Guardian mind. Ferals work hard to seem so ordinary. How they came to produce him, and how he came to leave them, is lost to the Earth, but their faces are interesting, at least.

...Of Warrant, and black-walled rooms carved into layered volcanic rock. Gentle hands, pitying voices. Schaffa doesn't remember the hands' or voices' owners. He is helped into a wire chair. (No, the nodes were not the first to use these.) This chair is sophisticated, automated, working smoothly even though something about it seems old to Schaffa's eye. It whirs and reconfigures and turns him until he is suspended facedown beneath bright artificial lights, with his face trapped between unyielding bars and the nape of his neck bared to the world. His hair is short. Behind and above him he hears the descent of ancient mechanisms, things so esoteric and bizarre that their names and original purposes have long been lost. (He remembers learning, around this time, that original purposes can be perverted easily.) Around him he can hear the snuffling and pleading of the others brought with him to this place—children's snuffling and pleading. *He* is a child in this memory, he realizes. Then he hears the other children's screams, followed by and mingling into whirring, cutting sounds. There is also a low watery hum that he will never hear again (yet it will be very familiar to you and any other orogene who has ever been near an obelisk), because from this moment forth his own sessapinae will be repurposed, made sensitive to orogeny and not to the perturbations of the earth.

Schaffa remembers struggling, and even as a child he's stronger than most. He gets his head and upper body almost free before the machinery reaches him. This is why the first cut goes so wrong, slicing far lower on his neck than it should and nearly killing him right there. The equipment adjusts, relentless. He feels the cold of it as the sliver of iron is inserted, feels the coldness of the other presence within him at once. Someone stitches him up. The pain is horrific and it never really ends, though he learns to mitigate it enough to function; all those who survive the implantation do. The smiling, you see. Endorphins ease pain.

...Of the Fulcrum, and a high-ceilinged chamber at the heart of Main, and familiar artificial lights that march toward and around a yawning pit from whose walls grow endless slivers of iron. He and the other Guardians gaze down at a small, shredded body crumpled at the bottom of the pit. Every now and again the children find the place; poor foolish creatures. Don't they understand? The Earth is indeed evil, and it is cruel, and Schaffa would protect them all from it, if he could. There is a survivor: one of the children attached to Guardian Leshet. The girl cringes as Leshet approaches, but Schaffa knows Leshet will let her live. Leshet has always been softer, kinder than she should be, and her children suffer for it...

...Of the road, and the endless flinching eyes of strangers who see his icewhite irises and unchanging smiles and know that they are seeing *something wrong* even if they don't know what it is. There is a woman one night, at an inn, who tries to be intrigued rather than frightened. Schaffa warns her, but she's insistent, and he cannot help but think of how the pleasure will keep the pain at bay for hours, perhaps the whole night. It's good to feel human for a while. But as he warned her, he circuits back in a few months. She's got a child in her belly, which she says isn't his, but he cannot permit the uncertainty. He uses the black-glass poniard, which is a thing made in Warrant. She was kind to him, so he targets only the child; hopefully she'll pass its corpse, and live. But she's furious, horrified, and she calls out for help and draws a knife of her own as they struggle. Never again, he resolves as he slaughters all of them—her whole family, a dozen bystanders, half the town as they attack him en masse. Never again can he forget that he is not, and has never been, human.

...Of Leshet again. He can barely recognize her this time: Her hair has gone white and her once-smooth face is all over lines and sagging skin. She's *smaller*, her softening bones compressing her into a hunched posture, which often happens to Arctics when they grow old. But Leshet has seen more centuries even than Schaffa. *Old* is not supposed to mean this for them: feebleness, senescence, shrinking. (Happiness, and a smile that means something other than mere mitigation of the pain. They're not supposed to have these either.) He stares at her broad, *welcoming* smile as she hobbles toward him from the cottage to which he has tracked her. He is filled with dim horror and a burgeoning disgust that he's not even aware of until she stops before him and he reaches out to reflexively break her neck.

...Of the girl. *The girl.* One of dozens, hundreds; they blur together over the endless years...but not this one. He finds her in a barn, poor frightened sad thing, and she loves him instantly. He loves her, too, wishes he could be kinder to her, is as gentle as he can be while he trains her to obedience with broken bones and loving threats and chances he should not give. Has Leshet infected him with her softness? Maybe, maybe... but *her face. Her eyes.* There's something about her. He is not surprised later, when he receives word that she is involved in the raising of an obelisk in Allia. His special one. He does not believe she is dead after. Indeed, he is filled with pride as he goes to reclaim her, and as he prays to the voice in his head that she will not force him to kill her. The girl...

...whose face causes him to wake with a soft cry. *The girl.*

The other two Guardians look at him with the Earth's judging eyes. They are as compromised as he, more. All three of them are everything the Guardian order has warned them against. He remembers his name but they do not remember theirs. That's the only real difference between him and them... isn't it? Yet they seem so much *less* than he, somehow.

Irrelevant. He pushes himself up from the cot, rubs his face, and heads outside.

The children's cabin. It's time to check on them, Schaffa tells himself, though he makes a beeline to Nassun's cot. She's asleep as he lifts a lantern to examine her face. Yes. It has always been there in her eyes and maybe cheekbones, tickling his mind, the fragments of his memory and the solidity of her features finally coming together. His Damaya. The girl who did not die, reborn.

He remembers breaking Damaya's hand and flinches with it. Why would he do such a thing? Why did he do any of the horrible things he did, in those days? Leshet's neck. Timay's. Eitz's family. So many others, whole towns of them. Why?

Nassun stirs in her sleep, murmuring softly. Automatically Schaffa reaches out to stroke her face, and she quiets at once. There is a dull ache in his chest that perhaps might be love. He remembers loving Leshet and Damaya and others, and yet he did such things to them.

Nassun stirs a little, and half wakes, blinking in the lantern light. "Schaffa?"

"It's nothing, little one," he says. "I'm sorry." Many degrees of sorry. But the fear is in him, and the dream lingers. He cannot help trying to expunge it. He finally blurts, "Nassun. Are you afraid of me?"

She blinks, barely lucid—and then she smiles. It untwists something within him. "Never."

Never. He swallows, his throat suddenly tight. "Good. Go back to sleep."

She drifts off at once, and perhaps she was never really awake to begin with. But he lingers near her, keeping watch until her eyelids flicker into dreaming again.

Never.

"Never again," he whispers, and twitches with the memory of that, too. Then the feeling changes and his resolve refocuses. What happened before does not matter. That was a different Schaffa. He has another chance now. And if being less than himself means being less than the monster that he was, he cannot regret it.

There is a quicksilver lightning strike of pain along his spine, too fast for him to smile it away. Something disagrees with his resolve. Automatically his hand twitches toward the back of Nassun's neck . . . and then he stops himself. No. She is more to him than just relief from pain.

Use her, commands the voice. *Break her. So willful, like her mother. Train this one to obey.*

No, Schaffa thinks back, and braces himself to bear the lash of retaliation. It is only pain.

So Schaffa tucks Nassun in, and kisses her forehead, and puts out the light as he leaves. He heads for the ridge that overlooks the town, and stands there for the rest of the night grinding his teeth and trying to forget the last of who he was and promising himself a better future. Eventually the other two Guardians come out onto the steps of their cabin as well, but he ignores the alien pressure of their gazes against his back.

12

Nassun, falling up

Again, much of this is speculation. You know *of* Nassun, and she is part of you, but you cannot *be* Nassun... and I think we have established by now that you do not know her as well as you think. (Ah, but no parent does, with any child.) Another has the task of encompassing Nassun's existence. But you love her, and that means that some part of me cannot help but do the same.

In love, then, we shall seek understanding.

* * *

With her consciousness anchored deep within the earth, Nassun listens.

At first there is only the usual impingement upon the ambient sesuna: the minute flex-and-contract of strata, the relatively placid churn of the old volcano beneath Jekity, the slow unending grind of columnar basalt rising and cooling into patterns. She's gotten used to this. She likes that she can listen to this freely now, whenever she wants, instead of having to wait until the dark of night, lying awake after her parents have gone to bed. Here in Found Moon, Schaffa has given Nassun permission to use the crucible whenever she wants, for as long as she wants. She tries not to monopolize it, because the others need to learn, too...but they do not enjoy orogeny as much as she does. Most of them seem indifferent to the power they wield, or the wonders they can explore by mastering it. A few of the others are even afraid of it, which makes no sense to Nassun—but then, it also makes no sense to her now that once she wanted to be a lorist. Now she has the freedom to be fully who and what she is, and she no longer fears that self. Now she has someone who believes in her, trusts her, fights for her, as she is. So she will *be* what she is.

So now Nassun rides an eddy within the Jekity hot spot, balancing perfectly amid the conflicting pressures, and it does not occur to her to be afraid. She does not realize this is something a Fulcrum four-ringer would struggle to do. But then, she doesn't do it the way a four-ringer would, by taking hold of the motion and the heat and trying to channel both through herself. She reaches, yes, but just with her senses and not her absorption torus. But where a Fulcrum instructor would warn that she can't affect anything like this, she follows the lesson of her own instincts, which say she can. By settling into the eddy, swirling with it, she can relax enough to winnow down through its friction and pressure to what lies beneath: the silver.

This is the word she has decided to give it, after questioning Schaffa and the others and realizing they don't know what it is, either. The other orogene kids can't even detect it; Eitz thought he sessed something once, when she shyly asked him to concentrate on Schaffa instead of the earth, because the silver is easier to see—more concentrated, more potent, more *intent*—within people than it is in the ground. But Schaffa stiffened and glared at him in the next instant, and Eitz flinched and looked guiltier and more haunted than ever, so Nassun felt bad that she hurt him. She never asked him to try it again.

The others, however, can't do even that much. It is the other two Guardians, Nida and Umber, who help the most. "This is a thing that we culled for in the Fulcrum when we found it, when they heard the call, when they listened too closely," Nida begins, and Nassun braces herself because once Nida gets started there's no telling how long she'll run on. She stops only for the other Guardians. "The use of sublimates in lieu of controlling structures is dangerous, determinate, a warning. Important to cultivate for research purposes, but most such children we steered into node service. Among the others we cut—cut—*cut* them, for it was forbidden to reach for the sky." Amazingly, she shuts up after this. Nassun wonders what the sky has to do with anything, but she knows better than to ask, lest Nida get going again.

But Umber, who is as slow and quiet as Nida is fast, nods. "We allowed a few to progress," he translates. "For breeding. For curiosity. For the Fulcrum's pride. No more than that."

Which tells Nassun several things, once she sifts sense from the babble. Nida and Umber and Schaffa are not proper Guardians anymore, though they used to be. They have given up the credo of their order, chosen to betray the old ways. So the use of the silver is clearly an issue of violent concern to ordinary Guardians—but why? If only a few of the Fulcrum's orogenes were allowed to develop the skill, to "progress," what was the danger if too many did it? And why do these ex-Guardians, who once "culled for" the skill, allow her to do it unfettered now?

Schaffa is there for this conversation, she notes, but he does not speak. He merely watches her, smiling and twitching now and again as the silver sparks and tugs within him. That's been happening to him a lot, lately. Nassun isn't sure why.

Nassun goes home in the evenings after her days at Found Moon. Jija has settled into his Jekity house, and every time she comes back, there are new touches of hominess that she likes: surprisingly rich blue paint on the old wooden door; cuttings planted in the small housegreen, though they grow scraggly as the ash thickens in the sky overhead; a rug he has bartered a glassknife for in the small room that he designates as her own. It's not as big as the room she had back in Tirimo, but it has a window that overlooks the forest around Jekity's plateau. Beyond the forest, if the air is clear enough, she can sometimes see the coast as a distant line of white just beyond the forest's green. Beyond that is a spread of blue that fascinates her, though there's nothing to see but that slice of color, from here. She has never seen the sea up close, and Eitz tells her wonderful stories of it: that it smells of salt and strange life; that it washes up onto thin stuff called sand in which little grows because of the salt; that sometimes its creatures wiggle or bubble forth, like *crabs* or *squid* or *sandteethers*, though the lattermost are said to appear only during a Season. There is the constant danger of tsunami, which is why no one lives near the sea if they can avoid it—and indeed, a few days after Nassun and Jija reach Jekity, she sessed rather than saw the remnant of a big shake far to the east, well out to sea. She sessed, too, the reverberations this caused when something vast shifted and then pounded at the land along the coast. For once she was glad to be so far away.

Still, it is nice having a home again. Life begins to feel normal, for the first time in a very long while. One evening during dinner, Nassun tells her father what Eitz has said about the sea. He looks skeptical, then asks where she heard these things. She tells him about Eitz, and he grows very quiet.

"This is a rogga boy?" he says, after a moment.

Nassun, whose instincts have finally pinged a warning—she's gotten out of the habit of keeping vigilant for Jija's mood shifts—falls silent. But because he will get angrier if she doesn't speak, she finally nods.

"Which one?"

Nassun bites her lip. Eitz is Schaffa's, though, and she knows that Schaffa will allow none of his orogenes to come to harm. So she says, "The oldest. He's tall and very black and has a long face."

Jija keeps eating, but Nassun watches the flex of muscles in his jaw that have nothing to do with chewing. "That Coaster boy. I've seen him. I don't want you talking to him anymore."

Nassun swallows, and risks. "I have to talk with all of the others, Daddy. It's how we learn."

"Learn?" Jija looks up. It's banked, contained, but he's furious. "That boy is what, twenty? Twenty-five? And he's still a rogga. *Still*. He should have been able to cure himself by now."

For a moment Nassun is confused, because curing herself of orogeny is the last thing she thinks of at the end of her lessons. Well, Schaffa did say that it was possible. Ah—and Eitz, who is only eighteen but obviously aged up in Jija's head, is too old to have not utilized this cure, if he's going to. With a chill, Nassun realizes: Jija has begun to doubt Schaffa's claims that the erasure of orogeny is possible. What will he do if he realizes Nassun no longer *wants* to be cured?

Nothing good. "Yes, Daddy," she says.

This mollifies him, as it usually does. "If you have to talk to him during your lessons, fine. I don't want you making the Guardians angry. But don't talk to him outside of that." He sighs. "I don't like that you spend so much time up there."

He grumbles on about it for the rest of the meal, but says nothing worse, so eventually Nassun relaxes.

The next morning, at Found Moon, she says to Schaffa, "I need to learn how to hide what I am better."

Schaffa is carrying two satchels uphill to the Found Moon compound as she says this. They're heavy, and he's freakishly strong, but even he has to breathe hard to do this, so she does not pester him for a response while he walks. When he has reached one of the compound's tiny storeshacks, he sets the satchels down and catches his breath. It's easier to keep goods up here for things like the children's meals than to go back and forth to the Jekity storecaches or communal mealhouse.

"Are you safe?" he asks then, quietly. This is why she loves him.

She nods, biting her bottom lip, because it is wrong that she must wonder this about her own father. He looks at her for a long, hard moment, and there is a cold consideration to this look that warns her he's begun to think of a simple solution to her problem. "Don't," she blurts.

He lifts an eyebrow. "Don't . . . ?" he challenges.

Nassun has lived a year of ugliness. Schaffa is at least clean and uncomplicated in his brutality. This makes it easy for her to set her jaw and lift her chin. "Don't kill my father."

He smiles, but his eyes are still cold. "Something causes a fear like that, Nassun. Something that has nothing to do with you, or your brother, or your mother's lies. Whatever it is has left its wound in your father—a wound that obviously has festered. He will lash out at anything that touches upon or even near that reeking old sore . . . as you have seen." She thinks of Uche, and nods. "That cannot be reasoned with."

"I can," she blurts. "I've done it before. I know how to . . ." *manipulate him*, those are the words for it, but she's barely ten years old so she actually says, "I can stop him from doing anything bad. I always have before." Mostly.

"Until you fail to stop him, once. That would be enough." He eyes her. "I will kill him if he ever hurts you, Nassun. Keep that in mind, if you value your father's life more than your own. *I* do not." Then he turns back to the shed to arrange the satchels, and that's the end of the conversation.

Some while later, Nassun tells the others of this exchange. Little Paido suggests: "Maybe you should move into Found Moon with the rest of us."

Ynegen, Shirk, and Lashar are sitting nearby, relaxing and recovering after an afternoon spent finding and pushing around the marked rocks buried beneath the crucible floor. They nod and murmur agreement with this. "It's only right," says Lashar, in her haughty way. "You'll never be truly one of us if you continue living down there among *them*."

Nassun has thought this herself, often. But . . . "He's my father," she says, spreading her hands.

This elicits no understanding from the others, and a few looks of pity. Many of them still bear the marks of violence inflicted by the trusted adults in their lives. "He's a still," Shirk snaps back, and that is the end of the matter as far as most of them are concerned. Eventually Nassun gives up on trying to convince them otherwise.

These thoughts invariably begin to affect her orogeny. How can they not, when an unspoken part of her wants to please her father? It takes all of herself, and the confidence that comes of delight, to engage with the earth to her fullest. And that afternoon, when she tries to touch the spinning silver threads of the hot spot and it goes so horribly wrong that she gasps and claws her way back to awareness only to find that she has iced all ten rings of the crucible, Schaffa puts his foot down.

"You will sleep here tonight," he says, after walking across the crusted earth to carry her back to a bench. She's too exhausted to walk. It took everything she had not to die. "Tomorrow when you wake, I'm going with you to your house, and we'll bring back your belongings."

"D-don't want to," she pants, even though she knows Schaffa doesn't like it when the children say *no* to him.

"I don't care what you want, little one. This is interfering with your training. It is why the Fulcrum took children from their families. What you do is too dangerous to allow any distractions, however beloved."

"But." She does not have the strength to object more strongly. He holds her in his lap, trying to warm her up because the edge of her own torus was barely an inch from her skin.

Schaffa sighs. For a while he says nothing, except to shout for someone to bring a blanket; Eitz is the one who delivers it, having already gone to fetch it once he saw what happened. (Everyone saw what happened. It is embarrassing. As you realized back during Nassun's dangerous early childhood, she is a very, very proud girl.) As Nassun finally stops shivering and feeling as though her sessapinae have been methodically beaten, Schaffa finally says, "You serve a higher purpose, little one. Not any single man's desire—not even mine. You were not made for such petty things."

She frowns. "What... what was I made for, then?"

He shakes his head. The silver flashes through him, the webwork of it alive and shifting as the thing lodged in his sessapinae weaves its will again, or tries to. "To remedy a great mistake. One to which I once contributed."

This is too interesting to fall asleep to, though Nassun's whole body craves it. "What was the mistake?"

"To enslave your kind." When Nassun sits back to frown at him, he smiles again, but this time it is sad. "Or perhaps it is more accurate to say that we perpetuated their enslavement of themselves, under Old Sanze. The Fulcrum was nominally run by orogenes, you see—orogenes whom we had culled and cultivated, shaped and chosen carefully, so that they would obey. So that they knew their place. Given a choice between death and the barest possibility of acceptance, they were desperate, and we used that. We *made* them desperate."

For some reason he pauses here, sighs. Takes a deep breath. Lets it out. Smiles. This is how Nassun knows without sessing that the pain which lives always in Schaffa's head has begun to flare hotter again. "And my kind—Guardians such as I once was—were complicit in this atrocity. You've seen how your father knaps a stone? Hammering at it, flaking away its weaker bits. Breaking it, if it cannot bear the pressure, and starting over with another. That is what I did, back then, but with children."

Nassun finds this hard to believe. Of course Schaffa is

ruthless and violent, but that is to his enemies. A year commless has taught Nassun the necessity of cruelty. But with the children of Found Moon, he is so very gentle and kind. "Even me?" she blurts. It is not the clearest of questions, but he understands what she means: *If you had found me, back then?*

He touches her head, smooths a hand over it, rests his fingertips against the nape of her neck. He takes nothing from her this time, but perhaps the gesture comforts him, for he looks so sad. "Even you, Nassun. I hurt many children, back then."

So sad. Nassun decides he would not have *meant* it back then, even if he'd done something bad.

"It was wrong to treat your kind so. You're people. What we did, making tools of you, was wrong. It is *allies* that we need—more than ever now, in these darkening days."

Nassun will do anything that Schaffa asks. But allies are needed for specific tasks, and they are not the same thing as friends. The ability to distinguish this is also something the road has taught her. "What do you need us as allies for?"

His gaze grows distant and troubled. "To repair something long broken, little one, and settle a feud whose origins lie so far in our past that most of us have forgotten how it began. Or that the feud *continues*." He lifts a hand and touches the back of his head. "When I gave up my old ways, I pledged myself to the cause of helping to end it."

So that's it. "I don't like that it hurts you," Nassun says, staring at that blot on the silver map of him. It's so tiny. Smaller than one of the needles her father sometimes uses to stitch up holes in clothing. Yet it is a negative space against the glimmer, perceptible in silhouette only, or by its effects rather than in itself. Like the motionless spider at a quivering dew-laden web's heart. Spiders hibernate, though, during a Season, and the thing within Schaffa never stops tormenting him. "Why does it hurt you if you're doing what it wants?"

Schaffa blinks. Squeezes her gently, and smiles. "Because I will not *force* you to do what it wants. I present its wishes to you as a choice, and I will abide if you say no. It is... less trusting of your kind. Admittedly, for good reason." He shakes his head. "We can speak of this later. Now let your sessapinae rest." She subsides at once—though she had not really meant to sess him, and hadn't been really aware of doing so. Constant sessing is becoming second nature to her. "A nap will help you, I think."

So he carries her into one of the dormitory buildings and lays her down on an unclaimed cot. She curls up within the cocooning blanket and drifts off to the sound of his voice instructing the other children not to trouble her.

And she wakes, the next morning, to the echo of her own screams and strangled gasps as she fights her way out of the blanket. Someone grabs her arm and it is everything it should not be: not now, not on her, not who she wants, not tolerable. She flails toward the earth and it is not heat or pressure that answer her call but silver lacing light that screams in echo and reverberates with her unspoken need for force. That scream echoes across the land, not just in threads but in waves, not just through the land but through water and air, and

and then

and then

something answers her. Something in the sky.

She does not mean what she does. Eitz certainly does not

intend what happens as a result of his attempt to wake her from the nightmare. He likes Nassun. She's a sweet kid. And even though Eitz is no longer a trusting child and it has occurred to him in the years since they left his Coastal home that Schaffa smiled too much that day and smelled faintly of blood, he understands what it means that Schaffa is so taken with Nassun. The Guardian has been looking for something all this time, and in spite of everything, Eitz loves him enough to hope that he finds it.

Perhaps that will comfort you, as it will not Nassun, when in her frightened, disoriented flailing, she turns Eitz to stone.

This is not like the thing happening, far away and underground, to Alabaster. That is slower, crueler, yet much more refined. Artful. What hits Eitz is a catastrophe: a hammer blow of disordered atoms reordered at not quite random. The lattice that should naturally form dissolves into chaos. It starts on his chest when Nassun's hand tries to slap him away, and spreads in less time than it takes for the other children present to draw breath in gasps. It spreads over his skin, the brown hardening and developing an undersheen like tigereye, then into his flesh, though no one will see the ruby inside unless they break him. Eitz dies almost instantly, his heart solidifying first into a striated jewel of yellow quartz and deep garnet and white agate, with faint lacing veins of sapphire. He is a beautiful failure. It happens so fast that he has no time for fear. That may comfort Nassun later, if nothing else.

But in the moment, in the pent seconds after this happens, as Nassun writhes and tries to drag her mind back from *falling, falling upward through watery blue light*, and as Deshati's gasp turns into a scream (which sets off others) and Peek comes forward to stare openmouthed at the glossy, brightly colored facsimile of himself that Eitz has become, a number of things happen simultaneously elsewhere.

Some of these things you will have guessed. Perhaps a hundred miles away, a sapphire obelisk shimmers into solid reality for an instant, then flickers back to translucence—before ponderously beginning to drift toward Jekity. Many more miles in a different direction, somewhere deep within a magmatic vein of porphyry, a shape that is suggestive of the human form turns, alert with new interest.

Another thing happens that you may not have guessed—or perhaps you will have, because you know Jija as I do not. But in the precise moment that his daughter rips a boy's protons loose, Jija finishes his laborious climb to the plateau that houses the Found Moon compound. Too angry for courtesy after a night of seething, he shouts for his daughter.

Nassun does not hear him. She is convulsing in the dormitory. Hearing the other children's screams, Jija turns toward the building—but before he can start in that direction, two of the Guardians emerge from their building and move across the compound. Umber heads toward the dormitory at a brisk pace. Schaffa veers off to intercept Jija. Nassun will hear of all this later from the children who witness it. (So will I.)

"My daughter didn't come home last night," Jija says as Schaffa stops him in his tracks. Jija is alarmed by the children's screams, but not by much. Whatever madness is happening within the dorm, he expects nothing better of the den of iniquity that Found Moon surely must be. As he confronts Schaffa, he has a set to his jaw that you will recognize from other occasions on which he has felt himself righteous. He will therefore be unwilling to back down.

"She will be remaining here," Schaffa says, smiling politely. "We've found that returning to your home in the evenings is interfering with her training. Since your leg has clearly healed enough to allow you to make the climb, could you be so kind as to bring her things, later today?"

"She—" The screams get louder for a moment as Umber opens the door to go inside, but he closes it behind him and they stop. Jija frowns at this, but shakes his head in order to focus on what is important. "She will *not* be rusting staying here! I don't want her spending any more time than she has to with these—" He stops short of vulgarity. "She isn't one of them."

Schaffa tilts his head for an instant, as if he is listening to something only he can hear. "Isn't she?" His tone is contemplative.

Jija stares at him, momentarily confused into silence. Then he curses and tries to move past Schaffa. His leg has indeed mostly healed since his arrival at Jekity, but he still limps heavily, the harpoon having torn nerves and tendons that will be slow to heal, if they ever fully do. Even had Jija been able to move easily, however, he could not have evaded the hand that comes out of nowhere to cover his face.

It is Schaffa's big hand that splays over his face, moving so fast that it blurs before it seats itself. Jija doesn't see it till it's over his eyes and nose and mouth, picking him up bodily and slamming him to the ground on his back. As Jija lies there, blinking, he is too dazed to wonder what just happened, too stunned for pain. Then the hand pulls away, and from Jija's perspective the Guardian's face is just *there*, nose nearly touching Jija's own.

"Nassun does not have a father," Schaffa says softly. (Jija will remember later that Schaffa smiles the whole time that he says this.) "She needs no father, nor mother. She does not know this yet, though someday she will learn. Shall I teach her early how to do without you?" And he positions two fingertips just under Jija's jaw, pressing the tender skin there with enough force that Jija instantly understands his life depends on his answer.

Jija goes still for a long, pent breath. There's nothing in his head worth relating, even speculatively. He says nothing, though he makes a sound. When the children speak later of this tableau, they leave out this detail: the small, strangled whine uttered by a man who is trying not to loose his bladder and bowels, and who can think of nothing beyond imminent death. It is mostly nasal, back-of-the-throat sound. It makes him want to cough.

Schaffa seems to take Jija's whine for an answer in itself. His smile widens for a moment—a real, heartening smile, the kind that crinkles the corners of his eyes and makes his gums show. He is *delighted* that he does not have to kill Nassun's father with his bare hands. And then he very deliberately lifts the hand that had been positioned under Jija's jaw, waggling the fingers before Jija's eyes until Jija blinks.

"There," Schaffa says. "Now we may behave again like civilized people." He straightens, head turning toward the dormitory; it is clear he has forgotten Jija already, but for an afterthought. "Don't forget to bring her things, please." Then he rises, steps over Jija, and heads into the dormitory.

No one really cares what Jija does after that. A boy has been turned to stone, and a girl has manifested power that is strange and horrifying even for a rogga. These are the things everyone will remember about this day.

Everyone, I suspect, except Jija, who quietly limps home in the aftermath.

In the dormitory, Nassun has finally managed to withdraw her awareness from the watery column of blue light that nearly consumed it. This is an amazing feat, though she does not realize it. All she knows, as she finally comes out of the fit and finds Schaffa leaning over her, is that a scary thing happened, and Schaffa is there to take care of her in the aftermath.

(She is your daughter, at her core. It is not for me to judge her, but... ah, she is so very much yours.)

"Tell me," Schaffa says. He has sat on the edge of her cot, very close, deliberately blocking her view of Eitz. Umber is ushering the other children out. Peek is weeping and hysterical; the others are silent in shock. Nassun does not notice, having her own trauma to deal with in the moment.

"There was," she begins. She's hyperventilating. Schaffa cups a big hand over her nose and mouth, and after a few moments her breathing slows. Once she is closer to normal, he removes his hand and nods for her to continue. "There was. A blue thing. Light and... I fell up. Schaffa, I fell *up*." She frowns, confused by her own panic. "I had to get out of it. It hurt. It was too fast. It *burned*. I was so scared."

He nods as if this makes sense. "You survived, though. That's very good." She glows with this praise, even though she has no idea what he means. He considers for a moment. "Did you sess anything else, while you were connected?"

(She will not wonder at this word, *connected*, until much later.)

"There was a place, up north. Lines, in the ground. All over." She means all over the Stillness. Schaffa cocks his head with interest, which encourages her to keep babbling. "I could hear people talking. Where they touched the lines. There were *people* in the knots. Where the lines crossed. I couldn't figure out what anybody was saying, though."

Schaffa goes very still. "People in the knots. Orogenes?"

"Yes?" It's actually hard to answer that question. The grip of those distant strangers' orogeny was strong—some stronger than Nassun herself. Yet there was a strange, almost uniform smoothness to each of these strongest ones. Like running fingers over polished stone: There is no texture to catch on. Those were also the ones spread across the greatest distance, some of them even farther to the north than Tirimo—all the way up near where the world has gone red and hot.

"The node network," Schaffa says thoughtfully. "Hmm. Someone is keeping some of the node maintainers alive, up north? How interesting."

There's more, so Nassun has to keep babbling it out. "Closer by, there were a lot of them. Us." These felt like her fellows of Found Moon, their orogeny bright and darting like fish, many words schooling and reverberating along the silver lines connecting them. Conversations, whispers, laughter. A comm, her mind suggests. A community of some sort. A community of orogenes.

(She does not sess Castrima. I know you're wondering.)

"How many?" Schaffa's voice is very quiet.

She cannot gauge such things. "I just hear a lot of people talking. Like, houses full."

Schaffa turns away. In profile, she sees that his lips have drawn back from his teeth. It isn't a smile, for once. "The Antarctic Fulcrum."

Nida, who has quietly come into the room in the meantime, says from over near the door: "They weren't purged?"

"Apparently not." There is no inflection to Schaffa's voice. "Only a matter of time until they discover us."

"Yes." Then Nida laughs softly. Nassun sesses the flex of silver threads within Schaffa. Smiling eases the pain, he has said. The more a Guardian is smiling, laughing, the more something is hurting them. "Unless . . ." Nida laughs again. This time Schaffa smiles, too.

But he turns again to Nassun and strokes her hair back from her face. "I need you to be calm," he says. Then he stands and moves aside so that she can see Eitz's corpse.

And after she has finished screaming and weeping and shaking in Schaffa's arms, Nida and Umber come over and lift Eitz's statue, carrying it away. It is obviously much heavier than Eitz ever was, but Guardians are very strong. Nassun doesn't know where they take him, the beautiful sea-born boy with the sad smile and the kind eyes, and she never knows anything of his ultimate fate other than that she has killed him, which makes her a monster.

"Perhaps," Schaffa tells her as she sobs these words. He holds her in his lap again, stroking her thick curls. "But you are *my* monster." She is so low and horrified that this actually makes her feel better.

* * *

Stone lasts, unchanging. Never alter what is written in stone.

—Tablet Three, "Structures," verse one

13

you, amid relics

It begins to feel as though you've lived in Castrima all your life. It shouldn't. Just another comm, just another name, just another new start, or at least a partial one. It will probably end the way all the others have. But... it makes a difference that here, everyone knows what you are. That is the one good thing about the Fulcrum, about Meov, about being Syenite: You could be who you were. That's a luxury you're learning to savor anew.

You're topside again, in Castrima-over as they've been calling it, standing on what used to be the town's token greenland. The ground around Castrima is alkaline and sandy; you heard Ykka actually hoping for a little acid rain to make the soil better. You think the ground probably needs more organic matter for that to work... and there isn't likely to be much of that, since you saw three boilbug mounds on the way here.

The good news is that the mounds are easy to detect, even when they're only a little higher than the ash layer that covers the ground. The insects within them tickle your awareness as a ready source of heat and pressure for your orogeny. On the walk here, you showed the children how to sess for that pent difference from the cooler, more relaxed ambient around it. The younger ones made a game of it, gasping and pointing whenever they sensed a mound and trying to outdo one another in the count.

The bad news is that there are more of the boilbug mounds this week than there were last week. That's probably not a good thing, but you don't let the children see your worry.

There are seventeen children altogether—the bulk of Castrima's complement of orogenes. A couple are in the teen range, but most are younger, one only five. Most are orphans, or might as well be, and that does not surprise you at all. What does surprise you is that all of them must have relatively good self-control and quick wits, because otherwise they wouldn't have survived the Rifting. They would've had to sess it coming in time enough to get to someplace isolated, let their instincts save them, recover, and then go someplace else before anybody started trying to figure out who was at the center of the circle of non-destruction. Most are Midlatter mongrels like you: lots of not-quite-Sanzed-bronze skin, not-quite-ashblow hair, eyes and bodies on a continuum from the Arctic to the Coaster. Not much different from the kids you used to teach in Tirimo's creche. Only the subject matter, and by necessity your teaching methods, must be different.

"Sess what I do—just sess, don't imitate yet," you say, and then you construct a torus around yourself. You do it several times, each time a different way—sometimes spinning it high and tight, sometimes holding it steady but wide enough that its edge rolls close to them. (Half the children gasp and scramble away. That's exactly what they should do; good. Not good that the rest just stood there stupidly. You'll have to work on that.)

"Now. Spread out. You there, you there; all of you stay about that far apart. Once you're in place, spin a torus that looks *exactly* like the one I'm making now."

It isn't how the Fulcrum would've taught them. There, with years of time and safe walls and comforting blue skies overhead, the teaching could be done gently, gradually, giving the children time to get over their fears or outgrow their immaturities. There's no time for gentleness in a Season, though, and no room for failure within Castrima's jagged walls. You've heard the grumbling, seen the resentful looks when you join use-caste crews or head down to the communal bath. Ykka thinks Castrima is something special: a comm where rogga and still can live in harmony, working together to survive. You think she's naive. These children need to be prepared for the inevitable day that Castrima turns on them.

So you demonstrate, and correct their imitations with words when you can and once with a torus-inversion slap when one of the older children spins his too wide and threatens to ice one of his comrades. "You *cannot* be careless!" The boy sits on the icy ground, staring at you wide-eyed. You also made the ground heave under his feet to throw him down, and you're standing over him now, shouting, deliberately intimidating. He almost killed another child; he *should* be afraid. "People die when you make mistakes. Is that what you want?" A frantic headshake. "Then get up, and do it again."

You flog them through the exercise until every one of them has demonstrated at least a basic ability to control the size of their torus. It feels wrong to teach them only this without any of the theory that will help them understand why and how their power works, or any of the stabilizing exercises designed to perfect the detachment of instinct from power. You must teach them in days what you mastered over years; where you are an artist, they will be only crude imitators at best. They are subdued when you walk them back to Castrima, and you suspect some of them hate you. Actually, you're pretty sure they hate you. But they will be more useful to Castrima like this—and on the inevitable day that Castrima turns on them, they'll be ready.

(This is a familiar series of thoughts. Once, as you trained Nassun, you told yourself that it did not matter if she hated you by the end of it; she would know your love by her own survival. That never felt right, though, did it? You were gentler with Uche for that reason. And you always meant to apologize to Nassun, later, when she was old enough to understand... Ah, there are so many regrets in you that they spin, heavy as compressed iron, at your core.)

"You're right," Alabaster says as you sit on an infirmary cot and tell him about the lesson later. "But you're also wrong."

It's later than usual for you to be visiting Alabaster, and as a result he is restless and in visible pain amid his nest. The medications that Lerna usually gives him are wearing off. Being with him is always a competition of desires for you: You know there's not much time for him to teach you this stuff, but you also want to prolong his life, and every day that you wear him down grates on you like a glacier. Urgency and despair don't get along well. You've resolved to keep it brief this time, but he seems inclined to talk a lot today, as he leans against Antimony's hand and keeps his eyes closed. You can't help thinking of this as some kind of strength-saving gesture, as if just the sight of you is a drain.

"Wrong?" you prompt. Maybe there's a warning note in your

voice. You've always been protective of your students, whoever they are.

"For wasting your time, for one thing. They'll never have the precision to be more than rock-pushers." Alabaster's voice is thick with contempt.

"Innon was a rock-pusher," you snap.

A muscle flexes in his jaw, and he pauses for a moment. "So maybe it's a good thing that you're teaching them how to push rocks safely, even if you aren't doing it kindly." Now the contempt is gone from his words. It's as close to an apology as you're probably going to get from him. "But I stand by the rest: You're wrong to teach them at all, because *their* lessons are getting in the way of *your* lessons."

"What?"

He makes you sess one of his stumps again, and—oh. Ohhhh. Suddenly it's harder to grasp the stuff between his cells. It takes longer for your perception to adjust, and when it does, you keep having to reflexively jerk yourself out of a tendency to notice only the heat and jittering movement of the small particles. One afternoon of teaching has set your learning back by a week or more.

"There's a reason the Fulcrum taught you the way it did," he explains finally, when you sit back and rub your eyes and fight down frustration. He's opened his eyes now; they are hooded as they watch you. "The Fulcrum's methods are a kind of conditioning meant to steer you toward energy redistribution and away from magic. The torus isn't even necessary—you can gather ambient energy in any number of ways. But that's how they teach you to direct your awareness *down* to perform orogeny, never up. Nothing above you matters. Only your immediate surroundings, never farther." He shakes his head to the degree that he can. "It's amazing, when you think about it. Everyone in the Stillness is like this. Never mind what's in the oceans, never mind what's in the sky; never look at your own horizon and wonder what's beyond it. We've spent centuries making fun of the astronomests for their crackpot theories, but what we really found incredible was that they ever bothered to *look up* to formulate them."

You'd almost forgotten this part of him: the dreamer, the rebel, always reconsidering the way things have always been because maybe they should never have been that way in the first place. He's right, too. Life in the Stillness discourages reconsideration, reorientation. Wisdom is set in stone, after all; that's why no one trusts the mutability of metal. There's a reason Alabaster was the magnetic core of your little family, back when you were together.

Damn, you're nostalgic today. It prompts you to say, "I think you're not just a ten-ringer." He blinks in surprise. "You're always *thinking.* You're a genius, too—it's just that your genius is in a subject area that no one respects."

Alabaster stares at you for a moment. His eyes narrow. "Are you drunk?"

"No I'm not—" Evil Earth, so much for your fond memories. "Go on with the rusting lesson."

He seems more relieved by the change of subject than you. "So that's what Fulcrum training does to you. You learn to think of orogeny as a matter of effort, when it's really . . . perspective. And perception."

An Allia-shaped trauma tells you why the Fulcrum wouldn't have wanted every two-shard feral reaching for any obelisks nearby. But you spend a moment trying to understand the distinction he's explaining. It's true that using energy is something entirely different from using magic. The Fulcrum's method makes orogeny feel like what it is: straining to shove around heavy objects, just with will instead of hands or levers. Magic, though, feels effortless—at least while one is using it. The exhaustion comes later. In the moment, though, it is simply about *knowing it's there.* Training yourself to see it.

"I don't understand why they did this," you say, tapping your fingers on the mattress in thought. The Fulcrum was built by orogenes. At least some of them, at some point in the past, must have sessed magic. But . . . you shiver as you understand. Ah, yes. The most powerful orogenes, the ones who detect magic most easily and perhaps have trouble mastering energy redistribution as a result, are the ones who end up in the nodes.

Alabaster thinks in bigger pictures than just the Fulcrum. "I think," he says, "they understood the danger. Not just that roggas who lacked the necessary fine control would connect to obelisks and die, but that some might do it successfully—for the wrong reasons."

You try to think of a right reason to activate a network of ancient death machines. Alabaster reads your face. "I doubt I'm the first rogga who's wanted to tip the Fulcrum into a lava pit."

"Good point."

"And the war. Don't ever forget that. The Guardians who work with the Fulcrum are one of the factions I told you about, so to speak. They're the ones who want the status quo: roggas made safe and useful, stills doing all the work and thinking they run the place, Guardians *actually* in charge of everything. Controlling the people who can control natural disasters."

You're surprised by this. No, you're surprised you didn't think of it yourself. But then you haven't spent much time thinking about Guardians, when you weren't in the immediate vicinity of one. Maybe this is another kind of thought aversion you've been conditioned to: Don't look up, and don't think about those damned smiles.

You decide to make yourself think about them now. "But Guardians die during a Season..." Shit. "They *say* they die..." Shit. "Of course they don't."

Alabaster lets out a rusty sound that might be a laugh. "I'm a bad influence."

He always has been. You can't help smiling, though the feeling doesn't last, because of the conversation. "They don't join comms, though. They must go somewhere else to ride it out."

"Maybe. Maybe this 'Warrant' place. No one seems to know where it is." He pauses, grows thoughtful. "I suppose I should have asked mine about that before I left her."

No one just leaves their Guardian. "You said you didn't kill her."

He blinks, out of memory. "No. I *cured* her. Sort of. You know about the thing in their heads." Yes. Blood, and the sting of your palm. Schaffa handing something tiny and bloody to another Guardian, with great care. You nod. "It gives them their abilities, but it also taints them, twists them. The seniors at the Fulcrum used to speak of it in whispers. There are degrees of contamination..." He sets his jaw, visibly steering himself away from that topic. You can guess why. Somewhere along the way, it lands on the shirtless Guardians who kill with a touch. "Anyway, I took that thing out of mine."

You swallow. "I saw a Guardian kill another once, taking it out."

"Yes. When the contamination becomes too great. Then they're dangerous even to other Guardians, and must be purged. I'd heard they weren't gentle about it. Brutes even to their own."

It's angry, Guardian Timay had said, right before Schaffa killed her. *Readying for the time of return.* You inhale. The memory is vivid in your mind because that was the day that you and Tonkee—Binof—found the socket. The day of your first ring test, early and with your life in the balance. You'll never forget anything of that day. And now—"It's the Earth."

"What?"

"The thing that's in Guardians. The…contaminant." *It changed those who would control it. Chained them fate to fate.* "She started speaking for the Earth!"

You can tell you've actually surprised him, for once. "Then…" He considers for a moment. "I see. That's when they switch teams. Stop working for the status quo and Guardian interests, and start working for the Earth's interests instead. No wonder the others kill them."

This is what you need to understand. "What does the Earth want?"

Alabaster's gaze is heavy, heavy. "What does any living thing want, facing an enemy so cruel that it stole away a child?"

Your jaw tightens. *Vengeance.*

You shift down from the cot to the floor, leaning against the cot's frame. "Tell me about the Obelisk Gate."

"Yes. I thought that would get you interested." Alabaster's voice has gone soft again, but there is a look on his face that makes you think, *This is what he looked like on the day he made the Rift.* "You remember the basic principle. Parallel scaling.

Yoking two oxen together instead of one. Two roggas together can do more than each individually. It works for obelisks, too, just...exponential. A matrix, not a yoke. Dynamic."

Okay, you're following so far. "So I need to figure out how to chain all of them together."

He nods back minutely. "And you'll need a buffer, at least initially. When I opened the Gate at Yumenes, I used several dozen node maintainers."

Several dozen stunted, twisted roggas turned into mindless weapons...and Alabaster somehow turned them against their owners. How like him, and how perfect. "Buffer?"

"To cushion the impact. To...smooth out the connection flow..." He falters, sighs. "I don't know how to explain it. You'll know when you try it."

When. He assumes so much. "What you did killed the node maintainers?"

"Not precisely. I used them to open the Gate and create the Rift...and then they tried to do what they were made to do: Stop the shake. Stabilize the land." You grimace, understanding. Even you, in your extremity, weren't foolish enough to try to *stop* the shockwave, when it reached Tirimo. The only safe thing to do was divert its force elsewhere. But node maintainers lack the mind or control to do the safe thing.

"I didn't use all of them," Alabaster says thoughtfully. "The ones far to the west and in the Arctics and Antarctics were out of my reach. Most have died since. No one to keep them alive. But I can still sess active nodes in a few places. Remnants of the network: south, near the Antarctic Fulcrum, and north, near Rennanis."

Of course he can sess active nodes all the way in the

Antarctics. You can barely sess a hundred miles from Castrima, and you have to work to stretch that far. And maybe the roggas of the Antarctic Fulcrum have survived somehow, and chosen to care for their less fortunate brethren in the nodes, but... "Rennanis?" That can't be. It's an Equatorial city. More southerly and westerly than most; people in Yumenes thought it was only a step above any other Somidlats backwater. But Rennanis was Equatorial enough that it should be gone.

"The Rift wends northwesterly, along an ancient fault line that I found. It swung a few hundred miles wide of Rennanis... I suppose that was enough to let the node maintainers actually do something. Should've killed most of them, and the rest should've died of neglect when their staffs abandoned them, but I don't know."

He falls silent, perhaps weary. His voice is hoarse today, and his eyes are bloodshot. Another infection. He keeps getting them because some of the burned patches on his body aren't healing, Lerna says. The lack of pain meds isn't helping.

You try to digest what he's told you, what Antimony has told you, what you've learned through trial and suffering. Maybe the numbers matter. Two hundred and sixteen obelisks, some incalculable number of other orogenes as a buffer, and you. Magic to tie the three together... somehow. All of it together forging a net, to catch the Earthfires-damned Moon.

Alabaster says nothing while you ponder, and eventually you glance at him to see if he's fallen asleep. But he's awake, his eyes slits, watching you. "What?" You frown, defensive as always.

He quarter-smiles with the half of his mouth that hasn't been burned. "You never change. If I ask you for help, you tell me to flake off and die. If I don't say a rusting word, you work miracles for me." He sighs. "Evil Earth, how I've missed you."

This...hurts, unexpectedly. You realize why at once: because it's been so long since anyone said anything like this to you. Jija could be affectionate, but he wasn't much given to sentimentality. Innon used sex and jokes to show his tenderness. But Alabaster...this has always been his way. The surprise gesture, the backhanded compliment that you could choose to take for teasing or an insult. You've hardened so much without this. Without him. You seem strong, healthy, but inside you feel like he looks: nothing but brittle stone and scars, prone to cracking if you bend too much.

You try to smile, and fail. He doesn't try. You just look at each other. It's nothing and everything at once.

Of course it doesn't last. Someone walks into the infirmary and comes over and surprises you by being Ykka. Hjarka's behind her, slouching along and looking very Sanzedly bored: picking her sharp-filed teeth with a bit of polished wood, one hand on her well-curved hip, her ashblow hair a worse mess than usual and noticeably flatter on one side where she's just woken up.

"Sorry to interrupt," Ykka says, not sounding especially sorry, "but we've got a problem."

You're beginning to hate those words. Still, it's time to end the lesson, so you nod to Alabaster and get up. "What now?"

"Your friend. The slacker." Tonkee, who hasn't joined the Innovators' work crews, doesn't bother to pick up your household share when it's her turn, and who conveniently disappears whenever it's time for a caste meeting. In another comm they'd have already kicked her out for that kind of thing, but she gets extra leeway for being one of the companions of the second-most-powerful orogene in Castrima. It only goes so far, though, and Ykka looks especially pissed off.

"She's found the control room," Ykka says. "Locked herself inside."

"The—" What. "The control room for what?"

"*Castrima.*" Ykka looks annoyed to have to explain. "I told you when you got here: There are mechanisms that make this place function, the light and the air and so on. We keep the room secret because if somebody loses it and wants to smash things, they could kill us all. But your 'mest is in there doing Evil Earth knows what, and I'm basically asking you if it's okay to kill her, because that's about where I am right now."

"She won't be able to affect anything important," Alabaster says. It startles you both, you because you aren't used to seeing him interact with anyone else, and Ykka because she probably thinks of him as a waste of medicines and not a person. He doesn't think much of her, either; his eyes are closed again. "More likely to hurt herself than anything else."

"Good to know," Ykka says, though she looks at him skeptically. "I'd be reassured if you weren't talking out of your ass, seeing as you couldn't possibly know what's happening beyond this infirmary, but it's a nice thought, anyway."

He lets out a soft snort of amusement. "I knew everything I needed to know about this relic the instant I came here. And if any of you other than Essun had a chance of making it do what it's really capable of, I wouldn't stay here a moment longer." As you and Ykka stare, he lets out a heavy sigh. There's a little bit of a rattle in it, which troubles you, and you make a note to ask Lerna about it. But he says nothing more, and finally Ykka glances at you with a palpable *I am really sick of your friends* look, and beckons for you to follow her out.

It's a long way up to wherever this control room is. Hjarka's breathing hard after the first ladder, but she acclimates after that and settles into a rhythm. Ykka does better, though she's still sweating in ten minutes. You've still got your road conditioning, so you handle the climb well enough, but after the first three flights of stairs, a ladder, and a spiraling balcony built round one of the fatter crystals of the comm, you're even willing to start small talk to take your mind off the ground falling farther and farther below. "What's your usual disciplinary process for people who shirk their caste duties?"

"The boot, what else?" Ykka shrugs. "We can't just ash them out, though; have to kill them to maintain secrecy. But there's a process: one warning, then a hearing. Morat—that's the Innovator caste spokeswoman—hasn't made a formal complaint. I asked her to, but she waffled. Said your friend gave her a portable water-testing device that may save some of our Hunters' lives out in the field."

Hjarka utters a rusty laugh. You shake your head, amused. "That's a nice bribe. She's a survivor, if nothing else."

Ykka rolls her eyes. "Maybe. But it sends a bad message, one person not joining any work crews and going unpunished for it, even if she does invent useful things outside of work time. Others start to skive off, what do I do then?"

"Ash out the ones who haven't invented anything," you suggest. Then you stop, because Ykka has paused. You think it's because she's annoyed by what you just said, but she's looking around, taking in the expanse of the comm. So you stop, too.

This far up, you're well above the main inhabited level of the comm. The geode echoes with calls and someone hammering something and one of the work crews singing a rhythm song. You risk a look over the nearest railing and see that someone's made a simple rope-and-wooden-pallet cargo lift for the mid-level, but without a counterweight, the only way to get a heavy load up is to basically play tug-of-war with it. Twenty people are at it now. It looks surprisingly like fun.

"You were right about the assimilations," Hjarka says. Her voice is soft as she, too, contemplates the bustle and life of Castrima. "We couldn't have made this place work without more people. Thought you were full of shit, but you weren't."

Ykka sighs. "*So far* it's working." She eyes Hjarka. "You never said you didn't like the idea before."

Hjarka shrugs. "I left my home comm because I didn't want the burden of Leadership. Didn't want it here, either."

"You don't have to knife-fight me for the headwomanship to give an *opinion*, for Earth's sake."

"When a Season's coming on and I'm the only Leader in the comm, I'd better be careful even about opinions." She shrugs, then smiles at Ykka with an air of something like affection. "Keep figuring you'll have me killed any minute now."

Ykka laughs once. "Is that what you would've done in my place?" You hear the edge in this.

"It's the playbook I was taught to follow, yeah—but it'd be stupid to try that here. There's never been anything like this Season... or this comm." Hjarka eyes you, pointedly, as the latest example of Castrima's peculiarity. "Tradition's just going to rust everything up, in a situation like this. Better to have a headwoman who doesn't know how things *should* be, only how she *wants* them to be. A headwoman who'll kick all the asses necessary to make her vision happen."

Ykka absorbs this in silence for a few moments. Obviously whatever Tonkee's done isn't so urgent or terrible. Then she turns and begins climbing again, apparently deciding that the rest break is over. You and Hjarka sigh and follow.

"I think the people who originally built this place didn't think it through," Ykka says as the climb resumes. "Too inefficient. Too dependent on machinery that can break down or rust out. And *orogeny* as a power source, which is basically the least-reliable thing ever. But then sometimes I wonder if maybe they didn't intend to build it this way. Maybe something drove them underground fast, and they found a giant geode and just made the best of what they had." She runs a hand along a railing as you walk. This is one of the original metal structures that have been built throughout the geode. Above the inhabited levels, it's all old metalwork. "Always makes me think they really must have been the ancestors of Castrima. They respected hard work and adapting under pressure, like us."

"Doesn't everyone?" Except Tonkee.

"Some." She doesn't take the obvious bait. "I outed myself to everyone when I was fifteen. There was a forest fire somewhere to the south; drought season. The smoke alone was killing the older people and babies in the comm. We thought we'd have to leave. Finally I went to the edge of the fire, where a bunch of the other townsfolk were trying to create a firebreak. Six of them died doing that." She shakes her head. "Wouldn't have worked. The fire was too big. But that's my people, for you."

You nod. It does sound like the Castrimans you've gotten to know. It also sounds like the Tirimo-folk you've gotten to know, and the Meovites, and the Allians, and the Yumenescenes. No people in the Stillness would have survived to this point if they weren't fearsomely tenacious. But Ykka needs to think of Castrima as special—and it *is* special, in its own strange ways. So you wisely keep your mouth shut.

She says, "I stopped the fire. Iced the burning part of the forest and used that to make a ridge farther south as a windbreak in case anything set off a new blaze. Everyone saw me do it. They knew exactly what I was then."

You stop walking and stare at her. She turns back, half smiling. "I told them I'd go, if they wanted to call the Guardians and have me shipped off to the Fulcrum. Or if they wanted to just string me up, I promised not to ice anyone. Instead, they argued about the whole mess for three days. I thought they were trying to decide how to kill me." She shrugs. "So I went home, had dinner with my parents—they both knew, and they were terrified for me, but I talked them down from smuggling me out of town in a horse cart. Went to creche the next day, same as always. At the end of it, I found out the townsfolk had been arguing about *how to get me trained.* Without letting the Fulcrum on, see."

Your mouth falls open. You've seen Ykka's parents, who are still hale and strong and with an air of Sanzed stubbornness about them. You can believe it of them. But everyone else, too? All right. Maybe Castrima *is* special.

Hjarka says, "Huh. How did you get trained, then?"

"Eh, you know what these little Midlatter comms are like. They were still arguing about it when the Rifting happened. I trained my damn self." She laughs, and Hjarka sighs. "That's my people, too. Complete rust-heads, but good people."

You think, against your will, *If only I had brought Uche and Nassun here as soon as they were born.*

"Not all of your people like having us here," you blurt, almost as a rebuttal to your own thought.

"Yeah, I've heard the chatter. Which is why I'm glad you're training the kids, and that everyone saw you get the boilbugs off Terteis." She sobers. "Poor Terteis. But you proved again that it's better to have people like us around than to kill us or drive us out. Castrimans are practical people, Essie." You hate this nickname immediately. "Too practical to just do something because everybody else says do it."

With that, she resumes the climb. After a moment, you and Hjarka do, too.

You've gotten used to the unrelenting whiteness of Castrima; only a few of the building-crystals have touches of amethyst or smoky quartz about them. Here, though, the ceiling of the geode has been sealed off with a smooth, glasslike substance that is deep emeraldine green in color. The color is a bit of a shock. The final stairway that leads up into this is wide enough for five people to climb abreast, so you're unsurprised to find two of Castrima's Strongbacks flanking what looks like a sliding attic door made of the same green substance. One of the Strongbacks has a small wireglass utility knife in her hand; the other just has his big folded arms.

"Still nothing," says the male Strongback as the three of you arrive. "We keep hearing sounds from inside—clicking, buzzing, and sometimes she yells things. But the door's still jammed."

"Yells things?" asks Hjarka.

He shrugs. "Like, 'I knew it' and 'that's why.'"

Sounds like Tonkee. "How does she have the door rigged?" you ask. The female Strongback shrugs. It's a stereotype that Strongbacks are all muscle and no brain, but a few of them fit that description more than they should.

Ykka gives you another *This is your fault* look. You shake your head, then climb up to the top step and bang on the door. "Tonkee, rust it, open up."

There's a moment of silence, and then you hear a faint clatter. "Fuck, it's you," Tonkee mutters, from somewhere farther away than the door. "Hang on and don't ice anything."

A moment later there's the sound of something rattling against the door material. Then the door slides open. You, Ykka, Hjarka, and the Strongbacks climb up—though all of you except Ykka stop and stare, so it's left to her to fold her arms and give Tonkee the exasperated glare she's earned.

The ceiling is hollow above the door. The green substance forms a floor, and the resulting chamber is molded around the usual white crystals that jut down from the geode's rocky, grayish-green true ceiling, perhaps fifteen feet overhead. What makes you stop, your mouth falling open and your mind stuttering from annoyance into silence, is that the crystals on this side of the green barrier flicker and blink, transitioning at random from shimmering images of crystals into solidity, and back again. The shafts and tips of these crystals, which poke through the floor, weren't doing this outside. None of the other crystals in Castrima do this. Aside from glowing—which, granted, is a warning that they aren't just rocks—the crystals of Castrima are no different from any other quartz. Here, though . . . you suddenly understand what Alabaster meant about what Castrima is capable of. The truth of Castrima is suddenly, terrifyingly clear: The geode is filled with not crystals, but *potential obelisks.*

"Flaking rust," one of the Strongbacks breathes. This speaks for you as well.

Tonkee's junk is everywhere in the room: weird tools and slates and scraps of leather covered in diagrams, and a pallet in the corner that explains why she hasn't been sleeping in the apartment much lately. (It's been lonely without her and Hoa, but you don't like admitting this to yourself.) She's walking away from you now, glaring over her shoulder and looking distinctly irritated that you've arrived. "Don't rusting touch anything," she says. "No telling what an orogene of your caliber will do to this stuff."

Ykka rolls her eyes. "You're the one who shouldn't be touching anything. You're not allowed in here and you know it. Come on."

"No." Tonkee crouches near a strange, low plinth at the center of the room. It looks like a crystal shaft whose middle has been chopped out: You see the (flickering, unreal) base growing from the ceiling, and the plinth is its (flickering in tandem) continuation, but there's a five-foot section in between that's just empty space. The plinth's surface has been cut so smoothly that it gleams like a mirror—and the surface stays solid, even as the rest of the shaft flickers.

At first you think there's nothing on it. But Tonkee is peering at the plinth's surface so intently that you walk over to join her. When you hunker down for a better look, she glances up to meet your eyes, and you're shocked at the barely disguised glee in hers.

Not really shocked by that; you know her by now. You're shocked because this high gleam, plus the new undisguise of her clean, short hair and neat clothing, transforms her so obviously into an older version of Binof that you marvel again you didn't see it at once.

But that's unimportant. You focus on the plinth, even though there are other wonders to behold: a taller plinth near the back of the room, above which floats a foot-tall miniature obelisk the same emerald color as the floor; another plinth bearing an oblong hunk of rock, also floating; a series of clear squares set into one wall bearing strange diagrams of some sort of equipment; a series of panels along the wall beneath them, each bearing meters measuring something unknown in numbers that you can't decipher.

On the big plinth, though, are the least obtrusive objects in the room: six tiny metallic shards, each needle-thin and no longer than your thumbnail. They are not the same silvery metal that makes up Castrima's ancient structures; this metal is a smooth dark color dusted faintly with red. Iron. Amazing that it hasn't oxidized away over all the years of Castrima's existence. Unless—"Did you put these here?" you ask Tonkee.

She's instantly furious. "Yes, of course I would enter the control core of a deadciv artifact, find the most dangerous device in it, and immediately throw bits of rusty metal on it!"

"Don't be an ass, please." Though you did sort of deserve that, you're too intrigued to be really annoyed. "Why do you think this is the most dangerous device in here?"

Tonkee points to the beveled edge of the plinth. You look closer and blink. The material is not smooth like the rest of the crystal shaft; on the edge it has been heavily etched with symbols and writing. The writing is the same as that along the wall panels—oh. And they are glowing red, the color seeming to float and waver just over the surface of the material.

"And this," Tonkee says. She raises a hand and moves it toward the plinth's surface and the metal bits. Abruptly the red letters leap into the air—you don't have a better way to describe what's happening than that. In an instant they have enlarged and turned to face you, blazing the air at eye level with what is unmistakably some sort of warning. Red is the color of lava pools. It is the color of a lake when everything in it has died except toxic algae: one warning sign of an impending blow. Some things do not change with time or culture, you feel certain.

(You are wrong, generally speaking. But in this specific case, you're quite right.)

Everyone's staring. Hjarka comes close and lifts a hand to try to touch the floating letters; her fingers pass through them. Ykka moves around the plinth, fascinated despite herself. "I've noticed this thing before, but never really paid attention to it. The letters turn with me."

They haven't moved. But you lean to one side—and sure enough, as you do this the letters pivot slightly to remain facing you.

Impatiently, Tonkee pulls her hand back and waves Hjarka's hand out of the way, and the letters flatten and shrink back into quiescence along the plinth edge. "There's no barrier, though. Usually in a deadciv artifact—an artifact from *this* civilization—anything truly dangerous is sealed off in some way. There's either a physical barrier, or evidence that there was once a barrier that's failed with time. If they really didn't want you to touch something, you either didn't touch it or you'd have to work pretty damned hard to touch it. This? Just a warning. I don't know what that means."

"Can you actually touch those things?" You reach toward one of the bits of iron, ignoring the warning this time when it springs up. Tonkee hisses at you so sharply that you jerk back like a child caught doing something you weren't supposed to.

"I *said* don't rusting touch! What's wrong with you?" You clench your jaw, but you deserved that, too, and you're too much a mother to deny it.

"How long have you been coming in here?" Ykka's crouched next to Tonkee's sleeping pallet.

Tonkee's staring down at the iron bits, and at first you think she hasn't heard Ykka; she doesn't answer for a long moment. There is a look on her face that you're starting not to like. You can't say you really know her any more now than you did when you were a grit, but you do know that she isn't the grim sort. That she is grim now, the tightened muscle along her jawline making it stand out more than you know she likes, is a very bad sign. She's up to something. She says to Ykka, "A week. But I only moved in three days ago. I think. I lost track." She rubs her eyes. "I haven't slept a lot."

Ykka shakes her head and rises. "Well, at least you haven't destroyed the rusting comm already. Tell me what you've figured out, then."

Tonkee turns to eye her warily. "Those panels along the wall activate, and regulate, the water pumps and air circulation systems and cooling processes. But you knew that already."

"Yes. Since we're not dead." Ykka dusts off her hands from

where she touched the floor, sidling toward Tonkee in a way that is somehow simultaneously thoughtful and subtly menacing. She's not as big as most Sanzed women—a good foot shorter than Hjarka. Her dangerousness is not as obvious as it is with others, but you sense the slow readying of her orogeny now. She was fully prepared to smash or ice her way into this place. The Strongbacks shift and edge a little closer, too, reinforcing her unspoken threat.

"What I want to know," she continues, "is how *you* knew that." She stops, facing Tonkee. "We figured it out, in those early days, through trial and error. Touch one thing and it gets cooler, touch another and the communal pool water gets hotter. But nothing's changed in the past week."

Tonkee sighs a little. "I've learned how to decipher some of the symbols over the years. Spend enough time in these kinds of ruins and you see the same things repeated over and over."

Ykka considers this, then nods toward the warning text around the plinth rim. "What's that say?"

"No idea. I said *decipher*, not read. Symbols, not language." Tonkee walks over to one of the wall panels and points to a prominent design in its top right corner. It's nothing intuitive: something green and arrow-like but squiggly, sort of, pointed downward. "I see that one wherever there were water gardens. I think it's about the quality and intensity of the light that the gardens get." She eyes Ykka. "Actually, I know it's about the light the gardens get."

Ykka lifts her chin a little, just enough that you know Tonkee has guessed right. "So this place is no different from other ruins you've seen? The others had crystals in them, like this?"

"No. I've never seen anything like Castrima before. Except—" She glances at you, once and away. "Well. Not *exactly* like Castrima."

"That thing in the Fulcrum wasn't anything like this," you blurt. It's been more than twenty years, but you haven't forgotten a detail about the place. That was a pit, and Castrima is a rock with a hole in it. If both were made by the same kinds of people, to do similar things, there's no evidence of that anywhere.

"It was, actually." Tonkee comes back to the plinth and waves up the warning. This time she points at a symbol within the glowing red text: a solid black circle surrounded by a white octagon. You don't know how you missed it before; it stands out from the red.

"I saw that mark in the Fulcrum, painted onto some of the light panels. You were too busy staring into the pit; I don't think you saw. But I've been in maybe half a dozen obelisk-builder sites since, and that mark is always near something dangerous." She's watching you intently. "I find dead people near it sometimes."

Inadvertently you think of Guardian Timay. Not *found* dead, but dead nevertheless, and you almost joined her that day. Then you remember a moment in the room without doors, near the edge of the yawning pit. You remember small needlelike protrusions from the walls of the pit . . . exactly like these bits of iron.

"The socket," you murmur. That was what the Guardian called it. "A contaminant." A prickle dances across the nape of your neck. Tonkee looks sharply at you.

"'Something dangerous' can mean any rusting thing," says Hjarka, annoyed, as you stand there staring at the bits of rust.

"No, in this case it means a specific rusting thing." Tonkee glares Hjarka down, which is impressive in itself. "It was the mark of their enemy."

Fuck, you realize. Fuck, fuck, fuck.

"What?" asks Ykka. "What in the Evil Earth are you talking about?"

"Their *enemy.*" Tonkee leans against the edge of the plinth—carefully, you note, but emphatically. "They were at war, don't you understand? Toward the end, just before their civilization vanished into the dust. All their ruins, anything that's left from that time, are defensive, survival-oriented. Like the comms of today—except they had a lot more than stone walls to help protect them. Things like *giant rusting underground geodes.* They *hid* in those places, and studied their enemy, and maybe built weapons to fight back." She pivots and points up, at the upper half of the plinth crystal. It flickers just as she does so, obelisk-like.

"No," you say automatically. Everyone turns to look at you, and you twitch. "I mean..." Shit. But you've said it now. "The obelisks aren't..." You don't know how to say it without telling the whole damned story, and you're reluctant to do that. You're not sure why. Maybe for the same reason that Antimony said, when Alabaster started to tell you: They aren't ready. Now you need to finish in a way that won't invite further comment. "I don't think they're defensive, or any sort of... weapon."

Tonkee says nothing for a long moment. "What are they, then?"

"I don't know." It's not a lie. You *don't* know for sure. "A tool, maybe. Dangerous if misused, but not *meant* to kill."

Tonkee seems to brace herself. "I know what happened to Allia, Essun."

It's an unexpected blow, and it floors you emotionally. Fortunately, you've spent your life training to deflect your reactions to unexpected blows in safe ways. You say, "Obelisks aren't *made* to do that. That was an accident."

"How do you—"

"Because I was *connected to* the rusting thing when it went into burndown!" You snap this so sharply that your voice echoes in the room and startles you into realizing how angry you are. One of the Strongbacks inhales and something in her gaze shifts and all at once you are reminded of the Strongbacks at Tirimo, who looked at you the same way when Rask asked them to let you go through the gate. Even Ykka's watching you in a way that wordlessly says, *You're scaring the locals, calm the rust down.* So you take a deep breath and fall silent.

(It is only later that you will recall the word you said during this conversation. *Burndown.* You will wonder why you said it, what it means, and you will have no answer.)

Tonkee lets out a deep breath, carefully, and this seems to speak for the room. "It's possible I've made some wrong assumptions," she says.

Ykka rubs a hand over her hair. It makes her head look incongruously small for a moment until it floofs back up. "All right. We already know Castrima was used as a comm before. Probably several times. If you'd *asked* me, instead of coming in here and acting like a rusting child, I could have told you that. I would have told you everything I knew, because I want to understand this place just as much as you do—"

Tonkee utters a single braying laugh. "None of you are smart enough for that."

"—but by pulling *this shit*, you've made me mistrust you. I don't let people I don't trust do things that can hurt the people I love. So I want you out of here for good."

Hjarka frowns. "Yeek, that's kind of harsh, isn't it?"

Tonkee tenses at once, her eyes going wide with horror, and hurt. "You can't keep me out. Nobody else in this rusting comm has a clue what—"

"Nobody else in this rusting comm," Ykka says, and now the Strongbacks look at *her* uneasily, because she's nearly shouting, "would set us all on fire for the chance to study people who've been gone since the world was young. Somehow I'm getting the impression that you would."

"Supervised visits!" Tonkee blurts. She looks desperate now.

Ykka steps up to her, getting right in her face, and Tonkee goes silent at once. "I would rather understand nothing about this place," Ykka says, brutally quiet and cold now, "than risk destroying it. Can you say the same?"

Tonkee stares back at her, trembling visibly and saying nothing. But the answer's obvious, isn't it? Tonkee's like Hjarka. Both were raised Leadership, raised to put the needs of others first, and both chose a more selfish path. It's not even a question.

Which is why later, in retrospect, you really aren't surprised at what happens next.

Tonkee turns and lunges and the red warning flashes and then one of the iron bits is in her fist. She's already turning away by the time you register her grab. Bolting for the stair door. Hjarka gasps; Ykka's just standing there, a little startled and mostly resigned; the two Strongbacks stare in confusion and then belatedly start after Tonkee. But then an instant later

Tonkee gasps and stumbles to a halt. One of the Strongbacks grabs her arm—but drops it immediately when Tonkee *yells.*

You're moving before you think. Tonkee is yours somehow—like Hoa, like Lerna, like Alabaster, as if in the absence of your children you're trying to adopt everybody who touches you emotionally for even an instant. You don't even like Tonkee. Still, your belly clenches when you grab her wrist and see that blood streaks her hand. "What the—"

Tonkee looks at you: quick, animal panic. Then she jerks and cries out again, and you almost let go this time because *something moves under your thumb.*

"The rust?" Ykka blurts. Hjarka's hand claps over Tonkee's arm, too, helping, because Tonkee's strong in her panic. You master your inexplicable, violent revulsion enough to instead move your thumb and hold Tonkee's wrist so that you can get a good look at it. Yes. There's something moving just under her skin. It jumps and jitters, but moves inexorably upward, following the path of a large vein there. It's just large enough to be the iron fragment.

"Evil Earth," Hjarka says, throwing a quick worried look at Tonkee's face. You fight sudden hysterical laughter at the unintentional irony of Hjarka's oath.

"I need a knife," you say instead. Your voice sounds remarkably calm to your own ears. Ykka leans over, sees what you've seen, and breathes an oath.

"Oh, fuck, rust, shit," Tonkee moans. "Get it out! Get it out and I'll never come in here again." It's a lie, but maybe she means it for the moment.

"I can bite it out." Hjarka looks up at you. Her sharpened teeth are small razors.

"No," you say, certain it would just go into Hjarka and do the same thing. Tongues were harder to carve than arms.

Ykka barks, "Knife!" at the Strongbacks—the one with the wireglass knife. It's sharp but small, meant more for cutting rope than as a weapon; unless you hit a vital area right off, you'd have to stab someone a million times to kill them with it. It's all you've got. You keep hold of Tonkee's wrist because she's flailing and growling like an animal. Someone puts the knife in your hand, fumbling and blade-first. It feels like it takes a year to get it repositioned, but you keep your gaze on that jerking, moving lump in Tonkee's brown flesh. Where the rust is it going? You're too quietly horrified to speculate.

But before you can put the knife in place to carve the moving thing loose, it vanishes. Tonkee screams again, her voice breaking and horrible. It's gone into the meat of her.

You slash once, opening a deep cut just above the elbow, which should be ahead of the thing. Tonkee groans. "Deeper! I can feel it."

Deeper and you'll hit bone, but you set your teeth and cut deeper. There's blood everywhere. Ignoring Tonkee's pants and hisses, you try to probe for the thing—even though privately you're terrified you'll find it and it'll go into your flesh next.

"Arterial," Tonkee pants. She's shaking, keening through her teeth between every word. "Like a rusting highroad to—sessa-*ah*! Fuck!" She claps at the lower half of her bicep. It's farther up her arm than you expected. Moving faster now that it's reached the larger arteries.

Sessa. You stare at Tonkee for a moment, chilled by the realization that she was trying to say *sessapinae*. Ykka reaches over you and wraps a hand around Tonkee's arm just below the deltoid, squeezing tight. She looks at you, but you know there's only one thing left to do. You're not going to be able to manage it with the tiny knife . . . but there are other weapons.

"Hold her arm out." Without waiting to see whether Ykka and Hjarka comply, you grip Tonkee's shoulder. It's Alabaster's trick that you're thinking of—a tiny, fine-spun, localized torus like the ones he used to kill the boilbugs. This time you'll use it to burrow through Tonkee's arm and freeze the little iron shard. Hopefully. But as you extend your awareness and shut your eyes to concentrate, something shifts.

You're deep in the heat of her, seeking the metallic lattice of the iron shard and trying to sess the difference between its structure and that of the iron in her blood, and then—yes. The silver glimmer of magic is there.

You weren't expecting that, here amid the gelid bobble of her cells. Tonkee isn't turning into stone like Alabaster, and you've never sessed magic in any other living creature. Yet here, *here* in Tonkee, there is something that gleams steadily, silverish and threadlike, coming up through her feet—from where? doesn't matter—and ending at the iron shard. No wonder the thing can move so quickly, fueled as it is by *something else*. Using this power source, it stretches forth tendrils of its own to link into Tonkee's flesh and drag itself along. This is why it hurts her—because every cell it touches shivers as if burned, and then dies. The tendrils get longer with every contact, too; the fucking thing is *growing* its way through her, feeding on her in some imperceptible way. A lead tendril feels its way along, orienting always toward Tonkee's sessapinae, and you know instinctively that letting it get there will be Bad.

You try grabbing onto the root-thread, thinking maybe to stall it or starve it of strength, but

Oh

no

there is hate and

we all do what we have to do

there is anger and

ah; hello, little enemy

"Hey!" Hjarka's voice in your ear, a shout. "Wake the fuck up!" You jerk out of the fog you weren't aware of drifting into. Okay. You stay away from the root-tendril, lest you get another taste of whatever is driving the thing. That instant of contact was worth it, though, because now you know what to do.

You visualize scissors with edges of infinite fineness and blades of glimmering silver. Cut the lead. Cut the tendrils or they may grow again. Cut the contamination before it can set hooks any deeper in her. You're thinking of Tonkee as you do this. Wanting to save her life. But Tonkee is not Tonkee to you right now; she is a collection of particles and substances. You make the cut.

This isn't your fault. I know you won't ever believe it, but… it isn't.

And when you manage to relax your sessapinae and adjust your perception back to the macro scale and you find yourself covered, absolutely *covered* in blood, you're surprised. You don't quite understand why Tonkee is on the floor, gasping, her body surrounded by a spreading pool as Hjarka shouts at one of the Strongbacks to hand her his belt, now, now. You feel the jerk of the iron shard nearby and twitch in alarm, because you know

now what those things are trying to do, and that they are evil. But when you turn to look at the iron shard, you're confused, because all you see is smooth bronze skin streaked with blood and a scrap of familiar cloth. Then there is a sort of twitchy movement, weight making itself known in your hand, and. And. Well. You're holding Tonkee's severed arm.

You drop it. Fling it, more like, violent in your shock. It bounces just beyond Ykka and the two Strongbacks who are clustering around Tonkee and doing something, maybe trying to save her life, you can't even wrap your head around that, because now you see that the cut end of Tonkee's arm is a perfect, slightly slanted cross-section, still bleeding and twitching because *you just cut it off*, but wait no that is not the only reason.

From a small hole near the bone you see something wriggle forth. The hole is the cross-section of an artery. The something is the iron shard, which drops to the smooth green floor and then lies amid the splattered blood as if it is nothing more than a harmless bit of metal.

Hello, little enemy.

INTERLUDE

There is a thing you will not see happening, yet that is going to impact the rest of your life. Imagine it. Imagine me. You know what I am, you think, both with your thinking mind and the animal, instinctive part of you. You see a stone body clothed in flesh, and even though you never really believed I was human, you did think of me as a child. You still think it, though Alabaster has told you the truth—that I haven't been a child since before your language existed. Perhaps I was never a child. Hearing this and believing it are two different things, however.

You should imagine me as what I truly am among my kind, then: old, and powerful, and greatly feared. A legend. A monster.

You should imagine—

Castrima as an egg. Motes surround this egg, lurking in the stone. Eggs are a rich prize for scavengers, and easy to devour if left unguarded. This one is being devoured, though the people of Castrima are barely aware of the act. (Ykka alone, I think, and even she only suspects.) Such a leisurely repast isn't a thing most of your kind would notice. We are a very slow people. It will be deadly nevertheless, once the devouring is done.

Yet something has made the scavengers pause, teeth bared but not sinking in. There is another old and powerful one here: the one you call Antimony. She isn't interested in guarding the egg, but she could, if she chose. She will, if they attempt to poach her Alabaster. The others are aware of this, and wary of her. They shouldn't be.

I'm the one they should fear.

I destroy three of them on the first day after I leave you. As you stand sharing a mellow with Ykka, I tear apart Ykka's stone eater, the red-haired creature that she's been calling Luster and you've been calling Ruby Hair. Filthy parasite, lurking only to take and give nothing back! I despise her. We are meant for better. Then I take the two who have been stalking Alabaster, hoping to dart in should Antimony become distracted—this is not because Antimony needs the help, mind, but simply because our race cannot bear that level of stupidity. I cull them for the good of us all.

(They're not really dead, if that troubles you. We cannot die. In ten thousand years or ten million, they will reconstitute themselves from the component atoms into which I've scattered them. A long time in which to contemplate their folly, and do better next time.)

This initial slaughter makes many of the others flee; scavengers are cowards at heart. They don't go far, though. Of those who remain near, a few attempt parley. Plenty for us all, they say. If even one has the potential . . . but I catch some of these watching you and not Alabaster.

They confess to me, as I circle them and pretend that I might be merciful. They speak of another old one—one who is known to me from conflicts long ago. He, too, has a vision for our kind, in opposition to mine. He knows of you, my Essun, and he would kill you if he could, because you mean to finish what Alabaster began. He can't get to you with me in the way... but he can *push you to destroy yourself. He's even found some greedy human allies up north to help him do so.*

Ah, this ridiculous war of ours. We use your kind so easily. Even you, my Essun, my treasure, my pawn. One day, I hope, you will forgive me.

14

you're invited!

Six months pass in the undifferentiated white light of an ancient magic-fueled survival shelter. After the first few days you start wrapping cloth around your eyes when you're tired, to create your own day and night. It works passably.

Tonkee's arm survives the reattachment, though she gets a bad infection at one point, which Lerna's basic antibiotics seem powerless to stop. She lives, though by the time the fever and livid infection lines have faded, her fingers have lost some of their fine movement and she gets phantom tinglings and numbness throughout the limb. Lerna thinks this will be permanent. Tonkee mutters imprecations about it sometimes, whenever you track her down in the middle of core sampling or whatever she's doing and force her to go meet with the Innovator caste head. Whenever she gets too free with the "arm-chopper" insults, you remind her first that unleashing a piece of the Evil Earth to crawl through her flesh was her own damned fault, and second that you're the only reason Ykka hasn't had her killed yet, so maybe she should consider shutting up. She does, but she's still an ass about it. Nothing ever really changes in the Stillness.

And yet...sometimes things do.

Lerna forgives you for being a monster. That's not exactly it. You and he still can't talk about Tirimo easily. Still, he heard your raging fight with Ykka all through the surgery that he performed on Tonkee's arm, and that means something to him. Ykka wanted Tonkee left to die on the table. You argued for her life, and won. Lerna knows now that there's more to you than death. You're not sure you agree with that assessment, but it's a relief to have something of your old friendship back.

Hjarka starts courting Tonkee. Tonkee doesn't react well at first. She's mostly just confused when gifts of dead animals and books start appearing in the apartment, brought by with a too-casual, "In case that big brain of hers needs something to chew on," and a wink. You're the one who has to explain to Tonkee that Hjarka's decided, through whatever convoluted set of values the big woman holds dear, that an ex-commless geomest with the social skills of a rock represents the pinnacle of desirability. Then Tonkee is mostly annoyed, complaining about "distractions" and "the vagaries of the ephemeral" and the need to "decenter the flesh." You mostly ignore all of it.

It's the books that settle the issue. Hjarka seems to pick them by the number of many-syllabled words on their spines, but you come home a few times to find Tonkee engrossed in them. Eventually you come home to find Tonkee's room curtain drawn and Tonkee engrossed in Hjarka, or so the sounds from beyond would suggest. You didn't think they could do that much with her bum arm. Huh.

Perhaps it is this new sense of connection to Castrima that causes Tonkee to begin trying to prove her worth to Ykka. (Or maybe it's just pride; Tonkee bristles so when Ykka once says that Tonkee isn't as useful to the comm as its hardest-working Strongback.) Whatever the reason, Tonkee brings the council a new predictive model that she's worked out: Unless Castrima finds a stable source of animal protein, some comm members will start showing deprivation symptoms within a year. "It'll start with the meat stupids," she tells all of you. "Forgetfulness, tiredness, little things like that. But it's a kind of anemia. If it goes on, the result is dementia and nerve damage. You can figure out the rest."

There are too many lorist tales of what can happen to a comm without meat. It will make people weak and paranoid, the community becoming vulnerable to attack. The only choice that will prevent this outcome, Tonkee explains, is cannibalism. Planting more beans just isn't enough.

The report is useful information, but nobody really wanted to hear it, and Ykka doesn't like Tonkee any better for sharing it. You thank Tonkee after the meeting, since no one else did. Her lower jaw juts out a bit as she replies, "Well, I won't be able to continue my studies if we all start killing and eating each other, so."

You shunt the orogene children's lessons to Temell, another adult orogene in the comm. The children complain that he's not very good—none of your finesse, and while he goes easier on them, they're not learning as much. (It's nice to be appreciated, if after the fact.) You do start training Cutter as an alternative, after he asks you to show him how you cut off Tonkee's arm. You doubt he'll ever perceive magic or move obelisks, but he's at least first-ring level, and you want to see if you can make him a two- or three-ringer. Just because. Apparently higher-level teaching doesn't interfere with what you're learning from Alabaster—or at least, 'Baster doesn't complain about it. You'll take it. You've missed teaching.

(You offer an exchange of techniques to Ykka, since she shows no interest in lessons. You want to know how she does the things she does. "Nope," she says, winking at you in a way that's not really teasing. "Gotta keep some tricks up my sleeve so you won't ice me someday.")

An all-volunteer trading party goes north to try to reach the comm of Tettehee. They do not return. Ykka nixes all future attempts, and you do not protest this. One of your former orogeny students was with the missing party.

Aside from the food supply issue, however, Castrima thrives in those six months. One woman gets pregnant without permission, which is a big problem. Babies contribute nothing useful to a comm for years, and no comm can tolerate many useless people during a Season. Ykka decides that the woman's household of two married couples will not receive an increased share until someone elderly or infirm dies to clear the way for the unauthorized baby. You get into another fight with Ykka about that, because you know full well she meant Alabaster when she offhandedly added, "Shouldn't be long," to the woman. Ykka's unapologetic: She did mean Alabaster and she hopes he dies soon, because at least a baby has future value.

Two good outcomes result from that fracas: Everyone trusts you more after seeing you shout at the top of your lungs in the middle of Flat Top without causing so much as a tremor, and the

Breeders decide to speak up for the new baby in order to settle the dispute. Based on the favorable recent genealogy, they contribute one of their child-allocations to the family, though with the stipulation that it will have to join their use-caste if it is born perfect. That's not so terrible a price to pay, they say, spending one's reproductive years cranking out children for comm and caste, in exchange for the right to be born. The mother agrees.

Ykka hasn't shared the protein situation with the comm, of course, or the Breeders wouldn't be speaking up for anyone. (Tonkee figured it out on her own, naturally.) Ykka doesn't want to tell anyone, either, until it's clear there's no hope of an alternate solution to the problem. You and the other council members agree reluctantly. There's still a year left. But because of Ykka's silence, a male Breeder visits you a few days after you bring Tonkee home to finish recuperating. The Breeder is an ashblow-haired, strong-shouldered, sloe-eyed thing, and he's very interested to know that you've borne three healthy children, all powerful orogenes. He flatters you by talking about how tall and strong you are, how well you weathered months on the road with only travel rations to eat, and hinting that you're "only" forty-three. This actually makes you laugh. You feel as old as the world, and this pretty fool thinks you're ready to crank out another baby.

You turn down his tacit offer with a smile, but it's . . . strange, having that conversation with him. Unpleasantly familiar. When the Breeder is gone, you think of Corundum and wake Tonkee by throwing a cup at the wall and screaming at the top of your lungs. Then you go to see Alabaster for another lesson, which is utterly useless because you spend it standing before him and trembling in utter, rage-filled silence. After five minutes of this, he wearily says, "Whatever the rust is wrong with you, you're going to have to deal with it yourself. I can't stop you anymore."

You hate him for no longer being invincible. And for not hating you.

Alabaster suffers another bad infection during these six months. He survives it only by deliberately stoning what's left of his legs. This self-induced surgery so stresses his body that his few bouts of lucid time shrink to a half hour apiece, interspersed with long stretches of stupor or fitful sleeping. He's so weak when he's awake that you have to strain to hear him, though thankfully this improves over the course of a few weeks. You're making progress, connecting easily now to the newly arrived topaz and beginning to understand what he did to transform the spinel into the knife-like weapon he keeps nearby. (The obelisks are conduits. You flow through them, flow with them, as the magic flows. Resist and die, but resonate finely enough and many things become possible.)

That's a far cry from chaining together multiple obelisks, though, and you know you're not learning fast enough. Alabaster doesn't have the strength to curse you for your cloddish pace, but he doesn't have to. Watching him shrivel daily is what drives you to push at the obelisk again and again, plunging yourself into its watery light even when your head hurts and your stomach lurches and you want nothing more than to go curl up somewhere and cry. It hurts too much to look at him, so you mop yourself up and try that much harder to become him.

One good thing about all this: You've got a purpose now. Congratulations.

You cry on Lerna's shoulder once. He rubs your back and

suggests delicately that you don't have to be alone in your grief. It's a proposition, but one made in kindness rather than passion, so you don't feel guilty about ignoring it. For now.

Thus do things reach a kind of equilibrium. It's neither a time of rest, nor of struggle. You survive. In a Season, in *this* Season, that is itself a triumph.

And then Hoa returns.

* * *

It happens on a day of sorrows and lace. The sorrow is because more Hunters have died. In the middle of bringing back a rare hunting kill—a bear that was visibly too thin to safely hibernate, easy to shoot in its desperate aggression—the party was attacked in turn. Three Hunters died in a barrage of arrows and crossbow bolts. The two surviving Hunters did not see their assailants; the projectiles seemed to come from all directions. They wisely ran, though they circled back an hour later in hopes of recovering their fallen comrades' bodies and the precious carcass. Amazingly, everything had been left unmolested by either assailants or scavengers—but left behind with the fallen was an object: a planted stick, around which someone tied a strip of ragged, dirty cloth. It was secured with a thick knot, something caught in its fraying loops.

You come into Ykka's meeting room just as she begins to cut open the knot, even as Cutter stands over her and says in a tight voice, "This is completely unsafe, you have no idea—"

"I don't care," Ykka murmurs, concentrating on the knot. She's being very careful, avoiding the thickest part of the knot, which clearly contains something; you can't tell what, but it's lumpy and seems light. The room is more crowded than usual because one of the Hunters is here, too, grimy with ash and blood and visibly determined to know what her companions died for. Ykka glances up in acknowledgment as you arrive, but then resumes work. She says, "Something blows up in my face, Cuts, you're the new headman."

That flusters and shuts Cutter up enough that she's able to finish the knot undistracted. The loops and strands of once-white cloth are lace, and if you don't miss your guess, it was of a quality that would once have made your grandmother lament her poverty. When the strands snap apart, what sits amid them is a small balled-up scrap of leather hide. It's a note.

WELCOME TO RENNANIS, it reads in charcoal.

Hjarka curses. You sit down on a divan, because it's better than the floor and you need to sit somewhere. Cutter looks disbelieving. "Rennanis is Equatorial," he says. And therefore it should be gone; same reaction you had when Alabaster told you.

"May not be Rennanis proper," Ykka says. She's still examining the scrap of leather, turning it over, scraping at the charcoal with the edge of the knife as if to test its authenticity. "A band of survivors from that city, commless now and little better than bandits, naming themselves after home. Or maybe just Equatorial wannabes, taking the chance to claim something they couldn't before the actual city got torched."

"Doesn't matter," snaps Hjarka. "This is a threat, whoever it's coming from. What are we going to *do* about it?"

They devolve into speculations and argument, all with a rising edge of panic. Without really planning to, you lean back against the wall of Ykka's meeting room. Against the wall of the crystal that her apartment inhabits. Against the rind of the geode, in which the crystal shaft is rooted. It is not an obelisk. Not even the flickering portions of crystal in the control room feel of power as they should; even if they are in an obelisk-like state of unreality, that is the only point of similarity they share with real obelisks.

But you've also remembered something that Alabaster told you a long time ago, on a garnet-hued afternoon in a seaside comm that is now smoldering ruins. Alabaster murmuring of conspiracies, watchers, nowhere was safe. *You're saying someone could hear us through the walls? Through the stone itself?* you remember asking him. Once upon a time, you thought the things he did were just miracles.

And now you're a nine-ringer, Alabaster says. Now you know that miracles are a matter of just effort, just perception, and maybe just magic. Castrima exists amid ancient sedimentary rock laced through with veins of long-dead forests turned to crumbly coal, all of it balanced precariously over a crisscross of ancient fault-scars that have all but healed. The geode has been here long enough, however awkwardly jammed amid the strata, that its outermost layers are thoroughly fused with local minerals. This makes it easy for you to push your awareness beyond Castrima in a fine, gradually attenuating extrusion. This is not the same thing as extending your torus; a torus is your power, this is you. It's harder. You can sense what your power cannot, though, and—

"Hey, wake up," Hjarka says, shoving you in the shoulder, and you snap back to glare at her.

Ykka groans. "Remind me, Hjar, to someday tell you what usually happens when someone interrupts high-level orogeny.

I mean, you can probably guess, but remind me to describe it in gory detail, so that maybe it can have some actual deterrent value."

"She was just sitting there." Hjarka sits back, looking disgruntled. "And the rest of you were just looking at her."

"I was trying to hear the north," you snap. They all look at you like you're crazy. Evil Earth, if only someone else here were Fulcrum-trained. Though this isn't something anyone but a senior would understand, anyway.

Lerna ventures, "Hear . . . the earth? Do you mean *sess?*"

It's so hard to explain with words. You rub your eyes. "No, I mean *hear.* Vibrations. All sound is vibrations, I mean, but . . ." Their expressions grow more confused. You're going to have to contextualize. "The node network is still there," you say. "Alabaster was right. I can sess it if I try, a zone of stillness where the rest of the Equatorials are a seething disaster. Someone *is* keeping them, the node maintainers around Rennanis, alive, so—"

"So this is really them," Cutter says, sounding troubled. "An Equatorial city really has decided to induct us."

"Equatorials don't induct," Ykka says. Her jaw is tight as she speaks, gazing at the scrap of leather in her hand. "They're Old Sanze, or what's left of it. When Sanze wanted something back in the day, Sanze took it."

After a tense silence, they start quietly panicking again. Too many words. You sigh and rub your temples and wish you were alone so you could try again. Or . . .

You blink. Or. You sess the hovering potentiality of the topaz, which drifts in the sky above Castrima-over, where it has been for the past six months, half-hidden amid the ash clouds. Evil

Earth. Alabaster isn't just sessing half the continent; he's using the spinel to do it. You haven't even thought about using an obelisk to extend your reach, but he does it like breathing.

"No one touch me," you say softly. "No one speak to me." Without waiting to see if they understand, you plunge into the obelisk.

(Because, well, some part of you *wants* to do this. Has dreamt of upward-falling water and torrential power for months. You are only human, whatever they say about your kind. It's good to feel powerful.)

Then you're in the topaz and through it and stretching yourself across the world in a breath. No need to be in the ground when the topaz is in air, *is* the air; it exists in states of being that transcend solidity, and thus you are capable of transcending, too; *you* become air. You drift amid the ash clouds and see the Stillness track beneath you in humps of topography and patches of dying forest and threads of roads, all of it grayed over after the long months of the Season. The continent seems tiny and you think, *I can make the equator in the blink of an eye*, but this thought scares you a little. You don't know why. You try not to think—how far of a leap is it from thrilling in such power to using it to destroy the world? (Did Alabaster feel this, when he . . . ?) But you are committed; you have connected; the resonance is complete. You launch yourself northward anyhow.

And then you stutter to a halt. Because there is something much closer than the equator that draws your attention. It is so shocking that you fall out of alignment with the topaz at once, and you are very lucky. There is a struck-glass instant in which you feel the shivering immensity of the obelisk's power and know that you survive only because of fortunate resonances and careful long-dead designers who obviously planned for mistakes like yours, and then you are gasping and back within yourself and babbling before you quite remember what words mean.

"Camp, fire," you say, panting a little. Lerna comes over and crouches in front of you, taking your hands and checking your pulse; you ignore him. This is important. "*Basin.*"

Ykka gets it instantly, sitting up straight and tightening her jaw. Hjarka, too; she's not stupid, or Tonkee would never put up with her. She curses. Lerna frowns, and Cutter looks at all of you in rising confusion. "Did that actually mean something?"

Asshole. "An army," you snap as you recover. But words are hard. "Th-there's a . . . a rusting *army*. In the forest basin. I could. Sess their campfires."

"How many?" Ykka is already getting up, fetching a longknife from a shelf and belting it round her thigh. Hjarka gets up, too, going to the door of Ykka's apartment and pulling open the curtain. You hear her shouting for Esni, the head of the Strongbacks. The Strongbacks sometimes do scouting and supplement the Hunters, but in a situation like this, they are charged primarily with the comm's defense.

You couldn't count all the little blots of heat that pinged on your awareness when you were in the obelisk, but you try to guess. "Maybe a hundred?" That was the campfires, though. How many people around each fire? You guess six or seven apiece. Not a large force, under ordinary circumstances. Any decent quartent governor could field an army ten times that size on relatively short notice. During a Season, though, and for a comm as small as Castrima—whose total population is not much larger—an army of five or six hundred is a dire threat indeed.

"Tettehee," Cutter breathes, sitting back. He's gone paler than usual. You follow him, though. Six months ago, the stand of impaled corpses set up as a warn-off in the forest basin. The comm of Tettehee is beyond the basin, near the mouth of the river that wends through Castrima's territory and ultimately empties into one of the great lakes of the Somidlats. You've heard nothing from Tettehee in months, and the trading party you sent past the warn-off failed to return. This army must have hit Tettehee around that time, then bunkered down there for a while, sending out scouting parties to mark territory. Replenishing stores, rebuilding arms, healing their wounded, maybe sending some of their spoils back north to Rennanis. Now that they've digested Tettehee, they're on the march again.

And somehow, they know Castrima's here. They're saying hello.

Ykka heads outside and shouts alongside Hjarka, and within a few minutes someone is ringing the shake alarm and shouting for a gathering of the household heads at the Flat Top. You've never heard Castrima's shake alarm—comm full of roggas—and it's more annoying than you expected, low and rhythmic and buzzy. You understand why: Amid a bunch of crystalline structures, ringing bells aren't the best idea. Still. You and Lerna and the rest follow Ykka as she strides along a rope bridge and around two larger shafts, her lips pressed together and face grim. By the time she reaches the Flat Top there's a small crowd already there; by the time she yells for someone to stop blowing the rusting alarm and the alarm actually stops, the sheared-off crystal is starting to look dangerously packed with murmuring, anxious people. There's a railing, but still. Hjarka shouts at Esni, and Esni in turn shouts at the Strongbacks amid the gathering, and they move clumsily to turn people away so there won't be any horrible tragedies distracting from the possible horrible tragedy that looms imminent.

When Ykka raises her hands for attention, everyone falls silent instantly. "The situation," she begins, and lays everything out in a few terse sentences.

You respect her for holding nothing back. You respect the people of Castrima, too, for doing nothing more than gasping or murmuring in alarm, and not panicking. But then, they are all good stolid commfolk, and panic has always been frowned upon in the Stillness. The lorists' tales are full of dire warnings about those who cannot master their fear, and few comms will grant such people comm names unless they're wealthy or influential enough to push the issue. Those things tend to sort themselves out once a Season rolls around.

"Rennanis was a big city," says one woman, once Ykka's stopped talking. "Half the size of Yumenes but still millions of people. Can we fight that?"

"It's a Season," Hjarka says, before Ykka can reply. Ykka shoots her a dirty look, but Hjarka shrugs it off. "We have no choice."

"We can fight because of the way Castrima's built," Ykka adds, throwing Hjarka one last quelling look. "They can't exactly come at us from the rear. If push comes to shove, we can block off the tunnels; then nothing can get down here. We can wait them out."

Not forever, though. Not when the comm needs both hunting

and trading to supplement its storecaches and water gardens. You respect Ykka for *not* saying this. There's a somewhat relieved stir.

"Do we have time to send a messenger south to one of our allied comms?" Lerna asks. You can feel him trying to skirt around the supply issue. "Would any of them be willing to help us?"

Ykka snorts at the last question. Lots of other people do, a few throwing pitying looks Lerna's way. It's a Season. But— "Trading's a maybe. We could load up on critical supplies, medicines, and be more ready if there's a siege. The forest basin takes days to get across with a small party; a big group will take a couple of weeks, maybe. Faster if they force-march it, but that's stupid and dangerous on terrain they don't know. We know their scouts are in our territory, but..." She glances at you. "How close are the rest of them?"

You're caught off guard, but you know what she wants. "The bulk of them were near the impaling." That's about halfway across the forest basin.

"They could be here in days," says someone, voice high-pitched with alarm, and many other people take up that murmur. They start getting louder. Ykka raises her hands again, but this time only some of the assembled people go quiet; the rest keep speculating, calculating, and you catch sight of a few people breaking for the bridges, clearly intent upon making their own plans, Ykka be damned. It's not chaos, not quite panic, but there's enough fear in the air to scent it faintly bitter. You get up, intending to move to the center of the gathering with Ykka, to try to add your voice to hers in calling for calm.

But you stop. Because someone is standing in the place you intended to move to.

It's not like with Antimony, or Ruby Hair, or the other stone eaters you've glimpsed around the comm from time to time. Those, for whatever reason, don't like to be seen moving; you'll catch a blur now and again, but then the statue is there, watching you, as if there has always been a statue of a stranger in that position, sculpted by someone long ago.

This stone eater is turning. It keeps turning, letting everyone see and hear it turn, watching as you finally register its presence, the gray granite of its flesh, the undifferentiated slick of its hair, the slightly greater polish of its eyes. Carefully sculpted length and weight of jaw, and its torso is finely carved with male human musculature rather than the suggestion of clothing that most stone eaters adopt. This one obviously wants you to think of it as male, so fine, it's male. He is allover gray, the first stone eater you have seen who looks like nothing more than a statue . . . except that he moves, and keeps moving, as everyone falls silent in surprise. He is taking all of you in, too, with a slight smile on his lips. He's holding something.

You stare as the gray stone eater turns, and as your mind makes out the oddly shaped, bloody thing he holds, it is recent experience that makes you suddenly realize it is an arm. It is a small arm. It is a small arm still partially wrapped in cloth that is familiar, the jacket that you bought a lifetime ago on the road. The red-smeared inhumanly white skin on the hand is familiar, and the size is familiar, even though the lump of splintered bone at the bloody end is clear and glasslike and finely faceted and not bone at all.

Hoa it is Hoa that is Hoa's arm

"I bear a message," says the gray stone eater. The voice is

pleasant, tenor. His mouth does not move, and the words echo up from his chest. This, at least, feels normal, insofar as you are currently capable of feeling normal, as you stare down at that dripping disaster of an arm.

Ykka stirs after a moment, perhaps pulling herself out of shock, too. "From whom?"

He turns to her. "Rennanis." Turn again, eyes shifting from face to face amid the crowd, same as a human would do when trying to make a connection, get a point across. His eyes skim over you as if you aren't there. "We wish you no harm."

You stare at Hoa's arm in his hand.

Ykka is skeptical. "So, the army camped on our doorstep . . . ?"

Turn. He ignores Cutter, too. "We have plentiful food. Strong walls. All yours, if you join our comm."

"Maybe we like being our own comm," Ykka says.

Turn. His gaze settles on Hjarka, who blinks. "You have no meat, and your territory is depleted. You'll be eating each other within a year."

Well, that sets off the murmuring. Ykka shuts her eyes for a moment in pure frustration. Hjarka looks around angrily, as if wondering who has betrayed you.

Cutter says, "Would all of us be adopted into your comm? With our use-castes intact?"

Lerna makes a tight sound. "I don't see how that's the point, Cutter—"

Cutter throws a slashing look at Lerna. "We can't fight an Equatorial city."

"But it *is* a stupid question," Ykka says. Her voice is deceptively mild, but in the part of your mind that is not stunned to silence by *that arm*, you note that she's never backed up Lerna before. You've always gotten the impression she doesn't much like him, and that it's mutual—she's too cold for him, he's too soft for her. This is significant. "If I were these people, I would lie, take us all north, and shove us into a commless buffer-shanty somewhere between an acid geyser and a lava lake. Equatorial comms have done that before, especially when they needed labor. Why should we believe this one's any different?"

The gray stone eater tilts his head. Between that and the little smile on his lips, it's a remarkably human gesture—a look that says, *Oh, aren't you cute.* "We don't have to lie." He lets those pleasant-toned words hang in the air for just the right amount of time. Oh, he's good at this. You see people exchange looks, hear them shift uncomfortably; you feel the pent silence as Ykka has no retort to that. Because it's true.

Then he drops the other boot. "But we have no use for orogenes."

Silence. Shocked stillness. Ykka breaks it by uttering a swift, "Fire-under-Earth." Cutter looks away. Lerna's eyes widen as he grasps the implications of what the stone eater has just done.

"Where is Hoa?" you ask into the silence. It's all you can think about.

The stone eater's eyes slide to you. The rest of his face does not turn. For a stone eater, this is normal body language; for *this* stone eater, it is conspicuous. "Dead," he says. "After leading us here."

"You're lying." You don't even realize you're angry. You don't think about what you're about to do. You just react, like Damaya in the crucibles, like Syenite on the beach. Everything in you crystallizes and sharpens and your awareness facets down to a razor point and you weave the threads that you barely noticed were there and it happens just like with Tonkee's arm; *shiiiiing.* You slice the stone eater's hand off.

It and Hoa's arm drop to the floor. People gasp. There is no blood. Hoa's arm hits the crystal with a loud, meaty thud—it's heavier than it looks—and the stone eater's hand makes a second, even more solid clack, separating from the arm. The cross-section of its wrist is undifferentiated gray.

The stone eater does not seem to react at first. Then you sess the coalescence of something, like the silver threads of magic but *so many.* The hand twitches, then leaps into the air, returning to the wrist-stump as if pulled by strings. He leaves Hoa's arm behind. Then the stone eater turns fully to face you, at last.

"Get out before I chop you into more pieces than you can put back together," you say in a voice that shakes like the earth.

The gray stone eater smiles. It's a full smile, eyes crinkling with crow's feet and lips drawing back from diamond teeth—and marvel of marvels, it actually looks like a smile and not a threat display. Then he vanishes, falling through the surface of the crystal. For an instant you see a gray shadow within the crystal's translucence, his shape blurred and not quite humanoid anymore, though that is probably the angle. Then, faster than you can track with eyes or sessapinae, he shoots down and away.

In the reverberating wake of his leaving, Ykka takes and lets out a deep breath.

"Well," she says, looking around at her people. What she believes to be her people. "Sounds like we need to talk." There is an uneasy stir.

You don't want to hear it. You hurry forward and pick up

Hoa's arm. The thing is heavy as stone; you have to put your legs into it or risk your lower back. You turn and people move out of your way and you hear Lerna say, "Essun?" But you don't want to hear him, either.

There are threads, see. Silver lines that only you can see, flailing and curling forth from the arm's stump, but they shift as you turn. Always pointing in a particular direction. So you follow them. No one follows you, and you don't care what that means. Not at the moment.

The tendrils lead you to your own apartment.

You step through the curtain and stop. Tonkee's not home. Must be either at Hjarka's or up in the green room. There are two more limbs on the floor in front of you, bloody stumps with diamond bones poking forth. No, they are not on the floor; they are *in* the floor, partially submerged in it, one down to the thigh, the other just a calf and foot. Caught, as if climbing out. There are twin trails of blood, thick enough to be worrisome, over the homey rug that you bartered one of Jija's old flintknives for. They go toward your room, so you follow them in. And then you drop the arm. Fortunately it does not land on your foot.

What is left of Hoa crawls toward the floor-mattress that passes for your bed. His other arm is also gone, you don't know where. Hanks of his hair are missing. He pauses when you come in, hearing or sessing you, and he lies still as you circle him and see that his lower jaw has been ripped away. He has no eyes, and there is a . . . a bite, just above his temple. That's why his hair is missing. Something has bitten into his skull like an apple, incising a chunk of flesh and the diamond bone underneath. You can't see what's inside his head for the blood. That's good.

It would frighten you, if you did not immediately understand. Beside your bed is the little cloth-wrapped bundle that he has carried since Tirimo. You hurry to it, open it up, bring it to the ruin of him, and hunker down. "Can you turn over?"

He responds by doing so. For a moment you're stymied by the lack of a lower jaw, and then you think *fuck it* and shove one of the stones from the bundle directly into the ragged hole of Hoa's throat. The feel of his flesh is warm and human as you push it down with your finger until the muscles of his swallowing reflex catch it. (Your gorge rises. You will it back down.) You start to feed him another, but after a few breaths he begins to shiver all over violently. You don't realize you're still sessing magic until suddenly Hoa's body becomes alive with glimmering silver threads, all of them whipping about and curling like the stinging tentacles of ocean creatures from lorists' tales. *Hundreds* of them. You draw back in alarm, but Hoa makes a raw, breathy sound, and you think maybe it means *more*. You push another stone into his throat, and then another. There weren't many left to begin with. When you're down to only three, you hesitate. "You want them all?"

Hoa hesitates, too. You can see that in his body language. You don't understand why he needs them at all; aside from that lashing of magic—he is *made* of it, every inch of him is alive with it, you've never seen anything like this—nothing about his damaged body is improving. Can anyone survive or recover from this degree of damage? He's not human enough for you to even guess. But finally he croaks again. It is a deeper sound than the first. Resigned, maybe, or maybe that is your imagination patterning humanity over the animal sounds of his animal flesh. So you push the last three stones into him.

Nothing happens for a moment. Then.

Silver tendrils billow and swell around him so rapidly, with such frenzy, that you scramble back. You know some of the things that magic can do, and something about this seems altogether wild and uncontrolled. It fills the room, though, and—and you blink. You can *see* it, not just sess it. All of Hoa glimmers now with silver-white light, growing rapidly too bright to look at directly; even a still would be able to see this. You move into the living room, peering through the bedroom door because that seems safer. The instant you cross the room's threshold, the substance of the whole apartment—walls, floor, everywhere there is crystal—shivers for an instant, becoming translucent and *obelisk-unreal*. Your bedroom furniture and belongings float amid the flickering white. There is a soft thump from behind you that makes you jump and whirl, but it's Hoa's legs, which are out of the living room floor and sliding along the trails of blood into your room. The arm you dropped is moving, too, already nudging up against the bright morass of him, becoming bright, too. Leaping to rejoin his body, as the gray stone eater's hand rejoined his wrist.

Something slides up from the floor—no. You see *the floor* slide up, as if it were putty and not crystal, and wrap itself around his body. The light dies when he does it; the material immediately begins to change into something darker. When you blink away the afterimages enough to see, there is something huge and strange and impossible where Hoa once was.

You step back into the bedroom—carefully, because the floor and walls might be solid again, but you know that's possibly a temporary state. The once-smooth crystal is rough beneath your feet. The thing takes up most of the room now, lying next to your disordered bed that is now half submerged in the resolidified floor. It's hot. Your foot tangles briefly in the strap of your half-empty runny-sack, which fortunately is still intact and unmerged with the room. You stoop quickly and grab it; the habits of survival. *Earthfires* it's hot in here. The bed does not catch fire, but you think that's only because it's not directly touching the big thing. You can sess it, whatever it is. No, you know what it is: chalcedony. A huge, oblong lump of gray-green chalcedony, like the outer shell of a geode.

You already know what's happening, don't you? I told you of Tirimo after the Rifting. The far end of the valley, where the shockwave of the shake loosed a geode that then split open like an egg. The geode hadn't been there all along, you realize; this is magic, not nature. Well, perhaps a bit of both. For stone eaters, there's little difference between the two.

And in the morning, after you spend the night at the living room table, where you meant to stay awake and watch the steaming lump of rock but instead fell asleep, it happens again. The cracking open of the geode is loud, explosively violent. A flicker of pressure-driven plasma curls forth and scorches or melts all the belongings you left in the room. Except the runny-sack, since you took it. Good instincts.

You're shaking from being startled awake. Slowly you stand and edge into the room. It's so hot that it's hard to breathe. Like an oven—though the waft of warmth causes the apartment's entry curtain to billow open. Quickly the heat diminishes to only uncomfortable, and not dangerous.

You barely notice. Because what rises from the split in the

geode, moving too human-smoothly at first but rapidly readjusting to a familiar sort of punctuated stillness... is the stone eater from the garnet obelisk.

Hello, again.

* * *

> Our position is thoroughly identified with the physical integrity of the Stillness—for the obvious interest of long-term survival. Maintenance of this land is peculiarly dependent upon seismic equilibrium, and by an imperious law of nature, none but the orogenic can establish such. A blow at their bondage is a blow at the very planet. We rule, therefore, that though they bear some resemblance to we of good and wholesome lineage, and though they must be managed with kind hand to the benefit of both bond and free, any degree of orogenic ability must be assumed to negate its corresponding personhood. They are rightfully to be held and regarded as an inferior and dependent species.
>
> —*The Second Yumenescene Lore Council's Declaration on the Rights of the Orogenically Afflicted*

15

Nassun, in rejection

What I remember of my youth is color. Greenness everywhere. White iridescence. Deep and vital reds. These particular colors linger in my memory, when so much of the rest is thin and pale and nearly gone. There is a reason for that.

* * *

Nassun sits in an office within the Antarctic Fulcrum, suddenly understanding her mother better than ever before.

Schaffa and Umber sit on either side of her. All three of them are holding cups of safe that the Fulcrum people have offered them. Nida is back at Found Moon, because someone must remain to watch over the children there and because she has the hardest time emulating normal human behavior. Umber is so quiet that no one knows what he's thinking. Schaffa's doing all the talking. They've been invited inside to speak with three people who are called "seniors," whatever that means. These seniors wear uniforms that are all black, with neatly buttoned jackets and pleated slacks—ah, so that is why they call Imperial Orogenes blackjackets. They feel all over of power and fear.

One of them is obviously Antarctic-bred, with graying red hair and skin so white that green veins show starkly just underneath. She has horsey teeth and beautiful lips, and Nassun cannot stop staring at both as she talks. Her name is Serpentine, which does not seem to fit her at all.

"Of course we have no new grits coming in," Serpentine says. For some reason she looks at Nassun as she speaks and spreads her hands. The fingers shake slightly. That's been happening since this meeting began. "It's a difficulty we hadn't quite anticipated. If nothing else, it means we have grit dormitories going unused in a time when safe shelter is quite valuable. That would be why we extended an offer to nearby comms to take in their unparented children, those too young to have earned acceptance into a comm. Only sensible, yes? And we took in a few refugees, which would be why we had no choice but to open trade negotiations with the locals for supplies and such. With no resupply coming from Yumenes..." Her expression falters. "Well. It's understandable, isn't it?"

She's whining. Doing it with a gracious smile and impeccable manners, doing it with two other people nodding sagely along with her, but doing it. Nassun isn't sure why these people bother her so much. It has something to do with the whining, and with the falseness of them: They are clearly uncomfortable with the arrival of Guardians, clearly afraid and angry, and yet they pretend courtesy. It makes her think of her mother, who pretended to be kind and loving when Father or anyone else was around, and who was cold and fierce in private. Thinking of the Antarctic Fulcrum as a place populated by endless variants of her mother makes Nassun's teeth and palms and sessapinae itch.

And she can see by the icy placidity of Umber's face, and the brittle-edged friendliness of Schaffa's smile, that the Guardians don't like it, either. "Understandable indeed," Schaffa says. He turns the cup of safe in his hands. The cloudy solution has remained white as it should, but he hasn't taken a single sip. "I imagine the local comms are grateful to you for housing and feeding their surplus population. And it is only sensible that you would put those people to work, too. Guarding your walls. Tending your fields—" He pauses, smiles more widely. "Gardens, I mean."

Serpentine smiles back, and her companions shift uncomfortably. It is something Nassun doesn't understand. The Season hasn't yet taken full hold here in the Antarctic region, so it does seem wise that a comm would plant its greenland and put Strongbacks on its walls and start preparing for the worst. Somehow it is bad that the Antarctic Fulcrum has done this, however. Bad that this Fulcrum is functional at all. Nassun has stopped drinking the cup of safe the seniors gave her, even though she's only had safe a couple of times before and sort of likes being treated like a grown-up—but Schaffa isn't drinking, and that warns her the situation is not really safe.

One of the seniors is a Somidlats woman who could pass for a relative of Nassun's: tall, middling brown, curling thick hair, a body that is thick-waisted and broad-hipped and heavy-thighed. They introduced her, but Nassun can't remember her name. Her orogeny feels the sharpest of the three, though she is the youngest; there are six rings on her long fingers. And she is the one who finally stops smiling and folds her hands and lifts her chin, just a little. It is another thing that reminds Nassun of her mother. Mama often held herself the same way, feeling of soft dignity layered over a core of diamond obstinacy. The obstinacy is what comes to the fore now as the woman says, "I take it you are unhappy, Guardian."

Serpentine winces. The other Fulcrum orogene, a man who introduced himself as Lamprophyre, sighs. Schaffa and Umber's heads tilt in near-unison, Schaffa's smile widening with interest. "Not unhappy," he says. Nassun can tell that he is pleased to be done with the pleasantry. "Merely surprised. It is, after all, standard protocol for any Fulcrum facility to be shut down in the event of a declared Season."

"Declared by whom?" the six-ringed woman asks. "Until your arrival today, there have been no Guardians here to declare anything of the sort. The local comm Leaderships have varied: Some declared Seasonal Law, some are only in lockdown, some are business as usual."

"And had they all declared Seasonal Law," Schaffa says, in that very quiet voice he uses when he knows the answer to a question already and only wants to hear you say it yourself, "would you truly have all killed yourselves? Since, as you note, there are no Guardians here to take care of the matter for you."

Nassun catches herself before she would have started in surprise. Kill themselves? But she is not quite good enough at controlling her orogeny to keep it from twitching where she does not. All three of the Fulcrum people glance at her, and Serpentine smiles thinly. "Careful, Guardian," she says, looking at Nassun but speaking to Schaffa. "Your pet seems uncomfortable with the idea of mass extermination for no reason."

Schaffa says, "I hide nothing from her," and Nassun's surprise is swallowed up by love and pride. He glances at Nassun. "Historically, the Fulcrum has survived on the sufferance of its neighbors, depending on the walls and resources of comms nearby. And as with all who have no viable use during a Season, there is most certainly an expectation that Imperial Orogenes will remove themselves from the competition for resources—so that normal, healthy people have a better chance to survive." He pauses. "And since orogenes are not permitted to exist outside the supervision of a Guardian or the Fulcrum..." He spreads his hands.

"We *are* the Fulcrum, Guardian," says the third senior, whose name Nassun has forgotten. This is a man from some Western Coastal people; he is slender and straight-haired and has a high-cheekboned, nearly concave face. His skin is white, too, but his eyes are dark and cool. His orogeny feels light and many-layered, like mica. "And we are self-sufficient. Quite apart from being a drain on resources, we provide needed services to the nearby communities. We have even—unasked and uncompensated—worked to mitigate the aftershakes of the Rifting on the occasions when they reach this far south. It is because of us that few Antarctic comms have suffered serious harm since the start of this Season."

"Admirable," says Umber. "And clever, making yourselves invaluable. Not a thing your Guardians would have permitted, though. I imagine."

All three of the seniors grow still for a moment. "This is Antarctic, Guardian," says Serpentine. She smiles, though the expression does not reach her eyes. "We are a fraction of the size of the Fulcrum at Yumenes—barely twenty-five ringed orogenes, a handful of mostly grown grits. There were never many Guardians permanently stationed here. Most of what we got were visiting Guardians on circuit, or delivering us new grits. None at all since the Rifting."

"Never many Guardians stationed here," agrees Schaffa, "but there *were* three, as I recall. I knew one." He pauses, and for a fleeting instant his expression goes distant and lost and a little confused. "I remember knowing one." He blinks. Smiles again. "Yet now there are none."

Serpentine is tense. They are all tense, these seniors, in a way that makes the itch at the back of Nassun's mind grow. "We endured several raids by commless bands before we finally put up a wall," Serpentine says. "They died bravely, protecting us."

It's so blatant a lie that Nassun stares at her, mouth open.

"Well," Schaffa says, setting down his cup of safe and letting out a little sigh. "I suppose this went about as well as could be expected."

And even though Nassun has guessed by now what is coming, even though she has seen Schaffa move with a speed that is not humanly possible before, even though the silver within him and Umber ignites like matchflame and blazes through them in the instant just before, she is still caught off guard when Schaffa lunges forward and puts his fist through Serpentine's face.

Serpentine's orogeny dies as she does. But the other two seniors are up and moving in the next instant, Lamprophyre falling backward over his chair to escape Umber's blurring reach for him and the six-ringed woman drawing a blowgun from one sleeve. Schaffa's eyes widen, but his hand is still stuck in Serpentine; he tries to lunge at her, but the corpse is deadweight on his arm. She lifts the gun to her lips.

Before she can get off a puff, Nassun is up and in the earth and beginning to spin a torus that will ice the woman in an instant. The woman jerks in surprise and flexes *something* that shatters Nassun's torus before it can form completely; it is a thing her mother used to do during their practices, if Nassun did something she wasn't supposed to. The shock of this realization causes Nassun to stagger and stumble back.

Her mother learned that trick here, in the Fulcrum, this is how people from the Fulcrum train young orogenes, everything Nassun has known of her mother is tainted by this place and has always been—

But the fleeting distraction is enough. Schaffa rips his hand free of the corpse at last and is across the room in another breath, grabbing the blowgun and snatching it away and stabbing it into the woman's throat before she can recover. She falls to her knees, choking, reaching instinctively for the earth, but then something sweeps the room in a wave and Nassun gasps when suddenly she cannot sess a single thing. The woman gasps, too, then wheezes, scrabbling at her throat. Schaffa grabs her head and breaks her neck with a swift jerk.

Lamprophyre is scrambling backward as Umber stalks him, fumbling at his clothing where some kind of small, heavy object has gotten lodged in cloth. "Evil Earth," he blurts, jerking at the buttons of his jacket. "You're contaminated! Both of you!"

He gets no further, though, because Umber blurs and Nassun flinches as something splatters her cheek. Umber has stomped the man's head in.

"Nassun," Schaffa says, releasing the six-ringed woman's body and staring down at it, "go to the terrace and wait for us there."

"Y-yes, Schaffa," Nassun says. She swallows. She's shaking. She makes herself turn despite this, and walk out of the room. There are approximately twenty-two other ringed orogenes around somewhere, after all, Serpentine said.

The Antarctic Fulcrum isn't much bigger than the town of Jekity. Nassun is leaving the big two-story house that serves as the administrative building. There's also a cluster of tiny cottages that apparently the older orogenes live in, and several long barracks near the big glass-walled greenhouse. Lots of people are around, moving in and out of the barracks and cottages. Few of them wear black, even though some of the civilian-dressed ones feel like orogenes. Beyond the greenhouse is a sloping terrace that hosts a number of small garden plots—too many, altogether, to really qualify as gardens. This is a farm. Most of the plots are planted heavily with grains and vegetables, and there are a number of people out working on them, since it's a nice day and no one knows the Guardians are busily killing everyone in the admin building.

Nassun walks the cobbled path above the terrace briskly, with her head down so that she can concentrate on not stumbling, since she can't sess anything after whatever Schaffa did to the six-ringed woman. She's always known that Guardians can shut down orogeny, but never felt it before. It's hard to walk when she can only perceive the ground with her eyes and feet, and also when she's shaking so hard. Carefully she puts one foot in front of the other and suddenly someone else's feet are just *there* and Nassun pulls up short, her whole body going rigid with shock.

"Watch where you're going," the girl says reflexively. She's thin and white, though with a shock of slate-gray ashblow hair, and she's maybe Nassun's age. She stops, though, when she gets a good look at Nassun. "Hey, there's something on your face. It looks like a dead bug or something. Gross." She reaches up and flicks it off with one finger.

Nassun jerks a little in surprise, then remembers her manners. "Thanks. Uh, sorry for getting in your way."

"It's all right." The girl blinks. "They said some Guardians had come and brought a new grit. Are you the new one?"

Nassun stares in confusion. "G-grit?"

The other girl's eyebrows rise. "Yeah. Trainee? Imperial-Orogene-to-be?" She's carrying a bucket of gardening supplies, which doesn't fit the conversation at all. "The Guardians used to bring kids here before the Season started. That's how I got here."

Technically that's how Nassun got here, too. "The Guardians brought me," she echoes. She is hollow inside.

"Me, too." The girl sobers, then looks away. "Did they break your hand yet?"

Nassun's breath stops in her throat.

At her silence, the girl's expression turns bitter. "Yeah. They do it to every grit at some point. Hand bones or fingers." She shakes her head, then takes a quick, gulping breath. "We're not supposed to talk about it. But it's not you, whatever they say. It's not your fault." Another quick breath. "I'll see you around. I'm Ajae. I don't have an orogene name yet. What's your name?"

Nassun can't think. The sound of Schaffa's fist crushing bone echoes in her head. "Nassun."

"Nice to meet you, Nassun." Ajae nods politely, then moves on, walking down the steps toward a terrace. She hums, swinging her bucket. Nassun stares after her, trying to understand.

Orogene name?

Trying not to understand.

Did they break your hand yet?

This place. This... Fulcrum. Is why her mother broke her hand.

Nassun's hand twitches in phantom pain. She sees again the rock in her mother's hand, rising. Holding a moment. Falling.

Are you sure you can control yourself?

The Fulcrum is why her mother never loved her.

Is why her father does not love her anymore.

Is why her brother is dead.

Nassun watches Ajae wave to a thin older boy, who is busy hoeing. This place. These people, who have no right to exist.

The sapphire isn't far off—hovering over Jekity, where it has been for the two weeks since she and Schaffa and Umber left to travel to the Antarctic Fulcrum. She can sess it in the distance, though it's too far off to see. It seems to flicker as she reaches for it, and for an instant she marvels that she *knows* this somehow. Instinctively she has turned to face it. Line of sight. She doesn't need eyes, or orogeny, to use it.

(This is an orogene's nature, the old Schaffa might have told her, if he still existed. Nassun's kind innately react to all threats the same way: with utterly devastating counterforce. He would have told her this, before breaking her hand to drive home the lesson of control.)

There are so many silver threads in this place. The orogenes are all connected through practice together, shared experience.

DID THEY BREAK YOUR HAND

It is over in the span of three breaths. Then Nassun lets herself fall out of the watery blue, and stands there shaking in its wake. Some while later, Nassun turns and sees Schaffa standing in front of her, with Umber.

"They weren't supposed to be here," she blurts. "You *said*."

Schaffa isn't smiling, and he is still in a way that Nassun knows well. "Did you do this to help us, then?"

Nassun can't think enough to lie. She shakes her head. "This place was wrong," she said. "The Fulcrum is wrong."

"Is it?" It is a test, but Nassun has no idea how to pass it. "Why do you say that?"

"Mama was wrong. The Fulcrum made her that way. She should have been a, a, an, an ally to you," *like me*, she thinks, reminds. "This place made her something else." She cannot articulate it. "This place made her *wrong*."

Schaffa looks at Umber. Umber tilts his head, and for an instant there is a flicker in the silver, a flicker between them. The things lodged in their sessapinae resonate in a strange way. But then Schaffa frowns, and she sees him push back against the silver. It hurts him to do this, but he does it anyway, turning to gaze at her with eyes bright and jaw tight and fresh sweat dotting his brow.

"I think you may be right, little one," is all he says. "It follows:

Put people in a cage and they will devote themselves to escaping it, not cooperating with those who caged them. What happened here was inevitable, I suppose." He glances at Umber. "Still. Their Guardians must have been very lax, to let a group of orogenes get the drop on them. That one with the blowgun . . . born feral, most likely, and taught things she shouldn't have been before being brought here. She was the impetus."

"Lax Guardians," says Umber, watching Schaffa. "Yes."

Schaffa smiles at him. Nassun frowns in confusion. "We've destroyed the threat," Schaffa says.

"Most of it," Umber agrees.

Schaffa acknowledges this with an incline of his head and a faintly ironic air before turning to Nassun. He says, "You were right to do what you did, little one. Thank you for helping us."

Umber is gazing steadily at Schaffa. At the back of Schaffa's neck, specifically. Schaffa suddenly turns to glare back at him, smile gone fixed and body deadly still. After a moment, Umber looks away. Nassun understands then. The silver has gone quiet in Umber, or as quiet as it ever gets in any of the Guardians, but the glimmering lines within Schaffa are still alive, active, tearing at him. He fights them, though, and is prepared to fight Umber, too, if necessary.

For her? Nassun wonders, exults. For her.

Then Schaffa crouches and cups her face in his hands. "Are you well?" he asks. His eyes flick toward the sky to the east. The sapphire.

"Fine," Nassun says, because she is. Connecting with the obelisk was much easier this time, partly because it was not a surprise, and partly because she is growing used to the sudden advent of strangeness in her life. The trick is to let yourself fall into it, and fall at the same speed, and think like a big column of light.

"Fascinating," he says, and then gets to his feet. "Let's go."

So they leave the Antarctic Fulcrum behind, with new crops greening in its fields and cooling corpses in its administrative building and a collection of shining, multi-colored human statues scattered about its gardens and barracks and walls.

* * *

But in the days that follow, as they walk the road and forest trails between the Fulcrum and Jekity, sleeping each night in strangers' barns or around their own fires...Nassun thinks.

She has nothing to do but think, after all. Umber and Schaffa do not speak to one another, and there is a new tension between them. She understands it enough to take care never to be alone in Umber's presence, which is easy because Schaffa takes care never to let her be. This is not strictly necessary; Nassun thinks that what she did to Eitz and the people in the Antarctic Fulcrum, she can probably do to Umber. Using an obelisk is not sessing, the silver is not orogeny, and thus not even a Guardian is safe from what she can do. She sort of likes that Schaffa goes with her to the bathhouse, though, and forgoes sleep—Guardians can do that, apparently—to keep watch over her at night. It feels nice to have someone, anyone, protecting her again.

But. She thinks.

It troubles Nassun that Schaffa has damaged himself in the eyes of his fellow Guardians by choosing not to kill her. It troubles her more that he suffers, gritting his teeth and pretending that this is another smile, even as she sees the silver flex and burn within him. It never stops doing so now, and he will not let her ease his pain because this makes her slow and tired the next day. She watches him endure it, and hates the little thing in his head that hurts him so. It gives him power, but what good is power if it comes on a spiked leash?

"Why?" she asks him one night as they camp on a flat, elevated white slab of something that is neither metal nor stone and which is all that remains of some deadciv ruin. There have been some signs of raiders or commless in the area, and the tiny comm they stayed at the night before warned them to be wary, so the elevation of the slab will at least afford them plenty of advance warning of an attack. Umber is gone, off setting snares for their breakfast. Schaffa has used the opportunity to lie down on his bedroll while Nassun keeps watch, and she does not want to keep him awake. But she needs to know. "Why is that thing in your head?"

"It was put there when I was very young," he says. He sounds weary. Fighting the silver for days on end without sleep is taking its toll. "There was no 'why' for me; it was simply the way things had to be."

"But..." Nassun does not want to be annoying by asking why again. "*Did* it have to be? What is it for?"

He smiles, though his eyes are shut. "We are made to keep the world safe from the dangers of your kind."

"I know that, but..." She shakes her head. "*Who* made you?"

"Me, specifically?" Schaffa opens one eye, then frowns a little. "I... don't remember. But in general, Guardians are made by other Guardians. We are found, or bred, and given over to Warrant for training and... alteration."

"And who made the Guardian before you, and the one before that? Who did it *first*?"

He is silent for a time: trying to remember, she guesses from his expression. That something is very wrong with Schaffa, chiseling holes in his memories and putting fault-line-heavy pressure on his thoughts, is something Nassun simply accepts. He is what he is. But she needs to know why he is the way he is . . . and more importantly, she wants to know how to make him better.

"I don't know," he says finally, and she knows he is done with the conversation by the way he exhales and shuts his eyes again. "In the end, the why does not matter, little one. Why are you an orogene? Sometimes we must simply accept our lot in life."

Nassun decides to shut up then, and a few moments later Schaffa's body relaxes into sleep for the first time in days. She keeps watch diligently, extending her newly recovered sense of the earth to catch the reverberations of small animals and other moving things in the immediate vicinity. She can sess Umber, too, still moving methodically at the edge of her range as he sets up his snares, and because of him she weaves a thread of the silver into her web of awareness. He can evade her sessing, but not that. It will catch any commless, too, should they sneak into arrow or harpoon range. She will not let Schaffa be injured as her father was injured.

Aside from something heavy and warm that treads along on all fours not far from Umber, probably foraging, there is nothing of concern nearby. Nothing—

—except. Something very strange. Something . . . immense? No, its boundaries are small, no bigger than those of a mid-sized rock, or a person. But it is directly underneath the white not-stone slab. Under her feet, practically, barely more than ten feet down.

As if noticing her attention, it moves. This feels like the movement of the world. Involuntarily Nassun gasps and leans away, even though nothing changes but the gravity around her, and that only a little. The immensity whips away suddenly, as if it senses her scrutiny. It doesn't go far, however, and a moment later, the immensity moves again: up. Nassun blinks and opens her eyes to see a statue standing at the edge of the slab, which was not there before.

Nassun is not confused. Once, after all, she wanted to be a lorist; she has spent hours listening to tales of stone eaters and the mysteries that surround their existence. This one does not look as she thought it would. In the lorist tales, stone eaters have marble skin and jewel hair. This one is entirely gray, even to the "whites" of his eyes. He is bare-chested and muscular, and he is smiling, lips drawn back from teeth that are clear and sharp-faceted.

"You're the one who stoned the Fulcrum, a few days ago," says his chest.

Nassun swallows and glances at Schaffa. He's a heavy sleeper, and the stone eater didn't speak loudly. If she yells, Schaffa will probably wake—but what can a Guardian do against such a creature? She isn't even sure she can do anything with the silver; the stone eater is a blazing morass of it, swirls and whirls of thread all tangled up inside him.

The lore, however, is clear on one thing about stone eaters:

They do not attack without provocation. So: "Y-yes," she says, keeping her voice low. "Is that a problem?"

"Not at all. I wanted only to express my admiration for your work." His mouth does not move. Why is he smiling so much? Nassun is more certain with every passing breath that the expression is not *just* a smile. "What is your name, little one?"

She bristles at the *little one*. "Why?"

The stone eater steps forward, moving slowly. This sounds like the grind of a millstone, and looks as wrong as a moving statue should look. Nassun flinches in revulsion, and he stills. "Why did you stone them?"

"They were wrong."

The stone eater steps forward again, onto the slab. Nassun half expects the slab to crack or tilt beneath the creature's terrible weight, which she knows is immense. He is a mountain, compacted into the size and shape of a human being. The slab of deadciv material does not crack, however, and now the creature is close enough for her to see the fine detailing of his individual hair strands.

"*You* were wrong," he says, in his strange echoing voice. "The people of the Fulcrum, and the Guardians, are not to blame for the things they do. You wanted to know why your Guardian must suffer as he does. The answer is: He doesn't have to."

Nassun stiffens. Before she can demand to know more, the stone eater's head turns toward him. There is a flicker of... something. An adjustment too infinitely fine to see or sess, and...and suddenly, the alive, vicious throb of silver within Schaffa dies into silence. Only that dark, needle-like blot in his sessapinae remains active, and immediately Nassun sesses its effort to re-assert control. For the moment, though, Schaffa exhales softly and relaxes further into sleep. The pain that has been grinding at him for days is gone, for now.

Nassun gasps—softly. If Schaffa has the chance to truly rest at last, she will not destroy it. Instead she says to the stone eater, "How did you do that?"

"I can teach you. I can teach you how to fight his tormentor, his *master*, too. If you wish."

Nassun swallows hard. "Y-yeah. I wish." She isn't stupid, though. "In exchange for what?"

"Nothing. If you fight his master, then you fight my enemy, too. It will make us . . . allies."

She knows now that the stone eater has been lurking nearby, listening in on her, but she doesn't care anymore. To save Schaffa . . . She licks her lips, which taste faintly of sulfur. The ash haze has been getting thicker in recent weeks. "Okay," she says.

"What is your name?" If it's been listening, it knows who she is. This is a gesture toward alliance.

"Nassun. And you?"

"I have no name, or many. Call me what you wish."

He needs a name. Alliances don't work without names, do they? "S-Steel." It's the first thing that pops into her mind. Because he's so gray. "Steel?"

The sense that he does not care lingers. "I will come to you later," Steel says. "When we can speak uninterrupted."

An instant later he is gone, into the earth, and the mountain vanishes from her awareness in seconds. A moment later,

Umber emerges from the forest around the deadciv slab and begins walking up the hill toward her. She's actually glad to see him, even though his gaze sharpens as he draws nearer and sees that Schaffa is asleep. He stops three paces away, more than close enough for a Guardian's speed.

"I'll kill you if you try anything," Nassun says, nodding solemnly. "You know that, right? Or if you wake him up."

Umber smiles. "I know you'll try."

"I'll try and I'll actually do it."

He sighs, and there is great compassion in his voice. "You don't even know how dangerous you are. To far, far more than me."

She doesn't, and that bothers her a lot. Umber does not act out of cruelty. If he sees her as a threat, there must be some reason for it. But it doesn't matter.

"Schaffa wants me alive," she says. "So I live. Even if I have to kill you."

Umber appears to consider this. She glimpses the quick flicker of the silver within him and knows, suddenly and instinctively, that she's no longer talking to Umber, exactly.

His master.

Umber says, "And if Schaffa decides you should die?"

"Then I die." That's what the Fulcrum got wrong, she feels certain. They treated the Guardians as enemies, and maybe they once were, like Schaffa said. But allies must trust in one another, be vulnerable to one another. Schaffa is the only person in the world who loves Nassun, and Nassun will die, or kill, or remake the world, for his sake.

Slowly, Umber inclines his head. "Then I will trust in your

love for him," he says. For an instant there is an echo in his voice, in his body, through the ground, reverberating away, so deep. "For now." With that, he moves past her and sits down near Schaffa, assuming a guard stance himself.

Nassun does not understand Guardian reasoning, but she's learned one thing about them over the months: They do not bother to lie. If Umber says he will trust Schaffa—no. Trust *Nassun's love for Schaffa*, because there is a difference. But if Umber says this has meaning to him, then she can rely on that.

So she lies down on her own bedroll and relaxes in spite of everything. She doesn't sleep for some while, though. Nerves, maybe.

Night falls. The evening is clear, apart from the faint haze of ash blowing from the north, and a few broken, pearled clouds that periodically drift southward along the breeze. The stars come out, winking through the haze, and Nassun stares at them for a long while. She's begun to drift, her mind finally relaxing toward sleep, when belatedly she notices that one of the tiny white lights up there is moving in a different direction from the rest—downward, sort of, while the other stars march west to east across the sky. Slow. Hard to unsee it now that she's made it out. It's a little bigger and brighter than the rest, too. Strange.

Nassun rolls over to turn her back to Umber, and sleeps.

* * *

These things have been down here for an age of the world. Foolish to call them bones. They go to powder when we touch them.

But stranger than the bones are the murals. Plants I've never seen, something that might be a language but it just looks like shapes and wiggling. And one: a great round white thing amid the stars, hanging over a landscape. Eerie. I didn't like it. I had the blackjacket crumble the mural away.

—Journal of Journeywoman Fogrid Innovator Yumenes. Archives of the Geneer Licensure, Equatorial East

16

you meet an old friend, again

I WANT TO KEEP TELLING THIS as I have: in your mind, in your voice, telling you what to think and know. Do you find this rude? It is, I admit. Selfish. When I speak as just myself, it's difficult to feel like part of you. It is lonelier. Please; let me continue a bit longer.

* * *

You stare at the stone eater that has burst forth from the chalcedony chrysalis. It stands hunched and perfectly still, watching you sidelong through the slight heat-waver of the air around the split geode. Its hair is as you remember from that half-real, half-dream moment within the garnet obelisk: a frozen splash, what happens to ashblow hair when a hard gust of wind lifts it up and back. Translucent white-ish opal now instead of simply white. But unlike the fleshly form that you grew to know, this stone eater's "skin" is as black as the night sky once was before the Season. What you thought were cracks back then, you now realize are actually white and silver marbling veins. Even the elegant drape of pseudo-clothing wrapped around the body, a simple chiton that hangs off one shoulder, is marbled black. Only the eyes lack the marbling, the whites now matte smooth darkness. The irises are still icewhite. They stand out from the black face, stark and so atavistically disturbing that it actually takes you a moment to realize the face around it is still Hoa's.

Hoa. *He* is older, you see at once; the face is that of a young man and not a boy. Still too wide, with too narrow a mouth, racially nonsensical. You can read anxiety in those frozen features, though, because you learned to read it on a face that was once softer and designed to elicit your compassion.

"Which was the lie?" you ask. It is the only thing you can think to ask.

"The lie?" The voice is a man's now. The same voice, but in the tenor range. Coming from his chest somewhere.

You step into the room. It's still unpleasantly hot, though cooling off quickly. You're sweating anyway. "Your human shape, or this?"

"Both have been true at different times."

"Ah, yes. Alabaster said all of you were human. Once, anyway."

There is a moment of silence. "Are you human?"

At this, you cannot help but laugh once. "Officially? No."

"Never mind what others think. What do you feel yourself to be?"

"Human."

"Then so am I."

He stands steaming between the halves of a giant rock from which he just hatched. "Uh, not anymore."

"Should I take your word for that? Or listen to what I feel myself to be?"

You shake your head, walking as far as you can around the geode. Inside it there is nothing; it's a thin stone shell bare of crystals or the usual precipitant lining. Probably doesn't qualify as a geode, then. "How'd you end up in an obelisk?"

"Pissed off the wrong rogga."

This surprises you into a laugh, which makes you stop and stare at him. It's an uncomfortable laugh. He's watching you the way he always used to, all eyes and hope. Should it really matter that the eyes are so strange now?

"I didn't know that could be done," you say. "Trapping a stone eater, I mean."

"You could do it. It's one of the only ways to stop one of us."

"Not kill you, obviously."

"No. There's only one way to do that."

"Which is?"

He flicks to face you. This seems instantaneous; suddenly the statue's pose is completely different, serene and upright, with one hand raised in . . . invitation? Appeal? "Are you planning to kill me, Essun?"

You sigh and shake your head and extend a hand to touch one of the stone halves, out of curiosity.

"Don't. It's still too hot for your flesh." He pauses. "This is how I get clean, without soap."

A day along the side of the road, south of Tirimo. A boy who stared at a bar of soap in confusion, then delight. It's still him. You can't shake it off. So you sigh and also let go of the part of yourself that wants to treat him as something else, something frightening, something other. He's Hoa. He wants to eat you, and he tried to help you find your daughter even though he failed. There's an intimacy in these facts, however strange they are, that means something to you.

You fold your arms and pace slowly around the geode, and him. His eyes follow. "So who kicked your ass?" He has regenerated the eyes that were missing, and the lower jaw. The limbs that had been torn off are part of him again. There's still blood in the living room, but whatever there had been in your bedroom is now gone, along with a layer of the floor and walls. Stone eaters are said to have control over the very smallest particles of matter. Simple enough to reappropriate one's own detached substance, repurpose unused surplus material. You guess.

"A dozen or so of my kind. Then one in particular."

"That many?"

"They were children to me. How many children would it take to overwhelm you?"

"*You* were a child."

"I looked like a child." His voice softens. "I only did that for you."

There is a greater difference between this Hoa and that Hoa than their states of being. When adult Hoa says things like this, the words have an entirely different texture from when child Hoa said them. You're not certain you like that texture.

"So you've been off getting into fights all this time," you say, adjusting the subject back toward comfort. "There was a stone eater at the Flat Top. A gray—"

"Yes." You didn't think it was possible for a stone eater to look disgruntled, but Hoa does. "That one isn't a child. He was the one who defeated me, finally, though I managed to escape without too much damage." You marvel for a moment that he thinks having all his limbs and jaw torn off is not much damage. But you're a little glad, too. The gray stone eater hurt Hoa, and you hurt him back. Ephemeral revenge, maybe, but it makes you feel like you look out for your own.

Hoa still sounds defensive. "It was also... unwise for me to face him while clothed in human flesh."

It's too damned hot in the room. Mopping sweat from your face, you move into the living room, push aside and tie off the main-door curtain so cooler air will circulate in more easily, and sit down at the table. By the time you turn back, Hoa is in the door of your bedroom, framed beautifully by the arch of it: study of a youth in wary contemplation.

"Is that why you changed back? To face him?" You didn't see the bit of rag that contained his rocks while you were in the bedroom. Maybe it caught fire and is just charred cloth amid the rest, purpose served.

"I changed back because it was time." There's that tone of resignation again. He sounded that way when you first realized what he was. Like he knows he's lost something in your eyes, and he can't get it back, and he has no choice but to accept that—but he doesn't have to like it. "I could have kept that shape only for a limited time. I made a choice to decrease the time, and increase the chance you will survive."

"Oh?"

Beyond him, in your room, you suddenly notice that the leftover shell of his, er, egg, is melting. Sort of. It is dissolving and lightening in color and merging back into the clear material of the crystal, parting around the detritus of your belongings as it rejoins its former substance and solidifies again. You stare at that instead of him for a moment, fascinated.

Until he says, "They want you dead, Essun."

"They—" You blink. "Who?"

"Some of my kind. Some merely want to use you. I won't let them."

You frown. "Which? You won't let them kill me, or you won't let them use me?"

"*Either.*" The echoing voice grows sharp suddenly. You remember him crouching, baring his teeth like some feral beast. It occurs to you, with the suddenness of an epiphany, that you haven't seen as many stone eaters around lately. Ruby Hair, Butter Marble, Ugly Dress, Toothshine, all the regulars; not a glimpse in months. Ykka even remarked on the sudden absence of "hers."

"You ate her," you blurt.

There is a pause. "I've eaten many," Hoa says. It is inflectionless.

You remember him giggling and calling you weird. Curling against you to sleep. Earthfires, you can't deal with this.

"Why me, Hoa?" You spread your hands. They are ordinary, middle-aged woman hands. A bit dry. You helped with the leather-tanning crew a few days ago, and the solution made your skin crack and peel. You've been rubbing them with some of the nuts you got in the previous week's comm share, even though fat is precious and you should be eating it rather than using it for your vanity. In your right palm there is a small, white, thumbnail-shaped crescent. On cold days that hand's bones ache. Ordinary woman hands.

"There's nothing special about me," you say. "There must be other orogenes with the potential to access the obelisks. Earthfires, Nassun—" No. "Why are you *here*?" You mean, why has he attached himself to you.

He is silent for a moment. Then: "You asked if I was all right."

This makes no sense for a moment, and then it does. Allia. A beautiful sunny day, a looming disaster. As you hovered in agony amid the cracked, dissonant core of the garnet obelisk, you saw him for the first time. How long had he been in that thing? Long enough for it to be buried beneath Seasons' worth of sediment and coral growth. Long enough to be forgotten, like all the dead civilizations of the world. And then you came along and asked how he was doing. Evil Earth, you thought you hallucinated that.

You take a deep breath and get up, going to the entrance of the apartment. The comm is quiet, as far as you can tell. Some people are going about their usual business, but there are fewer of them around than usual. The ones following routine are no proof of peace; people went about their business in Tirimo, too, right before they tried to kill you.

Tonkee didn't come home again last night, but this time you're not so sure that she's with Hjarka or up in the green room. There is a catalyst alive in Castrima now, accelerating unseen chemical reactions, facilitating unexpected outcomes. *Join us and live*, the gray one had told them, *but not with your roggas*.

Will the people of Castrima stop to think that no Equatorial comm really wants a sudden influx of mongrel Midlatters, and at best will make slaves or meat of them? Your mothering instinct is alive with warning. *Look after your own*, it whispers in the back of your mind. *Gather them close and guard them well. You know what happens when you turn your back for even a minute.*

You shoulder the runny-sack that's still in your hand. Keeping it with you isn't even a question at this point. Then you turn to Hoa. "Come with me."

Hoa's suddenly smiling again. "I don't walk anymore, Essun."

Oh. Right. "I'm going to Ykka's, then. Meet me there."

He does not nod, simply vanishes. No wasted movement. Eh, you'll get used to it.

People don't look at you as you cross the bridges and walkways of the comm. The center of your back itches from their stares as you pass. You cannot help thinking of Tirimo again.

Ykka's not in her apartment. You look around, follow the patterns of movement in the comm with your eyes, and finally head toward the Flat Top. She cannot still be there. You've gone home, watched a child turn into a stone eater, slept several hours. She can't be.

She is. You see that only a few people are still on the Flat Top now—a gaggle of maybe twenty, sitting or pacing, looking angry and exasperated and troubled. For the twenty you see, there are surely another hundred gathering in apartments and the baths and the storage rooms, having the same conversation in hushed tones with small groups. But Ykka is here, sitting on one of the divans that someone has brought from her apartment, still talking. She's hoarse, you realize as you draw close. Visibly exhausted. But still talking. Something about supply lines from one of the southern allied comms, which she's directing at a man who is walking in circles with his arms folded, scoffing at everything she says. It's fear; he's not listening. Ykka's trying to reason with him anyway. It's ridiculous.

Look after your own.

You step around people—some of whom flinch away from you—and stop beside her. "I need to talk to you in private."

Ykka stops midsentence and blinks up at you. Her eyes are red and sticky-dry. She hasn't had any water for a while. "What about?"

"It's important." As a sop to courtesy you nod to the people sitting around her. "Sorry."

She sighs and rubs her eyes, which just makes them redder. "Fine." She gets up, then pauses to face the remaining people. "Vote's tomorrow morning. If I haven't convinced you . . . well. You know what to do, then."

They watch in silence as you lead her away.

Back in her apartment, you pull the front curtain shut and open the one that leads into her private rooms. Not much to this space to indicate her status: She's got two pallets and a lot of pillows, but her clothes are just in a basket, and the books and scrolls on one side of the room are just stacked on the floor. No bookcases, no dresser. The food from her comm share is stacked haphazardly against one wall, beside a familiar gourd that the Castrimans tend to use for storing drinking water. You snag the gourd with your elbow and pick from the food pile a dried orange, a stick of dry bean curd that Ykka's been soaking with some mushrooms in a shallow pan, and a small slab of salt fish. It's not exactly a meal, but it's nutrition. "On the bed," you say, gesturing with your chin and bringing the food to her. You hand her the gourd first.

Ykka, who has observed all this in increasing irritation, snaps, "You're not my type. Is this why you dragged me here?"

"Not exactly. But while you're here, you need to rest." She looks mutinous. "You can't convince anyone of anything—" Let alone people whose hate can't be reasoned with. "—if you're too exhausted to think straight."

She grumbles, but it is a measure of how tired she is that she actually goes to the bed and sits down on its edge. You nod at the gourd, and she dutifully drinks—three quick swallows and down for now, as the lorists advise after dehydration. "I stink. I need a bath."

"Should've thought of that before you decided to try to talk down a brewing lynch mob." You take the gourd and push the dish of food into her hand. She sighs and starts grimly chewing.

"They're not going to—" She doesn't get far into that lie, though, before she flinches and stares at something beyond you. You know before you turn: Hoa. "Okay, no, not in my rusting room."

"I told him to meet us here," you say. "It's Hoa."

"You told—it's—" Ykka swallows hard, stares a moment longer, then finally resumes eating the orange. She chews slowly, her gaze never leaving Hoa. "Got tired of playing the human, then? Not sure why you bothered; you were too weird to pass."

You go over to the wall near the bedroom door and sit down against it, on the floor. The runny-sack has to come off for this, but you make sure to keep it near to hand. To Ykka you say,

"You've talked to the other members of your council and half your comm, still and rogga and native and newcomer. The perspective you're missing is theirs." You nod at Hoa.

Ykka blinks, then eyes Hoa with new interest. "I *did* ask you to sit on my council once."

"I can't speak for my kind any more than you can for yours," Hoa says. "And I had more important things to do."

You see Ykka blink at his voice and blatantly stare at him. You wave a hand at Hoa wearily. Unlike Ykka, you've slept, but it wasn't exactly quality sleep, while you sat in a sweltering apartment waiting for a geode to hatch. "Speaking what you know will help." And then, prompted by some instinct, you add, "Please."

Because somehow, you think he's reticent. His expression hasn't changed. His posture is the one he showed you last, the young man in repose with one hand upraised; he's changed his location, but not his position. Still.

The proof of his reticence comes when he says, "Very well." It's all in the tone. But fine, you can work with reticent.

"What does the gray stone eater want?" Because you're pretty rusting sure he doesn't really want Castrima to join some Equatorial comm. Human nation-state politics just wouldn't mean much to them, unless it was in service to some other goal. The people of Rennanis are his pawns, not the other way around.

"There are many of us now," Hoa replies. "Enough to be called a people in ourselves and not merely a mistake."

At this apparent non sequitur, you exchange a look with Ykka, who looks back at you as if to say, *He's your mess, not mine*. Maybe it's relevant somehow. "Yes?" you prompt.

"There are those of my kind who believe this world can safely bear only one people."

Oh, Evil Earth. This is what Alabaster talked about. How had he described it? Factions in an ancient war. The ones who wanted people . . . neutralized.

Like the stone eaters themselves, 'Baster had said.

"You want to wipe us out," you say. Whisper. "Or . . . change us into stone? Like what's happening to Alabaster?"

"Not all of us," Hoa says softly. "And not all of you."

A world of only stone people. The thought of it makes you shiver. You envision falling ash and skeletal trees and creepy statues everywhere, some of the latter moving. How? They are unstoppable, but until now they've only preyed on each other. (That you know of.) Can they turn all of you into stone, like Alabaster? And if they wanted to wipe humankind out, shouldn't they have been able to manage it before now?

You shake your head. "This world *has* borne two people, for Seasons. Three, if you count orogenes; the stills do."

"Not all of us are content with that." His voice is very soft now. "Such a rare thing, the birth of a new one of our kind. We wear on endlessly, while you rise and spawn and wilt like mushrooms. It's hard not to envy. Or covet."

Ykka is shaking her head in confusion. Though her voice holds its usual unflappable attitude, you see a little frown of wonder between her brows. Her mouth pulls to one side, though, as if she cannot help but show at least a little disgust. "Fine," she says. "So stone eaters used to be us, and now you want to kill us. Why should we trust you?"

"Not 'stone eaters.' Not all of us want the same thing. Some like things as they are. Some even want to make the world better…though not all agree on what that means." Instantly his posture changes—hands out, palms up, shoulders lifted in a *What can you do?* gesture. "We're people."

"And what do *you* want?" you ask. Because he didn't answer Ykka's question, and you noticed.

Those silver irises flick over to you, stay. You think you see wistfulness in his still face. "The same thing I've always wanted, Essun. To help you. Only that."

You think, *Not everyone agrees on what "help" means.*

"Well, this is touching," Ykka says. She rubs her tired eyes. "But you're not getting to the point. What does Castrima being destroyed have to do with…giving the world one people? What's this gray man up to?"

"I don't know." Hoa's still looking at you. It's not as unnerving as it should be. "I tried to ask him. It didn't go well."

"Guess," you say. Because you know full well there's a reason he asked the gray man in the first place.

Hoa's eyes shift down. Your distrust hurts. "He wants to make sure the Obelisk Gate is never opened again."

"The what?" Ykka asks. But you're leaning your head back against the wall, floored and horrified and wondering. Of course. *Alabaster.* What easier way to wipe out people who depend on food and sunlight to survive than to simply let this Season wear on until they are extinct? Leaving nothing but the stone eaters to inherit the darkening Earth. And to make sure it happens, kill the only person with the power to end it.

Only person besides you, you realize with a chill. But no. You can manipulate an obelisk, but you haven't got a clue how to activate two hundred of the rusting things at once. And can Alabaster do it anymore? Every use of orogeny kills him slowly. Flaking rust—*you're* the only one left who even has the potential to open the Gate. But if Gray Man's pet army kills both of you, his purpose is served either way.

"It means Gray Man wants to wipe out orogenes in particular," you say to Ykka. You're abbreviating heavily, not lying. That's what you tell yourself. That's what you need to tell Ykka, so that she never learns that orogenes have the potential power to save the world, and so that she never attempts to access an obelisk herself. This is what Alabaster must have constantly had to do with you—telling you some of the truth because you deserve it, but not enough that you'll skewer yourself on it. Then you think of another bone you can throw. "Hoa was trapped in an obelisk for a while. He said it's the only thing that can stop them."

Not the only way, he'd said. But maybe Hoa's giving you only the safe truths, too.

"Well, shit," Ykka says, annoyed. "You can do obelisk stuff. Throw one at him."

You groan. "That wouldn't work."

"What would, then?"

"I have no idea! That's what I've been trying to learn from Alabaster all this time." And failing, you don't want to say. Ykka can guess it, anyway.

"Great." Ykka abruptly seems to wilt. "You're right; I need to sleep. I had Esni mobilize the Strongbacks to secure weapons in the comm. Ostensibly they're making them ready for use if we have to fight off these Equatorials. In truth..." She shrugs, sighs, and you understand. People are frightened right now. Best not to tempt fate.

"You can't trust the Strongbacks," you say softly.

Ykka looks up at you. "Castrima isn't wherever you came from."

You want to smile, though you don't because you know how ugly the smile will be. You're from so many places. In every one of them you learned that roggas and stills can never live together. Ykka shifts a little at the look on your face anyway. She tries again: "Look, how many other comms would've let me live after learning what I was?"

You shake your head. "You were useful. That worked for the Imperial Orogenes, too." But being useful to others is not the same thing as being equal.

"Fine, then I'm useful. We all are. Kill or exile the roggas and we lose Castrima-under. Then we're at the mercy of a bunch of people who would as soon treat *all of us* like roggas, just because our ancestors couldn't pick a race and stick to it—"

"You keep saying 'we,' " you say. It is gentle. It bothers you to puncture her illusions.

She stops, and a muscle in her jaw flexes once or twice. "Stills *learned* to hate us. They can learn differently."

"Now? With an enemy literally at the gate?" You're so tired. So tired of all this shit. "Now is when we'll see the worst of them."

Ykka watches you for a long moment. Then she slumps—completely, her back bowing and her head hanging and her ash-blow hair sliding off to the sides of her neck until it looks utterly ridiculous, a butterfly mane. It hides her face. But she draws in a long, weary breath, and it sounds almost like a sob. Or a laugh.

"No, Essun." She rubs her face. "Just...no. Castrima is my home, same as theirs. I've worked for it. Fought for it. Castrima wouldn't be here if not for me—and probably some of the other roggas who risked themselves to keep it all going, over the years. I'm not giving up."

"It isn't giving up to look out for yourself—"

"*Yes. It is.*" She lifts her head. It wasn't a sob or a laugh. She's furious. Just not at you. "You're saying these people—my parents, my creche teachers, my friends, my lovers—You're saying just leave them to their fate. You're saying they're nothing. That they're not people at all, just beasts whose nature it is to kill. You're saying roggas are nothing but, but *prey* and that's all we'll ever be! No! I won't accept that."

She sounds so determined. It makes your heart ache, because you felt the same way she did, once. It would be nice to still feel that way. To have some hope of a real future, a real community, a real life...but you have lost three children relying on stills' better nature.

You grab the runny-sack and get up to leave, rubbing a hand over your locs. Hoa vanishes, reading your cue that the conversation is over. Later, then. When you're almost at the curtain, though, Ykka stops you with what she says.

"Pass the word around," she tells you. The emotion is gone from her voice. "No matter what happens, *we* can't start anything." Loaded into that delicate emphasis is an acknowledgment that orogenes are the *we* she means, this time. "We shouldn't even finish it. Fighting back could set off a mob. Only talk to the others in small groups. Person to person's best, if you can, so no one *thinks* we're getting together to conspire. Make sure the children know all this. Make sure none of them are ever alone."

Most of the orogene children do know how to defend themselves. The techniques you taught them work just as well for deterring or stopping attackers as for icing boilbug nests. But Ykka's right: There are too few of you to fight back—not without destroying Castrima, a pyrrhic victory. It means that some orogenes are going to die. You're going to *let* them die, even if you could save them. And you did not think Ykka cold enough to think this way.

Your surprise must show on your face. Ykka smiles. "I have hope," she says, "but I'm not stupid. If you're right, and things get hopeless, then we don't go without a fight. We make them regret turning on us. But up to that point of no return . . . I hope you're not right."

You know you're right. The belief that orogenes will never be anything but the world's meat dances amid the cells of you, like magic. It isn't fair. You just want your life to matter.

But you say: "I hope I'm not right, too."

* * *

The dead have no wishes.

—Tablet Three, "Structures," verse six

17

Nassun, versus

It has been so long since Nassun was proud of herself that when she becomes capable of healing Schaffa, she runs all the way through town and up to Found Moon to tell him.

"Healing" is how she thinks of it. She has spent the past few days out in the forest, practicing her new skill. It is not always easy to detect the wrongness in a body; sometimes she must carefully follow the threads of silver within a thing to find its knots and warps. The ashfalls have grown more frequent and sustained lately, and most of the forest is patchy with grayness, some plants beginning to wilt or go dormant in response. This is normal for them, and the silver threads prove this by their uninterrupted flow. Yet when Nassun goes slowly, looks carefully, she can usually find things for which change is not normal or healthy. The grub beneath a rock that has a strange growth along its side. The snake—venomous and more vicious now that a Season has begun, so she only examines it from a distance—with a broken vertebra. The melon vine whose leaves are growing in a convex shape, catching too much ash, instead of concavity, which would shake the ash off. The few ants in a nest who have been infected by a parasitic fungus.

She practices extraction of the wrongness on these things, and many others. It's a difficult trick to master—like performing surgery using only thread, without ever touching the patient. She learns how to make the edge of one thread grow very sharp, and how to loop and lasso with another, and how to truncate a third thread and use the burning tip of it to cauterize. She gets the growth off the grub, but it dies. She stitches together the edges of broken bone within the snake, though this only speeds what was already happening naturally. She finds the parts of the plant that are saying *curve up* and convinces them to say *curve down*. The ants are best. She cannot get all or even most of the fungus out of them, but she can sear the connections in their brains that make them behave strangely and spread the infection. She's very, very glad to have brains to work on.

The culmination of Nassun's practice occurs when commless raiders strike again, one morning as dew still dampens the ash and ground litter. The band that Schaffa devastated is gone; these are new miscreants who don't know the danger. Nassun is not distracted by her father anymore, not helpless anymore, and after she ices one of the raiders, most of the others flee. But she detects a snarl of threads in one of them at the last instant, and then must resort to old-style orogeny (as she has come to think of it) in order to drop the ground beneath the raider and trap her in a pit.

The raider throws a knife at Nassun when she peeks over the edge; it's only luck that it misses. But carefully, while staying out of sight, Nassun follows the threads and finds a three-inch wooden splinter lodged in the woman's hand, so deep that it scrapes bone. It is poisoning her blood and will kill her; already the infection is so advanced that it has swollen her hand to twice its size. A comm doctor, or even a decent farrier, could extract the thing, but the commless do not have the luxury of skilled care. They live on luck, what little there is in a Season.

Nassun decides to become the woman's luck. She settles nearby so that she can concentrate, and then carefully—while the woman gasps and swears and cries *What is happening?*—she pulls the splinter free. When she looks into the pit again, the woman is on her knees and groaning as she holds her dripping hand. Belatedly Nassun realizes she will need to learn how to anesthetize, so she settles against the tree again and casts her thread to try to catch a nerve this time. It takes her some time to learn how to numb it, and not just cause more pain.

But she learns, and when she is done she feels grateful to the raider woman, who lies groaning and in a stupor in the pit. Nassun knows better than to let the woman go; if she lives, she will only either die slowly and cruelly, or return and perhaps next time threaten someone Nassun loves. So Nassun casts her threads one last time, and this time slices neatly through the top of her spine. It is painless, and kinder than the fate the woman intended for Nassun.

Now she runs up the hill toward Found Moon, elated for the first time since she killed Eitz, so eager to see Schaffa that she barely notices the other children of the compound as they stop whatever they're doing and favor her with cool stares. Schaffa has explained to them that what she did to Eitz was an accident, and he has assured her they will eventually come around. She hopes he is right because she misses their friendship. But none of that is important now.

"Schaffa!" She first pokes her head into the Guardians' cabin. Only Nida is there, standing in the corner as she so often does, staring into the middle distance as if lost in thought. She focuses as soon as Nassun comes in, however, and smiles in her empty way.

"Hello, Schaffa's little one," she says. "You seem cheerful today."

"Hello, Guardian." She is always polite to Nida and Umber. Just because they want to kill her is no reason to forget her manners. "Do you know where Schaffa is?"

"He is in the crucible with Wudeh."

"Okay, thanks!" Nassun hurries off, undeterred. She knows that Wudeh, as the next most skilled with Eitz gone, is the only other child in Found Moon who has some hope of connecting to an obelisk. Nassun thinks it is hopeless because no one can train him in the way he needs to be trained, given that he is so small and frail. Wudeh would never have survived Mama's crucibles.

Still, she is polite to him, too, running up to the edge of the outermost practice circle and bouncing only a little, keeping her orogeny still so as not to distract him while he raises a big basalt column from the ground and then tries to push it back in. He's already breathing hard, though the column isn't moving very fast. Schaffa is watching him intently, his smile not as big as usual. Schaffa sees it, too.

Finally Wudeh gets the column back into the ground. Schaffa takes his shoulder and helps him over to a bench, which is plainly necessary because Wudeh can barely walk at this point. Schaffa glances at Nassun, and Nassun nods at once and turns to run back into the mess hall to fetch a glass from the pitcher of fruit-water there. When she brings it to Wudeh, he blinks at her once, then looks ashamed of hesitating, and finally takes it with a shy nod of thanks. Schaffa is always right.

"Do you need help back to the dormitory?" Schaffa asks him.

"I can make it back myself, sir," Wudeh says. His eyes dart to Nassun, by which Nassun understands that Wudeh probably would like help back, but knows better than to get in between Schaffa and his favorite student.

Nassun looks at Schaffa. She's excited, but she can wait. He lifts an eyebrow, then inclines his head and extends a hand to help Wudeh up.

Once Wudeh is safely abed, Schaffa comes back over to where Nassun now sits on the bench. She's calmer for the delay, which is good, because she knows she's going to need to seem calm and cool and professional in order to convince him to let some half-grown, half-trained girl experiment on him with magic.

Schaffa sits down beside her, looking amused. "All right, then."

She takes a deep breath before beginning. "I know how to take the thing out of you."

They both know exactly what she's talking about. She has sat beside Schaffa, quietly offering herself, as he has huddled on this very bench clutching his head and whispering replies to a voice she cannot hear and shuddering as it punishes him with lashes of silver pain. Even now it is a low, angry throb inside him, pushing him to obey. To kill her. She makes herself available because her presence eases the pain for him, and because she does not believe he will actually kill her. This is folly, she knows. Love is no inoculation against murder. But she needs to believe it of him.

Schaffa frowns at her, and it is part of why she loves him that he shows no sign of disbelief. "Yes. I have sensed you growing... sharper lately, by increments. This happened to the orogenes at the Fulcrum, too, when they were allowed to progress to this point. They become their own teachers. The power guides them along particular paths, by lines of natural aptitude." His brow furrows slightly. "Generally we steered them away from *this* path, though."

"Why?"

"Because it's dangerous. To everyone, not just the orogene in question." He leans against her, shoulder warm and supportive. "You've survived the point that kills most: connecting with an obelisk. I... remember how others died, making the attempt." For a moment he looks troubled, lost, confused, as he probes gingerly at the raw edges of his torn memories. "I remember something of it. I'm glad..." He winces again, looks troubled again. This time it isn't the silver that's hurting him. Nassun guesses he's either remembered something he dislikes, or can't remember something he thinks he should.

She won't be able to take the pain of loss away from him, no matter how good she gets. It's sobering. She can remove the rest of his pain, though, and that's the part that matters. She touches his hand, her fingers covering the thin scars that she has seen him inflict with his own nails when the pain grows too great even for his smiles to ease. There are more of them today than there were a few days ago, some still raw. "I didn't die," she reminds him.

He blinks, and this alone is enough to snap him back into the here and now of himself. "No. You didn't. But Nassun." He adjusts their hands; now he is holding hers. His hand is huge and she can't even see a glimpse of her own within it. She has always liked this, being enveloped so completely by him. "My compassionate one. I do not *want* my corestone removed."

Corestone. Now she knows the name of her nemesis. The word makes no sense because it is metal, not stone, and it is not at the core of him, just in his head, but that doesn't matter. She clenches her jaw against hate. "It hurts you."

"As it should. I have betrayed it." His jaw tightens briefly. "But I accepted the consequences of doing so, Nassun. I can bear them."

This makes no sense. "It *hurts* you. I could stop the hurt. I can even make it stop hurting without taking it out, but only for a little while. I'd have to stay with you." She learned this from that conversation with Steel, and watching what the stone eater did. Stone eaters are full of magic, so much more than people, but Nassun can approximate. "But if I take it out—"

"If you take it out," Schaffa says, "I will no longer be a Guardian. Do you know what that means, Nassun?"

It means that then Schaffa can be her father. He is in every way that matters already. Nassun does not think this in so many words because there are things she is not yet prepared to confront about herself or her life. (This will change very soon.) But it is in her mind.

"It means that I will lose much of my strength and health," he says in reply to her silent wishing. "I will no longer be able to *protect* you, my little one." His eyes flick toward the Guardians' cabin, and she understands then. Umber and Nida will kill her.

They will try, she thinks.

His head tilts; of course he is instantly aware of her defiant intent. "You couldn't defeat them both, Nassun. Even you aren't that powerful. They have tricks you haven't yet seen. Skills that..." He looks troubled again. "I don't want to remember what they're capable of doing to you."

Nassun tries not to let her bottom lip poke out. Her mother always said that was pouting, and that pouting and whining were things only babies did. "You shouldn't say no because of *me*." She could take care of herself.

"I'm not. I mention that only in hopes that the urge for self-preservation will help convince you. But for my own part, I do not want to grow weak and ill and *die*, Nassun, which is what would happen if you took the stone. I am older than you realize—" The blurry look returns for a moment. By this she knows he does not remember how old. "Older than *I* realize. Without the corestone to stop it, that time will catch up with me. A handful of months and I'll be an old man, trading the pain of the stone for the pains of old age. And then I'll die."

"You don't know that." She is shaking a little. Her throat hurts.

"I do. I've seen it happen, little one. And it is a cruelty, not a kindness, when it does." Schaffa's eyes have narrowed, as if he must strain to see the memory. Then he focuses on her. "My Nassun. Have I hurt you so?"

Nassun bursts into tears. She's not really sure why, except... except maybe because she's been *wanting* this, working toward it, so much. She's wanted to do something good with orogeny, when she has used it to do so many terrible things already—and she wanted to do it for him. He is the only person in the world who understands her, loves her for what she is, protects her despite what she is.

Schaffa sighs and pulls Nassun into his lap, where she wraps herself around him and blubbers into his shoulder for a long while, heedless of the fact that they are out in the open.

When the weeping has spent itself, though, she realizes that he is holding her just as tightly. The silver is alive and searing within him because she's so close. His fingertips are on the back of her neck, and it would be so easy for him to push in, destroy her sessapinae, kill her with a single thrust. He hasn't. He's been fighting the urge, all this while. He would rather suffer this, risk this, than let her help him, and that is the worst thing in all the world.

She sets her jaw, and clenches her hands on the back of his shirt. Dance along the silver, flow with it. The sapphire is nearby. If she can make both flow together, it will be quick. A precise, surgical yank.

Schaffa tenses. "Nassun." The blaze of silver within him suddenly goes still and dims slightly. It is as if the corestone is aware of the threat she poses.

It is for his own good.

But.

She swallows. If she hurts him because she loves him, is that still hurt? If she hurts him a lot now so that he will hurt less later, does that make her a terrible person?

"Nassun, please."

Is that not how love should work?

But this thought makes her remember her mother, and a chilly afternoon with clouds obscuring the sun and a brisk wind making her shake as Mama's fingers covered hers and held her hand down on a flat rock. *If you can control yourself through pain, I'll know you're safe.*

She lets go of Schaffa and sits back, chilled by who she has almost become.

He sits still for a moment longer, perhaps in relief or regret. Then he says quietly, "You've been gone all day. Have you eaten?"

Nassun is hungry, but she doesn't want to admit it. All of a sudden, she feels the need of distance between them. Something that will help her love him less, so that the urge to help him against his will does not ache so within her.

She says, looking at her hands, "I . . . I want to go see Daddy."

Schaffa is silent a moment longer. He disapproves. She doesn't need to see or sess to know this. By now, Nassun has heard of what else transpired on the day that she killed Eitz. No one heard what Schaffa said to Jija, but many people saw him knock Jija down, crouch over him, and grin into his face while Jija stared back with wide, frightened eyes. She can guess why it happened. For the first time, however, Nassun tries not to care about Schaffa's feelings.

"Shall I come with you?" he asks.

"No." She knows how to handle her father, and she knows that Schaffa has no patience for him. "I'll be back right after."

"See that you are, Nassun." It sounds kindly. It's a warning.

But she knows how to handle Schaffa, too. "Yes, Schaffa." She looks up at him. "Don't be afraid. I'm strong. Like you made me."

"As you made yourself." His gaze is soft and terrible. Icewhite eyes can't be anything but, though there's love layered over the terrible. Nassun is used to the combination by now.

So Nassun climbs out of his lap. She's tired, even though she hasn't done anything. Emotion always makes her tired. But she heads down the hill into Jekity, nodding to people she knows whether they nod back or not, noticing the new granary the village is building since they've had time to increase their stores while the ashfalls and sky occlusions are still intermittent. It's an ordinary, quiet day in this ordinary, quiet comm, and in some ways it feels much like Tirimo. If not for Found Moon and Schaffa, Nassun would hate it here the same way. She may never understand why, if Mama had the whole of the world open to her after somehow escaping her Fulcrum, she chose to live in such a placid, backwater place.

Thus it is with her mother on her mind that Nassun knocks on the door of her father's house. (She has a room here, but it isn't her house. This is why she knocks.)

Jija opens the door almost immediately, as if he was about to leave and go somewhere, or as if he has been waiting for her. The scent of something redolent with garlic wafts out of the house, from the little hearth near the back. Nassun thinks maybe it is fish-in-a-pot, since the Jekity comm shares have a lot of fish and vegetables in them. It's the first time Jija has seen her in a month, and his eyes widen for a moment.

"Hi, Daddy," she says. It's awkward.

Jija bends and before Nassun quite knows what's happening, he's picked her up and swept her into an embrace.

Jekity feels like Tirimo, but in a good way now. Like back when Mama was around but Daddy was the one who loved her most and the stuff on the stove would be duck-in-a-pot instead of fish. If this were then, Mama would be yelling at the neighbors' kirkhusa pup for stealing cabbages from their housegreen; Old Lady Tukke never did tie the creature up the way she should. The air would smell like it does now, rich cooking food mingled with the more acrid scents of freshly chipped rock and the chemicals Daddy uses to soften and smooth his knappings. Uche would be running around in the background, making *whoosh* sounds and yelling that he was falling as he tried to jump up in the air—

Nassun stiffens in Jija's embrace as she suddenly realizes: Uche. Jumping up. *Falling* up, or pretending to.

Uche, whom Daddy beat to death.

Jija feels her tense and tenses as well. Slowly he lets go of her, easing her to the ground as the joy in his expression fades to unease. "Nassun," he says. His gaze searches her face. "Are you all right?"

"I'm okay, Daddy." She misses his arms around her. She can't help that. But the epiphany about Uche has reminded her to be careful. "I just wanted to see you."

Some of the unease in Jija fades a little. He hesitates, seems to fumble for something to say, then finally stands aside. "Come in. Are you hungry? There's enough for you, too."

So she heads inside and they sit down to eat and he fusses over how long her hair has gotten and how nice the cornrows and puffs look. Did she do them herself? And is she a little taller?

She might be, she acknowledges with a blush, even though she knows for certain that she is a whole inch taller than the last time Jija measured her; Schaffa checked one day because he thought he might need to requisition some new clothes with Found Moon's next comm share. She's such a big girl now, Jija says, and there is such real pride in his voice that it disarms her defenses. Almost eleven and so beautiful, so strong. So much like—he falters. Nassun looks down at her plate because he's almost said, *so much like your mother.*

Is this not how love should work?

"It's okay, Daddy," Nassun makes herself say. It is a terrible thing that Nassun is beautiful and strong like her mother, but love always comes bound in terrible things. "I miss her, too." Because she does, in spite of everything.

Jija stiffens slightly, and a muscle along the curve of his jaw flexes a little. "I don't miss her, sweetening."

This is so obviously a lie that Nassun stares and forgets to pretend to agree with him. Forgets lots of things, apparently, including common sense, because she blurts, "But you do. You miss Uche, too. I can tell."

Jija goes rigid, and he stares at her in something that falls between shock that she would say this out loud and horror at *what* she has said. And then, as Nassun has come to understand is normal for her father, the shock of the unexpected abruptly transforms into anger.

"Is that what they're teaching you up in that...*place*?" he asks suddenly. "To disrespect your father?"

Suddenly Nassun is more tired. So very tired of trying to dance around his senselessness.

"I wasn't disrespecting you," she says. She tries to keep her voice even, inflectionless, but she can hear the frustration there. She can't help it. "I was just saying the truth, Daddy. But I don't mind that you—"

"It isn't the truth. It's an insult. I don't like that kind of language, young lady."

Now she is confused. "*What* kind of language? I didn't say anything bad."

"Calling someone a rogga-lover is bad!"

"I . . . didn't say that." But in a way, she did. If Jija misses Mama and Uche, then that means he loves them, and that makes him a rogga-lover. But. *I'm a rogga.* She knows better than to say this. But she wants to.

Jija opens his mouth to retort, then seems to catch himself. He looks away, propping his elbows on the table and steepling his hands in the way he so often does when he's trying to rein in his temper.

"*Roggas*," he says, and the word sounds like filth in his mouth, "lie, sweetening. They threaten, and manipulate, and use. They're evil, Nassun, as evil as Father Earth himself. You aren't like that."

That's a lie, too. Nassun has done what she had to do to survive, including lying and murder. She's done some of these things in order to survive *him*. She hates that she's had to, and is exasperated by the fact that he apparently never realized it. That she's doing it now and he doesn't see.

Why do I even love him anymore? Nassun finds herself thinking as she stares at her father.

Instead she says: "Why do you hate us so much, Daddy?"

Jija flinches, perhaps at her casual *us*. "I don't hate you."

"You hate Mama, though. You must have hated U—"

"I did not!" Jija pushes back from the table and stands. Nassun flinches despite herself, but he turns away and starts to pace in short, vicious half circles around the room. "I just—I know what they're capable of, sweetening. You wouldn't understand. I needed to protect you."

In a sudden blur of understanding as powerful as magic, Nassun realizes Jija does not remember standing over Uche's body, his shoulders and chest heaving, his teeth clenched around the words *Are you one, too?* Now he believes he has never threatened her. Never shoved her off a wagon seat and down a hill of sticks and stones. Something has rewritten the story of his orogene children in Jija's head—a story that is as chiseled and unchangeable as stone in Nassun's mind. It is perhaps the same thing that has rewritten Nassun for him as *daughter* and not *rogga*, as if the two can be fissioned from each other somehow.

"I learned about them when I was a boy. Younger than you." Jija's not looking at her anymore, gesticulating as he talks and paces. "Makenba's cousin." Nassun blinks. She remembers Miss Makenba, the quiet old lady who always smelled like tea. Lerna, the town doctor, was her son. Miss Makenba had a cousin in town? Then Nassun gets it.

"I found him behind the spadeseed silo one day. He was squatting there, shaking. I thought he was sick." Jija's shaking his head the whole time, still pacing. "There was another boy with me. We always used to play together, the three of us. Kirl went to shake Litisk and Litisk just—" Jija stops abruptly. He's baring his teeth. His shoulders are heaving the same way they were on that day. "Kirl was *screaming* and Litisk was saying he couldn't stop, he didn't know how. The ice ate up Kirl's arm and his arm broke off. The blood was in chunks on the ground. Litisk said he was sorry, he even cried, but he just kept freezing Kirl. He wouldn't *stop*. By the time I ran away Kirl was reaching for me, and the only thing left of him that wasn't frozen was his head and his chest and that arm. It was too late, though. I knew that. It was too late even before I ran away to get help."

It does not comfort Nassun to know that there is a reason—a specific reason—for what her father has done. All she can think is, *Uche never lost control like that; Mama wouldn't have let him.* It's true. Mama had been able to sess, and still, Nassun's orogeny from all the way across town sometimes. Which means Uche didn't do anything to provoke Jija. Jija killed his own son for what a completely different person did, long before that son's birth. This, more than anything, helps her finally understand that there is no reasoning with her father's hatred.

So Nassun is almost prepared when Jija's gaze suddenly shifts to her, sidelong and suspicious. "Why haven't you cured yourself yet?"

No reasoning. But she tries, because once upon a time, this man was her whole world.

"I might be able to soon. I learned how to make things happen with the silver, and how to take things out of people. I don't know how orogeny works, or where it comes from, but if it's something that can be taken out, then—"

"None of the other monsters in that camp have cured themselves. I've asked around." Jija's pacing has gotten noticeably faster. "They go up there and they don't get better. They live there with those Guardians, more of them every day, and none of them have been cured! Was it a lie?"

"It isn't a lie. If I get good enough, I'll be able to do it." She understands this instinctively. With enough fine control and the sapphire obelisk's aid, she will be able to do almost anything. "But—"

"Why aren't you good enough now? We've been here almost a year!"

Because this is hard, she wants to say, but she realizes he does not want to hear it. He does not want to know that the only way to use orogeny and magic to transform a thing is to become an expert in the use of orogeny and magic. She doesn't answer because there's no point. She cannot say what he wants to hear. It isn't fair that he calls orogenes liars and then demands that she lie.

He stops and rounds on her, instantly suspicious of her silence. "You aren't trying to get better, are you? Tell the truth, Nassun!"

She is so *rusting* tired.

"I am trying to get better, Daddy," Nassun replies at last. "I'm trying to become a better orogene."

Jija steps back, as if she has hit him. "That isn't why I let you live up there."

He isn't *letting* anything; Schaffa made him. He's even lying to himself now. But it is the lies he's telling her—as he has been, Nassun understands suddenly, her whole life—that really break her heart. He's said that he loved her, after all, but that obviously isn't true. He cannot love an orogene, and that is what she is. He cannot be an orogene's father, and that is why he constantly demands she be something other than what she is.

And she is tired. Tired and done.

"I like being an orogene, Daddy," she says. His eyes widen. This is a terrible thing that she is saying. It is a terrible thing that she loves herself. "I like making things move, and doing the silver, and falling into the obelisks. I don't like—"

She is about to say that she hates what she did to Eitz, and she especially hates the way that others treat her now that they know what she is capable of, but she doesn't get the chance. Jija takes two swift steps forward and the back of his hand swings so fast that she doesn't even see it before it has knocked her out of the chair.

It's like that day on the Imperial Road, when she suddenly found herself at the bottom of a hill, in pain. It must have been like this for Uche, she realizes, in another swift epiphany. The world as it should be one moment and completely wrong, completely broken, an instant later.

At least Uche didn't have time to hate, she thinks, in sorrow.

And then she ices the entire house.

It isn't a reflex. She's intentional about it, precise, shaping the torus to fit the dimensions of the house exactly. No one past the walls will be caught in it. She shapes twin cores out of the torus, too, and centers each on herself and her father. She feels cold along the hairs of her skin, the tug of lowered air pressure on her clothing and plaited hair. Jija feels the same thing and he *screams*, his eyes wide and wild and sightless. The memory of a boy's cruel, icy death is in his face. By the time Nassun gets to her feet, staring at her father across a floor slick with plates of solid ice and around the fallen-over chair that is now too warped to ever use again, Jija has stumbled back, slipped on the ice, fallen, and slid partially across the floor to bump against the table legs.

There's no danger. Nassun only manifested the torus for an instant, as a warning against further violence on his part. Jija keeps screaming, though, as Nassun gazes down at her huddled, panicking father. Perhaps she should feel pity, or regret. What she actually feels, however, is cold fury toward her mother. She knows it's irrational. It is no one's fault except Jija's that Jija is too afraid of orogenes to love his own children. Once, however, Nassun could love her father without qualification. Now, she needs someone to blame for the loss of that perfect love. She knows her mother can bear it.

You should have had us with someone stronger, she thinks at Essun, wherever she is.

It takes care to walk across the slick floor without slipping, and Nassun has to jiggle the latch for a few seconds to scrape it open. By the time she does, Jija has stopped screaming behind her, though she can still hear him breathing hard and uttering a little moan with every exhalation. She doesn't want to look back at him. She makes herself do it anyway, though, because she wants to be a good orogene, and good orogenes cannot afford self-deception.

Jija jerks as if her gaze has the power to burn.

"Bye, Daddy," she says. He does not reply in words.

* * *

And the last tear she shed, as he burned her alive with ice, broke like the Shattering upon the ground. Stone your heart against roggas, for there is nothing but rust in their souls!

—From lorist tale, "Ice Kisses," recorded in Bebbec Quartent, Msida Theater, by Whoz Lorist Bebbec. (Note: A letter signed by seven Equatorial itinerant lorists disavows Whoz as a "pop lorist hack." Tale may be apocryphal.)

18

you, counting down

When the Sanzed woman is gone, I pull you aside. Figuratively speaking.

"The one you call Gray Man doesn't want to prevent the opening of the Gate," I say. "I lied."

You're so wary of me now. It troubles you, I can see; you *want* to trust me, even as your very eyes remind you of how I've deceived you. But you sigh and say, "Yeah. I thought there might be more to it."

"He'll kill you because you can't be manipulated," I say, ignoring the irony. "Because if you open the Gate, you would restore the Moon and end the Seasons. What he really wants is someone who will open the Gate for *his* purposes."

You understand the players now, if not the totality of the game. You frown. "So which purpose would that be? Transformation? Status quo?"

"I don't know. Does it matter?"

"Suppose not." You rub a hand over your locs, which you've

retwisted recently. "I guess that's why he's trying to get Castrima to kick out all its roggas?"

"Yes. He'll find a way to make you do what he wants, Essun, if he can. If he can't... you're no use to him. Worse. You're the enemy."

You sigh with the weariness of the Earth, and do not reply other than to nod and walk away. I am so afraid as I watch you leave.

* * *

As you have in other moments of despair, you go to Alabaster.

There's not much left of him anymore. Since he gave up his legs he spends his days in a drugged stupor, tucked up against Antimony like a pup nursing its mother. Sometimes you don't ask for lessons when you come to see him. That's a waste, because you're pretty sure the only reason he's forced himself to keep living is so that he can pass on the art of global destruction to you. He's caught you at it a few times: You've woken up curled next to his nest to find him gazing down at you. He doesn't chide you for it. Probably doesn't have the strength to chide. You're grateful.

He's awake now as you settle beside him, though he doesn't move much. Antimony has moved fully into the nest with him these days, and you rarely see her in any pose other than "living chair" for him—kneeling, legs spread, her hands braced on her thighs. Alabaster rests against her front, which is only possible now because, perversely, the few burns on his back healed even as his legs rotted. Fortunately she has no breasts to make the position less comfortable, and apparently her simulated clothing isn't sharp or rough. Alabaster's eyes shift to follow as you sit, like a stone eater's. You hate that this comparison occurs to you.

"It's happening again," you say. You don't bother to explain the "it." He always knows. "How did you . . . at Meov. You *tried.* How?" Because you can't find it in yourself anymore to bother fighting for this place, or building a life here. All your instincts say to grab your runny-sack, grab your people, and run before Castrima turns against you. That's a probable death sentence, the Season having well and truly set in topside, but staying seems more certain.

He draws in a deep, slow breath, so you know he means to answer. It just takes him a while to muster the words. "Didn't mean to. You were pregnant; I was . . . lonely. I thought it would do. For a while."

You shake your head. Of course he knew you were pregnant before you did. That's all irrelevant now. "You fought for them." It takes effort to emphasize the last word, but you do. For you and Corundum and Innon, sure, but he fought for Meov, too. "They would've turned on us, too, one day. You know they would have." When Corundum proved too powerful, or if they'd managed to drive off the Guardians only to have to leave Meov and move elsewhere. It was inevitable.

He makes an affirmative sound.

"Then why?"

He lets out a long, slow sigh. "There was a chance they wouldn't." You shake your head. The words are so impossible to believe that they sound like gibberish. But he adds, "Any chance was worth trying."

He does not say *for you*, but you feel it. It is a subtext that is nearly sessable beneath the words' surface. So your family could have a normal life among other people, as one of them. Normal opportunities. Normal struggles. You stare at him. On impulse you lift your hand to his face, drawing fingers over his scarred lips. He watches you do this and offers you that little quarter-smile, which is all he can muster these days. It's more than you need.

Then you get up and head out to try to salvage Castrima's thin, cracked nothing of a chance.

* * *

Ykka has called a vote for the next morning—twenty-four hours after Rennanis's "offer." Castrima needs to deliver some kind of response, but she doesn't think it should be up to only her informal council. You can't see what difference the vote will make, except to emphasize that if the comm gets through the night intact it will be a rusting miracle.

People look at you as you walk through the comm. You keep your gaze ahead and try not to let them visibly affect you.

In brief, private visits you pass Ykka's orders on to Cutter and Temell, and tell them to spread the word. Temell usually takes the kids out for lessons anyway; he says he'll visit his students at home and encourage them to form study groups of two and three, in the homes of trusted adults. You want to say, "No adults are trustworthy," but he knows that. There's no way around it, so it's pointless to say aloud.

Cutter says he'll pass on the word to the few other adult roggas. Not all of them have the skill to throw a torus or control themselves well; except for you and Alabaster, they're all ferals. But Cutter will make sure the ones who can't stick near those who can. His face is impassive as he adds, "And who'll watch your back?"

Which means he's offering. The revulsion that shivers through you at this idea is surprising. You've never really trusted him, though you don't understand why. Something about the fact that he's hidden all his life—which is hypocritical as hell after your ten years in Tirimo. But then, sweet flaking rust, do you trust anyone? As long as he does his job it doesn't matter. You force yourself to nod. "Come find me after you're done, then." He agrees.

With that, you decide to get some rest, yourself. Your bedroom is wrecked thanks to Hoa's transformation, and you're not much interested in sleeping in Tonkee's bed; it's been months, but the memory of mildew dies hard. Also, you've realized belatedly that there's no one to watch Ykka's back. She believes in her comm, but you don't. Hoa ate Ruby Hair, who at least had an assumable interest in keeping her alive. So you borrow another pack from Temell, and scrounge your apartment for a few basic supplies—not quite a runny-sack, there's plausible deniability if Ykka protests—and then head to her apartment. (This will have the added purpose of making it hard for Cutter to find you.) She's still asleep, from the sound of her breathing through the bedroom curtain. Her divans are pretty comfortable, especially compared to sleeping rough when you were on the road. You use your runny-sack for a pillow and curl up, trying to forget the world for a while.

And then you wake when Ykka curses and stumbles past you at full speed, half ripping down one of the apartment curtains in her haste. You struggle awake and sit up. "What—" But by then you, too, hear the rising shouts outside. *Angry* shouts. A crowd, gathering.

So it's begun. You get up and follow, and it's not an afterthought that you grab the packs.

The knot of people is gathered on the ground level, near the communal baths. Ykka scrambles to that level in ways you will not—sliding down metal ladders, hopping over the railing of one platform to swing down to the one she knows is below, running across bridges that sway alarmingly beneath her feet. You go down in the sensible, non-suicidal way, so by the time you get to the knot of people, Ykka is in full shout, trying to get everyone to shut up and listen and back the fuck off.

At the center of the knot is Cutter, clad in nothing but a towel, for once looking something other than indifferent. Now he's tense, jaw set, defiant, braced to flee. And five feet away, the iced corpse of a man sits on the ground, frozen in mid-scrabble backward, a look of abject terror permanently on his face. You don't recognize him. That doesn't matter. What matters is that a rogga has killed a still. This is a match thrown right into the middle of a comm that is dried-out, oil-soaked kindling.

"—how this happened," Ykka is shouting, as you reach the knot of people. You can barely see her; there are nearly fifty people here already. You could push to the front, but you decide to hang back instead. Now is not the time to call attention to yourself. You look around and see Lerna also lurking at the rear of the crowd. His eyes are wide and his jaw tight as he looks back at you. There's also—oh, burning Earth—a cluster of three rogga kids here. One of them is Penty, who you know is the ringleader of some of the braver, stupider rogga children. She's standing on tiptoe, craning her neck for a better look. When she tries to push forward through the crowd, you catch her eye and give her a Mother Look. She flinches and subsides at once.

"Who the rust cares how it happened?" That's Sekkim, one of the Innovators. You only know him because Tonkee constantly complains that he's too stupid to rightly be part of the caste and should instead be dumped into something nonessential, like Leadership. "This is why—"

Someone else shouts him down. "*Fucking rogga!*"

Someone else shouts her down. "Fucking listen! It's Ykka!"

"Who the rust cares about another rogga monster—"

"Rusty son of a cannibal, I will beat you bloody if you—"

Someone shoves someone else. There are shoves back, more curses, vows of murder. It's a catastrophe.

Then a man rushes forward from the crowd, crouching beside the iced corpse and trying his best to fling his arms around it. The resemblance between him and the body is obvious even through the ice: brothers, perhaps. His wail of anguish causes a sudden, flustered silence to ripple across the crowd. They shuffle uneasily as his wail subsides into deep, soul-tearing sobs.

Ykka takes a deep breath and steps forward, using the opportunity that grief has provided. To Cutter, she says tightly, "What did I say? What did I rusting *say*?"

"He attacked me," Cutter says. There's not a scratch on him.

"Bullshit," Ykka says. Several people in the crowd echo her, but she glares them down until they subside. She looks at the dead man, her jaw tight. "Betine wouldn't have done that. He couldn't even kill a chicken that time it was his turn to look after the flock."

Cutter glares. "All I know is, I wanted to take a bath. I sat down to wash and he moved away from me. I figured fine, that's how it's going to be, and I didn't care. Then I went past him to get into the pool and he *hit* me. Hard, in the back of the neck."

There is a low, angry murmur at this—but also a troubled shuffle. The back of the neck is rumored to be the best place to strike a rogga. It's not true. Only works if you hit hard enough for a concussion or a cracked skull, and then that's what takes them down, not any sort of damage to the sessapinae. It's still a popular myth. And if it's true, it might be reason enough for Cutter to fight back.

"*Rust that.*" This is growled; the man who holds Betine's faintly hissing corpse. "Bets wasn't like that. Yeek, you *know* he wasn't—"

Ykka nods, going over to touch the man's shoulder. The crowd shuffles again, pent fury shifting with it. With her, tenuously, for the moment. "I know." A muscle in her jaw flexes once, twice. She looks around. "Anybody else see the fight?"

Several people raise hands. "I saw Bets move away," says one woman. She swallows, looking at Cutter; sweat dots her upper lip. "I think he just wanted to get closer to the soap, though."

"He looked at me," Cutter snaps. "I know what it rusting means when somebody looks at me like that!"

Ykka cuts him off with a wave of her hand. "I know, Cutter, but shut up. What else?" she asks the woman.

"That was it. I looked away and then when I looked back there was that—swirl. Wind and ice." She grimaces, her jaw tightening. "You know how you people kill."

Ykka glares back at her, but then flinches as there are more shouts, this time in agreement with the woman. Someone tries to shove through the crowd to get at Cutter; someone else holds the attacker back, but it's a near thing. You see the realization come over Ykka that she's losing them. She's not going to make her people see. They're working themselves into a mob, and there's nothing she can do to stop them.

Well. You're wrong about that. There's one thing she can do.

She does it by turning and laying a hand on Cutter's chest and sending something through him. You're not actively sessing at the moment, so you only get the backwash of it, and it's—what? It's like... the way Alabaster once slammed a hot spot into submission, years ago and a fifth of a continent away. Just smaller. It's like what that Guardian did to Innon, except localized, and not overtly horrific. And you didn't realize roggas could do anything like it.

Whatever it is, Cutter doesn't even have a chance to gasp. His eyes fly wide. He staggers back a step. Then he falls down, with a look of shock on his face to match that of Betine's fear.

Everyone's silent. Yours is not the only mouth that hangs open.

Ykka catches her breath. Whatever she did took a lot out of her; you see her sway a little, then get a hold of herself. "That's enough," she says, turning to look at everyone in the crowd. "More than enough. Justice has been done, see? Now all of you, go the rust home."

You don't expect that to work. You figure it'll only whet the crowd's bloodthirst... but shows how much you know. People mill a little, mutter a little more, but then begin to disperse. A grieving man's quiet sobs follow them all away.

That's midnight, the time-keeper calls. Eight hours till the vote in the morning.

* * *

"I had to do it," Ykka murmurs. You're in her apartment again, sort of, standing beside her. The curtain's open so she can see her people, so they can see her, but she's leaning against the doorsill and she's trembling. It's only a little. No one would see it from afar. "I had to."

You offer her the respect of honesty. "Yes. You did."

It's two o'clock.

* * *

By five o'clock, you're thinking about sleeping. It's been quieter than you expected. Lerna and Hjarka have come to join you at Ykka's. No one says you're keeping vigil, commiserating in silence, mourning Cutter, waiting for the world to end (again), but that's what you're doing. Ykka's sitting on a divan with her arms wrapped around her knees and her head propped against the wall, gaze weary and empty of thought.

When you hear shouts again, you close your eyes and think about ignoring them. It's the high-pitched screams of children that drag you out of this complete failure of empathy. The others get up and you do, too, and all of you go out onto the balcony. People are running toward one of the wide platforms that surround a crystal shaft too small to hold any apartments. You and the others head that way, too. The comm uses such platforms for storage, so this one is stacked with barrels and crates and clay jars. One of the clay jars is rolling around but looks intact; you see this as you and the others reach the platform. Which does not at all explain what else you're seeing.

It's the rogga kids again. Penty's gang. Two of them are doing all the screaming, tugging and hitting at a woman who has pinned Penty down and is shouting at her, gripping her throat. Another woman stands by, yelling at the kids, too, but no one's paying any attention to her. Her slurred voice is just the goad.

You know the woman that's got Penty down, sort of. She's maybe ten years younger than you, with a heavier build and longer hair: Waineen, one of the Resistants. She's been nice enough when you've done shifts in the fungus flats or latrines, but you've heard the others gossip behind her back. Waineen makes the mellows that Lerna periodically smokes, and the moonshine that a few people in the comm drink. Sometime back before the Season she had quite a lucrative sideline helping the native Castrimans perk up their lives of tedious mining and trading, and she stored the product down in Castrima-under to keep the quartent tax inspectors from ever finding it. Convenient, now that the world has ended. But she's her own biggest customer, and it's not unusual to find her stumbling about the comm, red-faced and too loud, emitting more fumes than a fresh blow.

Waineen's not usually a mean drunk, and she shares freely, and she never misses a shift, which is why nobody really cares what she does with her stuff. Everybody handles the Season in their own way. Still, something's set her off now. Penty *is* aggravating. Hjarka and some of the other Castrimans are striding forward to pull the woman off the girl, and you're telling yourself it's a good thing Penty has enough self-control to not ice the whole damned platform, when the woman lifts an arm and makes a fist.

a fist that

you've seen the imprint of Jija's fist, a bruise with four parallel marks, on Uche's belly and face

a fist that

that

that

no

You're in the topaz and between the woman's cells in almost the same instant. There is no thought in this. Your mind falls, *dives*, into the upward wash of yellow light as if it belongs there. Your sessapinae flex around the silver threads and you draw them together, you are part of both obelisk and woman and you will *not* let this happen, not again, not again, you could not stop Jija but—

"Not one more child," you whisper, and your companions all look at you in surprise and confusion. Then they stop looking at you, because the woman who was egging on the fight is suddenly screaming, and the kids are screaming louder. Even Penty is screaming now, because the woman on top of her has turned to glittering, multicolored stone.

"Not one more child!" You can sess the ones nearest you—the other council members, the screaming drunk, Penty and her girls, Hjarka and the rest, all of them. Everyone in Castrima. They trod upon the filaments of your nerves, tapping and jittering, and *they are Jija.* You focus on the drunk woman and it is almost instinctual, the urge to begin squeezing the movement and life out of her and replacing that with whatever the by-product of magical reactions really is, this stuff that looks like stone. This stuff that is killing Alabaster, the father of your other dead child, NOT ONE MORE RUSTING CHILD. For how many centuries has the world killed rogga children so that everyone else's children can sleep easy? *Everyone* is Jija, the whole damned world is Schaffa, Castrima is Tirimo is the Fulcrum NOT ONE MORE and you turn with the obelisk torrenting its power through you to begin killing everyone within and beyond your sight.

Something jars your connection to the obelisk. Suddenly you have to fight for power that it so readily gave you before. You bare your teeth without thinking, growl without hearing yourself, clench your fists and shout in your mind NO I WON'T LET HIM DO IT AGAIN and you are seeing Schaffa, thinking of Jija.

But you are *sessing* Alabaster.

Feeling him, in blazing white tendrils that lash at your obelisk link. That is Alabaster's strength contending against yours and... not winning. He does not shut you down the way you know he can. Or the way you thought he could. Is he weaker? No. You're just a lot stronger than you used to be.

And suddenly the import of this slaps through the fugue of memory and horror that you're trapped in, bringing you back to cold, shocking reality. You've killed a woman with magic. You're about to wipe out Castrima with magic. You're fighting Alabaster with magic—*and Alabaster cannot bear more magic.*

"Oh, uncaring Earth," you whisper. You stop fighting at once. Alabaster dismantles your connection to the obelisk; he's still got a more precise touch than you. But you feel his weakness when he does so. His fading strength.

You're not even aware of running at first. It barely qualifies as running, because the contest of magic and the abrupt disconnection from the obelisk have left you so disoriented and weak that you lurch from railing to rope as if drunk, yourself. Someone's shouting in your ear. A hand grabs your upper arm and you shake it off, snarling. Somehow you make it to the ground floor without falling to your death. Faces blur past you, irrelevant. You can't see because you're sobbing aloud, babbling, *No, no, no.* You know what you've done, even as you deny it with your words and body and soul.

Then you are in the infirmary.

You are in the infirmary, looking down at an incongruously small, yet finely made, stone sculpture. No color to this one, no polish, just dull sandy brown all over. It is almost abstract, archetypal: *Man in His Final Moment. Truncation of the Spirit. Neverperson, Unperson. Once Found but Now Lost.*

Or maybe you can just call it *Alabaster.*

It's five thirty.

* * *

At seven o'clock, Lerna comes to where you huddle on the floor in front of Alabaster's corpse. You barely hear him settle nearby, and you wonder why he's come. He knows better. He should go, before you snap again and kill him, too.

"Ykka's talked the comm into not killing you," he says. "I told them about your son. It's been, ah, mutually agreed that Waineen could've killed Penty, hitting her like that. Your overreaction was... understandable." He pauses. "It helps that Ykka killed Cutter earlier. They trust her more now. They know she's not speaking for you just out of..." He inhales, shrugs. "Kinship."

Yes. It's as the teachers told you back in the Fulcrum: Roggas are one and the same. The crimes of any are the crimes of all.

"No one will kill her." That's Hoa. Of course he's here now, guarding his investment.

Lerna shifts uneasily at this. But then another voice agrees, "No one will kill her," and you flinch because it is Antimony.

You push yourself up from the huddle slowly. She sits in the same position as always—she's been here all along—with the stone lump that was Alabaster resting against her as his living body once did. Her eyes are already on you.

"You can't have him," you say. Snarl. "Or me, either."

"I don't want you," Antimony says. "You killed him."

Oh, shit. You try to maintain abject fury, try to use it to focus and reach for the power to defy her, but the fury dissolves into shame. And anyway, you only get as far as that damned obelisk-longknife of Alabaster's. The spinel. It kicks back your flailing grab for it almost at once, as if spitting in your face. You *are* worthy of contempt, aren't you? The stone eaters, the humans, the orogenes, even the flaking obelisks all know it. You are nothing. No; you are death. And you've killed yet another person you loved.

So you sit there on your hands and knees, bereft, rejected, so hurt that it is like a clockwork engine of pain gear-ticking at the core of you. Maybe the obelisk-builders could have invented some way to harness pain like this, but they are all dead.

There is a sound that drags you out of grief. Antimony is standing now. Her pose is imposing, straight-legged and implacable. She looks down her nose at you. In her arms is the brown lump of Alabaster's remains. From this angle it doesn't look like anything that used to be human. Officially, it wasn't.

"No," you say. No defiance this time; it is a plea. *Don't take him.* Yet this is what he asked for. This is what he wanted—to be given to Antimony and not Father Earth, who took so much from him. That's the choice here: Earth or a stone eater. You're not on the list.

"He left you a message," she says. Her inflectionless voice is no different, and yet. Somehow. Is that pity? "'The onyx is the key. First a network, then the Gate. Don't rust it up, Essun. Innon and I didn't love you for nothing.'"

"What?" you ask, but then she flickers, becoming translucent. For the first time it occurs to you that the way stone eaters move through rock and the way obelisks shift between real and unreal states are the same.

It is a useless observation. Antimony vanishes into the Earth that hates you. With Alabaster.

You sit where she's left you, where he's left you. There are no thoughts in your head. But when a hand touches your arm, and a voice says your name, and a connection that is not the obelisk presents itself, you turn toward it. You can't help it. You need something, and if it is not to be family or death, then it must be something else. So you turn and grab and Lerna is there for you, his shoulder is warm and soft, and you need it. You need him. Just for now, please. Just once, you need to feel human, never mind the official designations, and maybe with human arms around you and a human voice murmuring, "I'm sorry. I'm sorry, Essun," in your ear, maybe you can feel like that. Maybe you *are* human, just for a little while.

* * *

At seven forty-five you sit alone again.

Lerna's gone to speak to one of his assistants, and maybe to the Strongbacks who are watching you from the infirmary doorway. At the bottom of your runny-sack is a pocket for hiding things. It's why you bought this particular runny-sack, years ago, from this particular leatherworker. When he showed you the pocket, you thought immediately of something that you wanted to put in it. Something that, as Essun, you didn't let yourself think about often, because it was a thing of Syenite's and she was dead. Yet you kept her remains.

You dig through the sack until your fingers find the pocket and wriggle inside. The bundle is still there. You tug them out, unfold the cheap linen. Six rings, polished and semiprecious, sit there.

Not enough for you, a nine-ringer, but you don't care about the first four, anyway. They clack and roll across the floor as you discard them. The last two, the ones he made for you, you put on the index finger of each hand.

Then you get to your feet.

* * *

Eight o'clock. Representatives of the comm's households gather at the Flat Top.

One vote per comm share is the rule. You see Ykka at the center of the circle again, her arms folded and face carefully blank, though you can sess an undertone of tension in the ambient that is mostly hers. Someone has brought out an old wooden box, and people are milling around, talking to each other, writing on scraps of paper or leather, dropping these into the box.

You walk toward the Flat Top with Lerna in tow. People don't notice you until you're nearly across the bridge. Nearly on top of them. Then someone sees you coming and gasps loudly. Someone else yelps an alarm: "*Oh, rust, it's her.*" People scramble to get out of your way, almost tripping over themselves.

They should. In your right hand is Alabaster's ridiculous pink longknife, the miniaturized and reshaped spinel obelisk. By now you have tapped it, resonated with it; it is yours. It rejected you before because you were unstable, floundering, but now you know what you need from it. You've found your focus. The spinel won't hurt anyone as long as you don't let it. Whether you will or not is an entirely different matter.

You walk into the center of the circle, and the man holding the ballot box scrambles back from you, leaving it there. Ykka frowns and steps forward and says, "Essun—" But you ignore her. You lunge forward and it is suddenly instinctual, easy, natural, to grip the hilt of the pink longknife with both hands and turn and swivel your hips and swing. The instant the sword touches the wooden box, the box is obliterated. It isn't cut, it isn't smashed; it disintegrates into its component microscopic particles. The eye processes this as dust, which scatters and glitters in the light before vanishing. Turned to stone. A lot of people are gasping or crying out, which means they're inhaling their votes. Probably won't hurt them. Much.

Then you turn and lift the longknife, pivoting slowly to point it at each face.

"No vote," you say. It's so quiet that you can hear water trickling out of the pipes in the communal pool, hundreds of feet below. "Leave. Go join Rennanis if they'll have you. But if you stay, no part of this comm gets to decide that any other part of this comm is expendable. No *voting* on who gets to be people."

Some of them shuffle or look at each other. Ykka stares at you like you are a possibly dangerous creature, which is hilarious. She should know by now that there's no "possibly" about it. "Essun," she starts to say, in the kind of even voice one uses with pets or the mad, "this is..." She stops because she doesn't know what it is. But you do. It's a fucking coup. Doesn't matter who's in charge, but on this one issue, you're going to be the dictator. You will not allow Alabaster to have died saving these people from you for nothing.

"*No vote*," you say again. Your voice is pitched to carry, as if they are twelve-year-olds in your old creche. "This is a community. You will be unified. You will fight for each other. *Or I will rusting kill every last one of you.*"

True silence this time. They don't move. Their eyes are white and so far beyond frightened that you know they believe you.

Good. You turn and walk away.

INTERLUDE

In the turning depths, I resonate with my enemy—or attempt to. "A truce," I say. Plead. There has been so much loss already, on all sides. A moon. A future. Hope.

Down here, it's nearly impossible to hear a reply in words. What comes to me is furious reverberation, savage fluctuations of pressure and gravitation. I'm forced to flee after a time, lest I be crushed—and though this would be only a temporary setback, I cannot afford to be incapacitated right now. Things are changing amid your kind, quickly as your kind so often do things when you finally make real decisions. I have to be ready.

The rage was my only answer, in any case.

19

you get ready to rumble

It has been one month since you last went aboveground. It has been two days since you killed Alabaster, in your folly and pain. All things change in a Season.

Castrima-over is occupied. The tunnel that you first passed through to enter the comm is blocked; one of the comm's orogenes has pulled a big slab of stone up from the earth to effectively seal it off. Probably Ykka, or Cutter before Ykka killed him; they were the two others in the comm with the best fine control besides you and Alabaster. Now two of those four are dead, and the enemy is at the gates. The Strongbacks who are clustered in the tunnel mouth behind the stone seal jump up as you walk into the electric-light circle, and the ones who were already standing stand straighter. Xeber, Esni's second-in-command among the Strongbacks, actually smiles at the sight of you. That's how bad things are. That's how worried everyone is. They've so lost their minds as to think of you as their champion.

"I don't like this," Ykka has said to you. She's back in the comm, organizing the defense that will be necessary if the tunnels are breached. The real danger is if the Rennanis scouts discover the ventilation ducts of Castrima's geode. They're well hidden—one in the cavern of an underground river, others in equally out-of-the-way places, as if the people who built Castrima feared attack themselves—but the comm's people will be forced out if those are sealed off. "And they've got stone eaters working with them. You're dangerous and ruster enough to fuck up an army, Essie, I'll give you that, but none of us can fight stone eaters. If they kill you, we lose our best weapon."

She said this to you at Scenic Overlook, where the two of you went to work things out. It was awkward for about a day, between you. By forbidding a vote, you undercut Ykka's authority and destroyed everyone's illusion of having a say in the comm's management. That was necessary, you still believe; everyone *shouldn't* have a say in whose life is worth fighting for. She actually agreed, she admitted as you talked. But it damaged her.

You didn't apologize for that, but you've tried to spackle the cracks. "*You* are Castrima's best weapon," you said firmly. You even meant it. That Castrima has lasted this far, a comm of stills who have repeatedly failed to lynch the roggas openly living among them, is miraculous. Even if "hasn't yet committed genocidal slaughter" is a low bar to hop, other communities haven't even managed that much. You'll give credit where it's due.

It eased the awkwardness between you. "Well, just don't rusting die," she told you at last. "Not sure I can keep this mess together without you, at this point." Ykka's good at that, making people feel like they've got a reason to do something. That's why she's the headwoman.

And that is why, now, you walk through a Castrima-over that has been turned into a camp by the soldiers of Rennanis, and you are actually afraid. It's always harder to fight for other people than for the self.

The ash has been falling steadily for a year now, and the comm is knee-deep in the stuff. There's been at least one rain to tamp it down recently, so you can sess a kind of damp-mud crust underneath the powdery layer on top, but even that's substantial. Enemy soldiers crowd the porches and doorways of the once-empty houses, watching you, and the untamped ash under the eaves is halfway up most of the houses' walls. They've had to dig out the windows. The soldiers look like… just people, because they don't wear uniforms, but there is a uniformity to them nevertheless: They are all fully Sanzed or very Sanzed-looking. Where you can see color in their ash-faded travel clothing, you spot that telltale scrap of prettier, more delicate cloth tied around their upper arms or wrists or foreheads. No longer displaced Equatorials, then; they've found a comm. Something older and more primal than a comm: They are a *tribe*. And now they're here to take what's yours.

But beyond that they are just people. Many are your age or older. You guess that a lot of them are surplus Strongbacks or commless trying to prove their usefulness. There are slightly more men than women, but that follows, too, since most comms are quicker to kick out those who can't produce babies than those who can—but the number of women here means that Rennanis isn't hurting for healthy repopulators. A strong comm.

Their eyes follow you as you walk down Castrima-over's main street. You stand out, you know, with your ashless skin and clean hair and your clothes bright with color. Just brown leather pants and unbleached white in your shirt, but these are colors that have become rare in this world of gray streets and gray dead trees and a gray, heavily clouded sky. You're the only Midlatter that you see, too, and you're small compared to most of them.

Doesn't matter. Behind you floats the spinel, remaining precisely one foot behind the back of your head and turning slowly. You aren't making it do that. You don't know why it's doing that, really. Unless you hold it in your hand, that's what the thing does: You tried to set it down, but it floated back up and moved behind you like this. Should've asked Alabaster how to make it behave before you killed him, oh well. Now it's flickering a little, real to translucent to real again, and you can hear—not sess, *hear*—the faint hum of its energies as it turns. You see people's faces twitch as they notice. They might not know what it is, but they know a bad thing when they hear it.

At the center of Castrima-over is a domed, open pavilion that Ykka tells you was once the comm's gathering center, used for wedding dances and parties and the occasional comm-wide meeting. It's been turned into some sort of operations center, you see as you walk toward it: A gaggle of men and women stand, squat, or sit around within it, but one knot of them stands around a freshly made table. When you get close enough, you see that they've got a crudely made diagram of Castrima and map of the local area side by side, which they're discussing.

To your dismay, you can see that they've marked at least one of the ventilation ducts—the one that's behind a small waterfall at the nearby river. They probably lost a scout or two finding it: The river's banks are by now infested with boilbug mounds. Doesn't matter; they found it, and that's bad.

Three of the people talking over the maps look up as you approach. One of them elbows another, who turns and shakes awake someone else as you walk into the pavilion and stop a few feet from the table. The woman who gets up, rubbing her face blearily as she comes to join the others, does not look particularly impressive. She's cut her hair on the sides to just above her ears—a painfully blunt chop that looks to have been done with a knife. It makes her look small, even though she's not particularly: Her torso is a smooth barrel, brief breasts blending into a belly that's probably carried at least one child, and legs like basalt pillars. She's not wearing anything more than the others; her sash of tribe membership is just a fading yellow silk kerchief hanging loosely around her neck. But there's a gravity in her gaze, even half-asleep, that makes you focus on her.

"Castrima?" she asks you, by way of greeting. It's all that really matters about who you are, anyway.

You nod. "I speak for them."

She rests her hands on the table, nodding. "Our message got delivered, then." Her gaze flicks to the spinel hovering behind you, and something adjusts in her expression. It's not hate that you're seeing. Hate requires emotion. What this woman has simply done is realize you are a rogga, and decide that you aren't a person, just like that. Indifference is worse than hate.

Well. You can't muster indifference in response; you can't

help but see her as human. Have to make do with hate, then. And what's more interesting is that she somehow knows what the spinel is, and what it means. Very interesting.

"We're not joining you," you say. "You want to fight over that, so be it."

She tilts her head to one side. One of her lieutenants chuckles into their hand, but is swiftly glared silent by another. You like the silencing. It's respectful—of your abilities if not of you per se, and of Castrima even if they don't think you have a chance. Even if you actually, probably, *don't* have a chance.

"We don't even have to attack, you realize," the woman says. "We can just sit up here, kill anybody who comes up to hunt or trade. Starve you out."

You manage not to react. "We have a little meat. It'll take awhile—months at least—for the vitamin deficiencies to set in. Our stores are pretty solid otherwise." You force a shrug. "And other communities have gotten around meat shortages easily enough."

She grins. Her teeth aren't sharpened, but you think momentarily that her canines are longer than they strictly need to be. It's probably projection. "True, if that's your taste. Which is why we're also working on finding your vents." She taps the map. "Close them up and suffocate you till you're weak, then break down those barriers you've put across the tunnels and dance right in. Stupid to live underground; once someone knows you're there, you're actually an easier target, not a harder one."

This is true, but you shake your head. "We can be hard enough, if you push us. But Castrima isn't rich, and our storecaches aren't any better than those of another comm that's not full of roggas." You pause for effect. The woman doesn't flinch, but there's a shuffle among the other people in the pavilion as they realize. Good. That means they're thinking. "So many easier nuts to crack out there. Why are you bothering with us?"

You know why they're really doing this, because Gray Man's after orogenes who can open the Obelisk Gate, but that can't be what he's told them. What could induce a strong, stable Equatorial comm to turn conqueror? Wait, no; it can't be stable. Rennanis is relatively close to the Rift. Even with living node maintainers, life in such a comm would be hard. Daily blow-throughs of noxious gas. Ashfall much worse than here, requiring people to wear masks at all times. Earth help them if it rains; it could be pure acid, and that's if rain is even possible with the Rift cranking out heat and ash nearby. Doubtful they have any livestock…so maybe they're facing a meat shortage, too.

"Because this is what it will take to survive," the woman says, to your surprise. She straightens and folds her arms. "Rennanis has too many people for our stores. All the survivors of every other Equatorial city have come to camp on our doorstep. We would've had to do this anyway, or have problems with too large of a commless population in the area. Might as well weaponize them into feeding themselves, and bringing what's left back home to the comm. You know this Season isn't going to end."

"It will."

"Eventually." She shrugs. "Our 'mests have calculated that if we grow enough 'shrooms and such, and strictly limit our population, we might achieve enough sustainability to survive until the Season ends. The odds are better if we take the storecaches of every other comm we encounter, though—"

You roll your eyes because you can't help it. "You think cachebread's going to last *a thousand years*?" Or two. Or ten. And then a few hundred thousand years of ice.

She pauses until you're done. "—and if we set up supply lines from every comm with renewables. We'll need some Coastal comms with oceanic resources, some Antarctics where growing low-light plants might still be possible." She pauses, also for effect. "But you Midlatters eat too much."

Well. "So basically, you're here to wipe us out." You shake your head. "Why didn't you just say so? Why the foolishness about getting rid of the orogenes?"

Someone from beyond the pavilion calls, "Daniel!" and the woman looks up, nodding absently. This is apparently her name. "Always a chance you'd turn on each other. Then we could just walk in and scrape up the leftovers." She shakes her head. "Now things have to be hard."

The dull, insistent buzz that suddenly impinges itself on your sessapinae is a warning as blatant as a scream.

It's too late the instant you sess it, because that means you're within range of the Guardian's ability to negate your orogeny. You turn anyway, half tripping even as you start to spin a huge torus that will flash-freeze the whole rusting town, and it is because you were expecting negation and did not deploy a tight shielding torus that the disruption knife pegs you in the right arm.

You remember Alabaster saying that these knives hurt. The thing is small, made for throwing, and it *should* hurt given that it's sunk into your bicep and probably chipping bone. But what Alabaster did not specify—you are irrationally furious with him hours after his death, stupid useless *ruster*—was that something about this knife seems to set your entire nervous system on fire. The fire is hottest, *incandescent*, in your sessapinae, even though those are nowhere near your arm. It hurts so much that all your muscles spasm at once; you flop onto your side and can't even scream. You just lie there twitching, and staring at the woman who steps through the gaggle of Rennanis soldiers to grin down at you. She's surprisingly young, or so she seems, though appearances are meaningless because she is a Guardian. She's naked from the waist up, her skin shockingly dark amid all these Sanzeds, her breasts small and almost entirely areola, reminding you of the last time you were pregnant. You thought your tits would never shrink back down after Uche... and you wonder if it will hurt, when you are shaken to pieces the way Innon was.

Everything goes black. You don't understand what's happened at first. Are you dead? Was it that quick? Everything's still on fire, and you think you're still trying to scream. But you become aware of new sensations then. Movement. Rushing. Something rather like wind. The touch of foreign molecules against infinitesimal receptors in your skin. It is... oddly peaceful. You almost forget your pain.

Then light, startling against the eyelids you hadn't realized you'd closed. You can't open them. Someone curses nearby and comes near and hands press you down, which nearly makes you panic because you can't do orogeny with your nerves exploding like this. But then someone yanks the knife out of your arm.

It is as though a shake siren within you has been suddenly silenced. You slump in relief, into just ordinary pain, and open your eyes now that you can control your voluntary muscles again.

Lerna's there. You're on the floor of his apartment, the light is from his crystal walls, and he's holding the knife and staring down at you. Beyond him, Hoa stands in a pose of entreaty, which he must have been directing toward Lerna. His eyes have shifted to you, though he hasn't bothered to adjust the pose.

"Burning rusty *fuck*," you groan-sigh. And then, because now you know what must have happened, you add, "Thanks," to Hoa. Who pulled you down into the earth and away before the Guardian could kill you. Never thought you'd be grateful for something like that.

Lerna's dropped the knife and already turned away to find bandages. You're not bleeding much; the knife went in vertically, paralleling rather than cutting across the tendons, and it seems to have missed the big artery. Hard to tell when your hands are still shaking a little; shock. But Lerna's not moving at that blurring, near-inhuman speed he tends to use when a life is on the line, so you're encouraged by that.

Lerna says, his back to you as he assembles items, "I take it your attempt at parley didn't go well."

Things have been awkward between you and him lately. He's made his interest clear, and you haven't responded in kind. You haven't rejected him, either, though, thus the awkwardness. At one point a few weeks back, Alabaster grumbled that you should just roll the boy already, because you were always crankier when you were horny. You called him an ass and changed the subject, but really—Alabaster's why you've been thinking about it more.

You keep thinking about Alabaster, too, though. Is this grief? You hated him, loved him, missed him for years, made yourself forget him, found him again, loved him again, killed him. The grief does not feel like what you feel about Uche, or Corundum, or Innon; those are rents in your soul that still seep blood. The loss of Alabaster is simply . . . a thinning of who you are.

And maybe now is not the time to consider your cataclysm of a love life.

"No," you say. You shrug off your jacket. Underneath you're wearing a sleeveless shirt good for Castrima's warmth. Lerna turns back and crouches and begins swabbing away the blood with a pad of soft rags. "You were right. I shouldn't have gone up there. They had a Guardian."

Lerna's eyes flick up to yours, then back to your wound. "I heard they could stop orogeny."

"This one didn't have to. That damned knife did it for her." You think you know why, too, as you remember Innon. That Guardian didn't negate him, either. Maybe the skin thing only works on roggas whose orogeny is still active. That's how she wanted to kill you. But Lerna's jaw muscle is already tight, and you decide maybe he doesn't need to know that.

"I didn't know about the Guardian," Hoa says unexpectedly. "I'm sorry."

You eye him. "I didn't expect stone eaters to be omniscient."

"I said I would protect you." His voice is more inflectionless, now that he's not in flesh-shape anymore. Or maybe his voice is the same, and you just read it as inflectionless because he has no body language to embellish it. Despite this, he sounds . . . angry. With himself, maybe.

"You did." You wince as Lerna starts winding a bandage around your arm tightly. No stitches, though, so that's good. "Not that I *wanted* to be dragged into the earth, but your timing was excellent."

"You were hurt." Definitely angry with himself. This is the first time he's sounded to you like the boy he appeared to be for so long. Is he young for one of his kind? Young at heart? Maybe just so open and honest that he might as well be young.

"I'll live. That's what matters."

He falls silent. Lerna works in silence. Between the collective air of disapproval that the two of them exude, you can't help feeling a little guilty.

Afterward you leave Lerna's apartment to head to Flat Top, where Ykka has set up an operations center of her own. Someone's brought the rest of the divans from her apartment, and she's set them up in a rough semicircle, basically bringing her council out into the open. In token of this, Hjarka sprawls over one divan as she usually does, head propped on fist and taking up the whole thing so no one else can sit down, and Tonkee is pacing in the middle of the semicircle. There are others around, anxious or bored people who've brought their own chairs or are sitting on the hard crystal floor, but not as many as you would've expected. There's a lot of activity around the comm, you noticed as you headed to the Flat Top: people fletching arrows in one chamber that you pass, building crossbows in another. Down on the ground level you can see what looks like a longknife-wielding class; a slender young man is teaching about thirty people how to do an over-and-under strike. Over by Scenic Overlook some of the Innovators seem to be rigging what looks like a dropped-rocks trap.

The spectators perk up as you and Lerna come onto the Flat Top, though; that's hilarious. Everyone knows you volunteered to go topside to deliver Castrima's answer to Rennanis. You did this in part to show publicly that you weren't taking over; Ykka's still in charge. Everyone seems to be reading it as a sign that you may be crazy, but at least you're on their side. Such hope in their eyes! It dies down quickly, though. That you are back, and that there is a visibly bloody bandage around one arm, is reassuring to no one.

Tonkee's in full rant about something. Even she's ready for battle, having traded her skirt for billowy pantaloons, tied her hair up atop her head in a scruffy pile of curls, and strapped twin glassknives to both thighs. She actually looks kind of stunning. Then you pay attention to what she's saying. "The third wave will need to be the most delicate touch. Pressure sets them off, see? A temperature differential should make the wind gust enough, the air pressure drop enough. But it has to happen *fast*. And no shaking. We're going to lose the forest either way, but shaking will just make them dig in. We need them moving."

"I can handle that," Ykka says, though she looks troubled. "At least, I can handle part of it."

"No, it has to be done all at once." Tonkee stops and glowers at her. "That's not rusting negotiable." She sees you then and stops, her eyes going immediately to the bandage around your arm.

Ykka turns and her eyes widen, too. "Damn."

You shake your head wearily. "I agreed it was worth a shot. And now we know they can't be reasoned with."

Then you sit down, and the people on the Flat Top fall silent as you impart what intelligence you were able to glean from your trip topside. An army of surplus people occupying the houses, a general named Danel, at least one Guardian. Adding this to what you already know—stone eaters on their side, a whole city more of them somewhere in the Equatorials—paints a bleak picture. But it is the unknowns that are most alarming.

"How did they know about the meat shortage?" No one seems to be holding the gray stone eater's revelation against Ykka, or at least they aren't doing it right now, even though they now know she was keeping the information from them. Headwomen are supposed to make choices like that. "How are they finding the rusting vents?"

"With enough people, it's not hard to search," you start to suggest, but she cuts you off.

"It is. We've been using this geode in one way or another for fifty years. We know the land—and it took us years to find those vents. One's in a damned peat bog further along the river, which stinks to the heavens and occasionally catches fire." She sits forward, propping her elbows on her knees and sighing. "How did they even know we were *here*? Even our trading partners have only ever seen Castrima-over."

"Maybe they have orogenes working with them, too," Lerna says. After so many weeks of hearing mostly *rogga*, his polite *orogene* sounds strained and artificial to your ears. "They could—"

"No," says Ykka. She looks at you then. "Castrima's huge. When you came into the area, did you notice a giant hole in the ground?" You blink in surprise. She nods before you can answer, since your face has said it all. "Yeah, you should have, but something about this place sort of... I don't know. *Shunts away* orogeny. Once you're in it, it's the opposite, of course; the geode feeds on us to power itself. But next time you're topside, and not being almost killed I mean, try sessing this place. You'll see what I'm talking about." She shakes her head. "Even if they've got pet roggas, they shouldn't have known we were here."

Hjarka sighs and rolls onto her back, muttering under her breath. Tonkee bares her teeth, probably a habit she's picking up from Hjarka. "That's not relevant," Tonkee snaps.

"Because you don't want to hear it, babe," Hjarka says. "Doesn't mean it's wrong. You like things neat. Life's not neat."

"*You* like things messy."

"Ykka likes things *explained*," Ykka says pointedly.

Tonkee hesitates, and Hjarka sighs and says, "It's not the first time I've thought there might be a spy in the comm."

Oh, rust. There's an immediate murmur and shuffle among the people listening. Lerna stares at her. "That makes no sense," he says. "None of us has any reason to betray Castrima. Anyone taken into this comm had nowhere else to go."

"That isn't true." Hjarka rolls to sit upright, grinning and flashing her sharp teeth. "I could have gone to my mom's birthcomm. She was Leadership there before she left to go to my birthcomm—too much competition, and she wanted to be a headwoman. I left my comm because I *didn't* want to be headwoman after her. Comm full of assholes. But I definitely wasn't planning to live out my useless years in a hole in the ground." She looks at Ykka.

Ykka sighs in a long-suffering way. "I can't believe you're still mad I didn't ash you. I told you, I needed the help."

"Right. But just saying: I wouldn't have stayed if you'd asked me at the time."

"You'd rather have some overcrowded Equatorial comm with delusions of being Old Sanze reborn?" Lerna frowns.

"*I* wouldn't." Hjarka shrugs. "I like it here now. But I'm saying that somebody else might prefer Rennanis. Enough to sell us out for a place in it."

"We need to find this spy!" shouts someone from over near the rope bridge.

"No," you say then, sharply. It's your teacher voice, and everyone jumps and looks at you. "Danel *said* she hoped to make Castrima tear itself apart. We're not starting any rogga-hunts, here." This has two meanings, but you're not trying to be clever. You know full well that your teacher voice isn't the only reason everyone's staring at you in palpable unease. The spinel still floats behind you, having followed you down from the surface.

Ykka rubs her eyes. "You gotta stop threatening people, Essie. I mean, I know you grew up in the Fulcrum and don't really know any better, but... it's not good community behavior."

You blink, a little thrown and a lot insulted. But... she's right. Comms survive through a careful balance of trust and fear. Your impatience is tilting the balance too far out of true.

"Fine," you say. Everyone relaxes a little, relieved that Ykka can talk you down, and there are even a few nervous chuckles. "But I still don't think it's relevant to discuss whether there's a spy right now. If there is, Rennanis knows what they know. All we can do is try to come up with a plan they won't anticipate."

Tonkee points at you and glares at Hjarka with a wordless *See?*

Hjarka sits forward, planting a hand on one knee and glaring at all of you. She doesn't usually argue much—that was Cutter's role—but you see stubbornness in the set of her jaw now. "It rusting matters if the spy is still here, though. Good luck keeping them from anticipating if—"

The commotion begins at Scenic Overlook. It's hard to see from Flat Top, but someone's shouting for Ykka. She's on her feet at once, heading in that direction, but a small figure—one of the comm's children working as a runner—comes darting along the pathways to meet her before she's even crossed the main bridge from Flat Top. "Message from the topside tunnels!" the boy calls even before he halts. "Says the Rennies are sledgehammering in!"

Ykka looks at Tonkee. Tonkee nods briskly. "Morat said the charges were set."

"Wait, what?" you ask.

Ykka ignores you. To the child, she says, "Tell them to fall back and follow the plan. Go." The boy turns and runs off, though only to a point where he's got a clear sight line to Scenic; he holds up a hand, clenches a fist, and then releases it in a splay of fingers. There's a series of whistles throughout the comm as this signal gets relayed, and a lot of bustling as clusters of people gather and head off into the tunnels. You recognize some of them: Strongbacks and Innovators. You have no idea what's going on.

Ykka seems remarkably calm as she turns back to face you. "Going to need your help," she says softly. "If they're using sledgehammers, then that's good; they don't have any roggas. But collapsing the tunnels will only hold them for a short time, if they're really determined to come down here. And I don't much like the idea of being trapped. Will you help me build an escape tunnel?"

You draw back a little, stunned. Collapsing the tunnels? But of course it is the only strategy that makes sense. Castrima cannot fight off an army that outnumbers them, out-weapons them, and out-allies them in stone eaters and Guardians. "What are we supposed to do, flee?"

Ykka shrugs. You understand now why she looks so tired—not just dealing with the comm almost turning on its roggas, but fear for the future. "It's a contingency. I've had people carrying critical stores into side caverns for days now. We can't carry it all, of course, or even most of it. But if we leave and go hide somewhere—we've got a place, before you ask, storage cavern a few miles away—then even if the Rennies break in, they'll find a comm that's dark and worthless and that will suffocate them if they stay too long. They'll take what they can and go, and maybe we can come back when they're done."

And this is why she's the headwoman: While you've been caught up in your own dramas, Ykka's been doing all this. Still . . . "If they have even one rogga with them, the geode will function. It'll be theirs. We'll be commless."

"Yeah. As a contingency plan, it blows, you're right." Ykka sighs. "Which is why I want to try Tonkee's plan."

Hjarka looks furious. "I rusting *told* you I don't want to be a headwoman, Yeek."

Ykka rolls her eyes. "You'd rather be commless? Suck it up."

You turn from her to Tonkee and back, feeling completely lost.

Tonkee sighs in frustration, but forces herself to explain. "Controlled orogeny," she says. "Sustained bursts of slow cooling at the surface, in a ring around the area but closing inward, centered on the comm. This will excite the boilbugs into a swarm state. The other Innovators have been studying their behavior for weeks." She flicks her fingers a little, perhaps unconsciously dismissing that sort of research as lesser. "It should work. But it has to be done fast, by someone who has the necessary precision and endurance. The bugs just dig in and go into hibernation otherwise."

Suddenly you understand. It's monstrous. It could also save Castrima. And yet—you look at Ykka. Ykka shrugs, but you think you read tension in her shoulders.

You have never understood how Ykka does the things she does with orogeny. She's a feral. In theory she's *capable* of doing anything you can; a dedicated self-teacher could conceivably master the basics and then refine them from there. Most self-taught roggas just…don't. But you've sessed Ykka when she's working, and it's obvious that in the Fulcrum she'd be ringed, though only two or three rings. She can shift a boulder, not a pebble.

And yet. She can somehow lure every rogga in a hundred-mile

radius to Castrima. And yet, there's whatever she did to Cutter. And yet there is a solidity to her, a stability and implication of strength even though you've seen nothing to explain it, which makes you doubt your Fulcrum-ish assessment of her. A two- or three-ringer doesn't sess like that.

And yet. Orogeny is orogeny; sessapinae are sessapinae. Flesh has limits.

"That army fills both Castrima-over and the forest basin," you say. "You'll pass out before you can ice half of a circle that big."

"Maybe."

"Definitely!"

Ykka rolls her eyes. "I know what I'm rusting doing because I've done it before. There's a way I know. You sort of—" She falters. You decide, if you manage to live through this, that the roggas of Castrima should start trying to come up with words for the things they do. Ykka sighs in frustration herself, as if hearing your thought. "Maybe this is a Fulcrum thing? When you run with another rogga, keep everybody at the same pace, train yourself to the capabilities of the least but use the endurance of the greatest . . . ?"

You blink . . . and then a chill passes through you. "Earthfires and rustbuckets. You know how to—" Alabaster did it to you twice, long ago, once to seal a hot spot and once to save himself from poisoning. "Parallel scale?"

"Is that what you call it? Anyway, when you form a whole group working in parallel, in a . . . a mesh, I could do it with Cutter and Temell before . . . Anyway, I can do that now. Use the other roggas. Even the kids can help." She sighs. You've guessed already. "Thing is, the person who holds the others together . . ."

The yoke, you think, remembering a long-ago angry conversation with Alabaster. "That's the one that burns out first. Has to, to take on the . . . the *friction* of it. Or everybody in the mesh will just cancel each other out. Nothing happens."

Burns out. *Dies*. "Ykka." You're a hundred times more skilled, more precise, than her. You can use the obelisks.

She shakes her head, bemused. "You ever, uh, 'meshed' with anyone before? I told you, it takes practice. And you've got another job to do." Her gaze is intent. "I hear your friend finally kicked off, in the infirmary. He teach you what you needed to know, before?"

You look away, bitterness in your mouth, because the proof of your mastery of individual obelisks is the fact that you killed him with one. But you're no closer to understanding how to open the Gate. You don't know how to use many obelisks together.

First a network, then the Gate. Don't rust it up, Essun.

Oh, Earth. *Oh, you amazing ass*, you think. It's self-directed as well as a thought thrown toward Alabaster.

"Teach me how to build a . . . mesh, with you," you blurt at Ykka. "A network. Let's call it a network."

She frowns at you. "I just told you—"

"That's what he wanted me to do! Flaking, fucking rust." You turn and start pacing, simultaneously excited and horrified and furious. Everyone's staring at you. "Not networking orogeny, networking—" All those times he made you study the threads of magic in his body, in your own body, getting a feel for how they connect and flow. "And of course he couldn't just rusting *tell* me, why would he ever do anything that sensible?"

"Essun." Tonkee's eying you sidelong, a worried look on her face. "You're starting to sound like me."

You laugh at her, even though you didn't think you'd be able to laugh ever again after what you did to 'Baster. "Alabaster," you say. "The man in the infirmary. My friend. He was a ten-ring orogene. He's also the man who broke the continent, up north."

Lots of murmurs at this. Tlino the baker says, "A *Fulcrum* rogga? He was from the *Fulcrum* and he did this?"

You ignore him. "He had reasons." Vengeance, and the chance to make a world that Coru could have lived in, even if Coru was no longer alive. Do they need to know about the Moon? No, there's no time, and it would just confuse everyone as much as the whole mess confuses you. "I didn't understand how he did it until now. 'First a network, then the Gate.' I need to learn how to do what you're about to do, Ykka. You can't die till you teach me."

Something shakes the ambient. It's small, relative to the power of a shake, and localized. You and Ykka and any other roggas on Flat Top immediately turn and look up, orienting on it. An explosion. Someone's set off small shaped charges and brought down one of the tunnels that leads out of Castrima. A few moments later there are shouts from Scenic Overlook. You squint in that direction and see a party of Strongbacks—the ones who were guarding the main tunnel into the comm when you went up to speak with Danel and the Rennanis people—trotting to a halt, breathless and anxious-looking...and dusty. They blew the tunnel as they fled.

Ykka shakes her head and says, "Then let's work together on the escape tunnel. Hopefully we won't kill each other in the process."

She beckons, and you follow, and together you half walk, half trot toward the opposite side of the geode. This happens by unspoken agreement; both of you instinctively know exactly where the best additional point to breach the geode lies. Around two platforms, across two bridges, and then the far wall of the geode is there, buried in stubby crystals too short to house any apartments. Good.

Ykka raises her hands and makes a rectangular shape, which confuses you until you sess the sudden sharp force of her orogeny, which pierces the geode wall at four points. It's fascinating. You've observed her before when she does orogeny, but this is the first time she's tried to be precise about something. And—it's completely not what you expected. She can't shift a pebble, but she can slice out corners and lines so neatly that the end result looks machine-carved. It's better than you could have done, and suddenly you realize: Maybe she couldn't shift a pebble because who the rust needs to shift pebbles? That's the Fulcrum's way of testing precision. Ykka's way is to simply *be precise*, where it is practical to do so. Maybe she failed your tests because they were the wrong tests.

Now she pauses and you sess her "hand" being extended to you. You're standing on a platform around a crystal shaft too narrow for apartments, which instead harbors storerooms and a small tool shop. It's recently made, so the railing is made of wood, and you don't much like entrusting your life to it. But you grip the railing and close your eyes anyway, and orogenically reach for the connection that she offers.

She seizes you. If you hadn't been used to this from Alabaster, you would have panicked, but it's the same as what happened back then: Ykka's orogeny sort of melds with and consumes yours. You relax and let her take control, because instantly you realize you are stronger than her and could, should, take control yourself—but you are the learner here, and she is the teacher. So you hold back, to learn.

It is a dance, of sorts. Her orogeny is like...a river with eddies, curling and flowing in patterns and at a pace. Yours is faster, deeper, more straightforward, more forceful, but she modulates you so efficiently that the two flows come together. You flow slower and more loosely. She flows faster, using your depth to boost her force. For an instant you open your eyes, see her leaning against the crystal column and sliding down to crouch at its base so that she doesn't have to pay attention to her body while she concentrates...and then you are within the geode's crystal substrate, through its shell and burrowing into the rock that surrounds it, flowing around the warps and wends of ancient cold stone. Flowing with Ykka, so easily that you are surprised. Alabaster was rougher than this, but maybe he wasn't used to doing it when he first tried it with you. Ykka has done this with others, and she is as fine a teacher as any you have ever had.

But—

But. Oh! You see it so easily now.

Magic. There are threads of it interwoven with Ykka's flow. Supporting and catalyzing her drive where it is weaker than yours, soothing the layer of contact between you. Where's all this coming from? She drags it out of the rock itself, which is another wonder, because you have not realized until now that there is any magic *in* the rock. But there it is, flitting between the infinitesimal particles of silicon and calcite as easily as it did between the particles of Alabaster's stone substance. Wait. No. Between the calcite and the calcite, specifically, though it touches the silicon. It is being generated by the calcite, which exists in limestone inclusions within the stone. At some point millions or billions of years ago, you suspect, this whole area was at the bottom of an ocean, or perhaps an inland sea. Generations of sea life were born and lived and died here, then settled to that ocean's floor, forming layers and compacting. Are those glacier scrapings that you see? Hard to tell. You're not a geomest.

But what you suddenly understand is this: Magic derives from life—that which is alive, or was alive, or even that which was alive so many ages ago that it has turned into something else. All at once this understanding causes something to shift in your perception, and

and

and

You see it suddenly: *the network*. A web of silver threads interlacing the land, permeating rock and even the magma just underneath, strung like jewels between forests and fossilized corals and pools of oil. Carried through the air on the webs of leaping spiderlings. Threads in the clouds, though thin, strung between microscopic living things in water droplets. Threads as high as your perception can reach, brushing against the very stars.

And where they touch the obelisks, the threads become another thing entirely. For of the obelisks that float against the map of your awareness—which has suddenly become vast, miles and miles, you are perceiving with far more than your sessapinae now—each hovers as the nexus of thousands, millions, *trillions* of threads. This is the power holding them up. Each blazes silvery-white in flickering pulses; Evil Earth, *this is what the obelisks are when they aren't real.* They float and they flicker, solid to magic to solid again, and on another plane of existence you inhale in awe at the beauty of them.

And then you inhale again, as you notice close by—

Ykka's control tugs at you, and belatedly you realize she has used your power even as you meandered through epiphany. Now there is a new tunnel slanting up through the layers of sedimentary and igneous rock. Within it is a staircase of broad, shallow steps, straight up except for wide regular landings. Nothing has been excavated to make room for these stairs; instead, Ykka has simply deformed the rock away, pressing it into the walls and compressing it down to form the stairs and using the increased density to stabilize the tunnel against the weight of the rock around it. But she has stopped the tunnel just shy of breaching the surface, and now she unweaves you from the network (that word again). You blink and turn to her, understanding why at once.

"You can finish it," Ykka says. She's getting up from the platform, dusting off her butt. Already she looks weary; it must have tired her, trying to modulate your surprised fluctuations. She cannot do this thing she has chosen to do. She'll burn out before she's made it halfway around the valley.

And she doesn't have to now. "No. I'll take care of it."

Ykka rubs her eyes. "Essie."

You smile. For once, the nickname doesn't bother you. And then you use what you just learned from her, grabbing her the way Alabaster once did, grabbing all the other roggas in the comm, too. (There is a collective flinch as you do this. They're used to it from Ykka, but they know a different yoke when they sess it. You have not earned their trust as she has.) Ykka stiffens, but you don't do anything, just hold her, and now it's obvious: You really can do it.

Then you drive the point home by connecting to the spinel. It is behind you, but you sess the instant that it stops flickering and instead sends forth a silent, earth-shivering pulse. *Ready*, you think it's saying. As if it speaks.

Ykka's eyes widen suddenly as she sesses just how the obelisk's catalysis... charges? awakens? awakens—the network of roggas. That's because you're now doing the thing that Alabaster tried to teach you for six months: using orogeny and magic together in a way that supports and strengthens each, making a stronger whole. Then integrating this into a network of orogenes working toward a single goal, all of them together stronger than they are individually, and plugged into an obelisk that amplifies their power manifold. It is amazing.

Alabaster failed to teach it to you because he was like you—Fulcrum-trained and Fulcrum-limited, taught only to think of power in terms of energy and equations and geometric shapes. He mastered magic because of who he was, but he did not truly understand it. Neither do you, even now. Ykka, feral that she is, with nothing to unlearn, was the key all along. If you hadn't been so arrogant...

Well. No. You cannot say Alabaster would be alive. He was dead the instant he used the Obelisk Gate to rip the continent in half. The burns were killing him already; that you finished it was mercy. Eventually you'll believe that.

Ykka blinks and frowns. "You okay?"

She knows the magic of you, and tastes your grief. You swallow against the lump in your throat—carefully, keeping tight hold of the power held pent within you. "Yeah," you lie.

Ykka's gaze is too knowing. She sighs. "You know . . . we both get through this, I have a stash of Yumenescene seredis in one of the storecaches. Want to get drunk?"

The tightness in your throat seems to snap, and you laugh it out. Seredis is a distilled liqueur made from a fruit of the same name that was harvested in the foothills just outside Yumenes. The trees didn't grow well anywhere else, so Ykka's stash might be the last seredis in the whole of the Stillness. "*Pricelessly* drunk?"

"*Disastrously* drunk." Her smile is weary, but real.

You like the sound of this. "If we get through this." But you're pretty sure that you will now. There's more than enough power in the orogene network and the spinel. You'll make Castrima safe for stills and roggas and anything else that's on your side. No one needs to die, except your enemies.

With that, you turn and raise your hands, splaying fingers as your orogeny—and magic—stretch forth.

You perceive Castrima: over, under, and all the matter between and below and above. Now the army of Rennanis is before you, hundreds of points of heat and magic on your mental map, some clustering in houses that do not belong to them and the rest clustering around the three tunnel mouths that lead into the underground comm. In two of the tunnels, they've broken through the boulders that one of Castrima's roggas positioned to seal them. In one of these, rocks have collapsed the passageway. Some of the soldiers are dead, their bodies cooling.

Other soldiers are working to clear the blockage. You can tell that's going to take a few days, at least.

But in the other—flaking *rust*—they've found and disabled the charges. You taste the acridity of unspent chemical potential, and the sourness of bloodlust-sweat; they are making their way unobstructed toward Castrima-under, and are more than halfway to Scenic Overlook. In minutes the first of them, several dozen Strongbacks bristling with longknives and crossbows and slingshots and spears, will hit the comm's defenses. Hundreds more file into the tunnel mouth behind them.

You know what you have to do.

You withdraw from this close view. Now the forest around Castrima spreads below you. Wider view: Now you taste the edges of Castrima's plateau, and the nearby depression that is the forest basin. Obvious now that there was once a sea here, and a glacier before that, and more. Obvious, too, are the knots of light and fire that comprise the life of the region, scattered throughout the forest. More of it than you thought, though much of it is hibernating or hidden or otherwise guarding itself against the Season's onslaught. Very bright along the river: Boilbugs infest both its banks and most of the plateau and basin beyond.

You begin with the river, then, delicately chilling the soil and air and stone along its length. You do this in pulsing waves, there and cool and there again and a little cooler. You drop the air pressure just on the inside of the circle of cold you're shaping, which causes wind to blow inward, toward Castrima. It is encouragement and warning: *Move and you'll live. Stay and I'll ice you little bastards to extinction.*

The boilbugs move. You perceive them as a wave of bright heat that surges out of underground nests and aboveground feeding piles that have formed around their many victims—hundreds of nests, millions of bugs, you had no idea the forest of Castrima was so riddled with them. Tonkee's warning about the meat shortage is meaningless and too late; you could never have competed against such successful predators. You were always going to have to get used to the taste of human anyway.

That's neither here nor there. The ring of cold around Castrima's territory is complete, and you direct the energy inward in waves, pushing, herding. The bugs are *fast*—and rusting hell, they can fly. You'd forgotten the wing covers.

And . . . oh, burning Earth. Suddenly you're glad you can only sess what's happening topside, not see or hear it.

What you perceive is painted in pressure and heat and chemical and magic. Here is a bright living cluster of Rennanis soldiers, bunched up within confines of wood and brick, as a swarm of blazing-hot boilbug motes reaches it. Through the foundation of the house you sess pounding feet, the slam of a door, the fleshier slam of bodies against each other and the floor. Mini-shakes of panic. The shapes of the soldiers glow brighter upon the ambient as the bugs land and do their work, boiling and steaming.

Terteis Hunter Castrima was unlucky; only a few bugs got him, which is why he didn't die of it. This is dozens of boilbugs per soldier, covering every accessible bit of flesh, and it is a kindness. They do not thrash for long, your enemies, and one by one the houses of Castrima-over become still and silent once more.

(The network shudders in your yoke. None of the others like

this. You steer them firmly, keeping them on task. There can be no mercy now.)

Now the swarms move into the basements, falling upon the soldiers gathered there, finding the hidden tunnels that lead down into Castrima-under. You lean on the spinel's power more here, trying to sess which of the living motes in the tunnels are Rennanis soldiers and which are Castrima's defenders. They're in clusters, fighting. You have to help your people—*ach*—rusting—shit. Ykka bucks against your control, and though you are too embedded in the network to hear what she says out loud, you get the idea.

You know what you have to do.

So you pull a chunk out of the walls and use this to seal off the tunnels. Some of Castrima's Strongbacks and Innovators are on the boilbug side of the seal. Some of Rennanis's soldiers are on the safe side of it. No one ever gets everything they want.

Through the stone of the tunnels, you cannot help sessing the vibration of screams.

But before you can force yourself to ignore this, there is another scream, nearer-by, a vibration that you perceive with eardrums and not sessapinae. Startled, you begin to dismantle the network—but not fast enough, not nearly, before something yanks at your yoke. *Breaks* it, throwing you and all the other roggas tumbling over each other and canceling one another's toruses as you come out of alignment. What the rust? Something has ripped two of your number loose.

You open your eyes to find yourself sprawled on the wooden platform, one arm painfully twisted under you, your face pressed against a storage crate. Confused and groaning—your knees are weak, being the yoke is *hard*—you push yourself up. "Ykka? What was . . . ?"

There is a sound beyond the crates. A gasp. A groan of wood from the platform beneath you, as something incomprehensibly heavy stresses the supports. A crunch of stone, so startlingly loud that you flinch even as you realize you've heard this sound before. Grabbing the edge of the crate and the wooden railing, you haul yourself up on one knee. That's enough for you to see:

Hoa, in a pose that your mind immediately and half-consciously names *Warrior*, stands with one arm extended. From the hand dangles a head. A *stone eater's* head, hair a curling coiffure in mother-of-pearl, face gone below the top lip. The rest of the stone eater, lower jaw on down, stands in front of Hoa, frozen in a posture of reaching for something. You can see Hoa's face in partial side view. It isn't moving or chewing, but there's pale stone dust on his finely carved black-marble lips. There's a divot about the size of a bite wound in what's left of the stone eater's nape. That was the familiar crunch.

An instant later the stone eater's remains *shatter*, and you realize Hoa's position has changed to put a fist through its torso. Then his eyes slide toward you. He doesn't swallow that you can see, but then he doesn't need his mouth to speak anyway. "Rennanis's stone eaters are coming for Castrima's orogenes."

Oh, Evil Earth. You make yourself get up, though you feel light-headed and unsteady on your feet. "How many?"

"Enough." Flick and Hoa's head has turned away, toward Scenic Overlook. You look and see heavy fighting there—the people of Castrima fighting back against the Rennanese who've made it down the tunnel. You spy Danel among the attackers, laying on with twin longknives against two Strongbacks as nearby, Esni shouts for another crossbow; hers has jammed. She drops her useless weapon and draws a knapped agate knife that flashes white in the light, then throws herself into the Danel fight.

And then your attention focuses on the nearer distance, where Penty has gotten herself tangled in a rope bridge. You see why: On the metal platform behind her stands another strange stone eater, this one allover citrine-gold but for the white mica around her lips. It stands with one hand extended, the fingers curled in a beckoning gesture. Penty is far from you, maybe fifty feet, but you can see tears streaking the girl's face as she struggles to extract herself from the ropes. One of her hands flops uselessly. Broken.

Her hand is broken. Your skin prickles all over. "Hoa."

There is a thunk against the wooden platform as he drops the head of his enemy. "Essun."

"I need to go topside fast." You can sess it up there, magic-feel it, looming and huge. It's been here all along, but you've been shying away from it. Too much for what you needed before. Exactly what you need now.

"Topside's crawling, Essie. Nothing but boilbugs." Ykka is standing, just, by bracing herself against the crystal's wall. You want to warn her—the stone eaters can come through the crystal—but there isn't time. If you're too slow, they'll get her regardless.

You shake your head and stagger over to Hoa. He can't come to you; he's so damned heavy that it's a wonder the wooden platform hasn't collapsed already. His pose has changed again, now that the other stone eater is just chunks scattered around him; now he has moved to place one hand on the crystal's wall, though the rest of him is facing you. His other hand extends toward you, open with invitation. You remember a day by a riverside, after Hoa fell into the mud. You offered him a hand to help him up, not realizing he weighed of diamond bones and ancient tales untold. He refused you to keep his secret, and you were hurt, though you tried not to be.

Now his hand is cool compared to the warmth of Castrima. Solid—although he does not sess quite of stone, you realize in fleeting fascination. There's a strange texture to his flesh. A very slight yielding to the pressure of your fingers. He has fingerprints. That surprises you.

Then you look up at his face. He's reshaped his expression from the coldness that you saw when he destroyed his enemy. Now there is a slight smile on his lips. "Of course I'll help you," he says. So much of the boy is still in him that you almost smile back.

There isn't time to parse this further, because all at once Castrima blurs into whiteness around you and then there is darkness, earthen-black. Hoa's hand is on yours, however, so you do not panic.

Then you stand before the pavilion of Castrima-over, amid the dead and dying. Around you on the walkways and pavilion flagstones lie the soldiers of Rennanis, their bodies twisted, some of them impossible to see beneath carpets of insects, a very few of them still crawling and screaming. The table that Danel used to plan the attack is overturned nearby; beetles crawl over its surface. There's that smell again, of meat in brine. The air swirls with boilbugs and the low-pressure breeze you created.

One of the bugs darts toward you and you cringe. An instant later Hoa's hand is where the bug was, dripping hot water as the teakettle whistle of the crushed creature fizzles away. "You should probably raise a torus," he advises. Flaking rust yes. You begin to pull away from him so you can do this safely, but his hand tightens on your own, just a little. "Orogeny can't hurt me."

You have more power at your disposal than just orogeny, but he knows that, so all right, then. You raise a high, tight torus around yourself, swirling with snow from the humidity, and immediately the boilbugs begin avoiding you. Perhaps they track prey by body heat. It's all irrelevant.

You look up then, at the blackness that blots out the sky.

The onyx is like no obelisk you've ever seen. Most are shards—double-pointed hexagonal or octagonal columns—though you've seen a few that were irregular or rough-ended. This one is an ovoid cabochon, at your summons descending slowly through the cloud layer that has hidden it since its arrival a few weeks before. You can't guess at its dimensions, but when you turn your head to take in the bowl of Castrima-over's sky, the onyx nearly fills it, south to north, gray-clouded horizon to underlit red. It reflects nothing, and does not shine. When you look up into it—this is surprisingly hard to do without cringing—only scuds of cloud around its edges tell you that it is actually hovering high above Castrima. Looking at it, it feels closer. Right above you. You have but to lift your hand... but some part of you is terrified of doing this.

There is a strata-shaking thud as the spinel drops to the ground behind you, as if in supplication to this greater thing. Or perhaps it is only that, with the onyx here and pulling at you, drawing you in, drawing you up—

—oh, Earth, it draws you *so fast*—

—there is nothing left of you that can command any other obelisk. You've got nothing to spare. You are falling up, flying into a void that does not so much rush you along as *suck* at you. You have learned from other obelisks to submit to their current, but at once you know better than to do that here. The onyx will swallow you whole. But you cannot fight it, either; it will rip you apart.

The best you can manage is a kind of precarious equilibrium, in which you pull against it yet still drift through its interstices. And too much of it is in you already, so much. You need to use this power or, or, but no, something is wrong, something is slipping out of equilibrium, suddenly there is light lashing around you and you realize you are tangled in a trillion, quintillion threads of magic and they are tightening.

On another plane of existence you scream. This was a mistake. *It's eating you*, and it is awful. Alabaster was wrong. Better to let the stone eaters kill every rogga in Castrima and destroy the comm than die like this. Better to let Hoa chew you to pieces with his beautiful teeth; at least you like him

love him

lo lo lo lo l o v e

Whiplash tightening of magic, in a thousand directions. Light-lattice blazing alive, suddenly, against the black. *You see.* This is so far past your normal range that it is nearly incomprehensible. You see the Stillness, the whole of it. You perceive the half shell of this side of the planet, taste whiffs of the other side. It's too much—and fire-under-Earth, you're a fool. Alabaster told you: first a network, then the Gate. You cannot do this alone; you need a smaller network to buffer the greater. You fumble toward the orogenes of Castrima again, but you cannot grasp them. There are fewer of them now, their numbers flaring and snuffing out even as you reach, and they are too panicked for even you to claim.

But there, right beside you, is a small mountain of strength: Hoa. You don't even try to reach for him, because that strength is alien and frightening, but he reaches for you. Stabilizes you. Holds you firm.

Which allows you to finally remember: *The onyx is the key.*

The key unlocks a gate.

The gate activates a network—

And suddenly the onyx pulses, magma-deep and earthen-heavy, around you.

Oh Earth not a network of orogenes he meant a network of

The spinel is first, right there, as it is. The topaz is next, its bright airy power yielding to you so easily.

The smoky quartz. The amethyst, your old friend, plodding after you from Tirimo. The kunzite. The jade.

oh

The agate. The jasper, the opal, the citrine...

You open your mouth to scream and do not hear yourself.

the ruby the spodumene THE AQUAMARINE THE PERIDOT THE

"It's too much!" You don't know if you're screaming the words in your mind or out loud. "Too much!"

The mountain beside you says, "They need you, Essun."

And everything snaps into focus. Yes. The Obelisk Gate opens only for a *purpose.*

Down. Geode walls. Flickering columns of proto-magic; what Castrima is made of. You sess-feel-know the contaminants within its structure. Those that crawl over its surfaces you permit.

(Ykka, Penty, all the other roggas, and the stills who depend on them to keep the comm going. They all need you.)

Yet there are also those interfering with its crystal lattices, riding along its strands of matter and magic, lurking within the rock around the geode shell like parasites trying to burrow in. They are mountains, too—But they are not *your* mountain.

Pissed off the wrong rogga, Hoa said of his own incarceration. Yes, these enemy stone eaters rusting did.

You shout again but this time it is effort, it is aggression. SNAP and you break lattices and magic strands and reseal them to your own design. CRACK and you lift whole crystal shafts to throw them like spears and grind your enemies beneath. You look for Gray Man, the stone eater who hurt Hoa, but he is not among the mountains that threaten your home. These are just his minions. Fine. You'll send him a message, then, written in their fear.

By the time you're done, you've sealed at least five of the enemy stone eaters into crystals. Easy to do, really, when they are so foolish as to try to transit through them while you're watching. They phase into the crystal; you simply de-phase them, freezing them like bugs in amber. The rest are fleeing.

Some flee north. Unacceptable, and distance is nothing for you now. You pull up and wheel and pierce down again, and there is Rennanis, nestled within its lattice of nodes like a spider among its bundled, sucked-dry prey. The Gate is meant to do things on a planetary scale. It is nothing to you to drive power down and inflict upon every citizen of Rennanis the same thing you did to the woman who would've beaten Penty to death. Bullies are bullies. So simple to twist the flickering silver between their cells until those cells grow still, solid. Stone. It is done, and Castrima's war won, in the span of a breath.

Now it's dangerous. Now you understand: To wield the power of this network of obelisks without a focus is to *become* its focus, and die. The wise thing to do, now that Castrima is safe, would be to dismantle the Gate and withdraw from the connection before it destroys you.

But. There are other things you want besides Castrima's safety.

The Gate is like orogeny, you see. Without conscious control, it responds to all desires as if they are the desire to destroy the world. And you will not control this. You cannot. This desire is as quintessential to you as your past or your defensive personality or your many-times-broken heart.

Nassun.

Your awareness spins. South. Tracking.

Nassun.

Interference. It hurts. The pearl the diamond the

Sapphire. It resists being pulled into the network of the Gate. You barely noticed before, overwhelmed as you were by dozens, hundreds of obelisks, but you notice now because

NASSUN

IT'S HER

It is your daughter, it's Nassun, you know the stolid complexity of her as you know your own heart and soul, *it's her, written all over this obelisk* and you have found her, she is alive.

Its (your) goal accomplished, the Gate automatically begins to disengage. The other obelisks disconnect; the onyx releases you last, albeit with a whiff of cold reluctance. Next time.

And as your body sags and lists to one side because something suddenly throws off your balance, hands take hold of you and pull you upright. You can barely lift your head. Your body feels distant, heavy, like the sensation of being in stone. You have not eaten in hours, but you feel no hunger. You know you've been taxed far beyond your own endurance, but you feel no exhaustion.

There are mountains around you. "Rest, Essun," says the one you love. "I'll take care of you."

You nod with a head heavy as a boulder. Then new presences pull at your attention, and you force yourself to look up one last time.

Antimony stands before you, impassive as ever, but there is something comforting about her presence nevertheless. You know instinctively that she is no enemy.

Beside her stands another stone eater: tall, slender, somehow awkward in its draped "clothing." Allover white, though the shape of its facial features is Eastern Coaster: full mouth and long nose, high cheekbones and a sculpture of neatly sculpted, kinky hair. Only its eyes are black, and though they watch you with only faint recognition, with a puzzled flicker of something that might be (but should not be) memory... something about those eyes is familiar.

How ironic. This is the first time you've ever seen a stone eater made of alabaster.

And then you are gone.

* * *

What if it isn't dead?

—Letter from Rido Innovator Dibars to Seventh University, sent via courier from Allia Quartent and Comm after the raising of the garnet obelisk, received three months after word of Allia's destruction spread via telegraph. Unknown reference.

INTERLUDE

You fall into my arms, and I take you to a safe place.

Safety is relative. You have driven off my unsavory brethren, those of my kind who would have killed you since they cannot control you. As I descend into Castrima, however, and emerge in a quiet space of familiarity, I smell iron on the air, amid the shit and stale breath and other scents of flesh, and smoke. The iron is a flesh scent, too: that variant of iron which is contained in blood. Outside, there are bodies along the walkways and steps. One even dangles from a ropeslide. The fighting is mostly over, however, because of two things. First, the invaders have realized they are trapped between the insect-infested surface and their enemies, who are greater in number now that most of the invading army is dead. Those who wish to live have surrendered; those who fear a worse death have flung themselves on the swords or crystals of Castrima.

The second thing that has stopped the fighting is the inescapable fact that the geode is badly damaged. All over the comm, the once-glowing crystals now flicker in irregular pulses. One of the longer ones has detached from the wall and broken, its dust and rubble scattered along the geode floor. On the ground level, warm water has stopped flowing into the communal pool, though occasionally there is a haphazard spurt of it. Several of the comm's crystals are completely dark, dead, cracked—but within each, a darker shape can be seen, frozen and trapped. Humanoid.

Fools. That's what you get for pissing off my rogga.

I lay you in a bed and make certain there is food and water nearby. Feeding you will be difficult, now that I have shed the quickened sheath I wore to friend you, but most likely someone will be along before I am forced to try. We are in Lerna's apartment. I've put you in his bed. He will like that, I think. You will, too, once you want to feel human again.

I do not begrudge you these connections. You need them.

(I do not begrudge you these connections. You need them.)

But I position you carefully, so that you will be comfortable. And I place your arm atop the covers, so you will know as soon as you awaken that you must now make a choice.

Your right arm, which has become a thing of brown, solidified, concentrated magic. No crudeness here; your flesh is pure, perfect, wholesome. Every atom is as it should be, the arcane lattice precise and strong. I touch it once, briefly, though my fingers barely notice the pressure. Leftover longing from the flesh I wore so recently. I'll get over it.

Your stone hand is shaped into a fist. There's a crack across the back of it, perpendicular to the hand bones. Even as the magic reshaped you, you fought. (You fought. This is what you must become. You have always fought.)

Ah, I grow sentimental. A few weeks' nostalgia in flesh and I forget myself.

Thus I wait. And hours or days later when Lerna returns to his apartment, stinking of other people's blood and his own weariness, he stops short at the sight of me, standing watchman in his living room.

He's still for only a moment. "Where is she?"

Yes. He's worthy of you.

"In the bedroom." He goes there immediately. There's no need for me to follow. He'll be back.

Some while later—minutes or hours, I know the words but they mean so little—he returns to the living room where I stand. He sits, heavily, and rubs his face.

"She will live," I say unnecessarily.

"Yes." He knows it's a coma and he will tend you well until you wake. A moment later he lowers his hands and gazes at me. "You didn't, uh." He licks his lips. "Her arm."

I know exactly what he means. "Not without her permission."

His face twists. I'm faintly repelled before I remember that not long ago I, too, was so constantly, wetly, in motion. Glad that's over with. "How honorable of you," he says, in a tone that he probably means as an insult.

No more honorable than his decision not to eat your other arm. Some things are simple decency.

Some while later, probably not years because he hasn't moved, possibly hours because he does look so very tired, he says, "I don't know what we're going to do now. Castrima's dying." As if to emphasize these words, the crystal around us stops glowing for a moment, dropping us into darkness lit harshly by the light from outside the apartment. Then the light returns. Lerna exhales, his breath redolent of fear-aldehydes. "We're commless."

It isn't worth pointing out that they would have also been commless if their enemies had succeeded in slaughtering Essun and the other orogenes. He'll figure it out eventually, in his plodding, sweaty way. But since there's one thing he does not know, I speak it aloud.

"Rennanis is dead," I say. "Essun killed it."

"What?"

He heard me. He just doesn't believe what he heard.

"You mean . . . she iced it? From here?"

No, she used magic, but all that matters is, "Everyone within its walls is now dead."

He ponders this for eternities, or maybe seconds. "An Equatorial city would have vast storecaches. Enough to last us years." Then his brow furrows. "Traveling there and bringing that many goods back would be a major undertaking."

He isn't a stupid man. I ponder the past while he figures things out. When he gasps, I pay attention to him again.

"Rennanis is empty." He stares at me, then gets to his feet, thumping and sloshing across the room. "Evil Earth—Hoa, that's what you're saying! Intact walls, intact homes, storecaches . . . and who the rust are we going to have to fight for it? No one with sense goes north, these days. We could live there."

At last. I return to my contemplations even as he mutters to himself and paces and finally laughs aloud. But then Lerna stops, staring at me. His eyes narrow in suspicion.

"You do nothing for us," he says softly. "Only for her. Why are you telling me this?"

I shape my lips into a curve, and his jaw tightens in disgust. I shouldn't have bothered. "Essun wants somewhere safe for Nassun," I say.

Silence, for maybe an hour. Or a moment. "She doesn't know where Nassun is."

"The Obelisk Gate permits sufficient precision of perception."

A flinch. I remember the words for movement: flinch, inhale, swallow, grimace. "Earthfires. Then—" He sobers and turns to look at the bedroom curtain.

Yes. When you wake, you will want to go find your daughter. I watch this realization soften Lerna's face, weigh down the tension of his muscles, slacken his posture. I have no idea what any of these things means.

"Why?" It takes a year for me to realize he's speaking to me and not himself. By the time I figure it out, however, he has finished the question. "Why do you stay with her? Are you just . . . hungry?"

I resist the urge to crush his head. "I love her, of course." There; I've managed a civil tone.

"Of course." Lerna's voice has grown soft.

Of course.

He leaves then, to ferry the information I've given him to the comm's other leaders. There follows a century, or a week, of frantic activity as the other people of the comm pack and prepare and gather their strength for what is sure to be a long, grueling, and—for a few—deadly journey. But they have no choice. Such is life, in a Season.

Sleep, my love. Heal. I'll stand guard over you, and be at your side when you set forth again. Of course. Death is a choice. I will make certain of that, for you.

(But not for you.)

20

Nassun, faceted

But also . . .

I listen through the earth. I hear the reverberations. When a new key is cut, her bittings finally ground and sharpened enough that she can connect to the obelisks and make them sing, we all know of it. Those of us who . . . hope . . . seek out that singer. We are forever barred from turning the key ourselves, but we can influence its direction. Whenever an obelisk resonates, you may be sure that one of us lurks nearby. We talk. This is how I know.

* * *

In the dead of the night Nassun wakes. It's dark in the barracks, still, so she's careful not to step on the creakier floorboards as she pulls on her shoes and jacket and makes her way across the room. None of the others stirs, if they even wake and notice. They probably just think she has to go to the outhouse.

Outside, it's quiet. The sky is beginning to lighten with dawn in the east, though it's harder to tell now that the ash clouds have thickened. She goes to the top of the downhill path and notices a few lights on in Jekity. Some of the farmers and fishers are up. In Found Moon, though, all is still.

What is it that tugs at her mind? The feel of it is irritating, *gummy*, as if something is caught in her hair and needs to be yanked free. The sensation is centered in her sessapinae—no. Deeper. This tugs at the light of her spine, the silver between her cells, the threads that bind her to the ground and to Found Moon and to Schaffa and to the sapphire that hovers just above the clouds of Jekity, visible now and again when the clouds break a little. The irritation is . . . it is . . . north.

Something is happening up north.

Nassun turns to follow the sensation, climbing the hill up to the crucible mosaic and stopping at its center as the wind makes her hair puffs shiver. Up here she can see the forest that surrounds Jekity spread before her like a map: rounded treetops and occasional outcroppings of ribbon-basalt. Part of her can perceive shifting forces, reverberating lines, connections, amplification. But of what? Why? Something immense.

"What you perceive is the opening of the Obelisk Gate," says Steel. She is unsurprised to find him suddenly standing beside her.

"More than one obelisk?" Nassun asks, because that's what she's sessing. *Lots* more.

"Every one stationed above this half of the continent. A hundred parts of the great mechanism beginning to work again as they were meant to." Steel's voice, baritone and surprisingly pleasant, sounds wistful in this moment. Nassun finds herself wondering about his life, his past, whether he has ever been a child like her. That seems impossible. "So much power. The very heart of the planet is channeled through the Gate...and she uses it for so frivolous a purpose." A faint sigh. "Then again, so did its original creators, I suppose."

Somehow, Nassun knows that Steel is talking about her mother with that *she*. Mama is alive, and angry, and full of so much power.

"What purpose?" Nassun makes herself ask.

Steel's eyes slide toward her. She has not specified whose purpose she means: her mother's, or those ancient people who first created and deployed the obelisks. "The destruction of one's enemies, of course. A small and selfish purpose that feels great, in the moment—though not without consequence."

Nassun considers what she has learned, and sessed, and seen in the dead smiles of the other two Guardians. "Father Earth fought back," she says.

"As one does, against those who seek to enslave. That's understandable, isn't it?"

Nassun closes her eyes. Yes. It's all so understandable, really, when she thinks about it. The way of the world isn't the strong devouring the weak, but the weak deceiving and poisoning and whispering in the ears of the strong until they become weak, too. Then it's all broken hands and silver threads woven like ropes, and mothers who move the earth to destroy their enemies but cannot save one little boy.

(Girl.)

There has never been anyone to save Nassun. Her mother warned her there never would be. If Nassun ever wants to be free of fear, she has no choice but to forge that freedom for herself.

So she turns, slowly, to face her father, who stands quietly behind her.

"Sweetening," he says. It's the voice he usually uses for her, but she knows it isn't real. His eyes are cold as the ice she left all over his house a few days ago. His jaw is tight, his body shaking just a little. She glances down at his tight fist. There's a knife in it—a beautiful one made from red opal, her favorite of his more recent work. It has a slight iridescence and a smooth sheen that completely disguises the razor-sharpness of its knapped edges.

"Hi, Daddy," she says. She glances toward Steel, who is surely aware of what Jija intends. But the gray stone eater has not bothered to turn away from the predawn forestscape, or the northern sky where so many earth-changing things are happening.

Very well. She faces her father again. "Mama's alive, Daddy."

If the words mean anything to him, it doesn't show. He just keeps standing there looking at her. Looking at her eyes in particular. She's always had her mother's eyes.

Suddenly it doesn't matter. Nassun sighs and rubs her face with her hands, as weary as Father Earth must be after so many eternities of hate. Hate is tiring. Nihilism is easier, though she does not know the word and will not for a few years. It's what she's feeling, regardless: an overwhelming sense of the meaninglessness of it all.

"I think I understand why you hate us," she says to her father as she drops her hands to her sides. "I've done bad things, Daddy, like you probably thought I would. I don't know how to *not* do them. It's like everybody wants me to be bad, so there's nothing else I can be." She hesitates, then says what's been in her mind for months now, unspoken. She doesn't think she'll have another chance to say it. "I wish you could love me anyway, even though I'm bad."

She thinks of Schaffa as she says this, though. Schaffa, who loves her no matter what, as a father should.

Jija just keeps staring at her. Elsewhere in the silence, on that plane of awareness that is occupied by sesuna and whatever the sense of the silver threads is called, Nassun feels her mother collapse. To be specific, she feels her mother's exertion upon the shifting, glimmering network of obelisks suddenly cease. Not that it ever touched her sapphire.

"I'm sorry, Daddy," Nassun says at last. "I tried to keep loving you, but it was too hard."

He's much bigger than her. Armed, where she is not. When he moves, it is with a mountainous lumber, all shoulders first and bulk and slow buildup to unstoppable speed. She weighs barely a hundred pounds. She has no real chance.

But in the instant that she feels the twitch of her father's muscles, small reverberating shocks against the ground and air, she orients her awareness toward the sky in a single, ringing command.

The transformation of the sapphire is instantaneous. It causes a concussion of air that rushes inward to fill the vacuum. The sound this makes is the loudest crack of thunder Nassun has ever heard. Jija, in mid-lunge, starts and stumbles, looking up. A moment later the sapphire slams into the ground before Nassun, cracking the central stone of the crucible mosaic and a six-foot radius of ground around her.

It isn't the sapphire as she's seen it up till now, although the sameness of it transcends things like shape. When she extends her hand to wrap around the hilt of the long, flickering knife of blue stone, she falls into it a little. Up, flowing through watery facets of light and shadow. In, down into the earth. Out, away, brushing against the other parts of the whole that is the Gate. The thing in her hand is the same monstrous, mountainous dynamo of silvery power that it has always been. The same tool, just more versatile now.

Jija stares at it, then at her. There is an instant in which he wavers, and Nassun waits. If he turns, runs . . . he was her father once. Does he remember that time? She wants him to. Nothing between them will ever be the same again, but she wants that time to matter.

No. Jija comes at her again, shouting as he raises the knife.

So Nassun lifts the sapphire blade from the earth. It's nearly the length of her body, but it weighs nothing; the sapphire floats, after all. It's just floating here in front of her instead of above. She doesn't lift it, either, strictly speaking. She wills it to move to a new position and it does. In front of her. Between her and Jija, so that when Jija angles his body to stab her, he cannot help bumping right into it. This makes it easy, inevitable, for her power to lay into him.

She doesn't kill him with ice. Nassun defaults to using the silver instead of orogeny most days. The shift of Jija's flesh is more controlled than what she did to Eitz, largely because she is aware of what she's doing, and also because she's doing it on purpose. Jija begins to turn to stone, starting at the point of contact between him and the obelisk.

What Nassun doesn't consider is momentum, which carries Jija forward even as he glances off the sapphire and twists and sees what is happening to his flesh and starts to inhale for a scream. He doesn't finish the inhalation before his lungs are solidified. He does, however, finish his lunge, though it is off-balance and out of control, more of a fall than an attack by now. Still, it is a fall with a knife as its focal point, and so the knife catches Nassun in the shoulder. He was aiming for her heart.

The pain of the strike is sudden and terrible and it breaks Nassun's concentration at once. This is bad because the sapphire flares as her pain does, flickering into its half-real state and back as she gasps and staggers. This finishes Jija in an instant, solidifying him completely into a statue with a frizz of smoky-quartz hair and a round red-ocher face and clothes of deep blue serendibite, because he wore dark clothing in order to stalk his daughter. This statue stands poised for only an instant, though—and then the flicker of the sapphire sends a ripple through him like a struck bell. Not unlike the concussion of turned-inward orogenic force that a Guardian once inflicted on a man named Innon.

Jija shatters in the same way, just not as wetly. He's brittle stuff, weak, poorly made. The pieces of him tumble into stillness around Nassun's feet.

Nassun gazes at the remains of her father for a long, aching moment. Beyond her, in Found Moon and down below in Jekity, lights are coming on in the cabins. Everyone's been woken up by the thunderclap of the sapphire. There is confusion, voices calling back and forth, frantic sessing and probes of the earth.

Steel now gazes down at Jija with her. "It never ends," he says. "It never gets better."

Nassun says nothing. Steel's words fall into her like a stone into water, and she does not ripple in their wake.

"You'll kill everything you love, eventually. Your mother. Schaffa. All your friends here in Found Moon. No way around it."

She closes her eyes.

"No way . . . except one." A careful, considered pause. "Shall I tell you that way?"

Schaffa is coming. She can sess him, the buzz of him, the constant torment of the thing in his brain that he will not let her remove. Schaffa, who loves her.

You'll kill everything you love, eventually.

"Yes," she makes herself say. "Tell me how not to . . ." She trails off. She can't say hurt them, because she has already hurt so many. She's a monster. But there must be a way for her monstrousness to be contained. For the threat of an orogene's existence to be ended.

"The Moon's coming back, Nassun. It was lost so long ago, flung away like a ball on a paddle-string—but the string has drawn it back. Left to itself, it will pass by and fly off again; it's done that before, several times now."

She can see one of her father's eyes, set into a chunk of his face, gazing up at her from amid the pile. His eyes were green, and now they have become a beautiful shade of clouded peridot.

"But with the Gate, you can . . . nudge it. Just a little. Adjust its tra—" A soft, amused sound. "The path that the Moon naturally follows. Instead of letting it pass again, lost and wandering, bring it home. Father Earth's been missing it. Bring it straight here and let them have a reunion."

Oh. *Oh*. She understands, suddenly, why Father Earth wants her dead.

"It will be a terrible thing," Steel says softly, nearly in her ear because he's moved closer to her. "It will end the Seasons. It will end *every* season. And yet . . . what you're feeling right now, you need never feel again. No one will ever suffer again."

Nassun turns to stare at Steel. He's bent toward her, a look of almost comical slyness chiseled on his face.

Then Schaffa trots to a stop before them. He's staring at the ruin of Jija, and she sees the moment when the realization of what he's seeing flickers across his face, a mobile shockwave. His icewhite gaze lifts to her, and she searches his expression with her belly clenched against imminent pain.

There is only anguish in his face. Fear for her, sorrow on her behalf, alarm at her bloodied shoulder. Wariness and protective anger, as he focuses on Steel. He is still her Schaffa. The ache of Jija fades within the ease of his regard. *Schaffa* will love her no matter what she becomes.

So Nassun turns then, to Steel, and says, "Tell me how to bring the Moon home."

APPENDIX 1

A catalog of Fifth Seasons that have been recorded prior to and since the founding of the Sanzed Equatorial Affiliation, from most recent to oldest

Choking Season: 2714–2719 Imperial. Proximate cause: volcanic eruption. Location: the Antarctics near Deveteris. The eruption of Mount Akok blanketed a five-hundred-mile radius with fine ash clouds that solidified in lungs and mucous membranes. Five years without sunlight, although the northern hemisphere was not affected as much (only two years).

Acid Season: 2322–2329 Imperial. Proximate cause: plus-ten-level shake. Location: unknown; far ocean. A sudden plate shift birthed a chain of volcanoes in the path of a major jet stream. This jet stream became acidified, flowing toward the western coast and eventually around most of the Stillness. Most coastal comms perished in the initial tsunami; the rest failed or were forced to relocate when their fleets and port facilities corroded and the fishing dried up. Atmospheric occlusion by clouds lasted seven years; coastal pH levels remained untenable for many years more.

Boiling Season: 1842–1845 Imperial. Proximate cause: hot spot eruption beneath a great lake. Location: Somidlats, Lake Tekkaris quartent. The eruption launched millions of gallons of steam and particulates into the air, which triggered acidic rain and atmospheric occlusion over the southern half of the continent for three years. The northern half suffered no negative impacts, however, so archeomests dispute whether this qualifies as a "true" Season.

Breathless Season: 1689–1798 Imperial. Proximate cause: mining accident. Location: Nomidlats, Sathd quartent. An entirely human-caused Season triggered when miners at the edge of the northeastern Nomidlats coalfields set off underground fires. A relatively mild Season featuring occasional sunlight and no ashfall or acidification except in the region; few comms declared Seasonal Law. Approximately fourteen million people in the city of Heldine died in the initial natural-gas eruption and rapidly spreading fire sinkhole before Imperial Orogenes successfully quelled and sealed the edges of the fires to prevent further spread. The remaining mass could only be isolated, where it continued to burn for one hundred and twenty years. The smoke of this, spread via prevailing winds, caused respiratory problems and occasional mass suffocations in the region for several decades. A secondary effect of the loss of the Nomidlats coalfields was a catastrophic rise in heating fuel costs and the wider adaption of geothermal and hydroelectric heating, leading to the establishment of the Geneer Licensure.

The Season of Teeth: 1553–1566 Imperial. Proximate cause: oceanic shake triggering a supervolcanic explosion. Location: Arctic Cracks. An aftershock of the oceanic shake breached a previously unknown hot spot near the north pole. This triggered a supervolcanic explosion; witnesses report hearing the sound of the explosion as far as the Antarctics. Ash went upper-atmospheric and spread around the globe rapidly, although the Arctics were most heavily affected. The harm of this Season was exacerbated by poor preparation on the part of many comms, because some nine hundred years had passed since the last Season; popular belief at the time was that the Seasons were merely legend. Reports of cannibalism spread from the north all the way to the Equatorials. At the end of this Season, the Fulcrum was founded in Yumenes, with satellite facilities in the Arctics and Antarctics.

Fungus Season: 602 Imperial. Proximate cause: volcanic eruption. Location: western Equatorials. A series of eruptions during monsoon season increased humidity and obscured sunlight over approximately 20 percent of the continent for six months. While this was a mild Season as such things go, its timing created perfect conditions for a fungal bloom that spread across the Equatorials into the northern and southern Midlats, wiping out then-staple-crop miroq (now extinct). The resulting famine lasted four years (two for the fungus blight to run its course, two more for agriculture and food distribution systems to recover). Nearly all affected comms were able to subsist on their own stores, thus proving the efficacy of Imperial reforms and Season planning, and the Empire was generous in sharing stored seed with those regions that had been miroq-dependent. In its aftermath, many comms of the middle latitudes and coastal regions voluntarily joined the Empire, doubling its range and beginning its Golden Age.

Madness Season: 3 Before Imperial–7 Imperial. Proximate cause: volcanic eruption. Location: Kiash Traps. The eruption of multiple vents of an ancient supervolcano (the same one responsible for the Twin Season of approximately 10,000 years previous) launched large deposits of the dark-colored mineral augite into the air. The resulting ten years of darkness was not only devastating in the usual Seasonal way, but resulted in a higher than usual incidence of mental illness. The Sanzed Equatorial Affiliation (commonly called the Sanze Empire) was born in this Season as Warlord Verishe of Yumenes conquered multiple ailing comms using psychological warfare techniques. (See *The Art of Madness*, various authors, Sixth University Press.) Verishe named herself Emperor on the day the first sunlight returned.

[**Editor's note:** Much of the information about Seasons prior to the founding of Sanze is contradictory or unconfirmed. The following are Seasons agreed upon by the Seventh University Archaeomestric Conference of 2532.]

Wandering Season: Approximately 800 Before Imperial. Proximate cause: magnetic pole shift. Location: unverifiable. This Season resulted in the extinction of several important trade crops of the time, and twenty years of famine resulting from pollinators confused by the movement of true north.

Season of Changed Wind: Approximately 1900 Before Imperial. Proximate cause: unknown. Location: unverifiable. For reasons unknown, the direction of the prevailing winds shifted for many years before returning to normal. Consensus agrees that this was a Season, despite the lack of atmospheric occlusion, because only a substantial (and likely far-oceanic) seismic event could have triggered it.

Heavy Metal Season: Approximately 4200 Before Imperial. Proximate cause: volcanic eruption. Location: Somidlats near Eastern Coastals. A volcanic eruption (believed to be Mount Yrga) caused atmospheric occlusion for ten years, exacerbated by widespread mercury contamination throughout the eastern half of the Stillness.

Season of Yellow Seas: Approximately 9200 Before Imperial. Proximate cause: unknown. Location: Eastern and Western Coastals, and coastal regions as far south as the Antarctics. This Season is only known through written accounts found in Equatorial ruins. For unknown reasons, a widespread bacterial bloom toxified nearly all sea life and caused coastal famines for several decades.

Twin Season: Approximately 9800 Before Imperial. Proximate cause: volcanic eruption. Location: Somidlats. Per songs and oral histories dating from the time, the eruption of one volcanic vent caused a three-year occlusion. As this began to clear, it was followed by a second eruption of a different vent, which extended the occlusion by thirty more years.

APPENDIX 2

A Glossary of Terms Commonly Used in All Quartents of the Stillness

Antarctics: The southernmost latitudes of the continent. Also refers to people from antarctic-region comms.

Arctics: The northernmost latitudes of the continent. Also refers to people from arctic-region comms.

Ashblow Hair: A distinctive Sanzed racial trait, deemed in the current guidelines of the Breeder use-caste to be advantageous and therefore given preference in selection. Ashblow hair is notably coarse and thick, generally growing in an upward flare; at length, it falls around the face and shoulders. It is acid-resistant and retains little water after immersion, and has been proven effective as an ash filter in extreme circumstances. In most comms, Breeder guidelines acknowledge texture alone; however, Equatorial Breeders generally also require natural "ash" coloration (slate gray to white, present from birth) for the coveted designation.

Bastard: A person born without a use-caste, which is only possible for boys whose fathers are unknown. Those who distinguish themselves may be permitted to bear their mother's use-caste at comm-naming.

Blow: A volcano. Also called firemountains in some Coastal languages.

Boil: A geyser, hot spring, or steam vent.

Breeder: One of the seven common use-castes. Breeders are individuals selected for their health and desirable conformation. During a Season, they are responsible for the maintenance of healthy bloodlines and the improvement of comm or race by selective measures. Breeders born into the caste who do not meet acceptable community standards may be permitted to bear the use-caste of a close relative at comm-naming.

Cache: Stored food and supplies. Comms maintain guarded, locked storecaches at all times against the possibility of a Fifth Season. Only recognized comm members are entitled to a share of the cache, though adults may use their share to feed unrecognized children and others. Individual households often maintain their own housecaches, equally guarded against non–family members.

Cebaki: A member of the Cebaki race. Cebak was once a nation (unit of a deprecated political system, Before Imperial) in the Somidlats, though it was reorganized into the quartent system when the Old Sanze Empire conquered it centuries ago.

Coaster: A person from a coastal comm. Few coastal comms can afford to hire Imperial Orogenes to raise reefs or otherwise protect against tsunami, so coastal cities must perpetually rebuild and tend to be resource-poor as a result. People from the western coast of the continent tend to be pale, straight-haired, and sometimes have eyes with epicanthic folds. People from the eastern coast tend to be dark, kinky-haired, and sometimes have eyes with epicanthic folds.

Comm: Community. The smallest sociopolitical unit of the Imperial governance system, generally corresponding to one city or town, although very large cities may contain several comms. Accepted members of a comm are those who have been accorded rights of cache-share and protection, and who in turn support the comm through taxes or other contributions.

Commless: Criminals and other undesirables unable to gain acceptance in any comm.

Comm Name: The third name borne by most citizens, indicating their comm allegiance and rights. This name is generally bestowed at puberty as a coming-of-age, indicating that a person has been deemed a valuable member of the community. Immigrants to a comm may request adoption into that comm; upon acceptance, they take on the adoptive comm's name as their own.

Creche: A place where children too young to work are cared for while adults carry out needed tasks for the comm. When circumstances permit, a place of learning.

Equatorials: Latitudes surrounding and including the equator, excepting coastal regions. Also refers to people from equatorial-region comms. Thanks to temperate weather and relative stability at the center of the continental plate, Equatorial comms tend to be prosperous and politically powerful. The Equatorials once formed the core of the Old Sanze Empire.

Fault: A place where breaks in the earth make frequent, severe shakes and blows more likely.

Fifth Season: An extended winter—lasting at least six months, per Imperial designation—triggered by seismic activity or other large-scale environmental alteration.

Fulcrum: A paramilitary order created by Old Sanze after the Season of Teeth (1560 Imperial). The headquarters of the Fulcrum is in Yumenes, although two satellite Fulcrums are located in the Arctic and Antarctic regions, for maximum continental coverage. Fulcrum-trained orogenes (or "Imperial Orogenes") are legally permitted to practice the otherwise-illegal craft of orogeny, under strict organizational rules and with the close supervision of the Guardian order. The Fulcrum is self-managed and self-sufficient. Imperial Orogenes are marked by their black uniforms, and colloquially known as "blackjackets."

Geneer: From "geoneer." An engineer of earthworks—geothermal energy mechanisms, tunnels, underground infrastructure, and mining.

Geomest: One who studies stone and its place in the natural world; general term for a scientist. Specifically geomests study lithology, chemistry, and geology, which are not considered separate disciplines in the Stillness. A few geomests specialize in orogenesis—the study of orogeny and its effects.

Greenland: An area of fallow ground kept within or just outside the walls of most comms as advised by stonelore. Comm greenlands may be used for agriculture or animal husbandry at all times, or may be kept as parks or fallow ground during non-Seasonal times. Individual households often maintain their own personal housegreen, or garden, as well.

Grits: In the Fulcrum, unringed orogene children who are still in basic training.

Guardian: A member of an order said to predate the Fulcrum. Guardians track, protect, protect against, and guide orogenes in the Stillness.

Imperial Road: One of the great innovations of the Old Sanze Empire, highroads (elevated highways for walking or horse traffic) connect all major comms and most large quartents to one another. Highroads are built by teams of geneers and Imperial Orogenes, with the orogenes determining the most stable path through areas of seismic activity (or quelling the activity, if there is no stable path), and the geneers routing water and other important resources near the roads to facilitate travel during Seasons.

Innovator: One of the seven common use-castes. Innovators are individuals selected for their creativity and applied intelligence, responsible for technical and logistical problem solving during a Season.

Kirkhusa: A mid-sized mammal, sometimes kept as a pet or used to guard homes or livestock. Normally herbivarous; during Seasons, carnivorous.

Knapper: A small-tools crafter, working in stone, glass, bone, or other materials. In large comms, knappers may use mechanical or mass-production techniques. Knappers who work in metal, or incompetent knappers, are colloquially called "rusters."

Lorist: One who studies stonelore and lost history.

Mela: A Midlats plant, related to the melons of Equatorial climates. Mela are vining ground plants that normally produce fruit aboveground. During a Season, the fruit grows underground as tubers. Some species of mela produce flowers that trap insects.

Metallore: Like alchemy and astronomestry, a discredited pseudoscience disavowed by the Seventh University.

Midlats: The "middle" latitudes of the continent—those between the equator and the arctic or antarctic regions. Also refers to people from midlats regions (sometimes called Midlatters). These regions are seen as the backwater of the Stillness, although they produce much of the world's food, materials, and other critical resources. There are two midlat regions: the northern (Nomidlats) and southern (Somidlats).

Newcomm: Colloquial term for comms that have arisen only since the last Season. Comms that have survived at least one Season are generally seen as more desirable places to live, having proven their efficacy and strength.

Nodes: The network of Imperially maintained stations placed throughout the Stillness in order to reduce or quell seismic events. Due to the relative rarity of Fulcrum-trained orogenes, nodes are primarily clustered in the Equatorials.

Orogene: One who possesses orogeny, whether trained or not. Derogatory: rogga.

Orogeny: The ability to manipulate thermal, kinetic, and related forms of energy to address seismic events.

Quartent: The middle level of the Imperial governance system. Four geographically adjacent comms make a quartent. Each quartent has a governor to whom individual comm heads report, and who reports in turn to a regional governor. The largest comm in a quartent is its capital; larger quartent capitals are connected to one another via the Imperial Road system.

Region: The top level of the Imperial governance system. Imperially recognized regions are the Arctics, Nomidlats, Western Coastals, Eastern Coastals, Equatorials, Somidlats, and Antarctics. Each region has a governor to whom all local quartents report. Regional governors are officially appointed by the Emperor, though in actual practice they are generally selected by and/or come from the Yumenescene Leadership.

Resistant: One of the seven common use-castes. Resistants are individuals selected for their ability to survive famine or pestilence. They are responsible for caring for the infirm and dead bodies during Seasons.

Rings: Used to denote rank among Imperial Orogenes. Unranked trainees must pass a series of tests to gain their first ring; ten rings is the highest rank an orogene may achieve. Each ring is made of polished semiprecious stone.

Roadhouse: Stations located at intervals along every Imperial Road and many lesser roads. All roadhouses contain a source of water and are located near arable land, forests, or other useful resources. Many are located in areas of minimal seismic activity.

Runny-sack: A small, easily portable cache of supplies most people keep in their homes in case of shakes or other emergencies.

Safe: A beverage traditionally served at negotiations, first encounters between potentially hostile parties, and other formal meetings. It contains a plant milk that reacts to the presence of all foreign substances.

Sanze: Originally a nation (unit of a deprecated political system, Before Imperial) in the Equatorials; origin of the Sanzed race. At the close of the Madness Season (7 Imperial), the nation of Sanze was abolished and replaced with the Sanzed Equatorial Affiliation, consisting of six predominantly Sanzed comms under the rule of Emperor Verishe Leadership Yumenes. The Affiliation expanded rapidly in the aftermath of the Season, eventually encompassing all regions of the Stillness by 800 Imperial. Around the time of the Season of Teeth, the Affiliation came to be known colloquially as the Old Sanze Empire, or simply Old Sanze. As of the Shilteen Accords of 1850 Imperial, the Affiliation officially ceased to exist, as local control (under the advisement of the Yumenescene Leadership) was deemed more efficient in the event of a Season. In practice, most comms still follow Imperial systems of governance, finance, education, and more, and most regional governors still pay taxes in tribute to Yumenes.

Sanzed: A member of the Sanzed race. Per Yumenescene Breedership standards, Sanzeds are ideally bronze-skinned and ashblow-haired, with mesomorphic or endomorphic builds and an adult height of minimum six feet.

Sanze-mat: The language spoken by the Sanze race, and the official language of the Old Sanze Empire, now the lingua franca of most of the Stillness.

Seasonal Law: Martial law, which may be declared by any comm head, quartent governor, regional governor, or recognized member of the Yumenescene Leadership. During Seasonal Law, quartent and regional governance are suspended and comms operate as sovereign sociopolitical units, though local cooperation with other comms is strongly encouraged per Imperial policy.

Seventh University: A famous college for the study of geomestry and stonelore, currently Imperially funded and located in the Equatorial city of Dibars. Prior versions of the University have been privately or collectively maintained; notably, the Third University at Am-Elat (approximately 3000 Before Imperial) was recognized at the time as a sovereign nation. Smaller regional or quartent colleges pay tribute to the University and receive expertise and resources in exchange.

Sesuna: Awareness of the movements of the earth. The sensory organs that perform this function are the sessapinae, located in the brain stem. Verb form: to sess.

Shake: A seismic movement of the earth.

Shatterland: Ground that has been disturbed by severe and/or very recent seismic activity.

Stillheads: A derogatory term used by orogenes for people lacking orogeny, usually shortened to "stills."

Stone Eaters: A rarely seen sentient humanoid species whose flesh, hair, etc., resembles stone. Little is known about them.

Strongback: One of the seven common use-castes. Strongbacks are individuals selected for their physical prowess, responsible for heavy labor and security in the event of a Season.

Use Name: The second name borne by most citizens, indicating the use-caste to which that person belongs. There are twenty recognized use-castes, although only seven in common use throughout the current and former Old Sanze Empire. A person inherits the use name of their same-sex parent, on the theory that useful traits are more readily passed this way.

Acknowledgments

Thanks to this trilogy, I now have greater respect for authors who write million-word sagas spanning five, seven, ten volumes or more. Like it or not, whether it makes you think "yay" or "nope" whenever you hear about it, let me tell you: Telling a single long involved story is *hard*, y'all. Mad respect to the multi-volumers.

And great thanks this time go to my day-job boss, who finagled me a flextime schedule that made finishing this book in one year possible; to my agent and editor, as usual, who both put up with my periodic hour-long phone rants about how "everything is wrong forever"; to Orbit's publicist Ellen Wright, who patiently puts up with my forgetting to tell her about, well, everything (stop checking work e-mail on holidays, Ellen); to fellow Altered Fluidian and medical consultant Danielle Friedman, who did a light-speed beta-read on short notice; to fellow Fluidian Kris Dikeman, who helped me design and build my own personal volcano (long story); to WORD Books in Brooklyn, which let me use their space free for the Magic Seismology Launch Party; to my father, who ordered me to slow down and breathe; to the girls of the Octavia Project, who reminded me of how far I've come and what all this is really for; to my therapist; and finally to my ridiculous cat KING OZZYMANDIAS, who seems to have perfected the art of jumping off the bookcase onto my laptop just when I need a writing break.

extras

www.orbitbooks.net

about the author

N. K. Jemisin is a Brooklyn author whose short fiction and novels have been nominated for the Hugo, the World Fantasy Award and the Nebula Award, shortlisted for the Crawford and the Tiptree, and have won the Locus Award. Her website is nkjemisin.com and she tweets at @nkjemisin.

Find out more about N. K. Jemisin and other Orbit authors by registering for the free monthly newsletter at www.orbitbooks.net

if you enjoyed

THE OBELISK GATE

look out for

WAKE OF VULTURES

by

Lila Brown

Nettie Lonesome lives in a land of hard people and hard ground dusted with sand. She's a half-breed who dresses like a boy, raised by folks who don't call her a slave but use her like one. She knows of nothing else. That is, until the day a stranger attacks her. When nothing, not even a sickle to the eye can stop him, Nettie stabs him through the heart with a chunk of wood and he turns to black sand.

And just like that, Nettie can see.

But her newfound sight is a blessing and a curse. Even if she doesn't understand what's under her own skin, she can sense what everyone else is hiding – at least physically. The world is full of evil, and now she knows the source of all the sand in the desert. Haunted by the spirits, Nettie has no choice but to set out on a quest that might lead her to find her true kin . . . if the monsters along the way don't kill her first.

CHAPTER 1

Nettie Lonesome had two things in the world that were worth a sweet goddamn: her old boots and her one-eyed mule, Blue. Neither item actually belonged to her. But then again, nothing did. Not even the whisper-thin blanket she lay under, pretending to be asleep and wishing the black mare would get out of the water trough before things went south.

The last fourteen years of Nettie's life had passed in a shriveled corner of Durango territory under the leaking roof of this wind-chapped lean-to with Pap and Mam, not quite a slave and nowhere close to something like a daughter. Their faces, white and wobbling as new butter under a smear of prairie dirt, held no kindness. The boots and the mule had belonged to Pap, right up until the day he'd exhausted their use, a sentiment he threatened to apply to her every time she was just a little too slow with the porridge.

"Nettie! Girl, you take care of that wild filly, or I'll put one in her goddamn skull!"

Pap got in a lather when he'd been drinking, which was pretty much always. At least this time his anger was aimed at a critter instead of Nettie. When the witch-hearted black filly had first shown up on the farm, Pap had laid claim and pronounced her a fine chunk of flesh and a sign of the Creator's good graces. If Nettie broke her and sold her for a decent price, she'd be closer to paying back Pap for taking her in as a baby when nobody else had wanted her but the hungry, circling vultures. The value Pap placed on feeding and housing a half-Injun, half-black orphan girl always seemed to go up instead of down, no matter that Nettie did most of the work around the homestead these days. Maybe that was why she'd not been taught her sums: Then she'd know her own damn worth, to the penny.

But the dainty black mare outside wouldn't be roped, much less saddled and gentled, and Nettie had failed to sell her to the cowpokes at the Double TK Ranch next door. Her idol, Monty, was a top hand and always had a kind word. But even he had put a boot on Pap's poorly kept fence, laughed through his mustache, and hollered that a horse that couldn't be caught couldn't be sold. No matter how many times Pap drove the filly away with poorly thrown bottles, stones, and bullets, the critter crept back under cover of night to ruin the water by dancing a jig in the trough, which meant another blistering trip to the creek with a leaky bucket for Nettie.

Splash, splash. Whinny.

Could a horse laugh? Nettie figured this one could.

Pap, however, was a humorless bastard who didn't get a joke that didn't involve bruises.

"Unless you wanna go live in the flats, eatin' bugs, you'd best get on, girl."

Nettie rolled off her worn-out straw tick, hoping there weren't any scorpions or centipedes on the dusty dirt floor. By the moon's scant light she shook out Pap's old boots and shoved her bare feet into into the cracked leather.

Splash, splash.

The shotgun cocked loud enough to be heard across the border, and Nettie dove into Mam's old wool cloak and ran toward the stockyard with her long, thick braids slapping against her back. Mam said nothing, just rocked in her chair by the window, a bottle cradled in her arm like a baby's corpse. Grabbing the rawhide whip from its nail by the warped door, Nettie hurried past Pap on the porch and stumbled across the yard, around two mostly roofless barns, and toward the wet black shape taunting her in the moonlight against a backdrop of stars.

"Get on, mare. Go!"

A monster in a flapping jacket with a waving whip would send any horse with sense wheeling in the opposite direction, but this horse had apparently been dancing in the creek on the day sense was handed out. The mare stood in the water trough and stared at Nettie like she was a damn strange bird, her dark eyes blinking with moonlight and her lips pulled back over long, white teeth.

Nettie slowed. She wasn't one to quirt a horse, but if the mare kept causing a ruckus, Pap would shoot her without a second or even a first thought—and he wasn't so deep in his bottle that he was sure to miss. Getting smacked with rawhide had to be better than getting shot in the head, so Nettie doubled up her shouting and prepared herself for the heartache that would accompany the smack of a whip on unmarred hide. She didn't even own the horse, much less the right to beat it. Nettie had grown up trying to be the opposite of Pap, and hurting something that didn't come with claws and a stinger went against her grain.

"Shoo, fool, or I'll have to whip you," she said, creeping closer. The horse didn't budge, and for the millionth time, Nettie swung the whip around the horse's neck like a rope, all gentle-like. But, as ever, the mare tossed her head at exactly the right moment, and the braided leather snickered against the wooden water trough instead.

"Godamighty, why won't you move on? Ain't nobody wants you, if you won't be rode or bred. Dumb mare."

At that, the horse reared up with a wild scream, spraying water as she pawed the air. Before Nettie could leap back to avoid the splatter, the mare had wheeled and galloped into the night. The starlight showed her streaking across the prairie with a speed Nettie herself would've enjoyed, especially if it meant she could turn her back on Pap's dirt-poor farm and no-good cattle company forever. Doubling over to stare at her scuffed boots while she caught her breath, Nettie felt her hope disappear with hoofbeats in the night.

A low and painfully unfamiliar laugh trembled out of the barn's shadow, and Nettie cocked the whip back so that it was ready to strike.

"Who's that? Jed?"

But it wasn't Jed, the mule-kicked, sometimes stable boy, and she already knew it.

"Looks like that black mare's giving you a spot of trouble, darlin'. If you were smart, you'd set fire to her tail."

A figure peeled away from the barn, jerky-thin and slithery in a too-short coat with buttons that glinted like extra stars. The man's hat was pulled low, his brown hair overshaggy and his lily-white hand on his gun in a manner both unfriendly and relaxed that Nettie found insulting.

"You best run off, mister. Pap don't like strangers on his land, especially when he's only a bottle in. If it's horses you want, we ain't got none worth selling. If you want work and you're dumb and blind, best come back in the morning when he's slept off the mezcal."

"I wouldn't work for that good-for-nothing piss-pot even if I needed work."

The stranger switched sides with his toothpick and looked Nettie up and down like a horse he was thinking about stealing. Her fist tightened on the whip handle, her fingers going cold. She wouldn't defend Pap or his land or his sorry excuses for cattle, but she'd defend the only thing other than Blue that mostly belonged to her. Men had been pawing at her for two years now, and nobody'd yet come close to reaching her soft parts, not even Pap.

"Then you'd best move on, mister."

The feller spit his toothpick out on the ground and took a step forward, all quiet-like because he wore no spurs. And that was Nettie's first clue that he wasn't what he seemed.

"Naw, I'll stay. Pretty little thing like you to keep me company."

That was Nettie's second clue. Nobody called her pretty unless they wanted something. She looked around the yard, but all she saw were sand, chaparral, bone-dry cow patties, and the remains of a fence that Pap hadn't seen fit to fix. Mam was surely asleep, and Pap had gone inside, or maybe around back to piss. It was just the stranger and her. And the whip.

"Bullshit," she spit.

"Put down that whip before you hurt yourself, girl."

"Don't reckon I will."

The stranger stroked his pistol and started to circle her. Nettie shook the whip out behind her as she spun in place to face him and hunched over in a crouch. He stopped circling when the barn yawned behind her, barely a shell of a thing but darker than sin in the corners. And then he took a step forward, his silver pistol out and flashing starlight. Against her will, she took a step back. Inch by inch he drove her into the barn with slow, easy steps. Her feet rattled in the big boots, her fingers numb around the whip she had forgotten how to use.

"What is it you think you're gonna do to me, mister?"

It came out breathless, god damn her tongue.

His mouth turned up like a cat in the sun. "Something nice. Something somebody probably done to you already. Your master or pappy, maybe."

She pushed air out through her nose like a bull. "Ain't got a pappy. Or a master."

"Then I guess nobody'll mind, will they?"

That was pretty much it for Nettie Lonesome. She spun on her heel and ran into the barn, right where he'd been pushing her to go. But she didn't flop down on the hay or toss down the mangy blanket that had dried into folds in the broke-down, three-wheeled rig. No, she snatched the sickle from the wall and spun to face him under the hole in the roof. Starlight fell down on her ink-black braids and glinted off the parts of the curved blade that weren't rusted up.

"I reckon I'd mind," she said.

Nettie wasn't a little thing, at least not height-wise, and she'd figured that seeing a pissed-off woman with a weapon in each hand would be enough to drive off the curious feller and send him back to the whores at the Leaping Lizard, where he apparently belonged. But the stranger just laughed and cracked his knuckles like he was glad for a fight and would take his pleasure with his fists instead of his twig.

"You wanna play first? Go on, girl. Have your fun. You think you're facin' down a coydog, but you found a timber wolf."

As he stepped into the barn, the stranger went into shadow for just a second, and that was when Nettie struck. Her whip whistled for his feet and managed to catch one ankle, yanking hard enough to pluck him off his feet and onto the back of his fancy jacket. A puff of dust went up as he thumped on the ground, but he just crossed his ankles and stared at her and laughed. Which pissed her off more. Dropping the whip handle, Nettie took the sickle in both hands and went for the stranger's legs, hoping that a good slash would keep him from chasing her but not get her sent to the hangman's noose. But her blade whistled over a patch of nothing. The man was gone, her whip with him.

Nettie stepped into the doorway to watch him run away, her heart thumping underneath the tight muslin binding she always wore over her chest. She squinted into the long, flat night, one hand on the hinge of what used to be a barn door, back before the church was willing to pay cash money for Pap's old lumber. But the stranger wasn't hightailing it across the prairie. Which meant…

"Looking for someone, darlin'?"

She spun, sickle in hand, and sliced into something that felt like a ham with the round part of the blade. Hot blood spattered over her, burning like lye.

"Goddammit, girl! What'd you do that for?"

She ripped the sickle out with a sick splash, but the man wasn't standing in the barn, much less falling to the floor. He was hanging upside-down from a cross-beam, cradling his arm. It made no goddamn sense, and Nettie couldn't stand a thing that made no sense, so she struck again while he was poking around his wound.

This time, she caught him in the neck. This time, he fell.

The stranger landed in the dirt and popped right back up into a crouch. The slice in his neck looked like the first carving in an undercooked roast, but the blood was slurry and smelled like rotten meat. And the stranger was sneering at her.

"Girl, you just made the biggest mistake of your short, useless life."

Then he sprang at her.

There was no way he should've been able to jump at her like that with those wounds, and she brought her hands straight up without thinking. Luckily, her fist still held the sickle, and the stranger took it right in the face, the point of the blade jerking into his eyeball with a moist squish. Nettie turned away and lost most of last night's meager dinner in a noisy splatter against the wall of the barn. When she spun back around, she was surprised to find that the fool hadn't fallen or died or done anything helpful to her cause. Without a word, he calmly pulled the blade out of his eye and wiped a dribble of black glop off his cheek.

His smile was a cold, dark thing that sent Nettie's feet toward Pap and the crooked house and anything but the stranger who wouldn't die, wouldn't scream, and wouldn't leave her alone. She'd never felt safe a day in her life, but now she recognized the chill hand of death, reaching for her. Her feet trembled in the too-big boots as she stumbled backward across the bumpy yard, tripping on stones and bits of trash. Turning her back on the demon man seemed intolerably stupid. She just had to get past the round pen, and then she'd be halfway to the house. Pap wouldn't be worth much by now, but he had a gun by his side. Maybe the stranger would give up if he saw a man instead of just a half-breed girl nobody cared about.

Nettie turned to run and tripped on a fallen chunk of fence, going down hard on hands and skinned knees. When she looked up, she saw butternut-brown pants stippled with blood and no-spur boots tapping.

"Pap!" she shouted. "Pap, help!"

She was gulping in a big breath to holler again when the stranger's boot caught her right under the ribs and knocked it all back out. The force of the kick flipped her over onto her back, and she scrabbled away from the stranger and toward the ramshackle round pen of old, gray branches and junk roped together, just barely enough fence to trick a colt into staying put. They'd slaughtered a pig in here, once, and now Nettie knew how he felt.

As soon as her back fetched up against the pen, the stranger crouched in front of her, one eye closed and weeping black and the other brim-full with evil over the bloody slice in his neck. He looked like a dead man, a corpse groom, and Nettie was pretty sure she was in the hell Mam kept threatening her with.

"Ain't nobody coming. Ain't nobody cares about a girl like you. Ain't nobody gonna need to, not after what you done to me."

The stranger leaned down and made like he was going to kiss

her with his mouth wide open, and Nettie did the only thing that came to mind. She grabbed up a stout twig from the wall of the pen and stabbed him in the chest as hard as she damn could.

She expected the stick to break against his shirt like the time she'd seen a buggy bash apart against the general store during a twister. But the twig sunk right in like a hot knife in butter. The stranger shuddered and fell on her, his mouth working as gloppy red-black liquid bubbled out. She didn't trust blood anymore, not after the first splat had burned her, and she wasn't much for being found under a corpse, so Nettie shoved him off hard and shot to her feet, blowing air as hard as a galloping horse.

The stranger was rolling around on the ground, plucking at his chest. Thick clouds blotted out the meager starlight, and she had nothing like the view she'd have tomorrow under the white hot, unrelenting sun. But even a girl who'd never killed a man before knew when something was wrong. She kicked him over with the toe of her boot, tit for tat, and he was light as a tumbleweed when he landed on his back.

The twig jutted up out of a black splotch in his shirt, and the slice in his neck had curled over like gone meat. His bad eye was a swamp of black, but then, everything was black at midnight. His mouth was open, the lips drawing back over too-white teeth, several of which looked like they'd come out of a panther. He wasn't breathing, and Pap wasn't coming, and Nettie's finger reached out as if it had a mind of its own and flicked one big, shiny, curved tooth.

The goddamn thing fell back into the dead man's gaping throat. Nettie jumped away, skitty as the black filly, and her boot toe brushed the dead man's shoulder, and his entire body collapsed in on itself like a puffball, thousands of sparkly motes piling up in the place he'd occupied and spilling out through his empty clothes. Utterly bewildered, she knelt and brushed the pile with trembling fingers. It was sand. Nothing but sand. A soft wind came up just then and blew some of the stranger away, revealing one of those big, curved teeth where his head had been. It didn't make a goddamn lick of sense, but it could've gone far worse.

Still wary, she stood and shook out his clothes, noting that everything was in better than fine condition, except for his white shirt, which had a twig-sized hole in the breast, surrounded by a smear of black. She knew enough of laundering and sewing to make it nice enough, and the black blood on his pants looked, to her eye, manly and tough. Even the stranger's boots were of better quality than any that had ever set foot on Pap's land, snakeskin with fancy chasing. With her own, too-big boots, she smeared the sand back into the hard, dry ground as if the stranger had never existed. All that was left was the four big panther teeth, and she put those in her pocket and tried to forget about them.

After checking the yard for anything livelier than a scorpion, she rolled up the clothes around the boots and hid them in the old rig in the barn. Knowing Pap would pester her if she left signs of a scuffle, she wiped the black glop off the sickle and hung it up, along with the whip, out of Pap's drunken reach. She didn't need any more whip scars on her back than she already had.

Out by the round pen, the sand that had once been a devil of a stranger had all blown away. There was no sign of what had almost happened, just a few more deadwood twigs pulled from the lopsided fence. On good days, Nettie spent a fair bit of time doing the dangerous work of breaking colts or doctoring cattle in here for Pap, then picking up the twigs that got knocked off and roping them back in with whatever twine she could scavenge from the town. Wood wasn't cheap, and there wasn't much of it. But Nettie's hands were twitchy still, and so she picked up the black-splattered stick and wove it back into the fence, wishing she lived in a world where her life was worth more than a mule, more than boots, more than a stranger's cold smile in the barn. She'd had her first victory, but no one would ever believe her, and if they did, she wouldn't be cheered. She'd be hanged.

That stranger—he had been all kinds of wrong. And the way that he'd wanted to touch her—that felt wrong, too. Nettie couldn't recall being touched in kindness, not in all her years with Pap and Mam. Maybe that was why she understood horses. Mustangs were wild things captured by thoughtless men, roped and branded and beaten until their heads hung low, until it took spurs and whips to move them in rage and fear. But Nettie could feel the wildness inside their hearts, beating under skin that quivered under the flat of her palm. She didn't break a horse, she gentled it. And until someone touched her with that same kindness, she would continue to shy away, to bare her teeth and lower her head.

Someone, surely, had been kind to her once, long ago. She could feel it in her bones. But Pap said she'd been tossed out like trash, left on the prairie to die. Which she almost had, tonight. Again.

Pap and Mam were asleep on the porch, snoring loud as thunder. When Nettie crept past them and into the house, she had four shiny teeth in one fist, a wad of cash from the stranger's pocket, and more questions than there were stars.

CHAPTER 2

Nettie barely slept a wink that night. Every time her eyes blinked shut, she imagined the stranger pulling himself together, the sand shifting back into the shape of something like a man and slithering into the house past Pap sleeping on the porch. One eye dripping black, he'd rise up like a rattler, snatch his teeth from inside her boot, poke them back into his gums, and rip her throat out.

After the third time she jolted up with a fright, alone in the dark with a stick-knife in her fist, she figured to hell with it and just got on up. Despite the drenching Durango heat, she'd taken to dressing like a bandito's grandmother with one of Pap's old, faded shirts over her bound chest, baggy pants held up by a rope, and a moth-gnawed serape over that. The less the folks of Gloomy Bluebird could see she was a girl, the less trouble they gave her.

Mam and Pap had taken to sending her on all their errands into town, considering they owed so many debts. Nettie'd learned that if she kept her head down and sucked in her cheeks, folks usually took pity and gave her the tail end of a sack of cornmeal or their most pitiful, nonlaying chicken. At first, she'd been embarrassed. But then she'd overheard two of the old biddy church ladies whispering about how shameful it was for Pap to send his half-breed slave pup around to beg, and she realized that they counted her for less than a dog and Pap only slightly more than that.

Mam and Pap Lonesome were of old East stock, pale as salt fish and just as odorous, with matching hay-colored hair and blue eyes that seemed ever confused thanks to eyelashes and eyebrows as light as dandelion fuzz. The pair were shapeless and old enough to look like someone else's aunt. Nettie couldn't have been more different, with medium brown skin that could've been called liver chestnut, if she'd been a horse worth noticing. Her hair was thick and frizzy, a dead giveaway to anyone trying to puzzle out her breed. Half black and half Injun, or maybe Aztecan; any way you added it up, the end result was somehow less than the individual components. She was built tall and narrow like a half-starved antelope, with eyes as dark and thick as a storm-mad creek and high cheekbones framing a mouth that had little reason to smile. She was ugly, was all they'd told her. But she didn't find them beautiful, so what did it matter? The entire town was an eyesore.

It was widely agreed that Gloomy Bluebird was a stupid name for a town, especially considering Old Ollie Hampstead had shot the only bluebird they had back in 1822, right outside what passed as a general store. The darnn thing had been stuffed and posed with little skill and now sat proudly on the storekeeper's counter as a reminder of what looking cheerful and bright would get you in a town as dusty as an old maid's britches. Nettie herself had seen a bluebird when she was just a little thing, hunting lizards out by the creek. When she'd run home to tell Mam, she'd been told to go fetch a switch for lying. Over time, she'd come to believe she must've seen a crow. But crows didn't have red bellies, did they? At least the town lived up to the gloomy part.

The excitement of last night had burned off, and Nettie was feeling downright gloomy herself, like some part of her had blown away with the impossible, sparkling sand. A strange thing had happened, and she had no one to tell, no one she trusted enough to question. Being alone wasn't so bad when nothing ever changed, but now Nettie didn't trust herself, and she was generally the only person she could trust.

Although Pap handled most of her punishment, Mam had once thrashed her for lying about a bluebird, and then thrashed her again when she'd started her monthlies and ruined an old striped mattress and screamed that she was dying. How was she supposed to know that was what women did? Nettie didn't reckon much about the world, but she knew that what happened last night had changed things as much as her flux blood. The world was suddenly more dangerous, but she had no idea why or how to protect herself from it. Seemed like the best way to keep her skin was to get on with breakfast and not say a danged thing, to hide it like she hid everything else.

When she went to shake her boots for scorpions, it was four pointed teeth that fell out. Considering no crevice of the shack was safe from Mam's quick fingers, Nettie shoved them into the little leather bag she kept tied around her waist with what few precious things she'd found over the years. A glittery white arrowhead, hardly chipped. A shiny gold button with a bugle on it. A wolf claw, or something like it. A penny given to her once in the town when she'd been kicked in the leg by a frachetty horse. She'd kept a piece of dirt-dusted ribbon candy some town brat had dropped in the pouch for two weeks once, allowing herself one suck a day. The four teeth added a weight barely felt, but she stood a mite taller. Whatever that stranger had been, she'd won. And that felt pretty goddamn good.

Mam and Pap weren't up, of course. They gave the sun time to stretch and get cozy before they stopped snoring. It was almost peaceful, setting up the porridge in the pot and watching the skillet shimmer with fatback grease. She always loved snatching warm eggs from under the scrawny, sleepy hens; this brood was the result of Pap's once-a-year victory at the poker table. They'd definitely seen harder times, although Nettie didn't much get to enjoy the bounty herself. If Mam and Pap left any eggs on their plates, that was usually treat enough.

The sun came up so fast that if you weren't watching careful, you'd miss it. For just a second, it was a flat circle, hot-red and bleeding all over the soft, purple clouds. Nettie stared at it as long as she could, not blinking, then leaned over to turn the eggs, and when she looked again, the sun sat high and white, relentlessly beating down on the endless prairie. Sunset, at least, took its time, nice and lazy. She liked the colors of it, and the way that no one could own the sun. It couldn't be compelled, couldn't be roped. You could yell at it all day long, threaten and plead and cuss, and the sun would not budge a goddamn inch. It was what it was, and it took its damn time about it.

But Nettie had fewer choices, so she quickly bolted down her small share of the porridge. Not only because Mam and Pap would give her an earful if they woke up with her in the house, but also because she wanted to mosey over to the Double TK before the surlier of the cowboys were awake and taking out their hangovers on whoever happened by. The ranch next door was far richer than Pap's, considering they had more than a one-eyed mule, two nags for renting, a herd of cattle too thin for the butcher to carve, and one milk cow that barely squirted enough milk for weak porridge. Mam had sent her toddling over to the Double TK for the first time to have a knife sharpened when she was just five years old, and Monty had taken her on like a lost pup. The old cowpoke had told her, years later, that they'd figured her for a boy at first, as she'd been in britches and had a shorn head. But since she'd been mannerly and offered to help the wranglers by sweeping out the pen or tossing rocks at vultures, they'd generally tolerated her presence.

Over the years, she'd learned by watching Monty and had figured out better ways to work a colt than using Pap's whip. She was awful shy of the other cowpokes and never went near the ranch house or Boss Kimble, but Monty said he was right glad for her calm hand with the horses and general quietude. He was still thin and tough as leather, with a luxurious mustache, but she'd noticed that in the last couple of years, Monty had saved the wilder horses for her visits and chosen gentler mounts for himself, and that his mustache had gone to gray.

On her way to the Double TK, she stopped to feed the few critters Pap hadn't used up yet. Blue greeted her with his usual hollering, and she gave him a once-over and a fine scratch and fed him a precious handful of grain, plus a bite she'd held back from the porridge. He pressed his big, ugly mule nose over her shoulder, and she leaned into his skinny chest and breathed in his good horse smell. He didn't know he wasn't a horse, and he didn't know he was ugly. Pap's swayback mare, Fussy, took the grain and turned her tail, just as sour as her owner, and the aged nag they called Dusty refused to get up off the ground. The wild black mare was still gone and the water trough still clean, thank heavens. Nettie had already fed the cow and scattered the morning's corn for the chickens, but the poor things crowded around her with hopeful clucking. It was a sad joke, calling it a ranch.

Before heading off, Nettie snuck into the other barn to see if the stranger's clothes were still there. They were, rolled up tight on the old rig's seat beside his hat, which was rugged and new and featured cunning strings to keep it on a feller's head. For a reason she couldn't explain, she tried it on and found it a good fit. With the wide brim pulled down and her pigtails tucked up underneath, maybe people would notice her even less. If asked, she could just say she'd found the hat floating in the creek. By the time she'd walked past the fence and Pap's ranch was just a shimmer on the horizon, the hat felt like it was part of her body and always had been.

Slipping under the fence to the Double TK, Nettie felt instantly calmer, almost at peace. It was business as usual on Boss Kimble's land, just a passel of grown men doing men's work, and she liked the feeling of being part of the simple but effective machinery. She headed toward the colt pens, where Monty and Poke sat on the rail as Jar clung to a bronc's back, and poorly at that. Monty shouted easy encouragement while old Poke leaned out and hollered through cupped, stubby hands about how Jar rode like a one-legged frog. Which he did, a little, as the young cowpoke was fine on his feet but all knees and elbows in the saddle. As Nettie got closer, she admired the bronc crow-hopping around the round pen—a big, bone-white stallion. No way a proud, uptight feller like Jar could break a mustang like that, especially not with his saddle cinched so tight. She couldn't help smirking.

"I got a penny says he falls off within a minute," she called, feeling lucky and reckless in her fine new hat.

Monty and Poke turned with good-natured smiles. Poke pulled out his dented watch while Monty fetched up a penny out of his disreputable pants, which looked as though they'd been made out of the curtains in a whore's bedroom, all velvet with gold curlicues.

"I'll take that bet, Nat," Monty hollered.

He never called her Nettie or treated her like a girl, even though he knew well enough what she was. When she'd started her monthlies, Mam had tried to set her up in skirts, but she'd ripped the hated things into strips and used them to bind her growing chest instead. Mam had given up and wished her quietly to Hell, so long as she kept cooking and cleaning and breaking colts. Monty had called her Little Lady once around that time, and she'd whipped out her jackknife, all fierce and cold, and told him that she was no girl, and he'd nodded, all thoughtful, and started calling her Nat instead. It was one of the many reasons she all but worshipped him.

Just now, he was looking at her with his head cocked and a friendly grin. "Nice hat. Who'd you kill for it?"

Goose bumps rose on her arms, and she pulled the hat down lower. "Nobody you know. Found it in the creek." Hitching up her too-big britches, Nettie climbed to sit by Monty on the top rail of the round pen. She'd always admired the clean, white boards of the Double TK's fencing. Of course, you couldn't stab a stranger in the heart with one of their fence boards, but they sure looked nice.

"How long's he been working that white stallion?"

Monty rubbed the curled end of his gray mustache between two fingers. "Not long. Big fellow came in with the raid last night. Boss wants him broke right fast. Might keep him for himself, if he has a gentle gait. Otherwise, he'll be the nicest fancy in the territory."

Jar flew off said horse in a graceful arc and landed, spread-eagled, in the dust. He rolled to the side right as the big bronc's dish-sized hooves hammered the dirt where the boy's so-called handsome face had been just seconds ago. Before the bronc could stomp again, Jar had skittered back to the edge of the round pen and rolled under the boards to safety. Monty held up a shiny penny and winked at Nettie.

"You beat his time, Nat, and I'll double your winnings. Hell, I'll give you a nickel."

Nettie admired the big bronc trotting around the pen, always keeping a sharp, intelligent eye on the four folks watching him back. Jar climbed up next to Poke and mopped off his face with a hanky that had seen better days.

"Big white bastard. Boss deserves him," Jar said.

Nettie slipped off the fence, wriggled out of her serape, and stood to face the bronc, watching him watch her. Poor feller's saddle was too narrow for his withers, his girth was too tight, and his bridle pulled at his lips, giving him a meaner look than she liked.

"Gimme a rope, Poke."

Poke threw his lasso to her, and she caught it in midair. The bronc stomped a foot, but before he could decide what sort of gangly, dangerous critter she might be, she'd looped him around the neck with a gentle toss. He reared back, first off, but she held tight and gentle, like Monty had taught her. When he stepped back, she went with him. *You can't force a horse, but you can't let him force you, neither*, the old cowpoke always said. As she approached the stallion, calm and murmuring sweet words, she looped the slack from the rope and watched for him to lick a little. The wranglers on the fence whispered, and she heard the clank of coins as they placed their bets.

When she'd got up to the bronc's side, she reached to stroke his neck. His white skin shivered, and dust came away on her fingertips.

"Ho, big feller. We're gonna be friends."

The horse's ears flickered back and his eye stuck to her as she undid the cinch and knocked the saddle off his back, leaving a sweaty stain. The bronc bowed his head and danced in place as he shook and blew air. Nettie smiled and touched him all over. When she got to his face, she went straight for the throat latch and then slipped the whole bridle off his ears. Once the reins were over his head, the horse stretched out his neck like he'd grown two sizes.

"Thought we taught you how to break a bronc, Nat. Nobody gets paid for settin' 'em free," Jar hollered, but Monty only snickered.

"Somebody else taught me you've got to loosen a creature up to get what you want," she whispered so only the bronc could hear.

A rope halter hung on the other side of the round pen, and she walked the bronc over there with Poke's lasso loose around his neck. He followed, not like he really wanted to, but like he was willing to see what her next idea might be. With fingers gentle as last night's rare breeze, she slipped the halter over the bronc's nose and ears and tossed down Poke's lariat. The horse let her pull his face close, and she blew into his twitching pink nostrils. Murmuring all along, she walked him a bit, turned him, got him to cross over his back hooves so she had control of his haunches. That was where all the power was—in the rump.

And when the horse had mostly got used to doing what she wanted, she slipped off her boots, grabbed a handful of mane and rein, kicked up off the fence boards, and launched herself onto the white bronc's broad, sweaty back.